The Scientific Romances of
J.-H. Rosny Aîné

HELGVOR
of the Blue River
THE GIANT FELINE

The Scientific Romances of
J.-H. Rosny Aîné

HELGVOR
of the Blue River

translated by
Georges Surdez

THE GIANT FELINE

translated by
The Honorable Lady Whitehead

A Black Coat Press Book

Acknowledgements: I should like to thank Serge Parmentier. Also thanks to Paul Wessels for his generous and extensive help in the final preparation of this text.

This translation of *Helgvor of the Blue River* was initially serialized in the issues of May 28, June 4, 11 and 18, 1932 of *Argosy*.

Visit our website at www.blackcoatpress.com

ISBN 978-1-935558-46-0. First Printing. September 2010. Published by Black Coat Press, an imprint of Hollywood Comics.com, LLC, P.O. Box 17270, Encino, CA 91416. All rights reserved. Printed in the United States of America.

Table of Contents

Introduction

This is the seventh and last volume of a collection of stories by J.-H. Rosny *Aîné* ("the Elder"). Volumes 1-6 include all of Rosny's scientific romances, and a number of other stories that have some relevance to his work in that genre, all translated by Brian Stableford. The first volume of the series includes a long general introduction to Rosny's life and works.

The contents of the previous six volumes are:
Volume 1. THE NAVIGATORS OF SPACE AND OTHER ALIEN ENCOUNTERS: The Xipehuz, The Skeptical Legend, Another World, The Death of the Earth, The Navigators of Space, The Astronauts.
Volume 2. THE WORLD OF THE VARIANTS AND OTHER STRANGE LANDS: Nymphaeum, The Depths of Kyamo, The Wonderful Cave Country, The Voyage, The Great Enigma, The Treasure in the Snow, The Boar Men, In the World of the Variants.
Volume 3. THE MYSTERIOUS FORCE AND OTHER ANOMALOUS PHENOMENA: The Cataclysm, The Mysterious Force, Hareton Ironcastle's Amazing Adventure.
Volume 4. VAMIREH AND OTHER PREHISTORIC FANTASIES: Vamireh, Eyrimah, Nomaï.
Volume 5. THE GIVREUSE ENIGMA AND OTHER STORIES: Mary's Garden, The Givreuse Enigma, Adventure in the Wild.
Volume 6. THE YOUNG VAMPIRE AND OTHER CAUTIONARY TALES: The Witch, The Young Vampire, The Supernatural Assassin, Companions of the Universe.

Helgvor du fleuve bleu was first published in 1930 by Cent centraux bibliophiles. It was translated into English by

Georges Surdez in 1932 as *Helgvor of the Blue River*, serialized in the May 28, June 4, 11 and 18 issues of *Argosy*.

Georges Surdez (Georges Arthur Surdez, 1900(?)-1949) was a prolific writer of action/adventure stories published in magazines such as the *Blue Book of Fiction and Adventure, Collier's*, the *Saturday Evening Post, Adventure, Argosy*, and many others. Much of his work featured the French Foreign Legion. He is credited with having brought the term *Russian Roulette* into existence through his short story of the same title published by *Collier's* in the January 30, 1937 issue. His short story *A Game in the Bush* (*Adventure* magazine, February 20, 1923) and novel *The Demon Caravan* (The Dial Press, 1927) were both made into films in 1927 and 1953 respectively. He was born in Switzerland, and came to the United States in 1912.

Le Félin géant was first serialized in 1918 in *Lectures pour Tous* then published in bookform by Plon in 1920. It was translated into English by "The Honorable Lady Whitehead" as *The Giant Cat* (McBride & Co., 1924), and later retitled as *Quest of the Dawn Man* (Ace, 1964).

The Honorable Lady Whitehead (née Marian Cecilia Brodrick, 1869-1932) was married to Sir James Whitehead, son of Robert Whitehead the inventor of the torpedo. Their daughter, Agathe Whitehead, married naval commander Georg Ludwig von Trapp who would use the torpedoes engineered by his wife's grandfather in an SM U-5 submarine built at the Whitehead Torpedo and Ship factory in Fiume (Rijeka) with deadly effect in WW1. Von Trapp re-married after the early death of Agathe Whitehead and his family later became the basis for the musical *The Sound of Music*. Lady Whitehead also translated Jérôme and Jean Tharaud's *Quand Israël est roi*, Plon, 1921 (*When Israel is King*, Robert M. McBride & Co., 1924) and Guglielmo Ferrero's *La ruine de la civilization antique*, Plon-Nourrit, 1921 (*The Ruin of the Ancient Civilization and the Triumph of Christianity*, G. P. Putnam's Sons, 1921) into English.

HELGVOR OF THE BLUE RIVER

I. The Devouring Mountain

The women at the entrance to the caverns contemplated the flames leaping toward the stars, and the sky lowered over the plain like a hollow rock.

"Our fathers have seen torrents of fire flowing," Old Man Urm said. "The fire melted the stone, and the men died like locusts."

He was the age of whitened crows: the Tzohs believed that he had been born with the stars, the river and the forest. The other old men stared at him with dull eyes. Because it was the time when the strong men of the tribe were away hunting for herbivorous, giant animals, the red flames seemed more frightening. The mountain growled within its ranks.

Urm spoke to the angry spirits which reside in the stone—one never knows when they may escape, "The Tzohs shall pour warm blood upon the mountain," he clamored. "Living hearts shall be torn from chests and shall feed the Hidden Lives."

He lifted supplicating hands, ashen and quivering like reeds. The flames paled. The moaning of the women was heard from cave to cave, and the voice of the mountain towered.

"The Tzohs will sacrifice at sunrise!" the old man promised. And he added, in a murmur, "The Tzohs are sons of the Great Boar which issued from the Rock, on a day when fire flowed in torrents. The Tzohs are the sons of the Red Boar and of the Rock."

The tribe had come from the east. It knew how to forge bronze and till the soil, while the men of the west still chipped stone instruments. The caverns sheltered 200 warriors, as many adult women, 300 children, but few old people for the race practiced the Law, which is to kill off the weak, and lived without blemish.

"Tomorrow," Urm went on softly, "three women and a warrior must perish! The Test of the Stones shall designate them."

This dictate, passing from the highest cave to the lowest, reassured the women. The mountain had understood. The faraway drone slackened, the flames of the crater became almost invisible. The women and the old people returned to the shadows of the rocks. Urm remained alone with Glava, daughter of Wokr, who belonged to a warrior, Wam the Lynx, for the children are the property of the mother's brother.

Glava was but a year beyond childhood. She did not have the cubical head of the Tzohs nor their slanting brows. She resembled a grandmother of another breed because of her light-colored face, of the tawny gleams in her eyes, of the long hair which grew constantly, while the hair of the true Tzohs remained short and snarled at the tips.

In her, Urm recognized the race of the Green Lakes from which Tzoh warriors had stolen women long ago. At that time, because of a prolonged period of starvation, the women had been decimated, for food must first be served to warriors. When they became too weak, a club felled them and their flesh fed the survivors.

Glava, thinking of the Test of the Stones, hated the Hidden Lives. Yet she was sure that she would not die, for, tall and lithe, with powerful muscles, stronger and more agile than any other woman in the three clans, she could lift the largest stones.

But Amhao, her sister, whom she preferred to the rest of the tribe, would be sacrificed. Terror and anger filled her breast. The chief, Kzahm, son of the Black Boar, was odious to her because of his roughness, his ferocity, and also because, when he returned from the great hunt, he would break off her canine teeth and make her his wife.

His head like that of an aurochs, his odor like that of a jackal, his frenzied eyes, disgusted her. And she did not want Amhao to perish; to save her, she would rebel against Kzahm, Urm and the Hidden Lives.

"The stars are cold!" Urm mumbled. "Why do you not go back into the cavern?"

Formerly, he had been the chief of the Men of the Rock. He was still heeded, because he alone knew all legends and all mysteries. Also, his strength surpassed that of aged men much younger than he; he scaled the crests; he could walk half a day. The belief was growing that he was immortal.

Glava did not like him. He constantly exacted human sacrifices and watched blood flow with grave joy.

"I shall go back into the cavern," she assented.

"Go! It is best that Urm be alone to hear the Great Word."

She left and searched for Amhao. Although she knew the fate awaiting her, the young woman was asleep with her child nearby. If he had been younger, she would have been safe, but he had passed his sixth season. Amhao's sleep was troubled and light. When Glava took her hand, she sat up in the shadows.

"Rise," Glava whispered, "and come with your little one."

Although she was the older and had cared for Glava as a child, Amhao now submitted to the stronger will of her sister. She rose. The night was stirred with wind. Bodies sprawled in their path. At the extremity of the cave they slipped through a narrow, rough gap, reached the torrent, almost dry, which poured between granite walls.

"Where are we going?" Amhao asked.

"Where you shall not die," replied the daughter of Wokr.

A deep rumble was heard in the flanks of the mountain; the red light again leaped toward the stars.

"The Hidden Lives will avenge themselves upon us!" moaned Amhao, who vacillated like a twig in the wind; terror choked her. Glava bent her head before the obscure horror of

11

the legend, but her instincts impelled her to rebel, to be incredulous, almost.

"If Amhao remains in the cave, it is to die!" she said. "What more can the Hidden Lives do to her?"

Her small, powerful hands grasped Amhao's arm. The red fire wrapped the crest, water flowed like blood, and the mountain roared like a gigantic lion. Then impetuous anger swept the daughter of Wokr. She defied the elements, the Hidden Lives and the Clans.

"The Hidden Lives are blind," she said. "They strike like a falling stone."

And she led Amhao, whose soul was as that of a child, away. The torrent became a river, and a distorted Moon appeared beyond the Black River. Glava walked rapidly, without hesitation, having chosen her path. The growling of the mountain could no longer be heard, but the red glow added to the light of the Moon.

Jackals, behind the women, yelped lugubriously, then a spotted beast emerged from a bush. Glava, recognizing a leopard, stopped to face it and uttered a strident yell. Stretched out like a reptile, eyes glowing in the darkness, it crept forward cautiously. Far away, between the tall, black poplar-trees, the shimmering of the river could be discerned.

Warriors armed with a bow, with a club or a bronze knife, do not dread the leopard, and it never attacks them; but in the Tzoh country it could recognize women and children.

"I shall break your bones and pierce your chest!" Glava cried, imitating the hunters. She saw a round stone. Picking it up, she lifted her arm high. This gesture stopped the beast.

"Walk toward the river, Amhao!" ordered the daughter of Wokr, "and take your child."

Amhao obeyed, and was followed by Glava, who walked backward, and each time the leopard drew nearer the young girl stopped threateningly. But the animal grew excited; hunger stirred its entrails. Glava, aware that all animals are afraid of the human glance, kept her eyes on it. Light-footed and furtive, the jackals followed the hunt.

Suddenly the leopard changed tactics. In a few oblique bounds it circled the fugitives and crouched before Amhao. Gripped by icy discouragement, she thought that the Hidden Lives were guiding the wild beast and remained motionless. It scented this fear and came forward.

But Glava forestalled it. The stone shot out and struck the animal on the nose. With a howl of pain and fury the leopard retreated toward the river. The jackals yelped shrilly in astonishment. Everywhere appeared their coppery pelts, their pointed ears; they were weak, cowardly, yet dangerous.

"The leopard will come back!" Amhao said.

Glava, who had picked up the stone, dispersed three jackals with a menacing gesture. But Amhao was not reassured: the leopard, as the pain dwindled, returned toward the two women. Again it was near, with its cortège of parasites.

"Glava will break off the leopard's teeth!" the young girl shouted.

Then the voice of thunder growled in the ground; the river became scarlet in hue. The mountain could be seen to vacillate, the whole plain palpitated like a chest. Glava and Amhao rolled on the grass; a cleft in the ground swallowed the leopard; the jackals moaned, flights of birds flapped above the trees. In the double light of the Moon and of the red flames, the eye of Glava, keen as an eagle's, saw the rocks crack and engulf the caverns.

"The Hidden Lives!" Amhao sighed.

"They have killed the tribe," Glava retorted, "and you are alive!"

The leopard had not reappeared but the jackals already scented the exciting odor of blood and were yelping on the lips of the cleft. In the ravaged plain and on the bank of the river, the trees were tilted, animals were fleeing, and hills were sinking gently.

Glava at last found what she sought: a canoe abandoned by the Tzohs.

"There!" she said, "we shall leave for unknown lands."

The caves, except one, had become the graves of the women, of the old people and the children. But Urm had survived. Standing on a boulder, he recalled the time when fire had flowed like water, and mused, "When the warriors return they will go and take the women from the men of the Blue River and of the Green Lakes. The blood of the prisoners we take shall appease the Hidden Lives."

Because he had escaped death once more, he thought that his life would never end and scorned those who died.

II. The Invasion

Helgvor, son of Shtra, walked up the bank of the river with two dogs, a wolf and a child. The skin of a bear covered the man's shoulders, the skin of a jackal those of the boy.

From Shtra and his ancestors, Helgvor had inherited height, tawny eyes and light hair. His agility was comparable to that of a deer. His strength was nearly that of Heigoun, the most powerful of the men gathered in the Red Peninsula.

For 20 generations, the clan had bred and trained dogs. Helgvor, on a day of hunting, had picked up a wolf cub; the animal with the oblique glance lived with the dogs whose glances were straight. Like them, obedient and faithful, it served man and helped him seek his prey.

It was autumn. The warriors of the Blue River were off in search of adventures. The clan was guarded by five warriors and 20 dogs, and many old men still knew how to throw a spear. There were more than 60 women, young and middle-aged. Each day two warriors went scouting afar with their dogs, for remote danger is the more to be feared when men are concerned.

Helgvor explored the south. The Men of the Rocks, with cubical heads, lived two moons' march away. He had never seen them, but Gmar and Shtra related that formerly they had raided in the region of the Blue River and the Green Lakes.

Their hatchets and knives, more to be dreaded than stone hatchets and oaken clubs, were made with fire.

Helgvor, followed by the dogs, the wolf and the boy, climbed a boulder on the river bank. From there he glanced about. Each thing was as new as his youth; the world started afresh each morning; the grass, the tree, the flower, the weed; water and clouds were eternal. There would always be horses and aurochs grazing on the plain; hippopotami among the reeds, rhinoceroses in great numbers, and surly boars; deer with bleating voices; megaceros elks with gigantic antlers; and even mammoths with hides like the bark of old sycamore-trees.

Never would the does depart from the brush, the crows cease to gather in black troops; the doves, the stork, the ducks, the cranes and the swallows would fly across the vast sky forever. A world in which vultures, eagles, cave lions, tawny leopards, black leopards, herons propped on their stilts, numberless insects and water animals did not exist could not be conceived by Helgvor.

His vigilant eyes followed those strange shapes moving among the motionless plants, armed with teeth, with talons, with hoofs, with horns, with venom, arms attached to their bodies, while he, Helgvor, carried spears, club, stone hatchet, bow and arrows which he could place aside on the rock.

Near him, their senses alert to all variations in the atmosphere, were the two dogs and the wolf, weapons themselves for the man, living weapons which increased his hold upon the world, weapons unknown to the Tzohs.

The boy, agile and tireless, small creature with a brave heart, hid in the grass, in the narrow crevices, behind swells of the ground, even in branches too weak to bear Helgvor's weight. He was already acquainted with human ruses.

The dogs growled, the wolf rose, bristling.

Mammoths were passing by. Their enormous bodies, the color of clay, seemed like moving boulders. With their snaky trunk, their curving tusks, they appeared to come from the depths of the ages. All in them was strange. Alone among living beings, they bore that nose which was a colossal arm, those teeth, each of which weighed as much as 100 clubs.

During their thousands of years of peaceful reign, their race had witnessed the vanishing of the giant felines and of the great cave bears. They themselves were the last of their breed. Already, their kind had vanished from the land of the Men of the Rock; they rarely reached the Green Lakes. But the Blue River still watered a sufficient number of their herds for Helgvor to deem them eternal.

He loved them. They satisfied his essential craving for power. And standing upon the boulder, he shouted, "The mammoth is mightier than the lion, the tiger and the rhinoceros!"

The wolf listened and sniffed; the dogs stopped growling. All three admitted they were unable to cope with those boulders of flesh. Helgvor watched them drinking with a dull exaltation. He dreamed that they might have been trained like dogs, for in him the instinct to transform the free beast into a tame animal was more developed than in any other man of the Blue River. Guarded by the mammoths, the tribe would be invincible, and the Men of the Rock would never dare approach the Red Peninsula.

A long quiver rippled the flesh of the nomad. Far off, thin and ominous, a bluish streamer of smoke rose behind a hillock, spreading wide at the crest. On this calm morning, on the humid plain, that smoke had a single, formidable meaning: the presence of men.

Worry dropped on Helgvor like the blow of a club. Then he clung to a slim hope, that perhaps the hunters had returned. But was that possible? The warriors had been away ten days, and a great hunt usually lasted half a moon. Doubtless they had encountered large herds of horses. For a long time, in the vicinity of the Red Peninsula, horses had been found only in small numbers. For the winter, captured horses were guarded by the dogs.

These were fed with grass picked by the women at the end of summer. When the hunting was poor, they were killed to feed the clans. Helgvor had desired to tame them, but because of obscure traditions the old men had opposed him. The horses, soon accustomed to captivity, lived behind barriers erected by men, near the huts.

"Hiolg, hide yourself!" the warrior addressed his small companion, while he himself sprawled close to the ground. The boy concealed himself behind a rock. Helgvor watched the menacing smoke. He waited a long time. At first, the smoke grew thicker, then lighter. And on both sides of the hillock, bushes spread, which kept all presence secret.

Helgvor, after scanning the soil, knew that even Hiolg could not approach them without being seen. The plain spread everywhere. Only the river bank afforded shelter, but upstream and downstream the river flowed far from the hillock.

"Have the men seen Helgvor?" he wondered.

Perhaps they were watching from behind the bushes as he watched them from the top of his boulder. Then they would not show themselves.

Suddenly he uttered an exclamation. An erect being had left the bushes to the left, and the keen eye of Helgvor saw at once that the cubical head, the squat body, were not those of a son of the Blue River. He breathed hard, for he felt that the clan and himself were running a fearful risk.

"Hiolg sees the man?" he asked.

"Hiolg sees him," the boy with the hawk's eyes answered.

Helgvor pulled up the bear skin over his skull, and Hiolg did the same with the jackal pelt wrapped about his shoulders.

"Helgvor and Hiolg must reach the river!" the man said.

They slid from the boulder, opposite the hillock. Then they slipped through the grass and crawled. The dogs and the wolf followed silently.

They marched a third of a day, making sure that no one followed their tracks. The Red Peninsula was near. Helgvor planned means to defend it. With the three warriors, the women and the dogs, it would be possible to beat back a few enemies, and doubtless the invaders would not attack unless they felt themselves much the stronger.

The small hillock, the appearance of a single warrior, all indicated a small hunting party. The entrance to the Peninsula, 20 paces wide, was defended by boulders. Helgvor believed that it would take more than a score of men to pass.

Hiolg interrupted his thoughts. He came up, panting, "Men are walking toward the river."

Helgvor again ascended the bank. At a distance, a troop of men, spread out, advanced prudently. All had massive heads and squat bodies. The warrior thought he recognized the man he had seen near the hillock. He counted seven silhouettes. If a surprise was to be avoided, there must be haste; but the child, although agile, delayed progress.

"Helgvor will run!" the warrior said. "Hiolg knows how to make himself invisible as a mole. He will follow."

The child was not afraid. If needed, he would enter the river, for he swam and dove like an otter. And on the opposite shore there were many hiding places among the rocks and in the forest.

"Hiolg will not be seen!" he answered briefly.

Helgvor ran. His speed was that of the roebuck; he soon neared the spot where the Peninsula opened at right angles to the shore. First, he heard a confused murmur, then shouts, fierce yells, long moans, cries of terror.

Helgvor stopped. The shiver of disaster shook him. The Red Peninsula was invaded. The Tzohs were cleaving skulls, piercing bellies, crushing limbs. The old men, the women and a surviving warrior were in flight before a howling horde. At every step a club fell, a spear sank into a chest, and once the victim was down, a Tzoh pounced upon the body to smash the head or tear at the heart.

Weak from his wounds, the last warrior faced his foes. It was to die. Chest drenched with blood, eyes blinded and legs quivering, he muttered insults and predicted the vengeance of the Ougmars. He lifted his hatchet with an effort, struck out at random. Ten clubs fell; the warrior tumbled to the grass, where the spears dug into his palpitating flesh.

Then, gripped by holy fury, trembling with the courage of his breed, Helgvor cried, "The Ougmars will crush the Tzohs!"

Startled, the invaders turned. And they saw nothing. Helgvor, understanding the uselessness of a struggle and the need to survive, had concealed himself in the thick bushes covering the Peninsula. Several Tzohs explored the space in vain; Helgvor, the wolf and the dogs remained invisible.

Helgvor already seemed out of reach. He was advancing under cover when the wolf bristled and the dogs growled. Two Tzoh warriors appeared from behind a boulder, which, at the same time as the breeze, had attenuated their scent. It was a stark scene, shaded by tall rocks and thick with bushes. Helgvor and his enemies watched each other, motionless. It was a merciless minute: life for the victor, death for the vanquished.

The Man of the Blue River gave the signal to the wolf and the dogs. Those cunning beasts slid through the vegetation and reappeared behind the Tzohs. Helgvor shot two arrows one after the other. The first creased the skull of a Tzoh, the second knocked out one eye, and as he uttered a howl of pain the wolf attacked him from the rear.

Hatchet brandished, Helgvor leaped forward.

The second Tzoh met his onslaught, while the first fought the wolf and the dogs. A spear gashed Helgvor's shoulder, then the two were face to face. The Tzoh was squat, with mighty shoulders and muscular hands. "The Tzohs have taken your women and killed your children! They shall massacre your warriors and there will be no more Ougmars on the Earth," he cried.

Helgvor did not understand the words, but knew them to be insulting. He retorted, "The Ougmars will wipe out the filthy race of the Tzohs!"

His hatchet whirled, the other lifted his club. Because they were both agile and keen of eye, handling their weapons well, neither was struck at first. Leaping like leopards, they struck and dodged at the same time.

Helgvor, fearing the arrival of other enemies, resolved to end it quickly. He lowered his weapon, allowed the club to fall. The heavy mace almost hit him, but he avoided its sweep with a light leap, and split the skull of his opponent who had been carried forward by his lunge. The beaten man dropped in a heap and lay dying upon the grass.

Aside, the victorious wolf and dogs were devouring the other warrior. Hiolg, who had contributed to the victory by clutching the Tzoh warrior's legs, threw himself toward Helgvor who shouted, "Thus will perish all the Tzohs, race of jackals and stinking hyenas."

But the Tzohs, who had not seen the combat, did not learn the fate of the two warriors until later. As they could not find Helgvor, they finished their task. They drove aside the adult women, methodically massacred the old people and the children. At times, when an old man or a woman knelt at their feet, the warriors would laugh and torture them longer. At last the killing ended. The chief, kneeling, with hands extended, called out, "Hidden Lives, the Tzohs have spilled blood for your drinking. You will lead back to the land of the Rocks the warriors and the captive women."

For a while longer, the Tzohs explored the Red Peninsula. When they discovered a trembling old fellow or a frightened child, the clubs or the spears were used, and ended matters.

III. The Pursuit Begins

The Sun blazed like a red furnace when Helgvor reached the Peninsula. The dogs and the wolf smelled the corpses, black birds swooped with hoarse cries, jackals were coming at their slinking gait, drawn by the odor of blood.

The Ougmars did not bury the dead, as did the Tzohs, and they had no definite rites. They knew, nevertheless, that the Ougmars were the children of the Giant Eagle and of the Blue River. The Giant Eagle came from an egg floating on the river. At that time, the water flowed over the forest and the rocks; the Eagle was larger than the tiger and the Ougmars respected the life of the Eagle.

The old men also knew that when starting for the hunt, a spear should be thrown toward the clouds, accompanied by words passed down from their ancestors, to propitiate luck.

"The Sons of the Eagle and of the River will slay the Tzohs!" Helgvor growled.

He did not chase away the crows, the hyenas and the jackals, for it was their task to purify the forest and the plain of dead bodies. From time to time he glanced at the corpses sprawled on the ground. The blood of his own people had not been spilled, for his mother had died ten years before; he had no sisters, and his father and brothers were away with the warriors.

But Hiolg had returned quickly enough to witness the kidnaping of his mother and the slaying of a grandfather. Adult hatred swelled his puny breast.

For a while it appeared that the Tzohs had massacred all save those they had taken captive. Then an old man appeared, his chest bloody, followed by a grown woman who had sheltered herself in the thicket. Then came a few children, and as the moments passed, a few others, women or old men.

The warrior addressed them, "Helgvor will follow the trail of the Tzohs. He will leave behind coals and smoke-blackened stones, sometimes he will stick twigs into the earth. Thus, when the warriors return here, they shall be able to follow him."

The old men had lost much blood; they listened as in a daze. But a woman understood and answered, "Malgwa will repeat Helgvor's words to the warriors."

Twilight spread upon the clouds a world of illusion, brighter, vaster than the real world. A depressing vapor steamed up from the river; the crows, the vultures, the jackals and hyenas enjoyed this hour.

Helgvor called the dogs and the wolf away from the human flesh. As he left the Peninsula, Hiolg came running after him. The boy had discovered the bodies of his little brothers among the dead, and moaned like a wolf cub. The son of Shtra said to him, "Hiolg is not swift enough. If the Tzohs find him, they will catch and kill him. Hiolg shall remain here to await the warriors."

Having spoken thus, Helgvor threw a spear toward the sky, uttered the words, and vanished, followed by the wolf and the dogs. Other dogs had reappeared, having escaped the general slaughter, and were joining the jackals and hyenas on the field of combat.

Helgvor had no trouble following the trail of the kidnapers, for the wolf and the dogs had understood what he expected of them, and their sensitive nostrils could discern a scent far better than the keenest human eye could discern a silhouette.

Because the Tzohs were slowed down by their captives, the Ougmar warrior felt no great haste. He could count on the dogs not to lose the trail and his own agility to catch up with his foes, and escape from them if they turned to pursue him.

The last ashen streak in the sky melted into the sunset, and nothing remained save the intense darkness of the night and the trembling glow of the stars.

Lights bloomed on the plain, indicating camp fires, the formidable, ominous signs of the erect beast, man. Helgvor had taken his station downwind, and crouched in a hollow of the soil. He counted five fires, saw the black silhouettes of warriors and women, at times their bodies glowing red in the flames' glare. Rage made his jaws lock savagely when he identified the youngest of the women. He was swept at once with anger at the outrage, and a glowing, primitive tenderness.

"The Tzohs are jackals," he muttered in a low, thick voice. "The Men of the River will break their bones and recapture their women!"

He tried to count his enemies. There were about twice as many as the Ougmars could gather. Despairing, dazed, the women seemed resigned, the majority already appeared on good terms with the victors. Helgvor felt an immense jealousy, a collective jealousy, but was not otherwise surprised. Women tremble like does, and do not wish to die!

He spied upon the camp a long time, growing used to the gestures, to the smells of the Tzohs. His attention was drawn to the leader, and all his hatred condensed upon that compact stature, on that enormous face, red as fresh blood. In the darkness, Helgvor lifted his club, aimed his spear; the madness of combat contracted his fists, dilated his heart.

At length he decided to rest. He found a safe haven in a depression of the plain, lit a small fire and roasted a piece of deer which he shared with the animals. Then he slept, but his ears and his nose continued to perceive the subtle emanations, the rumors of the night. About him, the wolf and the dogs watched also, seeming part of his being.

He could not be surprised.

Ten days passed, and Helgvor still trailed the Tzohs.

Because of his skill, his scent, his prudence, perhaps also because his foes had no dogs, nothing had betrayed his presence. At night he kept even further away than during the day.

The march of the Tzohs was made very slow by the women and by the need to carry the canoes, almost useless to them as they were progressing upstream. On occasions, when the river widened to form a sort of lake, the canoes were launched, and Helgvor feared he would be left behind. But soon the stream became narrow and rapid again, and the Tzohs resumed their march upon the plain.

On the morning of the 11th day the Men of the Rocks divided into two smaller bands. While the bulk of the party went on, the others scattered as if to surround a herd of animals.

Helgvor recognized their chief, the man seen near the hillock on the morning of the massacre.

Dogs and wolf, eyes glowing, panting and bristling, remained silent. They had followed the trail of the Tzohs so many days, without being sent in to attack, and knew them as enemies to be feared.

Undetected, Helgvor drew back, and as he no longer feared to lose the trail, retreated a considerable distance. He reached a line of rocks which formed a crenelated wall along the bank, and concealed himself. His line of retreat was secure; through the high grass, he could reach a clump of sycamore-trees.

The halt lasted a long time. The river flowed by, very wide, and islands could be distinguished upstream; a canoe emerged between two of them. Helgvor was startled to see that it was handled by women.

Nearer to the right bank than to the left, they paddled desperately. Soon, another canoe appeared, filled with warriors, gaining on the first one rapidly, obviously seeking to slide between the fugitives and the bank. The women swerved to the right at the precise moment that a third canoe appeared around the tip of an island.

Then Helgvor's flesh quivered with the hunting passion. And while he crawled, panting, a shadow appeared among the rocks. The warrior turned his head and recognized the boy, Hiolg.

IV. The Fugitives

Glava and Amhao had traveled downstream consistently. Amhao, skilled in the finding of plants and fruits which feed human beings, lit and kept alive the fire with more ability than her sister.

Glava showed a surer skill of the hunt, a sharper knowledge of animals. During her childhood she had learned to throw the sharpened stones and the spear; her hand was deft, her glance quick and sure. Each day she brought back meat for the night's fire.

As they spent almost the entire day in the canoe, they avoided lions, leopards and bears. At night, they sought a tall boulder or a cave, and their fire kept away the flesh-eaters. Often, also, they camped on an island in the river.

When there chanced to be game on the island, they remained two or three days, although they still had to beware of the large hydrosaurians. They had manufactured spears, two clubs, two darts, which although not as solid as those made by the warriors, were efficient nevertheless. Glava had roughed them out, and Amhao, more patient, had polished them with tireless persistence. And thus, day by day, they had become better adapted to combat. The energy and audacity of Glava bolstered the spirits of her elder, who practiced the throwing of stones and spears with docility.

Now they scarcely feared the panther, the leopard or the hyena, but when they heard the thunderous roar, the menacing yelp of the tiger, or the growling of the gray bear, lords of the plain and the forest, they were aware of their weakness. At the time when the caves were their refuge, the strength of the warriors had protected them: the whole tribe could scorn the flesh-eaters.

Memories of the cave dwellings were strongest when the shadows flooded the world, when dimly distinguished shapes prowled around their fire, even when the stars seemed threatening. Then Amhao sighed, thinking of Tsaouhm, her master, the father of her child.

"Tsaouhm is strong!" she chanted.

At the sound of this complaint, which seeped into her self-confidence in a subtle manner, audacity and anger would stir in Glava's chest.

"Amhao forgets she was to die!" she would grumble. "Long since her blood would have dried upon the rocks! The Tzohs are worse than the tiger or the lion!"

One night a hungry gray bear stopped by the bank of the river. Since the preceding day, wary beasts had caught his heavy scent and had avoided him. In vain he had hidden among the boulders, squatted in the brush, lurked in the high grasses. The saiga antelope, the elaph deer, the doe, the wild sheep, all discerned his effluvia above that of the leaves, of the grass, of the smelly sod.

His fury grew, stirred by hunger, and his opaque, dull soul was filled with indignation against the ruses or the agility of his prey.

Before the flames of the women's fire he opened his growling jaws wide, and when he shook his paws their enormous claws clattered together. The eyes, ferocious and alert, gleamed covetously at the two human beings. He was swathed in his pelt which hung in thick pleats on his chest; each of his movements revealed a supple strength; the habit of winning gave him an undefinable, formidable prestige.

At times he would prowl nervously before the flames, then stop short, oscillating, gaping, furious. A concave boulder sheltered the women; the fire seemed to form the string of a stone bow. The wild beast could have cleared it at a single leap, but the mysterious palpitation of the flames filled him with distrust. When he crept nearer he was dazzled, and the heat hurt his nostrils.

Glava, having closed the gap with care, kept the fire high with branches. Each time the monster closed in she would wave a blazing torch. Then, astonished, he would growl deeply and show his teeth. New stars appeared, others waned. The stubborn brute was still near, and the woman saw the heap of twigs and branches dwindle. Although they had gathered much wood at twilight and fed the fire stingily, it was probable the flames would die out before the red star fell beneath the horizon.

Then, their flesh would bleed between the jaws of the bear.

At intervals Glava brandished her spear, but she knew that the weapon could not penetrate to the heart of the huge animal and that a wound would but stir him to savage fury, to blind rage. She did not launch the weapon.

Then there was no more wood; the last flames fluttered, the crimson coals darkened, and the teeth of Amhao clashed together with fear. Glava made ready for her last combat.

A colossal mass in the shadow, the bear came forward. For a few moments, to the right and behind the rocks, yelps and cries had been heard. The murmur swelled into a roar. A very tall animal appeared, trotting with a perceptible limp, and the bear, through wide-open nostrils, identified a horse. Wounds in the legs were slowing the fugitive, and he had not covered 100 strides when five wolves appeared, then a horde of jackals.

With a joyous grunt the bear started forward. In the grip of immense terror, the horse halted then turned his head. He saw the five wolves across the path to the east, while the bear and the rocks barred the path to the west.

The horse spun on his hoofs and fled southward, pursued by the bear with oscillating, heavy leaps, and the wolves, now frightened by their new rival but kept in action by lingering hope. The hunted beast, reddening the trail with his blood, constantly lost ground. His wounded leg seemed dead, stiff, and hampered his strides. All about, avid lives sought to swallow this terrified life.

Soon, with the bear so near that the wolves howled with disappointment, the grass-eater saw nothing but greedy maws. A few seconds before there had remained a lane of escape, the open plain upon which, for so long, through his scent and speed, he had fled from the meat-eaters. Now, space was filled with famished beasts, and the horse, heavy as a rock, still as a tree, waited for death with a sinister moan. The bear split his throat, blood drenched the red hair; a wolf, bolder than the others, attacked him from behind.

That terrible night made the women even more prudent. When the haven was not sure, they upset their canoe, and this shelter disconcerted the crude intelligence of the wild beasts.

Between the ground and the rim of the craft there was space left through which to prick the nostrils that came scenting, or the groping paws. Mysteriously wounded by an invisible foe, the beasts beat a rapid retreat. Glava and Amhao took care not to wield their spears too violently, so as not to exasperate the larger meat-eaters.

Almost always the prowlers were only wolves, hyenas and jackals. Once a tiger came, and twice a lion. They did not linger, perhaps because they were puzzled, perhaps because they found easier game. Often, also, the fugitives avoided animals by taking shelter in the thickets. As they went further and further from the tribe they halted for longer periods. They made pointed stakes, as they had seen the Tzohs do, and used them to make a bristling barrier around their shelter.

On the river islands security was almost complete. Sometimes they would slide into crevices too narrow for the large meat-eaters, and when they chanced to discover an empty cave, easily defended, they would sojourn there for several days.

A moon after their flight from the clan, the women decided that they had come far enough to settle for a long period. They needed a section filled with game; a haven safe from beasts and storms, and in the proximity of the river. This they sought for many days. One morning, in a granite boulder, they saw a cleft wide enough to allow passage for a man, a large wolf or a leopard. This opening was four arms' lengths from the soil; the surface of the stone was smooth, slippery. It could not be reached by many animals lacking wings; even a panther would find the leap difficult to achieve.

Glava climbed on her sister's shoulders. Before sliding into the cleft, she looked in, sniffed, smelled nothing save the large bats. Then, crouching, she advanced. A dim light dropped from the vault, the cleft widened to form a cave in which several human beings could find shelter. The light penetrated through a vertical split that cleaved the rock from bottom to top.

Glava, supplied with a handful of dried twigs, lit a fire which rapidly flamed high. She then noted that the top was five or six arms' lengths above her head; the refuge was good. The daughter of the Rocks turned to her companion.

"Amhao and Glava shall rest here!" she said. "The entrance to the cave is too high for wolves, too narrow for the tiger, the lion or the gray bear. Stakes and stones shall defend it against the panther."

For the space of a half moon their life was as secure as if they had been living under the protection of the warriors, for they went forth only by day after inspecting the surroundings. The great felines were asleep. They found no tracks of the gray bear, no tracks of men.

There were beasts and plants in plenty. By lighting the fire beneath the opening of the roof, no smoke befouled the cave. The ruses and skill of the women grew day by day. Glava in particular could sense danger in advance, gifted as she was with the slyness of the jackal. When she pressed her ear against the ground, she heard the slightest sound; her glance pierced very far to espy beings which she identified by their gait, their movements.

Each day she made her traps more perfect, while Amhao shaped better and better weapons and tools. Provided with sharp spears, with a knotty club, with a harpoon, Glava lived with quiet audacity and her courage made Amhao feel secure.

Nevertheless, Amhao missed Tsaouhm, her man, who had been rough but not ferocious. He had shown her unexpected tenderness at times.

She remembered scenes that added to her homesickness. Although the women fed badly on what the warriors left, Amhao thought with uneasy longing of the immense fires on which roasted antelopes, deer or wild oxen, sheep, bustards and teals; of the endless gossip of the women; even of the hard work which followed the great hunting trip.

Glava thought less of her former existence, for the future rose before her. She brought the instinct of the race, still undetermined, to the new soil, and the thrill of new discoveries extinguished memory of the Rocks. Yet, on certain days, she felt a retrospective gentleness, saw in her mind's eye the native caves. But it was brief; hatred against Old Urm, the horror of human sacrifices, the thought of having her canine teeth broken as a symbol of her union to Kzahm, who smelled like a jackal, filled her breast with anger.

One morning Glava was inspecting the canoe, concealed in the bushes 100 arms' lengths from the river. With the help of Amhao she had repaired the cracks of the hull and had hewn new paddles. They used the craft to visit other islands or to reach the shores.

It was a long boat and split the stream easily. Glava granted it an undefined, unexplainable affection. Perhaps because the canoe bore the fugitives, skimmed over the river lightly, saving them much fatigue and many dangers; perhaps also because it had often been their sole refuge, she attributed life and understanding to it. So, almost every day, she came to see if the canoe was intact.

Before leaving the bushes, Glava paused, wishing to make sure that no prowler was near. She inhaled the scents, explored the surroundings with her keen glance, then pressed her ear against an ash-tree.

Steps were quivering in the tree; at once she knew they were not those of four-footed animals or of birds.

The heavy rhythm indicated a vertical being loaded with a burden, and Glava, thinking at first that it was Amhao and her child, was reassured. Then worry grew. Why was Amhao so near the river? Had she not agreed to await Glava's return from the hunt?

The woman slipped silently out of the bushes. The wood ended on her left, where the steps had been heard and Amhao was in sight. She walked a short distance from the fringe of the thicket so as to survey the plain without being seen. She did not notice her sister until she was very near.

"Why did Amhao leave the cave?"

"Amhao sought Glava." The older woman was ashen, her lips were bloodless. "Amhao has seen Tzohs!"

"Tzohs!" Glava repeated, frightened.

Amhao lifted the five fingers of her right hand and one finger of her left.

"Amhao recognized them?"

"There were Kamr, son of the Hyena, Ouaro, Tohr—"

"Did they see Amhao?"

"They were far, walking toward the rock. The marsh halted them and they disappeared into the woods. Then I came down, circled the rock and came through the bushes."

"Amhao hid the fire?"

"Yes."

Glava shook her head and scanned the scene again.

"We must reach the island and hide."

She turned back to the canoe, followed by Amhao. They bore the craft to the bank. The grass was high, the shore deserted and the rock invisible. The two women could be seen only by men following the beach or standing across the stream from them. When they were in the canoe they drew some distance away from land. The current bore the boat away, slowly, then more rapidly.

Glava wondered if the Tzohs had stopped at the rock. Even then they were unlikely to suspect that the cleft admitted people into an inhabited cave, and, as it was morning, they were in no need of seeking shelter therein.

Seeking to guess the motive of their presence, she rejected the thought that they were pursuing them or that a hunting trip had taken them such a long distance from home. It could not be a migration of the whole tribe, either, for the Tzohs sought to live only on rocky soil.

Recollections leaped into her mind like locusts through grass: Glava and Amhao were the daughters of an alien woman. Finding the caves fallen in, the majority of their women killed, the Tzohs had gone to seek new mates near the Green Lakes or the Blue River.

V. Flight

The canoe slid on the smooth surface of the stream
which was so wide that the far shore could not be discerned.
Then the island appeared, narrow and long, thickly covered
with vegetation. Centuries had reared there the trunks of the
black poplar-trees and sycamores. The willows were everywhere on the shore.

Before heading for the island Glava glanced long upon
the plain. As no vertical shape appeared, they plied the paddles and crossed the stream to a small cove sheltered by a bar-
ren jutting headland. They alighted quickly, then hid in the
bushes to wait.

Nothing revealed the presence of man. The hideous snout
of a hippopotamus, the scales of a crocodile, the shell of a
tortoise, the flight of a heron across the sky, then the appearance upon the beach of an elaph deer, of a rhinoceros, of an
antelope, drew the women's attention momentarily.

Suddenly Glava started. Erect beings had appeared! Dim
at first, they became more precise, and the fugitives recognized the men of their clan, among them Kazhm's well known
bull-like head.

"Women!" Amhao exclaimed.

The women followed the first detachment of warriors. Of
an alien breed, their faces lighter than those of the Tzohs, their
hair in some cases the hue of leaves in the autumn, they resembled Glava.

"They come from the Green Lakes or the Blue River!"
said the daughter of Wokr, "and are to replace those whom the
Mountain has killed."

Obscure jealousy palpitated in Amhao's flesh while, because they looked like her, Glava felt pity for the captives,
especially for those who belonged to the chief who smelled
like a jackal. Amhao's face grew pale again for she saw with

the rear guard the warriors who had frightened her: Ouaro, Tohr and the others. They closed in on the main body.

The chief called a halt, and questioned them. At intervals they scanned the river and their glances lingered on the island. At length Kzahm, son of the Black Boar, gave orders, and those who bore the canoes went to the shore and launched them. Two craft came toward the island.

"The Tzohs are on our trail!" Amhao moaned.

"No! They want to explore the island, perhaps camp."

"We must flee!"

The servile soul of the woman quivered within Amhao as she recalled convulsively the Law of the Rock and the vengeance of the Hidden Lives.

Glava hesitated. The island was vast, there were numerous hiding places, but the scent of the Tzohs was to be feared. The slightest indication would betray the fugitives. In particular, the canoe moored in the cove would at once reveal not only the presence of human beings but the identity of the two who had defied the might of the Hidden Lives.

"Amhao and Glava will flee!" she said.

The cove, behind the headland, was invisible to the new arrivals. Followed by her elder Glava crept to the canoe, cast off quickly, and slid alongside the shore of the island under the tall white willows. Had the Tzohs landed on the southern end they would have seen the fugitives. But they reached the central part where the island was considerably wider and where vision was screened by thick vegetation.

When the two women reached the northern end the river spread before them, immense, swarming with voracious lives; it was the place where the canoe would be in sight, and the women stopped paddling, thinking of the ruthless tribe, of the mysterious tortures, of the flames into which their quivering bodies would be thrown.

Glava slipped the canoe close to shore, within the veil of overhanging plants in which swarmed cold-blooded beasts: crocodiles, tortoises, snakes, gigantic spiders, enormous in-

33

sects; a young, frightened, pink hippopotamus-dove; a crocodile lifted his long, scaly snout; a toad hopped away heavily while tiny birds with azure and coral wings fluttered in the leafage.

She listened, peered between the lianas at the canoes sliding toward the island, and heard the voices of the men already ashore. There was no Tzoh rearguard already on the plain. She decided that by striking off toward the far shore they would remain undiscovered some time longer.

"Amhao and Glava will continue to flee!" she addressed her companion.

They started out again on the vast river, toward the left bank, where the stream turned a bend, 10,000 arms' lengths away. Should they succeed in reaching that turn and remain unseen, they would be saved.

Digging the paddles deep at each stroke, they strove desperately, and when they turned they saw no one on the dangerous zone of the island they had left. The turn! Already the canoe skirted the left shore, and they were under the overhanging bushes.

Kamr, son of the Hyena, had reached the opposite shore of the island. As he scanned the surface of the water his keen eyes espied the monstrous head of a hippopotamus emerging among floating branches, and, far off, something elongated skirting the left bank. He soon made out a canoe and two human beings aboard and the gave the alarm, although he did not suspect them to be women.

Several of his companions ran up to his side, among them Kzahm, the Black Boar, and they all saw the craft vanish at the turn of the stream. Because it was always preferable to investigate, Kzahm ordered a pursuit, forbidding, however, that it be kept up longer than a fourth of one day, ordering his men to retreat in case the strange canoe was joined by others.

Twelve strong and agile warriors, known to be excellent paddlers, leaped into two canoes. Kzahm counted that they would gain rapidly on the mysterious boat ahead, and suggested that its occupants should be brought back alive, if possible. After the craft had left, the chief became worried. Were the strangers warriors from the Green Lakes or the Blue River, or merely stragglers? A dim dread arose in his thick brain, but he put it aside with scorn. Did he not command 100 fighting men, while the Blue River clan could not muster over 60?

As for those of the Green Lakes, they were known to be hunting far away, in scattered groups. To have them mass their forces, they would need open warfare. And no war, for two generations, had clashed the Men of the Rocks with those of the Green Lakes. Nevertheless, because a leader must at one and the same time be very brave and very wise, the Black Boar sent out scouts on both shores of the stream.

Glava uttered a muffled cry, Amhao groaned, and hope shrunk as their distress increased like the shadows of the black poplar-trees, for a canoe had rounded the bend.

Then the women knew themselves to be as weak, as helpless, as the mosquitoes humming near the shore, and Amhao, discouraged, relaxed her grip on the paddle. Her spirit yielded to despair. She was ready to surrender to evil destiny, ready to acknowledge the might of the Tzohs and the power of the Hidden Lives.

"We cannot escape them," she moaned. "Amhao must die."

For a brief instant, bitter grief lowered Glava's head, but energy reawakened in her with the need to exhaust the resources of her being before surrendering to men and fate.

"Amhao and Glava will die if taken" she said bitterly, "but they are not yet caught."

"Look!" cried Amhao.

The second canoe had come in sight.

"Did we not escape Urm, the leopard and the bear?" Glava spoke roughly. And as she looked at Amhao with tender resolution, the older woman, dominated by a stronger will, picked up the paddle.

It became a hard and miserable struggle; the canoes of the pursuers, better constructed, shot forward by the might of muscular arms, devouring space. Glava saw her chances dwindle at each sweep of the flashing paddles. Before very long the Tzohs saw the fugitives clearly and lifted a clamor, a raucous, furious, insulting, vindictive clamor.

"The Tzohs have recognized us!" Amhao said.

One of their canoes shot directly toward the women's craft; the other kept close to the left bank, as close as the vegetation permitted, to cut off possible retreat. That one was the swifter of the two, and her diagonal course would bring it in position to intercept the fleeing craft.

Glava headed for the right bank. But Amhao, already very tired and almost fainting, no longer hoped. The tests and the perils had been useless, they would be taken back to their starting point, and their torture would be horrible.

Tzohs knew of suicide. Glava addressed her companion.

"Amhao and Glava can make the bank, and there, if Amhao wills it, they shall die." Amhao looked long toward the bank, then her sorrowing eyes rested on her child. Glava went on, "If we jump into the river, the Tzohs will rescue us. We have firm hands, we can stab ourselves with the spears."

This was reasonable. Moreover, a mighty instinct urged her to persist until the last chance was gone. The bank rose steeply, rocky and crested with tawny bushes. As she was about to land, Glava lowered her head and the tears flowed. Love of life sprang up in that young body; immense memories spread, of events lost in the night of her consciousness: the beauty of the dawn upon the plain, the marvel of the growing grass, the miracle of life. Even that morning, Glava and Amhao had been free to breathe, had been drunk with space and movement.

The craft struck land.

Three hundred arms' lengths behind appeared the leading Tzoh canoe, and the other came on obliquely. Amhao, uttering a weak moan, clasped her child passionately. She too loved life, in a slower, more inert fashion.

"Amhao must go first."

Obediently, her eyes streaming tears, Amhao landed, and as Glava grasped hatchet and spears, she felt within her the fear of death mingling with the elation of combat. She turned and cried, "The Tzohs are filthy and cowardly victors!"

"The Hidden Lives await the daughters of Wokr to devour them!" A warrior replied amid a chorus of jeers and laughter.

Glava understood the last minute had come, and she said gently, "Amhao is ready?"

"Amhao is ready," the older woman agreed, weeping.

VI. Strange Allies

The nearest canoe was not more than 100 arms' lengths away. Suddenly a loud voice called out; an arrow flew over the water and struck a Tzoh in the throat. A wolf howled, dogs barked.

Bewildered, the men of the Rocks stopped paddling, but a second arrow pierced the shoulder of a warrior, and the voice rose again, loud as the bellowing of an aurochs. The Tzohs were brave, but the law of plain and forest ordained care; the two canoes retreated before the unseen foe.

Quivering with mingled hope and fear, the two women scanned the rocks. A head appeared, young and covered with tawny hair, a face which did not resemble that of the Tzoh. Then a child was seen sliding between the ridges of granite, climbing to the top of the cliff, speaking words which the two women did not understand, although they guessed the meaning of his gestures: the hidden men were friends.

With other gestures he indicated that the canoe should proceed downstream. Despite many signs, he could not make the reason clear. At the sight of the child, the Tzohs seemed about to come back, but two shouts, one uttered in a deep voice, the other shrill, warned then off.

"The daughters of Wokr must obey!" Glava spoke. "The hidden men are friends."

She was not altogether sure of this but her fighter's soul comprehended the need of taking one side or the other. She picked up her paddle, and the canoe resumed its flight downstream, followed, within two arrow flights, by the Tzohs' craft.

The child had vanished and nothing revealed the presence of human beings other than fugitives and pursuers. The Tzohs hurled loud insults at the invisible enemy. The man struck in the throat lay at the bottom of the canoe; the one who had been hit in the shoulder could not stem the blood flowing from his wound.

The passion for life, fierce hope, animated Glava and Amhao. They paddled doggedly, keeping close to shore beside the tall cliff pitted with caves in which lived eagles, vultures and bats. This cliff suddenly seemed to cave in, a dark defile gaped, into which the river poured with the velocity of a torrent. A strong voice hailed the two women.

They saw a man, two dogs, a wolf and a boy scrambling down toward them. Amhao dropped her paddle from fear, but Glava was not shaken. The stature of the man reared beyond the height of Kzahm the Black Boar, but he was not as massive, and seemed more supple. The face was young, the skull long, and the eyes matched the hue of the river, with jade-green reflections. He made a few hasty signs, indicated the Tzohs with a gesture.

Without hesitation Glava made for the shore. In a flash, man, boy and animals were in the canoe. The stranger spoke:

"The Tzohs took the women of the Ougmars! Helgvor will bring warriors to wipe theirs out."

He had already snatched Amhao's paddle, for his sure instinct had informed him that she was the weaker, less resolute than her companion. He directed the craft into the gully. All distrust had left Glava. That warrior's face was lighter than were the faces of the Tzohs, its hue resembled that of her own visage, and that clear complexion, the sinewy, long limbs, pleased her more than the massive structures of men of her tribe. She was ready to obey him, to help him.

The rushing waters hurled the canoe into the defile, and the speed was that of a galloping man. At first, the pursuers did not understand this move, and those in the leading craft saw the fugitives' boat flash in the semi-darkness. Then they guessed that the stranger fleeing with Glava and her sister had no companions save the boy and beasts.

"We will pursue the canoe!" urged a warrior with enormous shoulders. The others hesitated, pointed at the two wounded men, and one of them voiced the general opinion.

"Are not other warriors hidden in those rocks?"

The crew of the second canoe, which had come near, overheard these words. One of them, Kamr, son of the Hyena, snorted sarcastically, "Had there been more warriors, Glava and Amhao would not have fled! Shall 12 Tzohs run before a man and two women?"

"Two of our warriors are hit, and Kzahm ordered prudence."

The son of the Hyena laughed ironically. His strength was as great as that of Kzahm, the Black Boar, and in his heart he craved for leadership. "Did Kazhm order us to be cowards? Let two warriors follow Kamr on the bank. If it is deserted, the Tzohs will pursue the women."

He spoke like a chief, and was a chief. His canoe made for the shore, and he landed with two comrades. They discovered no men among the rocks, saw none on the plain and the majority of the Tzohs were thus convinced: ambushed warriors would have fired arrows and spears at them.

"The Tzohs will pursue the canoe!" Kamr said, returning.

"Kzahm shall be discontented and will punish Kamr," the chief of the first boat objected.

"Kzahm cannot punish six warriors for pursuing a lone man. And the men of the Red Clan are not his slaves!"

The crew of the second canoe belonged to that clan, feared for its courage and spirit of independence. Kzahm had to handle its members carefully.

"Women lose days speaking," Kamr resumed arrogantly. "Let tongues be still. Warriors wish to fight!"

With a violent gesture he picked up the paddle and launched his craft into the rapids. The onrush of the current was such that it grew dangerous to increase progress, and the six men were content to keep their boat away from the rocky walls. At times, strong whirlpools spun the canoe, but the Tzohs were accustomed to water and its traps and did not worry. Kamr searched in vain for the fugitives. Helgvor had too long a lead.

Stubbornly, the warrior refused to be discouraged, and as no attack came from the cliffs, close enough to be within arrow range, he grew certain that there was but one combatant ahead. The cliffs towered by degrees and soon were no more than a low line of rocks, and the immense surface of the river reappeared. The surface was smooth and they slid silently along. On the right shore was the plain across which the Tzohs had marched, on the left bank was a virgin forest.

In the middle of the stream the canoe was safe from surprise, and Kamr triumphantly glanced over the river and looked for traces of the fugitives.

But nothing appeared on the broad river.

As long as the canoe was between the cliffs, Helgvor and Glava thought only of avoiding a wreck. Although the women had repaired the boat, it was more fragile and not as well balanced as the craft of the pursuers. At times the waves threatened to overturn it; then the man and the girl used all their skill to keep it afloat. Used to the river, both were capable.

They turned to look behind. No canoe appeared on the river, no silhouette rose ashore. The banks parted widely until the left strand was almost invisible. When it vanished, finally, the river resumed the aspect of a lake.

Helgvor now looked at the women. Amhao offered the swarthy face of the Tzohs, their bestial jaws, their small, beady eyes. Such appearance did not please men of the Blue River. But Glava was strangely like the women of the Ougmar clan, with her long oval face, her large clear eyes, her hair the color of gold and her flexible torso.

Looking at her, a sweet fervor flooded his chest, comparable to his elation when he roamed the plain in the early dawn. And Glava preferred, to the dark complexion and massive build of the Tzohs, this great body, supple as that of a leopard, this face pink as that of a baby.

He tried to make her understand, mingling words and gestures, that the Tzohs had stolen the Ougmars' women. She caught a 'word here and there, a word which recalled words uttered by her grandmother from the Green Lake, for the tongue of the Lakes resembled that of the men of the Blue River. The two races came from a common origin, and primitive terms had remained similar. And in her turn, she undertook to relate her flight, the earthquake in the mountain, the threat of death, the escape in the night.

Although he understood her less than she understood him, he knew that they had formed an alliance. At least he knew their names, repeated with signs. And they knew his name.

"Glava and Amhao will be Ougmar women," he said. "Helgvor will save them."

They progressed on the river, and the enemy did not appear. Nevertheless, Helgvor decided to increase his lead, and Glava helped him with an energy which amazed him. He considered landing, striking out through the forest, but they could not leave the canoe. And the boat, precious help on the river, would be a burden ashore.

Helgvor decided therefore to keep on water as long as no new peril presented itself. He paddled in silence while dim plans for the future came to mind. Vigilant as a warrior, Hiolg continuously scanned the surroundings. As they rounded a headland, he uttered an exclamation, then, his piercing glance directed upstream, spoke.

"The Tzohs are back."

Helgvor and Glava, while steering the craft out of a whirlpool, gazed behind, and saw, very far away, a canoe. Had they not expected it, they might have mistaken it for a crocodile or a tree-trunk floating on the water. Then their sharp eyes discerned dim silhouettes which were those of men, and Helgvor repeated, looking at Glava, "The Tzohs!"

VII. Besieged

The fugitives' canoe, close to a thickly bushed bank, must be difficult to discern. Helgvor steered still closer to land, so that the craft would be all the more difficult to espy from afar. Before rounding a bend, he cast a last glance behind.

There was still but one canoe in sight. Was the second one slower, or had it given up? He did not dwell long on the question, and came to a decision. Ten thousand arms' lengths away, the real bush started, where he could prepare an ambush. In the thicket, his wolf was capable of downing a warrior; his two dogs, less robust, could worry an enemy. Glava seemed ready to show fight, and he, Helgvor, was the best bowman among the Ougmars; and, with a single club-blow, he dropped his man.

Although she still paddled vigorously, Glava was beginning to show fatigue. She had been struggling since morning. Helgvor took her paddle and gave it to Amhao, who had rested somewhat. The pursuers were not seen again until the bush was within 5000 arms' lengths.

From then on, they gained steadily. Not only was their craft better constructed, but what availed Helgvor, seconded by a woman, against six mighty paddlers? He thought only of reaching the bush. To get there in time, it was enough for the canoe to go half as fast as that of the Tzohs.

For 2000 arms' lengths, he contrived to keep his distance very well. His strength was intact, and his skill made up for the weakness and clumsiness of Amhao. But before long, the woman tired again, and the advantage of the foes became considerable. Had Glava not picked up the paddle again, it would have been impossible to reach shelter in time.

"Glava is as brave as a warrior!" shouted Helgvor, warm admiration in his eyes.

She did not understand the words, but smiled at the gesture, while her heart swelled with happiness. Already, her effort showed results: the distance separating the two canoes dwindled slowly, and Helgvor could hope to reach his goal before danger became pressing. At the same time, he was elated because the second Tzoh boat had not come in sight. The last minutes were arduous; despite her courage, Glava faltered, but he, stiffening his muscles, fought against fate with frantic ardor.

"Oah!" he shouted triumphantly.

They had reached the bush and the Tzohs, 300 arms' lengths late, could not see the canoe bearing Helgvor and his companions skimming under the bending branches of the weeping willows, up a narrow tributary of the main river. This stream had two outlets. Helgvor paddled up one of them slowly. Before attaining the tip of the island formed by the delta, a marshy stretch appeared on the left bank, thick with reeds.

"If Glava has no strength left," he said, "Glava need not paddle longer."

The canoe reached a haven in the marsh, a cove sheltered by enormous willows and gigantic poplar-trees. Helgvor pushed the canoe into a tangle of reeds, then picked up his weapons.

All was quiet. The Tzohs must have gone by the river's mouth. But their return must be feared, for they would soon discover that the fugitives had vanished. Doubtless, they would hesitate a while before the two outlets, then before the marsh. Only luck would bring them upon the canoe hidden in the reeds!

Glava had watched Helgvor's stratagem with admiration, and with the eagerness of youth she wished to laugh despite the peril. But Helgvor was already dragging his companions through the bush. When it grew too thickly he sought an easier path; often he opened the way with his hatchet. Soon tall trees appeared with parasitic plants swirling in their shade. Then the fugitives came to a clearing in the center of which were several great boulders.

"Helgvor, Hiolg, Glava and Amhao will stop here."

The son of Shtra chose a space surrounded with stones, in which one found shelter from projectiles. He then spoke to the wolf and the dogs. They knew the words that ordered silence, watchfulness or fight: on this occasion he told them to remain quiet and alert. Their admirable senses caught all variations in the atmosphere; the scent of the dogs surpassed that of the wolf, but the wolf heard better.

Helgvor stationed them in the three inlets to the circle of stones, then examined his weapons. He had his club, the hatchet, a bow, two spears and five arrows. The weapons of the women consisted of a club, four spears, two hatchets and a sharpened stake. Hiolg had a child's bow and one spear. The wolf was to be counted upon; and the dogs, although small, might be of help in hand to hand combat.

The fugitives ate dried meat hastily, then Helgvor and Hiolg sought to make their enclosure more secure. They barred the outlets with spiny branches, leaving only narrow lanes for the animals; if any Tzoh sought to crawl in, he could be stunned with ease. Meanwhile, the women watched between the boulders.

Several times Helgvor felt a desire to increase the distance between them and the pursuers, but Amhao was too tired to carry on. Even Glava was struggling against utter fatigue. If the Tzohs found their tracks, they would soon make up for lost time, and the fight would be forced upon the ill-assorted group in the open. Here, the rocks afforded protection, and the women were recuperating enough to be of use.

In the depth of the forest the branches cast thicker shadow, and the Sun appeared to swell as it neared the tree-tops. Because their souls and their races were young, the thought of perils dwindled in Helgvor, Glava and Amhao: they grew certain that the Tzohs had lost their tracks.

Before a man could walk 10,000 paces, twilight kneaded the clouds into obscurity. Their shelter seemed sure. They would pass the night there. At times, Helgvor and Glava exchanged gestures or words. Already repetition had started a common speech. Glava grasped language quicker than the Ougmar, for the memory of her grandmother's muttered words, in the tongue of the Green Lakes, was growing clearer and she was thus better able to comprehend Helgvor's articulations.

Amhao took small part in those efforts at conversation. Passive, nonchalant in spirit, tired, occupied by her child, she yielded to the energy of her companions. The little one fascinated Hiolg, who brought laughter upon the flabby, round face of the baby. Habit was being formed among those people, and the sensation of strangeness and contrast was dwindling, even for Amhao, who, more than Glava, was aware that she was an alien to the tall nomad.

Shortly before nightfall the dogs stirred uneasily, and the wolf prowled outside the enclosure. Although Helgvor and his people listened intensely, they heard nothing save the murmur of the wind through the branches and the sounds of insects. But the dogs and the wolf could be depended upon; they scented a foe, man or beast, within the atmosphere. The eyes of the wolf glowered, and the dogs turned often to look at their master inquiringly.

Helgvor whistled gently. It was an order for silence. In any case, unless the man permitted, the dogs and the wolf never barked or howled before a prey or before danger. However, their agitation increased; the wolf slunk about softly, the dogs slid in and out of the openings left for them, returned with their teeth showing in a mute snarl.

"It is a tiger, a lion, a gray bear—or the Tzohs!" Helgvor stated, adjusting his bow. Glava clutched her club, preferring to leave her spear to the warrior.

Then Helgvor and Hiolg, with their ears pressed against the soil, heard distinct, soft steps which were unmistakable to them.

"The Tzohs are coming!"

Even Amhao understood the gesture, and Hiolg started to laugh at her fears, for he believed Helgvor invincible. Although less confident than the boy, Glava was elated at the thought of fighting at the warrior's side. The steps halted, and the nomad guessed that the enemy had paused on the fringe of the clearing and that the enclosure was being examined with great care. The same silence prevailed on both sides, the same prudence, as of felines in ambush.

The nearest tree was within arrow-shot, and all about the enclosure there was nothing but grass and a few bushes too thin and scattered to protect a man. For a while, the stillness was so complete that Helgvor might have believed he had been mistaken, had the attitude of his beasts allowed uncertainty. Identical rage stiffened their muscles and dilated their pupils.

Since he had identified human steps, the Ougmar did not permit them to roam outside, and, accustomed to ambush, they waited, at once patient and eager. The four fugitives were watching, each one at a loophole, and Amhao showed herself as alert as the others. At length Hiolg, who faced west, came to touch Helgvor's shoulder.

"A Tzoh in the trees!"

Helgvor turned gently, reaching out for his bow. A Tzoh was climbing an ash-tree, screened by the branches of a large sycamore. The fellow, having risen halfway up the trunk, could see into the enclosure. At that distance, no Tzoh bow could have reached him with an arrow, but the tall Ougmars had weapons that carried very far, and Helgvor had the mightiest one in the clan.

His eyes fastened on the climber, the nomad waited until the left shoulder and part of the torso showed; he tightened the string, released a missile. He meant to hit the chest, but the distance was too great; despite his calculations, the arrow only pierced the hand of the climbing man.

With a cry of rage, the Tzoh slid down along the bole, striking the ground heavily, while his comrades, knowing they had been discovered, roared frantically. The resounding voice of the Ougmar launched the war-cry, and because silence had become useless, Hiolg and Glava also shouted, while the dogs barked furiously and the wolf howled as on hunger nights.

"The Tzohs are vultures lacking courage! They shall perish under the hatchet, the spear and the arrow!"

"The Tzohs took the women from the Men of the Blue River," the chief of the enemy jeered. "The Men of the Blue River are stupid as sheep and slugs."

The clamors died out after leaving the mouths of the criers, and silence settled down again, weighted with anxiety. Helgvor was wondering if the warriors of the second canoe had joined those of the first. The voices he had heard revealed five or six men, but that might have been prearranged, some of the new arrivals might have purposely remained quiet.

The red furnace of the Sun seemed to devour the western forest, then the clouds, the hue of flowers and fire, created a universe wider than that of the forests, the lakes, the plains and the rivers. That limitless life was dying out with every quiver of the leaves; the strange ashes of darkness were spreading the murderous night.

It was the hour when weak animals know that meat-eaters are leaving their dens.

Formidable voices exchanged menaces. The lion roared, wolves howled, and the jackals added their sharp yelps to the sinister laughter of the hyena. When there remained no light save the weak glow of the stars, the aspect of the clearing became awe-inspiring.

In the granite enclosure, human beings and animals found their night-senses growing keener, while the Tzohs discerned the shelter of the Ougmars and the women only as a shadowy mass. All was still, the quiet of ambush.

The wild beasts were prowling. The Tzohs wished to surprise the tall nomad. They had scouted the obstacle, and knew where the spears and stones would come from, but an attack might be made in vain against those sheltered behind the protecting boulders.

Kamr with the bull's chest said: "If the Tzohs are to attack, why wait? Will not the man of the Blue River and his animals be ready for combat all night long? And Kzahm, our chief, is waiting for us on the island."

"How attack?" a warrior, whose face was seamed with deep scars, asked.

"Night is dark. The Tzohs shall crawl through the grass, and when Kamr gives the war-cry, we shall leap in all together."

"That's well," the other admitted. "But the bow of the River Man must be dreaded."

"The River Man cannot aim on a moonless night! Are five Tzohs afraid of a lone Ougmar?"

"Woum is not scared," proudly replied the one with the scars.

And the five men started the crawl. Half of the space which they must cross was thick with high grass and ferns, which concealed them from human eyes. But the nostrils of the wolf and dogs did not fail. From them, Helgvor knew that the Tzohs were approaching. But when he pressed his ear against the sod, the sounds made by roaming animals outside prevented discerning the progress of the enemy.

With a flint stone he lit an armful of dried grass in a hollow of the soil, and made torches from two branches. A strong glow lit the enclosure and cast some light into the clearing.

"When the Tzohs rise in the short grass," he addressed the boy, "Hiolg shall raise the torches so that Helgvor can see the enemy."

In their intense excitement, the dogs were pushing their pointed muzzles through the gaps; the wolf growled deeply. Almost simultaneously Hiolg, Helgvor and Glava perceived movements in the shorter grass. The boy picked up the torches and, standing on a boulder, illuminated the clearing. The quivering rays revealed the presence of the Tzohs. Helgvor bent his bow, discharged two arrows swiftly. One scratched a foe's shoulder, the second sank beneath the collar bone. The man dropped the club grasped in his right fist and uttered a great cry. Helgvor now had but two arrows left.

Startled by the torchlight and the skill of the tall nomad, the Tzohs hugged the ground to became invisible. The torches cast an oscillating radiance which made surprise out of the question. The enclosure must be besieged or stormed. Having engaged himself in the venture, already responsible for the wounding of two men, in the grip of mad fury and intense hatred against Kzahm whose scorn he feared, Kamr resolved to risk everything.

"The Tzohs will leap ahead," he ordered, "and kill the River Man."

"Two Tzohs have been wounded here, two were wounded in Houa's canoe," retorted the scarred man.

"Have the Tzohs forgotten vengeance?" Kamr snarled. "Do Tzohs tremble like storks before an eagle? If the River Man does not perish with the two women who have betrayed the clans, the Tzohs must go home trembling, and the Ougmars' women will laugh in their faces! The River Man is alone. I shall slay him with blows of my club!"

This was not too boastful. All knew that Kamr had attacked leopards with his hatchet, and on a day of great hunting he had slain a lion.

"While Kamr attacks the River Man, the warriors shall beat down the women and the beasts."

Kamr uttered the war-cry, and the four men bounded forward through the grass. An arrow hummed, struck the ground, then a second scratched the arm of a warrior without weakening him. Tzohs reached the enclosure and scaled it rapidly with the vigor of strong young men.

Helgvor held his spears, and Glava made ready to help him. Almost at the same moment, the warriors appeared on the crest of the rocks. Hiolg had quickly put out the fire and extinguished the torches. There remained only the light of the stars, and in the violet night, silhouettes were indistinct as vapors.

Plans were forgotten. Helgvor swung a club, Glava used a spear, and Hiolg threw stones. An assailant collapsed under the rain of blows, another was pierced through the shoulder by Glava's weapon, but despite his injury, he leaped down into the enclosure followed by Kamr and the remaining warrior. The dogs leaped; Glava fought desperately.

Hiolg was helping the wolf which had caught a warrior at the neck from behind. Frightened at first, Amhao darted forward to take her share of the struggle.

Kamr and Helgvor were face to face.

They were powerful fighting machines, equal in bulk, energy and courage, unlike in build. With his cubical head, his chest rounded as the chests of animals, Kamr represented the race of the Tzohs, sprung from volcanic soil, while Helgvor, with his long skull, his broad, flat chest, his long limbs, was the perfect descendant of the people who lived by the Green Lakes and the Blue River. The hatred of their ancestors flamed in them, they were animated by obscure legends, ancestral memories and incompatible instincts.

The clubs whirled. In that corner of the enclosure, where they had much space to move in, Kamr insulted Helgvor and his ancestors, while the Ougmar predicted the vengeance of his tribe. Each held a spear in the left hand. In the semi-darkness, Helgvor was lighter than Kamr, whose head melted into the night.

Kamr thrust with his spear, but Helgvor broke the weapon with a swing of his club. Then the club of Kamr fell like a stone. The heavy weapons clashed together, and Helgvor staggered. With a long howl, the Tzoh tried to complete his victory, but the tip of Helgvor's spear menaced his breast and Kamr prudently leaped to safety.

The spear, barely visible in the darkness, struck his shoulder, but did not sink beneath the skin. For a very brief moment they caught their breath, face to face, waiting for an opportunity. Near them, in the obscurity wolf, dogs, the women and the boy were fighting the other Tzohs.

Then Kamr resumed the attack, and again the clubs clashed with such mighty impact that they whirled from the men's fists.

"The River Man shall die!" Kamr growled.

He leaped forward, clasped Helgvor in his arms. Among the Tzohs, Kamr was admitted to be the strongest in a fight without weapons, where body and limbs clash. Even Kzahm, the Black Boar, so formidable with hatchet and club, would have been beaten. So Kamr was confident, and when he had grasped the Ougmar around the body, he panted with joy and lifted his foe off the ground.

Helgvor gripped Kamr by the throat. As they fell, then rolled over and over on the ground, Kamr had the advantage at first, having secured the better hold. But his breath grew short, his mouth gaped to inhale. His nerves weakened so that the Ougmar was able to throw aside the heavy body, and Kamr gurgled, flat on his back, the cartilage of his neck broken, smashed by the nomad's powerful fingers.

After a few quivers, the enormous body became motionless in a last spasm.

"Thus shall die the Tzohs, ravishers of women!" Helgvor cried.

Picking up the club, he ran to assist the women.

Amhao was down, struck by a bronze hatchet and a spear. Glava and the wolf had slain a man, but the girl, bloody

51

and battered, was about to give way before the onslaught of the remaining Tzoh, who had just stunned Hiolg.

The Ougmar leaped like a leopard.

It was not a fight. Twice the heavy weapon fell, and the last Tzoh dropped. The tall nomad shouted his victory to the gleaming stars.

VIII. Pain and Death

Helgvor relit the fire.

In the glare of the purple flames, he saw the blood flow on the face, the arms and the chest of Glava. Amhao seemed dead, pierced by deep wounds. Hiolg, stunned with a club, was beginning to regain consciousness. One of the dogs was dying. The other licked his wounds, while the wolf shook himself in an attempt to rid his flank of a protruding spear.

A grim sadness overcame Helgvor. He alone was strong, for without him, women, children and animals would have died. Yet he himself had been saved by their courage. The nomad left the enclosure to pluck the leaves and the bitter-tasting plants which Ougmars crushed to cover wounds. When he returned, he noticed that Hiolg's head, although swollen near the temple, was not bleeding. Life was coming back into the boy's eyes.

Having crushed the leaves and grasses, Helgvor applied them as he had seen done by those who knew ancestral secrets. Then he carried the bodies of the Tzohs and the carcass of the dog outside the enclosure, to avoid the annoyance of wild beasts attracted by freshly spilled blood. He saw the dead man left in the clearing, but he saw no trace of the man whose hand he had pierced with an arrow.

His fatigue was extreme. He looked at Amhao, who was motionless, at Glava, not much better off, at Hiolg, who stirred. Only the wolf and the dog could have resumed the fight.

"Helgvor shall watch until midnight," he murmured. "Then it will be Hiolg's turn."

Squatting near the fire, he listened to the sounds of the forest, haunted by furtive lives. At intervals there could be heard call and menace, cries of alliance, cries of murder, the voices of victory and despair, agonized plaints. Already the prowlers were crawling toward the fresh prey, still bleeding, which even the large beasts would not scorn.

The rising Moon, half-disk of burnished copper which paled as it rose, covered the clearing with uncertain light. The peaceful smells of vegetables passed in the light night-wind. A bat hovered on its membraned wings, fell to the ferns, then two hyenas appeared, their dirty gray pelts streaked with brown. Odd beasts, with blazing eyes, with backs sloping sharply from head to tail, luck had served them well, for their sense of smell was poor.

With sinister chuckles, they smelled the too fresh corpses, and their formidable jaws, powerful as those of lions or tigers, ripped bellies open. Rovers with subtle scent, eyes aglow, slinking forth lightly, the jackals came, light as cats, ears pointed. Here was prey in abundance, eternal hunger increased their avidity, but already five wolves emerged from the night, rough guests which growled threateningly. Then came a wildcat, sliding through the grass, and a screech-owl swooped silently.

When the wolves growled, the hyenas started. Bitter and mournful, the jackals yelped. Hatred and hunger stiffened their spines. Eyes gleamed, teeth glittered in the red maws, an identical instinct for life and death stirred in the timid jackals, in the cowardly hyenas, in the wise wolves.

The jackals were aware of their weakness, and even in numbers did not dare fight. The hyenas knew their jaws could crunch the wolves' bones. The wolves, alert and angry, estimated the prey; when they saw that there was a share for them, they howled louder to indicate their determination, and took two of the corpses. The jackals surrounded the body farthest from the rest. The hyenas, possessing Kamr, another warrior and the dead dog, understood that a truce had come about, and resumed eating.

Suddenly, twigs crackled, and a rough, thick body crushed small trees. The animal coming forward, supple and heavy at the same time in his gray fur, with his flat skull and enormous claws, disturbed the meal. All knew his might and his brutal temper.

At the sight of the gathering he halted, swayed on his massive paws, his tiny eyes gleaming through coarse hair. Then he stated his will with an imperious grunt. All stopped eating and stared at the intruder. Even those who had never encountered him before understood the menace. He was larger than a tiger, and yielded to none save the mammoth and the rhinoceros.

The wolves being nearer than the hyenas, he drove them away. With long howls, quivering with rage, indignation and hatred, they left. The bear laid one paw on a corpse. The wolves, slinking back, dragged the other away. Bending over his prey, the huge beast paid no attention to them; a cheek and a shoulder had been devoured, but the meat was fresh, oozing blood, and it would not have been otherwise had the bear made the kill himself. Satisfied, he set to work. His fangs sank into a thigh. He felt a sweet pleasure in sating a violent hunger.

While he was tearing strips of flesh, the forest sent forth a new prowler, the formidable odor of which had been scented by wolves and jackals for some time.

The head appeared first, compact, with two streaks of orange hair and great yellowish eyes which palpitated like enormous stars. The feline yawned, and revealed a crimson cavern in which the fangs stood out like long, white daggers. He roared and swelled his broad chest, his flanks streaked with somber marking, worked his sharp claws on the ground. All knew him at once, save the gray bear, who came from the mountain, and all were in the grip of terror.

If the gray bear did not know him, he did not know the gray bear. He knew only a brown bear which never dared face him. He was startled to see this one, with the ease of a victor, continue to eat his prey. It happened that if beasts, with the exception of mammoth and rhinoceros, avoided the tiger, in his home mountain, the gray bear acknowledged no rival.

The tiger roared a second time. As the bear was nearest to him, the bear must give up his place. Fury had come, the insane rage that distends the breast.

The bear understood that he was being threatened. He stopped feeding, turned his snout slowly toward the tiger. Before the immense, fiery eyes, his little bloodshot pupils seemed weak, lost in thick hair, pale as glow-worms. But the size of the bear was greater than that of the tiger.

Gathered on his broad paws, swinging his colossal body, the great bear answered the roar with a lordly grunt. He was the descendant of hot-tempered ancestors, and his rage was so swift, so intense, that his breath rustled the grass. Yet the effluvia met before the bodies came into contact, and each one knew dimly that the other was a worthy foe.

Because his breed is prudent, the tiger stalked aside to launch a flank attack. The bear waited no longer, and as the tiger came on, he clawed out, yet he did not stop that hairy mass hurtling like a bolt. Then teeth, claws, and muscles met, and blood dripped through the fur over the short hair. The bear had downed the tiger, but the feline rolled aside, put the larger beast off balance, and they formed a confused whirl of bodies from which rose raucous clamors.

The tiger leaped aside, and the bear sought to clutch him again. They were face to face, red with the blood of ten wounds, each now fully aware of the power of his opponent. Perhaps there was some hesitation. But pain, hatred, the lust for revenge, shot their quivering bulks to the fight.

The tiger fell, the bear sank his fangs in the depth of the flesh, but one of his paws became useless, crushed. The huge chests creaked with the effort. The tiger groped for another paw. But the jaws of the bear slashed into his enemy's throat, wrenched at it, pierced it, dug into it.

When the feline succumbed, the bear rose, staggering, uttered a grunt of pain, then, weakened by loss of blood, dropped back to the ground. Then a dim joy stirred the jackals, the wolves and the hyenas, and from everywhere frailer beasts who had witnessed the combat emerged from the grasses, the bushes, the forest.

It was a subtle swarming of pupils, of paws, of muzzles, the secret life, the unquenchable life, and already the devouring tiger, whose scent alone caused the multitude to flee, was sniffed by voracious nostrils, felt by small teeth.

Helgvor had indistinctly seen, through the brush and the tall ferns, the coming of hyenas, wolves and jackals, then the fierce battle. The wind brought together the sweet odors of the vegetation and the stench of the animals. He heard the gray bear growling, the tiger roar. Then came a prolonged silence, broken by pants, weak cries and muffled moans.

Which had won? Or had they both been wounded, and given up the struggle? He thought that one or the other might remain near the enclosure, and then danger would be feared, night or day. His tribe at times hunted the huge cats. Helgvor, with arrows, hatchet and club, had killed a lion. But he had been badly wounded himself and had remained unconscious for hours. Had he been alone, the prowling beasts would have devoured him.

As he remembered that, he knew he was tired. He feared that he would not fight well due to fatigue. For a space the wolf growled, the dog smelled the air. Then they sank to the ground, and slept.

IX. To The Victor...

Helgvor was still asleep when day came. Squatted near the ashes of the fire, Hiolg was dozing. There was joy in the trees and upon the earth. The night seemed eternal each time, because death roamed and all the weak feared they might fill the bellies of the strong. But when darkness was vanquished, hope was boundless as the birds sang, facing the rising Sun. Hiolg touched Helgvor gently, and the warrior rose instantly. Like a wild animal, he was always on the alert, and rose club in hand.

"The eyes of Hiolg no longer see, his ears no longer hear!" the child said. "Hiolg can sleep," the man said.

The Sun shed an amber light through the branches of the trees, dispelling the mists of the morning. Only the bones of the Tzohs were left, and the tiger was a skeleton also. The bear, still alive, kept the greedy jaws at bay.

Helgvor inhaled the fresh air, the creating air, and his youth swelled in a flooding of happiness, his victory filled him with limitless strength. Turning his eyes toward the two women and the child, he believed Amhao dead until he saw her chest rise and fall perceptibly. Glava, weak from bleeding, slumbered.

The wolf and the dog, awakened by hunger, turned trusting eyes toward their master. They were granted their share of the dry meat. Then, stirring up the fire, the Ougmar cooked his meal. The mysterious force of the food increased his joy of living, his tenderness; these women, these children, even the wolf and the dog, saved by his courage and his muscles, seemed part of his own being.

When the Sun had dissipated the fog, Helgvor left the enclosure and found the skeletons of the Tzohs, near the fleshless bones of the tiger. As the warrior drew near, the gray bear lifted his head, which was swarming with insects, and a veil appeared to screen his pupils. His gaping wounds festered, his death was certain. As Helgvor halted to stare at him, a painful snarl of menace lifted the hairy lips.

"The great bear shall not hunt any more!" the nomad said. "Long has he caused the horse, the stag, even the aurochs, to tremble. He has killed the tiger. The great bear is almost as mighty as the mammoth—and the great bear is about to die!"

The erect beasts loved to utter words to fit circumstances, and the Ougmar loved speech.

"The great bear is about to die," the hunter repeated. "He will be torn to pieces by the jackal, the wolf and the hyena. But his flesh is good for man also, and the Ougmar has not enough to feed his women and children. The great bear must give of his flesh."

A doe raced by, within arrow range. Helgvor felt that it was better to allow her to pass, for she was fitted to reproduce life. The doomed beast would supply meat without waste of life. He picked up his spear, selected a spot through which to reach the heart. The blade sank in, moved about. The bear uttered a groan of agony, but his weakness was so great, so like death, that he scarcely quivered.

"The great bear would have suffered until night," resumed the son of Shtra, "and perhaps the wolf and the hyena would have devoured him alive."

He picked up the scattered arrows, a few tools left by the Tzohs, spears, three bronze hatchets, then went back to the bear; he cut off both hams and some slices of tender meat. The pelt was very handsome. He would skin the animal later, if he had time. Thirst was searing his mouth, and he searched for water. Eventually he found a source and he drank deeply.

Going back to the enclosure, he found all quiet. The dog and the wolf were again asleep, but Glava was awakening. The flow of blood had stopped, her wounds were not deep, and she was moaning, bending over Amhao.

"Amhao shall not die!" the nomad assured her.

Glava understood his gestures, and a smile spread on her bloodstained face. Then, seeing her arms blackened and reddened, she desired to wash them. He guessed that she must be thirsty as well, and pointed to the forest.

"Helgvor found a spring."

There were three waterskins, roughly made. One belonged to Helgvor, the others he had found on the Tzohs. The warrior indicated that he was going to fill them, and Glava wished to go with him. But her legs still quivered under her weight.

"Helgvor shall go with Hiolg."

He also took the animals along.

When Glava had drunk, she hid behind a boulder to wash her body. Meanwhile, Helgvor cooked some meat for her, and as she ate, he found pleasure in watching that light-colored face in which gleamed eyes the hue of the river.

Why doesn't she resemble the Tzohs? he wondered.

Glancing at Amhao, he compared the cubical head, the wide face, the heavy jaws of the elder with the delicate features of the girl. Their complexions differed oddly, too. That of Amhao was the color of oak bark, with coppery glints; that of Glava almost white, like the petals of a flower. Amhao's torso was bulky as that of a sow, Glava's flexible like that of a doe. Glava was tall and lithe.

Amhao is a daughter of the Rocks. But Glava is like the daughters of the Green Lakes and the Blue River.

Proud to have saved her, he admired her because she had fought with the courage and skill of a warrior. Amhao awoke when her child cried. Although dazed and dull, she recognized her sister.

"Amhao is saved," Glava informed her. "The tall warrior of the River has killed off those who attacked us!"

The young woman listened vaguely. She could neither see nor hear clearly. She repeated: "Amhao is saved."

She drank water greedily, but could eat nothing. She fell asleep as Glava washed her face.

Helgvor thought as a warrior thinks: of the danger, of the human foes, of animals. He did not plan to pick up the trail of the Tzohs, for he counted upon Glava to guide the Ougmars to their homes. But what had become of the sixth enemy, of which the wolf and the dog found no trace?

He could not go away by canoe. Often the river was too rapid for the strength of several men; in a large craft, a single paddler would be helpless. Would the man join his clan on foot? The road was long, particularly for a wounded man. The Ougmar called the child.

"Hear me, Hiolg: Helgvor and the dog, Hiolg and the wolf, will seek the tracks of the wounded Man of the Rocks. Helgvor will not go far, for he must watch the enclosure. Hiolg must not fight. When he has seen the Tzoh, he comes back."

"The Man of the Rocks is wounded," the boy replied. "Perhaps the wolf can finish him."

"Hiolg shall not fight!" Helgvor ordered. "Hiolg shall remain unseen. And he shall return here when the Sun starts to set."

No warrior could conceal himself better than the boy in ferns and grass, in rocks or bushes.

"Hiolg will hide like a fox!" he stated.

They searched for tracks. Helgvor returned to the enclosure often, while Hiolg carried on into the forest. His memory for sites and trails was extraordinary, his mind retained the image of every step taken. Many heavy beasts had walked about, the tracks of the Tzoh could not be picked up. Hiolg walked toward the marsh and the river, but scouted to one side or the other often. The wolf helped him, but, being less docile when with the child than with the man, he roamed more or less as he liked.

The child and the animal found the tracks almost at the same time. It was on moist soil in which the man's feet had left deep imprints. Because there were many, perhaps also because he deemed his lead too great for pursuit, the Tzoh had made no effort to conceal them.

Hiolg allowed the wolf to scent them a long while, then resumed the hunt, increasing his wariness, dilating his sharp pupils. A great pride distended his puny chest, for the soul of a warrior welled within him.

At length he espied the man. Stretched on the ground, weakened, tired and fierce, feverish from his wound, the warrior thought gloomily of the defeat inflicted on Kamr and his companions. Lurking in the darkness, he had witnessed the struggle, and when all the Tzohs had fallen, he had gone into the forest. He had not slept much, constantly awakened by inner tremors of fear, gripped by panic, his right hand useless. Despite his bronze hatchet, he had become a weak animal.

This morning his head was not clear and he heard humming in his ears the threat of secret dangers; it was a bad omen, which often announced the death of wounded warriors. The hum increased as the Sun rose higher. Tzoum, son of the Stag, had applied grass to the wound, but the compress did not ease his pain: the hole was black and burning; he felt the pulse beat in the raw flesh.

Prone at the foot of a sycamore-tree, he felt the terror of being alone, far from friends, far from home caves. The defeat of Kamr depressed him as much as the wound; his race had proved the weaker, and that weakness he felt in his bowels.

"The Tzohs are mightiest," he muttered, to give himself cheer, and because he had a strong love for his breed.

Hidden in the bushes, Hiolg trembled as he identified him.

The wounded warrior was the very man who had captured the boy's mother and slain his grandfather. Because he was young, Hiolg was forgetting, he had consoled himself already, but the sight of the Tzoh made his memory flare up blindingly, and aroused the child to fury.

"The Tzoh has no spear," he mused. "His hand is sick. Hiolg and the wolf are stronger."

The warrior, a man of thick torso, short of legs, long of arms, had an enormous face and thick hair which fell down over his sloping forehead almost to the eyes, which, like those of the bison, were set high up toward the temples. His strength must be that of the great boar. The child held the wolf and said ardently,

"Hiolg must not fight. But the Tzoh took away Hiolg's mother."

The wolf sniffed the warrior's scent, stronger because of the man's illness. He recalled the Tzoh he had strangled on the preceding evening. Suddenly he broke free, and slid to the tree under which the warrior lay. His walk was as silent as the flight of a night bird, but he frightened a rabbit, which fled madly.

The Tzoh turned, saw the wolf, and rose proudly, hatchet in his left hand. "Tzoum has slain ten wolves. A wolf is no stronger than a deer before a Tzoh's hatchet. Tzoum laughs at the wolf!"

The eyes of the wolf glowered; those of Tzoum glittered with fever, and the man lied: he was afraid. He was afraid because he was on alien soil, because the unknown voices whistled shrilly in his ears, because Kamr had died despite his strength, and because the wolf's ways were not those of wild wolves.

"Tzoum shall offer a sacrifice to the Hidden Lives!" Tzoum promised.

The wolf circled the man. His neck was powerful, his teeth fine and pointed: he showed them, parting his jaws in a snarl of threat and defiance. Tzoum whirled the hatchet about his head. It was of the finest bronze, very sharp.

"Tzoum has slain larger wolves than the black wolf."

Backed against the tree, he did not see Hiolg, creeping near like a snake. The wolf scented the man's weakness, and seeing Hiolg coming, he did not move, held his ground, eyeing the warrior sideways. The son of the Stag, sure that he had frightened the beast, cried out louder,

"With a single stroke, Tzoum can cleave the skull of the wolf."

A sharp sting in his thigh made him quiver, his knee gave beneath his weight. Hiolg's spear had struck him. Startled, the warrior turned, and while he turned, with a single leap, the wolf was at his throat. Then the child drew out the spear, struck again. The big man crumpled like an uprooted tree, while the beast clung, strangling him. In a flash, Tzoum saw the caves, the warriors, the women, then he slipped into the shadows. The wolf lapped his hot blood.

Hiolg, recalling the words and gestures of warriors, clamored stridently, "Hiolg and the black wolf have slain the big warrior. Hiolg and the wolf are the stronger!"

When he reached the enclosure, with the bronze hatchet and the fur garment of the Tzoh, the child said, "Hiolg did not wish to fight. But he could not hold back the wolf. And the Tzoh had taken the mother of Hiolg. Hiolg stabbed his thigh twice, and the wolf strangled the warrior."

"That is well," Helgvor said, his hand on the little fellow's head.

"Hiolg shall be a warrior, and even a chief, when the time comes."

Boundless happiness flooded Hiolg.

At the end of two days, Glava's wounds were healing. The blood had ceased flowing, the flesh was dry and the ache was scarcely noticeable, save during the night, and the girl could walk easily. Amhao healed more slowly. Nevertheless, rich in youth, her life was resuming. Habit had already united the man and the two women. They admired his strength, his size and his courage.

According to ancestral instinct, Amhao was willing to obey the orders of Helgvor, who now seemed her master. Glava differed from her as a she-wolf differs from a doe: a will for freedom flamed in her, the same urge that had taken her away from the caves, the same which had brought her into the solitude of the forest and caused her to fight like a male warrior.

Unimpressed, she was near Helgvor as an equal. He, by instinct and in gratitude for her courage, understood and accepted her pride. In any case, she intimidated him somewhat, and this unusual timidity thrilled him so that he did not wish to react against it.

They combined their skill and knowledge. Glava knew how to handle a needle and could weave cloth. Helgvor made stout weapons and delicate tools with stone, with horn, with bones. They now had many weapons: the spears, hatchets, bows and arrows of the Tzohs had been collected, and Helgvor honed the edges and points.

The words and gestures they exchanged so often became less obscure. Glava was learning Ougmar. Her memories, formerly forgotten, welled to the surface of her mind. The words spoken by her grandmother made other words easy to understand. Helgvor made little effort to speak Tzoh, for he hated the language of his foes.

He learned that Amhao had been fated for sacrifice when Glava had forced her to flee. He now also knew that the Tzohs lived upstream, more than two moons' march from the Ougmar camp. Since her mother's death, Glava had only bad memories, save those of Amhao; she hated the Tzohs more than before the fight, aware that if the fugitives were recaptured, they would be put to death. Thus her fate was linked to that of the son of Shtra.

In the presence of Glava, the nomad experienced unknown sensations. Growing more slowly than the Tzohs, the young Ougmars, until at an age decided by the old men, had no right to take a woman.

Glava knew more, for the Tzohs obeyed brutal and sensual instinct. But what she had seen filled her with horrified disgust. The chief, Urm, or another old man broke the canine teeth of the girl with a stone, indicating that the woman was thereby submitted without defense to the will of her mate. Then the warrior came forward and struck the woman over the head, and when their union had thus been announced, she became his slave.

She worked for her man and her children. He could beat her and even kill her without punishment. For the one who could have avenged her, usually the brother of the mother, had to accept blood price if offered.

These traditions horrified Glava. She feared as a day of torture the time when she would be given to Kzahm, the Black Boar, whose odor was fetid. She knew also how harshly Amhao had been treated. She feared that the usages of the Ougmars were similar.

In reality, they were not as rough. Canine teeth were not broken off. Those who wished to be engaged to a maid or a widow had to obtain the mother's consent, or the permission of the mother's brother or his successor.

Glava did not know these things. She liked to be with Helgvor, she admired his stature and even his face, but she could not imagine that this man of an alien breed could be her companion for life. And she wished for no closer tie than that which, vague yet tender, now linked them.

He did not think clearly. He trembled when her eyes, the mingling hues of the river and of dead leaves, rested on him. He quivered when the long hair, which she washed in the stream so often, touched his arm or his shoulder. He appreciated the teeth, as white and strong as those of a wolf cub, the supple stride, the round neck, but he did not think of the future. Perhaps he was thus calm because there was no other man about, and the madness which blinds stags, felines and birds could not be aroused.

There were hours so sweet that the nomad forgot the menace of the outside world. In the morning, when the waves of light had driven away the fog, an immense and formless dream grew with the patience of ferns and trees, flowing steadily as the stream. Then Glava became the life of life, a fearsome mystery which astonished and worried the young man. At times, when he thought that she was of an alien race, he would think that she might be his slave, but when he saw the tawny glow of her eyes, there remained in his flesh but a dazzled humility.

The canoe of the women, and that of the Tzohs, larger and faster, had been found. On the sixth day, when Amhao was strong enough, they left the granite enclosure.

X. The Vengeance Trail

Helgvor found a few old men on the Peninsula, old women and children who had escaped the massacre, and also a number of adult women who had fled in time to avoid capture. He waited two days. He had given his hut to the fugitives while a new one was being constructed for him.

Then the warriors returned. They were bringing back many horses for the winter, the hunt had been successful, but their grief was deep and touching.

Akroun, chief of chiefs, was still as strong as a leopard, but years weighed heavily on his shoulders and sprinkled salt in his hair. Craft showed on his rough face, shone in his yellow eyes. Not as tall as Heigoun, the giant of the clan, or even as Helgvor, his shoulders spread like rocks and his torso was hooped with solid ribs.

He called for Helgvor, and spoke in a gruff voice.

"Akroun had left the huts filled with women and children. Five warriors watched over the Red Peninsula. What became of the women; where did the warriors go?"

He knew, for he had met Old Man Hagm far from the camp.

Helgvor replied without visible agitation, "The women were kidnapped, the warriors have died!"

"They fought?" the chief of chiefs swept the young man with a ferocious glance.

"They fought."

"What did Helgvor do? Did he not dare look the foes in the face?"

"It was on the day that Helgvor went scouting with his dog, his wolf and Hiolg. Helgvor saw the Men of the Rocks and came back. The Tzohs were on the Peninsula, Helgvor was alone."

"Helgvor alone did not fight."

"Helgvor fought. He killed two Tzohs. Later, he killed four others. He wounded two."

The warriors surrounded the young man. Heigoun laughed in derision. The chief's face darkened.

"No warrior witnessed Helgvor's deeds!"

"Hiolg saw all."

"Helgvor killed six Men of the Rocks," a shrill voice piped up, "and Hiolg, with the wolf, killed one." Boldly, the boy came to stand beside the tall warrior.

Then Iouk, brother of Helgvor, and Shtra his father, shouted,

"Helgvor is a warrior!"

"The word of a child weighs no more than a leaf," grumbled Heigoun.

The Ougmars believed Heigoun to be the strongest of men, and when Akroun was not present, he was chief.

"Here are my witnesses," Helgvor said.

From an otter skin he drew seven mummified hands, and Hiolg produced an eighth.

Then Akroun said, "Helgvor fought."

"Where did that seventh hand come from?" Heigoun asked.

"It is the hand of a Tzoh slain by a fugitive woman from the Rocks, and by the wolf," Helgvor said reluctantly.

Heigoun shouted, shaking a spear aloft, "Helgvor thus has made alliance with a stranger?"

There was hatred between the two men. Heigoun detested the strength of Helgvor, which increased moon by moon. Learning that the younger man had killed six foes, murderous fury whirled in his skull. All stepped aside as the heavy weapon swung high; the red hair of the warrior blazed like a torch; his chest was large as that of a lion, his arms were knotty with muscles, and his legs were stout as small trees.

"Helgvor allied himself with the fugitives," the young man answered, stepping back a pace, holding his club ready. "Thus Helgvor knows where the Men of the Rocks live, and the fugitives shall guide the Ougmars."

"Akroun wants to see those women!" the chief grunted.

"All the warriors want to see them!" Heigoun added.

"It is well."

When the women appeared, an astonished murmur spread among the Ougmars. All eyes turned from the wide face, the slanting eyes and the stocky body of Amhao, to fasten upon Glava.

With her golden hair, her tawny eyes with jade-hued lights, her high, flexible stature, she was comparable with the most beautiful maiden of the Blue River. Because the women were gone, she appeared more desirable.

"That Tzoh is worthy of entering a warrior's hut," said Heigoun, staring at her avidly, speaking in a masterful voice. As she stood straight and proud, an expression of scorn on her face, the man added, "Heigoun is a chief! The Tzoh woman shall be a chief's woman."

"Is Heigoun the chief of the clan?" Helgvor asked, vehement fury flooding his chest. "And did he make alliance with this maid?"

Akroun listened in silence. The passion for leadership held him entirely, and this quarrel left him indifferent. And if he disliked Heigoun, he feared him because of his strength and his numerous adherents. When Akroun grew old, all expected command to come to Heigoun, the colossal warrior.

"Helgvor is not even a warrior!" rasped Heigoun.

"Helgvor looks Heigoun face to face—and will fight with spear, bow or hatchet."

The spears lifted, and Akroun wished for the defeat and death of his rival. But he feared that Helgvor would be beaten, and he spoke imperiously, "No man of the Blue River shall have a new wife until the Tzohs have been chastised. Until the hour of revenge, the Ougmars will be like jackals or deer. After, the man who shall have fought best shall obtain the woman he desires."

A clamor of applause rose. Many of the warriors were lured by the captive woman, and jealousy already darkened their hearts. The majority, however, wanted to free their women and slay their ravishers. Thus, they all heard Akroun's words with satisfaction, and Shtra said, "The chief has spoken well. The Ougmars shall obey."

"Helgvor defied Heigoun!" the giant howled.

"The tribe needs all the warriors!" Akroun stated harshly. "If Heigoun, Helgvor, or the two of them, were wounded, the Tzohs would be the stronger!"

"Heigoun shall kill Helgvor after victory!"

"Helgvor shall beat down Heigoun!"

As he spoke, the young man stood straight, and his height was almost equal to that of his adversary; but the shoulders of the grown warrior were more massive, his limbs thicker. Startled by the daring of Shtra's son, many warriors admired his courage. Glava, aware that Heigoun was interested in her, was pale with anger and hatred.

The warriors, who were to start the following day, spent the afternoon repairing or sharpening their weapons. Worry depressed Helgvor, and, dimly, he felt how gentle and easy life had been within the enclosure. If the instinct of race and hatred for the Tzohs had not been strong, he would have thought of escape. Glava was as sad, and when the first stars appeared, she felt the threatening weight of the darkness.

Heigoun was as evil as Kzahm, hostility was aroused in her against the alien breed, and she experienced a certain resentment toward Helgvor for bringing her among these men.

Akroun called Helgvor to his shelter. "The maid will lead us to the land of the Tzohs?" he asked.

"Yes," the warrior replied, "if no one menaces her. Glava does not fear death. She fought like a man. And she will bow to none. If the chief wants her for a guide, let Heigoun stay aside. The maid will talk only to Helgvor."

The chief listened, worried, and at heart he approved Helgvor, but he foresaw trouble. Shaken by circumstances, his authority was swaying; he guessed that many among his people blamed him for carelessness. A few had murmured audibly. Heigoun, daring and eager to dominate, would leave him no respite. Because their natures were antagonistic, and perhaps because Heigoun had shown his greed for power too soon, the chief of chiefs did not wish to have him take leadership.

"How came Helgvor to meet the women and fight the Tzohs?" he asked.

Helgvor related his adventures, the first meeting with the Men of the Rocks, the massacre on the Red Peninsula, the pursuit and the meeting with the fugitives, the fighting on the shore, the combat at the enclosure.

Those many exploits astonished Akroun, for Helgvor was younger than any warrior who hunted the aurochs and horses. Nevertheless, his skill with the bow was well known; since childhood, he had fired arrows and thrown spears with surprising accuracy. His strength increased quicker than his size.

Akroun saw in him a rival for the giant; should Helgvor become the hero of the tribe, the chief of chiefs would have no rivals. A very young man would never aspire to command. Akroun no longer claimed physical supremacy. Age had drained his muscles of their suppleness and vigor.

At least seven men of the clan were better warriors than he; as he reigned through foresight and craftiness, he was the first to reproach himself for the catastrophe befallen the tribe during his absence. Doubtless it was true that the Men of the Rocks had not raided the Ougmars for two generations and had been thought to have migrated far to the east. But a chief should never have forgotten their existence!

"The daughter of the Rocks shall walk by day with Helgvor," he decided. "At night she shall be alone, watched by Akroun's dogs, which cannot be approached by anyone save the chief."

Deep sorrow gnawed at Helgvor's heart. He did not trust even the chief.

In the morning, Akroun counted the warriors. There were 58, all hardened to fatigue and skilled in the use of hatchet, stake, club and spear.

"The Men of the Rocks are much more numerous," Helgvor said. "There are three Tzohs for each Ougmar."

"Formerly, the warriors of the Green Lakes fought with us against them," Akroun said. "But their tribes are now more than a moon's march away."

"We must surprise the Tzohs," Heigoun grumbled.

"The Ougmars shall pass through the forests of the far bank," Akroun said with a somber laugh. "Ten days of marching along the High River will bring them to the Land of the Sun. There they shall try to make an alliance with the Gwahs, Men of the Night."

"They are jackals lacking in strength, they eat their dead!" Heigoun retorted harshly.

"The Gwahs are swift afoot and clever at preparing ambushes," Shtra stated. "For six generations they have been the friends of the Ougmars. Shtra has hunted with the Gwahs."

"Gaor also," put in another warrior. "It is a fact that they eat the dead men, but they are faithful to friends, trustworthy."

The Ougmars forded the river in well-built canoes. Although the forest was thick, the ancestors of the clan had many years ago traced a trail through it, a path often taken by mammoths, bison and other animals. Each craft was carried by four men who were relieved at intervals. This made the march slower, but once the western hills had been crossed, the river would be found in the high valley which led southward on a swift current.

The warriors traveled all day, stopping only to eat. The forest seemed endless and it grew on slopes ascending toward the sunset sky. At twilight, behind their fires, the Ougmars were stronger than all animals, even than the mammoths and bison which travel in herds. Only vertical beasts were to be feared, but only the Men of the Night were known to live in the forest, a strange people living in the trunks of old trees.

Glava had been isolated in the center of the camp. The warriors looked toward her often, with fierce yet tender glances. Heigoun roamed as near as he dared, but Akroun had stationed Shtra and some men around her who detested the gigantic warrior and his alert dogs.

"Akroun didn't know enough to protect the women," Heigoun told his friends. "He's keeping this maid for his friends."

And he turned his hairy face, the hue of dying ashes, toward Glava.

Crushed by fear and regret, she was bitterly resentful that she had followed Helgvor to the Red Peninsula. She had been separated from Amhao roughly, and her sister had been left behind with the old men and the survivors. She had resisted at first, then, understanding that this might prove dangerous for Amhao, she had yielded to superior force.

Now, she dreamed of circulating again, with her sister, on the solitary trails. As hateful as the Tzohs, and strangers moreover, the Ougmars, by their gestures, their habits, their weapons, their voices, inspired in the young girl an intense dislike. She would gladly have led Helgvor toward the Land of the Tzohs, but she meant to deceive the others, to take them on false roads.

Helgvor, looking at the maid in the firelight, understood her rancor, and was worried. Several times he had urged the chief to take Amhao on the trip. Heigoun and his friends had opposed this, explaining that the woman would delay the march unless her child was left behind.

"Helgvor will carry the child," the young nomad had said.

"Shtra and Iouk also," his father and brother had added.

Heigoun would not accept this and Akroun gave in, careless of what happened to Amhao. As he would not listen to Helgvor, the young man did not risk suggesting that Glava might avenge herself.

The next day, the first Men of the Night were encountered. Their faces lengthened like sheep's heads and their pointed ears were tufted with coarse hair. Black as slate, they showed small eyes, like squirrels' pupils, mouths shaped as if eternally sucking, thin limbs and hollow bellies. Their hair grew in islets on their skulls, faces and chests. Their skins oozed an evil-smelling oil, and the thick upper lip lifted to show fang-like teeth. For weapons, they had only sharp stones and pointed sticks.

Shtra had met them in the forest for a score of years. Knowing their tongue he spoke, with many gestures, "If the Gwahs will come with the Ougmars, they shall have flesh and blood aplenty."

"Why should the Gwahs go with the Ougmars?" asked the oldest black.

"To help in tracking down the Tzohs. Don't you remember the time when the Tzohs massacred the Men of the Night? The Gwahs shall have the carcasses of the fallen, for the Ougmars are the stronger!"

Despite their craftiness, the Gwahs had credulous souls. Tomorrow seemed to them an unlimited time ahead. They sniffed toward the roasting meat, and having been given a share, they ate as they walked beside the River Men. At times, other Gwahs, emerging from hollow trees or from branches, joined the detachment, lured by the example of the others.

"Flesh will be needed every day," Shtra said to Akroun. "If flesh is lacking, the Gwahs will stop."

Poor hunters, and poor fire-builders, the Gwahs often knew famine.

"They'll have flesh," Akroun assured. "There is much game in the forest." He counted on the Gwahs less to fight the Tzohs openly than to harass them and draw them into ambushes.

After a lapse of several days, there were about 50 Gwahs with the party. Despite their small bodies, they were always ready to eat, equally fitted to starve as to gorge. The Ougmar hunters sought stags, aurochs, boars, all large animals, to satisfy the voracity of their allies.

The Gwahs, inclined to laziness, scattered during the day on all sides of the marching clan, but at night gathered near the fires, inhaling the smells of cooking meat, warming their bodies with much pleasure. Their smells, which resembled those of foxes and skunks, inspired Glava with bitter disgust, but the warriors, after the first evenings, paid no further attention.

When the High River was reached, it was discovered that there were not enough canoes, and the Gwahs, directed by Ougmars, built rafts. They handled them with more skill than canoes, and did not fear water, for all of them swam like otters. The High River carried them impetuously; in three days they covered an enormous distance and found themselves near the Blue River.

The stream had overflowed. The water spread in the forest and beat against the lower slopes of the hills. It took six hours to find dry land on the shore. As the plain was broken by great ponds, the canoes and rafts had to be carried along. Akroun hardened his face to maintain his authority in the face of this additional hardship.

"The Ougmars crawl like worms," Heigoun cried late that afternoon. "Never shall they reach the land of the Tzohs."

"The flood must have delayed the kidnappers," Akroun replied harshly. "The Ougmars must pursue." He sent for Helgvor and asked him, "The Tzohs were further than we are upstream when Helgvor met the fugitives?"

"No, the Tzohs were two or three days' travel downstream from here."

"The Tzohs must have gone overland," Heigoun suggested. "We must leave the river bank."

"Not yet!" Akroun snapped. He stared at Heigoun. "Does Heigoun forget we are on the warpath?"

"Heigoun obeys the chief! But warriors have the right to group and confer."

Akroun grew ashen. There was no talk of gathering the warriors for a conference unless the authority of the chief was questioned.

"Akroun will call the warriors together when the fires are lit."

"If the Tzohs are nearby, they shall see the fires."

"Is Heigoun a child? Does he believe that the chief does not know fires must be screened?"

That night Akroun selected a depression rimmed with trees for the camping place. In any case the scouts, Ougmars and Gwahs, had discovered no tracks up to a distance from which the fires, even on the flat plain, would have been invisible. When the wood burned brightly, Akroun summoned the men.

"Let the warriors gather. The chief will listen to them."

Heigoun's supporters came first. There were 12 of them, not one of whom had seen over 30 autumns. Those who remained loyal to the chief, whether by trust, by fear or hatred of Heigoun, arrived more slowly. There were 15, among them Shtra, Iouk and Helgvor. The rest, undecided, ready to side with the stronger group, hovered behind.

Akroun, watching his rival's friends with anxiety, remembered with bitterness the days, not so far in the past, when the tribe had followed him blindly. Then, Heigoun had waited for the time to ripen. Now, the chief sensed distrust in the depths of his men's souls, knew that he was reproached with the loss of the women. He rose, and the fires cast red reflections in the amber eyes. His mighty face simulated confidence. And he spoke.

"The chief has gathered the warriors to consult their wisdom. The road alongside the river is flooded. But it is the shortest route. Must we follow it, or strike across land? Let the warriors think it over!"

Heigoun lurched to his feet, bulky, formidable. His shoulders oscillated slowly, his powerful jaws were contracted, and when he opened his mouth he showed white fangs.

"The experience of the chief is great and the warriors shall obey his orders. But if the river road is the shorter, it will take longer to follow. The Tzohs will not have followed it. The Tzohs have gone inland."

His enormous hand indicated the west, while his companions exclaimed approvingly. "Hunting is difficult near the shore! Tonight, the Gwahs will not get enough flesh, and the Gwahs are with the Ougmars only to eat. Do the Ougmars wish the Gwahs to go away? Then they shall not be numerous enough to attack the Tzohs!"

His backers agreed by words and gestures. The undecided looked on timidly, ready to fall in with the new power. When Akroun rose to answer, his chest was seen to quiver.

"Heigoun is a clever warrior! But what does he know of the enemy? What do the Ougmars know? The tracks have not been picked up. We must seek their trail. Here is what Akroun wishes. Seven warriors, with Gwahs and dogs, will scout along the river. All will bring back the flesh of animals they hunt. Thus will the Ougmars know the right way. The chief has spoken. The warriors shall obey."

Then the timid men who had waited for a decision again trusted the chief, while Heigoun's supporters were silent and still. Understanding that the occasion had not arrived, the son of the Wolf said,

"Heigoun can command scouts to march overland?"

The chief agreed. But a suspicion stirred the giant; he looked at Helgvor, he looked toward Glava. Akroun understood, and, being careful not to nurture a quarrel before the Tzohs had been beaten, he intervened.

"Shtra shall command the men who will follow the river, and Helgvor will be the guide."

Helgvor looked at Glava with despair. A deep rancor rose in his heart.

XI. The Enemy

At dawn, Heigoun started out inland with six warriors, a few Gwahs and dogs. Shtra, with Helgvor, left for the river, his troop bearing two canoes to ford the pond. When the sheets of water were narrow they circled them or at times waded across.

Gloomy thoughts depressed Helgvor. The image of Glava tormented his youth, and because he was incapable of analyzing his mind, that image dominated his acts and his impulses. Formerly, the defeat of the Tzohs would have absorbed his whole being. Now, he thought much more of winning Glava.

Shtra loved Helgvor. He was a warrior with peaceful ways, humble before the chief, and he detested Heigoun. With much experience and little intuition, without ambition to command, he loved his ease. On the trail, at war and during the hunt, he performed his duties without ardor. He killed animals calmly, he was ready to exterminate the Tzohs. In like fashion, he would have liked to deprive Heigoun and his friends of their lives, preferably by some trick, had Akroun so ordered. Death did not perturb him, neither did the sufferings of those toward whom he was indifferent, but he would have mourned for Iouk or Helgvor many days.

Iouk, brother of Helgvor, resembled Shtra. More alert, he hated strongly. Although born before Helgvor, he acknowledged without anger or envy the superior strength and skill of his brother; he even was proud of him. For he was of those men for whom others may seem happy parts of their own beings.

For the first hours the little expedition progressed slowly. The six dogs, the wolf, the Gwahs and the warriors searched in vain for tracks. When the Sun had crossed the first quarter of the sky, Shtra said,

"If the Tzohs passed here before the flood, they must be very far ahead."

"Is not the flood wider upstream?" Helgvor asked.

Shtra shrugged. His narrow face resumed its apathetic gentleness. They had crossed a submerged ravine, had circled rocks, and walked on dry soil. The Gwahs searched casually, for they were hungry and wished to rest. A halt was ordered.

Then Helgvor explored the plain, and to see better, climbed on a boulder. Furtive animals appeared in a flash and vanished. He saw a deer, horses, a triangular flight of cranes under a cloud. The dogs and the Ougmars also searched. At last the eyes of Helgvor lit up. A herd of aurochs had appeared in a ravine.

He slipped through the thickets, crawled in the tall grass, and came within arrow range of the herd. The aurochs had stopped in the ravine, where fresh grass grew.

Two enormous bulls protected the herd, and perhaps after an unsatisfactory combat, kept far from one another. Tawny hair grew on their shoulders and straggled over their eyes. Their limbs were slender for their tremendous bodies which tapered from their broad, shaggy chests to slim hindquarters. They gave an impression of immense strength united with extreme agility. Their horns, spread wide and sharp, were strong enough to toss aside lion, tiger or gray bear.

The herd grazed quietly. At intervals, one of the bulls would lift his monstrous head and seem to catch on his sensitive nostrils the emanations in the atmosphere, to catch within the radiance of his big, dark eyes the reflection of his surroundings.

Helgvor crept nearer, bent his bow.

One of the bulls bellowed; the cows lifted their melancholy heads as the dread effluvia of man drifted through the air. Several knew the smell, and one of the bulls who had already seen the erect beast on his horizon gave the signal for retreat.

An arrow struck him in the chest, a keen point stabbed for his heart. Furious, he charged for the center of the smell while the herd fled.

Helgvor stood up. Filled with admiration for the colossal beast, aware that he was protecting the herd, he felt a dim regret. But the Ougmars, the Gwahs, the animals, waited for the flesh that creates flesh. A second arrow dug into the chest, then Helgvor drew a spear from his belt. The wounded aurochs had lost all sense of preservation, thought only of crushing his attacker, longed to gore him with his horns. He came on like a boulder rolled in an avalanche.

Helgvor threw his spear. It penetrated near the shoulder. Rage and pain caused the aurochs to roar like a lion. When the gigantic beast was but a stride away, Helgvor leaped nimbly aside, and his club swung down. It struck on the skull, bounced off, fell back and broke the bull's foreleg. From then on the man was the master. Clumsy, almost helpless, the beast tried several attacks, which the hunter easily avoided.

"The warriors and the dogs need the flesh of the great aurochs!" he said.

He expressed in this way, without being aware of it, his admiration for the immense beast, and his sorrow to slay it. For the bull was dying. His large eyes were foggy. He no longer attacked, but waited motionless, in the dream of death, on the mysterious brink of Nothingness. Then he trembled, a raucous plaint rose from his deep throat, and suddenly he tumbled into the grass, dead.

Helgvor called the Gwahs and the Ougmars. All were coming near, their eyes avidly fastened on the enormous prey. The Gwahs grinned their silent, primitive grimace of a laugh, almost like that of the dogs.

"There!" Helgvor announced, "there is much flesh now."

"Helgvor is a great hunter!" Shtra said, while Iouk made a fire.

But Helgvor paid no heed to his praise. He had seen, not far away, a wide, dark spot in the grass, and joy dilated his breast. The Tzohs had camped there. The ashes still seemed fresh. Bones were strewn about, with rags of fur. Helgvor called his wolf and his dog, made them smell the encampment.

Behind, the Gwahs were watching Iouk striking flint. Their eyes gleaned like those of jackals. Shtra was laughing softly. "The Gwahs have forgotten famine. They will follow the warriors like dogs."

Helgvor announced, "The tracks of the Tzohs are found. They camped in this ravine last night."

The Ougmars were skinning the aurochs, and already large quarterings of meat emanated the heady aroma of cooking food.

If Helgvor thought of the Tzohs, who had to be exterminated, he thought even more of Glava; he could imagine her, somber and angry, near the fires; her breast would dilate as if to lift space, while her heart was heavy as a block of granite. And he intensely hated Heigoun with the hairy chest.

The dog and the wolf followed the tracks.

To avoid confusion, other animals were held behind. Because of the numbers of the Tzohs and their captives, their trail was easily followed for a long time. Across pools, plains and hills the scouts progressed for two-thirds of one day. A tributary river was reached, which rolled muddy waters rapidly, and on the far side of that stream the tracks had vanished.

As the Tzohs could not have gone upstream—the river was swift as a torrent—the scouts must seek downstream. In any case it was easier in that direction, for the ground was high and dry. The tracks of the Tzohs were found.

Then a bloodstained spear left behind announced that the Tzohs had passed here recently. Shtra, Iouk and Helgvor examined the weapon carefully.

"The Tzohs are near," Shtra concluded. "The blood is not yet black." He shook his head anxiously. "Did not Helgvor see 100 warriors before meeting the fugitives?"

"They were more than 100 when they attacked the Red Peninsula, and more than 100 also when Helgvor counted them on the plain."

"Then Shtra shall take care not to start a fight with them, having only a few warriors and the Gwahs."

"That fire of which Shtra saw the ashes was not a fire for 100 warriors!"

"Perhaps they didn't have enough dry wood!"

"Helgvor thinks the pursuit must be kept up."

"So does Iouk!"

"Let's follow the tracks," Shtra said with resignation. They walked for two hours, then the trail was evidently so recent that all were aware the Tzohs were very near. All doubts were removed when the distinct imprints of feet were discerned on moist soil. Some were so clear that Shtra commented, "Here passed the heavy feet of the Tzohs, and here the light feet of the women." A sudden rage swept this pacific man and his fists knotted.

Helgvor, trying to read the tracks, followed them for some hundreds of yards, then retraced his steps. "The Tzohs are not more numerous than the fingers of three hands!"

"The Gwahs and the Ougmars united are less numerous than the Tzohs! The Gwahs are weak and poorly armed."

"Helgvor's wolf will fight, and the dogs will harass the foes."

Shtra was silent, uncertain as to what should be done.

"Our arrows carry further than those of the Tzohs," the young man argued. "Their warriors aim badly. The men on our side who cannot shoot well can turn over their arrows to Helgvor."

"Yes, Helgvor has the eye of the hawk," Shtra agreed.

"Helgvor shall go first. He shall kill some Tzohs and lure the others into pursuit. Shtra and the warriors will lie in ambush."

While Shtra still hesitated, Iouk intervened. "Our women are with them!" he growled, and his eyes flashed.

"Let Helgvor guide us, then," Shtra said, filled with fury, speaking in a vehement voice. "When we get near the Tzohs, we shall ambush thern."

The little troop started again, preceded by Helgvor and Iouk. The tracks vanished, reappeared. A long hill, low and green, barred the horizon. They climbed the slopes slowly. On the crest they came upon a circular clearing studded with boulders and thick with bushes.

"Let Shtra await his son here," Helgvor said. "The Tzohs are down below."

He progressed alone, cautiously. A narrow granite plateau crowned the hill's crest. Coarse grass grew there, broken by small trees, bushes and low, stone masses. Since a moment ago, the dog showed an agitation which the wolf soon shared. They crept between the boulders with care.

A low whistle checked them. Helgvor had reached the rim of the plateau. Crouched on the ground, he crept, and his quicker breath revealed his emotion.

At the bottom of the hill, stopped by the flood, the Tzohs were lighting their fires. The captive women, squatted, huddled, were obviously exhausted. Perhaps 30 warriors were there on the nude soil, and although the majority seemed as worn out as the females, almost all were young men fitted for combat. Before those thick torsos, those mighty shoulders, the Gwahs would be as children. Only the strongest Ougmars might cope with them.

Nevertheless, Helgvor saw that the encampment, protected from direct attack, could be flanked and riddled with arrows. He cast a glance at the big bow suspended from his shoulder. He had five arrows, all tipped with nephrite stone points, and he knew that he could shoot them from a distance beyond the range of the Tzohs' puny bows.

His chest swelling with the fighting excitement of war, he went back to the crest of the hill. He addressed Shtra, "If Helgvor has many arrows, he will drop a good many Tzohs. The others can be wiped out by the warriors and the Gwahs."

He described the position occupied by the enemy.

"Shtra wants to look," the chief said.

He requisitioned a dozen arrows for Helgvor. The two warriors climbed to the crest and Shtra, having counted the Tzohs, yielded gloomily to the prestige of his tall son.

"Shtra and his warriors will wait among the boulders."

He went back to camp and Helgvor descended the far slope of the hill, very slowly, having ordered the dog and the wolf to wait for him, a command which they understood as well as men might have. Helgvor felt this would be a great day in his life; his heart was beating hard and a great lucidity reigned in his brain.

But the nearer he approached the more daring the adventure became. The faces and bodies of the Tzohs appeared to be more alive; he discerned clearly their broad, swarthy faces, the granite-like jaws, the jackals' pupils. If they surrounded him his death was near, and he sensed this fully as he advanced upon them.

Although he thought himself quicker than they, doubts assailed him like treacherous beasts. Among so many young warriors perhaps a few would possess, as he did, the speed of the stag and the spring of the leopard. Even a slight wound in the leg would cause his death, by placing Helgvor at his enemies' mercy. Skilled in the use of trees and grass to screen himself, he had arrived within two arrows' flight. The soil was bare, covered with silvery moss, save on the boulders where the growth was reddish and green.

Another step, and Helgvor would be visible.

For a moment his heart pounded so fast that his strength seemed puny before these gathered forces; the love of life stirred in him like the leaves of the sycamore in the breeze. Thinking of Glava, he faltered. Her glowing eyes and tawny hair appeared all the joy in the world. It was brief; the day was come when victory would make him a warrior feared by all. If he drew back now, Glava would scorn him and he would not dare reappear among his people.

XII. Lone Attack

A Tzoh saw him, another, and in succession the cubical heads lifted. Their stupefaction was so intense that they were silent at first. They stared at this lone warrior and searched for his companions. There were none, and the man was coming on, in long strides, charging upon the camp alone.

Then some of the Tzohs identified him. He was the very man who had rescued the fugitive women. Kamr had gone after him with five men, and none had come back. Trusting in their numbers and accustomed to battle, they rose and uttered the challenging death-yelp.

"Helgvor killed two Tzohs, then four of those in the big canoe," the nomad shouted. "Helgvor killed the chieftain with the wide shoulders. All the ravishers shall perish!"

The women, mute and filled with terror, with hope, listened to this ringing voice. Their youth, memories of the Red Peninsula, flooded them with quivering joy.

Helgvor ran nearer. He was soon within range, and stretched his bow. The arrow scarcely grazed the shoulder of a warrior and the Tzohs howled with rage. Two other missiles reached their targets. One pierced the breast of a warrior, the other sank into his belly.

The Tzohs returned his fire, but their bows did not carry far, the few arrows which reached the nomad were spent, powerless. Three more times the great bow hummed, and two enemies received deep wounds.

Enraged, the Tzohs started for the lone man. He retreated, and while retreating wounded two other men. The others rushed madly, save for six, staying to watch the captive women. Helgvor had three arrows left. He saved them for the supreme struggle and took flight, which scattered the pursuers. Three, faster afoot than were the others, had gained a long lead by the time the Ougmar reached the crest. They were young men, at the age when legs are very speedy but arms weak. They were together, armed with bronze hatchets and spears.

Suddenly they saw Helgvor no more. Fearing ambush, they slackened speed. A rustling caused them to turn. The Ougmar had risen behind them, between two boulders, a spear poised; the sharp weapon hurtled through the air, and the nearest Tzoh fell. The others launched their spears. One of them wounded Helgvor in the head, but rushing forward he swung his club, smashed the skull of one of the young warriors, while the point of a spear darted from the left hand, piercing the throat of the other.

The attack had been so swift that none of the other pursuers was within arrow range when Helgvor resumed his flight and scrambled down the slope. He shouted in a voice which resounded in the camp of his comrades,

"Helgvor wounded nine Tzohs. Let the warriors be ready for combat."

Within a few moments his strides seemed to falter. He lifted his hand to his head, from which blood flowed, and looked at that hand, reddened with blood. He gestured then, to make his injury obvious to the Men of the Rocks. Then, pretending to weaken, he stumbled. Sure that he was dropping, the most eager dared to leave the group of runners.

"Let our warriors attack!" he screamed.

He whirled when very near the ambush, and with the quick spring of a leopard he was on the nearest Tzoh, knocking him down. Another, coming on in great leaps, stopped too late. The enormous club smashed across his loins, fracturing his spine.

At the same moment, arrows, stones, spears spouted from the refuge of the Ougmars and the Gwahs. The dogs barked, the men bellowed like aurochs and wolves. Six tall warriors emerged, then others, blacks with pointed ears, sliding through grass as rapidly as the barking dogs.

It was a panic—the Tzohs believed themselves facing the whole clan, and the majority, filled with terror, scattered at random. But six or seven faced the unexpected foes. They slew two Gwahs and one Ougmar, but great clubs broke their bones, knocked out their bowels from ripped bellies. When they had been exterminated, the Men of the River and their beasts took up the chase. Those who were caught made no resistance. The pointed stakes of the Gwahs, the clubs, the hatchets, the spears of the Ougmars cut off their defenseless lives.

More agile than were the short-legged Tzohs, the victors had wiped out almost all the vanquished when they reached the camp and the women. Their guards, mediocre fighters, had fled. Those that were overhauled allowed themselves to be slain without a fight.

The day was about to end. The red Sun, half-buried in clouds, already slid down toward the river. Almost all the Tzohs had died.

Shtra, filled with admiration and enthusiasm, cried out,

"Helgvor, son of Shtra, is a mighty warrior—strong as the mammoth, swift as the tiger—Heigoun is only a wolf!"

The Ougmar warriors repeated,

"Helgvor, son of Shtra, is a mighty warrior!"

The women, overjoyed at their rescue, clamored with the men. They had seen Helgvor's first exploits.

And the clouds were twisted into mirages like all the mirages that had filled the clouds through aeons and aeons. It was a brilliant evening upon the perishable Earth; a soft breeze ran across the waters; and when the fires were lit, the joy of life filled those who had suppressed life.

Helgvor felt the pride of being a dreaded warrior, but his pride was laid before a remote fire, before a supple shape, and his heart quivered with sweet yet terrible anguish.

XIII. Glava in the Night

When Helgvor vanished beyond the hills, horror swooped upon Glava. Haggard, she stared at these unknown beings about her, found the sight of them less and less bearable.

Akroun had given strict orders that no one should go near the foreign woman. She was in the middle of the encampment. Men's glances went toward her, which irritated her. Because she was alone, the peril was not great and Akroun's protection surer. For almost all these warriors had lost their women, and were rivals.

The day passed dully, without incident. A heavy boredom crushed the men and many fell asleep. Akroun scanned the horizon, or dispatched small parties of warriors as scouts, instructing them not to go beyond the hills. These would soon return without anything to report.

The camp was guarded by six sentries, stationed at regular intervals and changed often. No surprise could be feared. The chief remained gloomy. The Ougmars' distrust weighed on his mind for he knew it would increase at the least failure. Then he would lose authority and would be put to death, for Heigoun would not tolerate a living rival.

The image of Heigoun oppressed Akroun as if the warrior had been near, with his cave bear's chest, his ferocious eyes and his enormous shoulders. He also thought of Helgvor, whom he admired grudgingly for his exploits, his skill and his vigor. Much too young to become a chief, Helgvor, no matter what happened, would not prove dangerous. In any event if he, Akroun, made good and recaptured the women taken by the Tzohs, he would be pitiless to his foes. But would he recapture them? The Tzohs were too numerous and his allies too weak! Dull doubt gnawed the chief's brain.

Night came.

Neither Shtra nor Heigoun had come back, and the sentries on the hills signaled nothing. Perhaps the scouts had been surprised by their foes and killed off. Then, all struggle rendered impossible, the Ougmars would return to their homes beaten, to live without women, without sons, and their race would die.

Glava also thought bitter, harsh thoughts. Her youth was weary as old age; her anxiety was increasing. A few stars appeared, gleaming a while to be extinguished by a light downpour, which turned into a torrential rain.

The rivers filled space. Water rose in the pools. Wild beasts sought their dens. Owls hooted mournfully and the jackals complained.

One by one the fires went out, and the night spread thick as velvet. Here and there men still stirred, but the water soaked through their furs, moistened hair and beards, seeped into ears and nostrils, extinguishing their lust as it had put out the fires.

Nevertheless, their snores annoyed Glava. Unable to bear the sounds longer, she crept away in the darkness. No definite plan was in her mind. She fled like a doe pursued by the wolf, like the stag pursued by the tiger.

She crept a long time with animal prudence, noiselessly circling the prone bodies. Dogs awoke with short growls, then they identified Glava, whose scent was familiar, and dropped back into their shivering torpor.

Then she was alone and crawling quicker; she soon left the camp behind. There were no more rough sounds, no odors save those of the moist sod, the grass and the trees. Weary, she remained motionless an instant to gather her scattered thoughts. She ardently wished to join Amhao. She also would have desired to see Helgvor. She loved him more than she herself knew, with a love similar to that she granted her sister.

But Helgvor was away, sent off purposely to leave her defenseless. She could not understand why he had gone, although she knew that he could not disobey a chief. The terrifying silhouette of Heigoun lifted in her mind. Why had Helgvor not come back? Death was all about.

She started forward again. Like an unchecked torrent the rain fell and its sounds muffled all other noises. Even the jackals were quiet. Glava was chilled to the bones, her limbs tired.

Then there was no time and no space, all melted into the dark, watery night. The water rose to the fugitive's chest, she did not know where to step. Everywhere her hands encountered the cold fluid which penetrated and submerged everything.

She struck a hard object, which moved. Glava identified a canoe. She held onto it, drew the craft near, and succeeded in climbing into the hull. There were paddles, which she handled at random. Then she felt the gentle, soft slide as she was borne away, faster and faster.

Dawn came at last, a smear of ashy white in the depth of the sky. Light increased, and the world was dripping with happiness. Far off, Glava discerned vegetation and rocks, and as the current shot the canoe along rapidly she knew that she was on the river. With this knowledge hope was reborn. She thought of rejoining Amhao on the Red Peninsula.

Despite her weariness she paddled long, to increase the distance between herself and the Ougmars. When she was tired she inspected her boat. There was only a pointed stake for a weapon and a sharp-edged stone for a tool. The point of the stake was worn dull, and could be employed only against weak beasts. For a long time she suffered from cold, then the rising Sun warmed her chilled limbs which resumed the suppleness and the spring of youth.

"Glava shall see Amhao!" she said.

Then the canoe slid slowly on the immense surface. Glava had gone near the left bank to be sheltered from sight. She was hungry, and she found a haven in which to land. It was a gently sloping stone platform in a rocky cliff at the end of which was a small cave. Glava, having made sure that no wild beast lived therein, dragged the canoe into a seam of the stone and fastened it with leather ropes left in the craft by the Ougmars.

The cave connected with the top of the cliff, through cracks. Glava picked up the stake, to hunt game and defend herself. By a corridor of basaltic rock she reached soil that the waters could not reach, a narrow plain fringed the thick forest which had spread over the universe long before the birth of the Gwahs, Sons of the Night.

Glava was afraid, less of the beasts than of the forest and of the unnamed things which menace living creatures. When

89

she had fled with Amhao, the presence of her sister and the child had populated the world. Now, she was wholly alone, to face the immensity of the river and of the forest, and hostile life.

She hesitated before plunging into the jungle, but nothing appeared on the plain save a few animals which remained too far away to be caught. In the forest, Glava found white mushrooms such as were eaten by the Tzohs. Raw, they smelled like mouldy wood, but she ate two to appease her intense hunger, before disgust overcame famine.

Two squirrels appeared on the lower branches of a sycamore-tree. Invisible behind a young tree, she spied upon the small beasts covered with gray fur, with brushy ears and extraordinarily hairy tails longer than their bodies. Their rats' eyes glittered and each of their movements was graceful. With a bow, or even with a spear, she could have killed one of them, but the clumsy stake would surely miss the target.

They gnawed peacefully and did not see, in the thick foliage, death nearing them. A lynx was there, strange feline with triangular ears, hair sprouting on each side of the jaws like a beard, and a spotted pelt. He was as silent as night. They saw him suddenly, and leaped. But the quick beast fell on them like a projectile, broke their backs with two strokes of his paws. They dropped to the ground and the lynx slid down the tree to get at them.

Rage at seeing his legitimate prey claimed by another vibrated through the slim body, and the lynx lifted a paw warningly. Glava held the point of the stake toward him. The animal measured the height and mass of the girl with a glance, and recalled Gwahs encountered in his native forest. They were beings such as this one, more dangerous than wolves, equipped with queer claws that they shot far from their bodies. A lynx should yield to them. But this was the first time one of the erect beings had seized prey from a lynx.

"Glava is stronger than the lynx!" the young girl shouted, knowing that animals must be menaced. The lynx growled, and she tossed the stake at him. Then, furious but resigned, the beast leaped away, vanished into the undergrowth. One of the squirrels was dying, the other dead. Glava, with their flesh, could face the unknown forces which destroy human beings. Laden with the small, tawny bodies, she went back to the canoe.

One of the squirrels contributed his mysterious energy to her body without driving off the need for sleep. She sought a shelter, but found none. Wild animals could come down to the river bank. She could not sleep in the canoe; tiger or lion would have reached her in one leap. And the craft was too heavy for her to turn over, as she had done on occasions while with Amhao.

An island would be the best refuge, but the flood had submerged the low ones, and of the larger, only the crests emerged. Glava would have preferred a small, easily explored islet, on which she could be sure no felines lived.

The canoe had started again, and now slid swiftly, bearing away the weak human beast.

After a long time, Glava espied two islands of different sizes. The largest was prolonged by long, slender headlands, at the tips of a thickly overgrown plateau. The sight of many large crocodiles and snakes which the flood had driven to the center of this island kept her from attempting a landing. The second island, smaller and very rocky, appeared more hospitable, there were few trees and the low grass revealed no suspicious presence.

Two boulders left between them a slit too narrow to give passage to tiger, lion or gray bear, which, in any case, would have had to come from one of the banks, something that Glava deemed impossible. To avoid risk, she further barred the way with twisted branches and lianas, and having moored the canoe, fell asleep.

The Sun was already low on the horizon when she awoke. Its yellow radiance flushed the right bank, and a deep, luminous peace reigned over the waters. An old hippopotamus, hideous and peaceful, slumbered at the tip of the island. A bird twittered, perched on a quivering bough.

Toward morning, a slight noise awoke her, and in the light of the stars she saw a head gnawing the small bones of the squirrel. It was a diminutive animal, the size of a young fox, with pointed ears and eyes that glowed like fireflies.

The immensity of the sky was still sprinkled with luminous flowers. In their weak glow, Glava identified a jackal. He did not appear to have attained his full growth, and his presence on the islet was astonishing. Doubtless he had been brought here by the flood, shaken on the rushing water and thrown upon this deserted rock. Was he alone?

She did not drive the jackal away but listened to the little sounds made by the teeth on the bones. Glava, no longer sleepy, stood slowly. The baby jackal fled, and she already regretted moving when she saw it returning, furtively, eyes on the heap of branches hiding the unknown beast.

It started gnawing the bones again, then, having discovered the pelt, it chewed it. Its presence became pleasing. At an age when distrust did not yet have roots in the depths of instinct and experience, the jackal grew accustomed to Glava's scent. Prompt to terror, it was also prompt to familiarity, once certain no harm would befall it.

The little stars vanished, the larger ones dimmed. And beyond the right bank, where the Ougmars pursued the Tzohs, light rose so slowly that it seemed it never would reach the bank. The forest was lit in turn, and an enormous Sun spilled its motionless flames in the clouds. The sky became a limitless world.

The jackal uttered a little, plaintive cry. Ceaselessly it fled, ceaselessly it came back. It was very graceful, with its brownish pelt, paler on the chest, its fine, mobile ears, its delicate paws. All its movements had the awkward ease of a stillgrowing animal. And, looking at him, obscure tenderness swept the young Tzoh girl.

Meanwhile, hunger had come again, and the islet produced no plant suitable to feed man. The Tzohs knew how to fish with a harpoon, even with bare hands. Motionless, Glava stared a long time at the perch, the trout and the pike which swam in the stream. But it was a tortoise which brought its strength. It had climbed upon a flat rock, and its snake-like head was over the stream, seeking prey, when it became prey. The head withdrew into the shell, and Glava seemed to hold nothing but a colorful stone.

She made a fire and cooked the tortoise. The jackal roamed about, constantly driven away by fear, brought back by hunger and hope. When it received the organs of the tortoise, it dropped all distrust. It joined Glava as it would have joined its breed. It rubbed against her legs, did not dread the touch of her hand, but when Glava took it into the canoe and it saw itself floating on the river, fever flared in its pupils.

Then the canoe itself became familiar, and in the infinite chances of life and death, the jackal followed the fate of the woman.

XIV. Men of the Night

A few days elapsed.

As long as light endured, Glava sailed on the river, upon which, despite whirlpools and rapids, she felt more secure than on land. Each evening she was nearer to Amhao, and her impatience waxed like the crescent of the Moon. Between her and the young jackal, alliance was complete. The young animal attached itself the more as it realized its weakness and the imperfection of its instinct.

In the vast solitude the little beast became very dear to the fugitive. It showed quick intelligence and already its subtle senses helped Glava in tracking down animals and discovering prey. By living with a human being, the jackal understood all that an animal may learn from man; and Glava, with her intuition of her companion's reactions, wondered how much it could make plain, by its action, its caresses and its glance.

It appeared scarcely less intelligent than certain human brutes, such as the son of the Sheep, a clumsy, loutish warrior, whose eyes remained still as those of a crocodile, while the eyes of the little jackal were alert and full of willingness to serve.

One night, when the fire had gone out, the jackal scratched her shoulder, and the girl, awakening with a start, sat up to see two tall black wolves creeping toward her. Had she been surprised asleep she would have succumbed to their fangs. She uttered a harsh cry and cast her stake, the point of which she had mended and hardened in fire. Moreover, Glava now had a club hewn from a locust-wood branch, and a provision of sharp stones. The wolves, seeing the vertical beast rise, startled by the shout, stood still.

The half moon revealed their necks and their keen fangs; they were wolves of the big breed, able to strangle a man, to fight a panther. But even hunger had not killed their prudence. The young jackal had taken shelter behind the woman, although it knew, by instinct inherited from generations, that it was not a good prey for these huge animals which resembled it somewhat.

"Men are mightier than wolves," Glava threatened them. "Glava will pierce their bellies with this stake, crush their bones with this club!"

The wolves listened attentively. The human voice was not unknown to them, for they had heard, rarely, the voices of the Gwahs. But the Gwahs spoke little, confined their speech to war howls. Higher pitched and changing in tone, Glava's voice awoke distrust, without, however, persuading them to avoid combat. Their entrails, ablaze with hunger, gave them courage.

"Let the wolves hunt the stag, the doe or the antelope!" the woman resumed.

The stronger wolf, excited by her scent, breathed hard and bared his teeth. All his flesh sensed the joy of a meal. It needed but one leap, teeth dug into an artery of the throat, and the prey would appease the call of his belly.

Filled with fury against the beast which kept food from him, the wolf howled. Glava tossed a sharp stone at him, not too hard, for the rage of wounded beasts was to be feared. The less bold of the wolves, struck on the head, uttered a cry of mingled pain and terror, retreated, while the other understood that this prey might be dangerous.

Nevertheless, he started an attack, and Glava hit him with another stone, on the flank. He retreated also. Though he knew the sound of human voices, he had not known that men could hit at a distance, for the Gwahs had never hunted him. Taking refuge behind a boulder, disconcerted by this bizarre prey, he showed less ardor. Had it not been for the scent quickening his hunger, he would have run off, but a foggy lust held him.

The Moon vanished. The girl still saw the eyes of the wolves, like four green stars. But they did not attack, and doubtless would attack only if they believed her asleep. To keep them in hesitation, she cried out, spoke. Sometimes, also, to spare her sharp stones, she picked up large pebbles which she threw at random.

The night was fearfully long. Often the wolves started forward, and toward dawn they came within three arms' lengths. Two more sharp stones, perhaps the smell of another prey, decided them to retreat at last. They were lost to sight in the morning's haze.

A new morning dawned on the river, the forests and the plains, heavy with fog. The girl shivered. Having ascertained that the way was clear she went to the canoe. She was hastening to leave this evil spot, to find herself on the waters again, rid of sinister animals.

Then fear flooded her arteries; the canoe had vanished.

There remained only fragments of the leather ropes, gnawed away by wild beasts. On the surface of the river there was nothing save scum, leaves and twigs carried by the current. A measureless sadness filled the girl. She wept bitterly, squatting on the shore. As on the night when she had fled from the Ougmars' camp, she conceived the horror of solitude, felt weaker than the little jackal moaning its hunger at her side.

The breeze swept the sky clear of fog. The Sun revealed limitless space, and Glava, frightened by the distance separating her from Amhao, despaired of the day to come. She still had some cooked meat left over from her evening meal. She gave a part to the jackal, eating the rest herself. But while the world became happy again for the satiated animal, it remained somber as agony to the daughter of the Rocks.

Nevertheless, she started forth. Between the shore and the forest spread a plain on which walking was easy, but while she had been fearless on the river, here peril might lurk anywhere. Although he hated daylight, the jackal trusted in her, and trotted contentedly.

Rounding a boulder, the fugitive stopped short and trembled throughout her body; the lordly beasts had come!

There were five of them, black as slate, with their horsy faces, their hairy, pointed ears, their slender limbs and hollow stomachs. She recognized them as Gwahs, allies of the Ougmars, ferocious as hyenas, men who ate the flesh of human beings. Armed with stakes and stones, they were completely naked. She remained as if petrified, her eyes on those fearsome, repulsive creatures.

They soon espied the maid. Despite the throbbing of her heart, she kept the half-calm of the grass-eaters before the carnivorous beasts, which ends only after they have been caught. The line of rocks, steep and without cleft, offered no shelter; the plain was open to the forest. She must retreat to the bushes.

But the Gwahs were only 500 arms' lengths away, arriving rapidly. Brief though it was, Glava's hesitation allowed them to gain 50 strides.

At last she sprang forward. In the land of Rocks her speed equaled that of the fastest runners, and doubtless she would have reached the thickets had not her path been barred by a passing herd of large deer, trotting to the forest. At sight of them the Gwahs hurried to cut her off, and the speediest one succeeded, calling his companions in a strident voice. The Gwahs hesitated an instant between the girl and the four-footed game. The deer were already far off, the human prey was near.

They started after Glava with a great outcry.

She no longer hoped to hide in the bushes where the Gwahs could have surrounded her easily, and counted solely on her speed. In fact, she ran quicker than those short-legged men, and after they had covered 2000 arms' lengths, she had gained 500.

Gradually she drew nearer the forest, although she had resolved not to enter it until she had attained a reassuring lead, for if the undergrowth offered many hiding places, it made running difficult. Moreover, the Gwahs were jungle people, skilled at sliding through spiny bushes and tangled growth. She turned at intervals, and perceived their odious silhouettes loping steadily, tirelessly.

The little jackal followed her without effort. Doubtless it vaguely understood this peril, which is never remote and which hovers eternally over jackals as well as antelopes and deer.

Glava's chest heaved. A sharp ache came below her ribs; her legs faltered. Two of the Gwahs were running now as fast as the girl. She knew it; her discouragement increased, despair leading to defeat and death. Nevertheless all her will power concentrated on escape, and she fought the weakness of her limbs.

The forest was near, its fringe gnawing irregularly into the plain. A last time she turned, and this time she saw that the leading Gwahs were progressing faster than she. Then they were out of sight, a jutting clump of trees screening them.

The terrible choice had come: should she keep running or hide? She hesitated until her labored breathing, the hammering of her heart, persuaded her. She leaped across a pond of water, trod on stones which would not reveal her passage, penetrated into the land of trees and numberless dens.

For a long time Glava roamed in the thickets, across clearings, without discovering a good hiding place. Branches struck her face as she sped by, spines brought blood on her hands, her knees, her feet. She paid no heed, and thought only of escaping the Men of the Night.

A brook barred her way. Instead of leaping across it, she waded on its bed, carrying the jackal, thus ensuring that her tracks would be washed out.

She hesitated before a thick clump of bushes, fearing that a wild boar might be hidden there. Urged by her fatigue, she decided to take the risk, and slid into a small clearing in the center. Worn out, she slumped to the ground and was half-conscious, in a sort of torpor which abolished worry without lessening her caution. And as the shadows of the branches crept over the soil, she grew to hope that the Gwahs had lost her trail.

In fact, they had lost it. For a long time they kept running through the fringe of the forest. Then they came to open country, saw nothing of their prey, and stopped. But their fierce instincts, their race hatred, had been aroused. They belonged to a clan which never had allied itself with the Ougmars. As they had seen Glava from behind, they did not know she was a woman.

Tired and out of breath, they halted to confer. If their souls were rudimentary, scarcely less so than those of wolves or jackals, words wielded a fearful power among them. Knowing few words, they completed thoughts with gesture, agreeing that they had run too far, and that they were to retrace their steps.

While they were arguing, other Gwahs appeared from the river bank, where they had captured fish among the stones.

One of them was a chief, a chief such as the Gwahs had, one whose sway waned or grew according to circumstances. His ruses were many, he was more intelligent than the rest. He was more successful when hunting and brought back more

flesh and fish than he needed, so that his surplus won him followers. He was told of the adventure.

"The stranger cannot live near the Gwahs!" he decided.
"Ouak and the warriors must eat the stranger!"

In an instant, he became chief again.

"The warriors must eat the stranger!" the others repeated.

Ouak made them understand that they must travel scattered, but remain in touch with one another. If this tactic
worked well when seeking wolves or boars, why would it not
succeed when seeking a man? Those who had fish ate it raw,
to avoid delay and be ready at once to follow Ouak. The tracks
must be found. The Gwahs entered the forest.

If the Gwahs did not possess the wisdom of the Ougmars, they were patient as ants. They searched the forest for a
fourth of one day. When they halted to rest, at a signal given
by Ouak, they kept their intervals. The forest, in which traveled mammoths, stags, and boars, remained secretive, yielded
no human trail. And Ouak's prestige dwindled with passing
time, each Gwah resuming his liberty of action.

But, when the day was two-thirds spent, one of the hunters heard a short yelp from a thicket. He remembered that the
running creature had been accompanied by a jackal, and signaled to his companions.

For some time Glava had sensed that humans were
prowling nearby. The jackal stretched out its sharp nose and
moved its little ears. The scent of man was heavy on the air.
The jackal yelped. She stood with an effort, still stiff from
running, and her feet were black with dried blood. She listened
and sniffed. Men were near!

She allowed a low moan to escape her lips, and despair
raked her like a poison. Prone, her ear against the ground, she
heard the crackling of twigs under feet, the soft crunching of
steps. These noises came from all about her. She thought feve-
rishly of flight, but she knew that she would meet men everywhere.

The steps came nearer, then a perceptible rustling announced a crawling man. Glava grasped club and stake. And

she saw a head rise above the nearer bushes, black, with small rat's eyes and thick ferocious lips.

As she lifted the stake, that head vanished. A call vibrated, steps resounded everywhere. Death! Glava remembered the women sacrificed by the Tzohs to the Hidden Lives. She had seen them die, their eyes dilated by terror; she had heard their screams of agony.

This was what the somber men were bringing.

XV. Return of the Scouts

The heavy rain had tormented the Ougmars until dawn. Without fire, in darkness so dense that they were as if buried in a black pit, with that soft and multiplied pattering of drops, bodies drenched by the cold liquid, they shuddered. At times they awoke from sodden slumber to intolerable sensations which stripped them of all strength, of all will power.

Those who surrounded Glava did not think of her, and the idea of an escape on such a night had not even entered their skulls. At last the rain stopped. Before dawn a cold wind blew upon their suffering flesh and a soft light seeped down. The nomads arose. One of them uttered a sharp exclamation and the others stared at him, puzzled.

"Where is the Tzoh woman?" the warrior asked.

Akroun gained his feet heavily. Slow aches twisted his muscles for he had reached the age when humidity is evil in effects. At the warrior's cry he looked about, saw the captive had gone. Fury beat against his temples and his voice rose loudly.

"What ailed the men set to watch the daughter of the Rocks? Where are their eyes, their ears, their hands, or are they like the worms crawling in the sod?"

The four warriors set on guard lowered their heads.

"Men who are blind and deaf cannot be called warriors. They deserve neither women nor sons. They are less useful than dogs!"

"The dogs did not bark!" one of the guards said humbly.

"The Tzoh girl was no longer a stranger to them. But she should have been for men."

He was silent, torn between the desire to punish the culprits and the fear of losing followers. Glava was to have served his plans, by keeping Heigoun and Helgvor in suspense, and finally throwing them against each other in mortal combat.

"Let the warriors scan the ground!" he ordered.

He looked for tracks himself, and was soon convinced that only chance would cause them to find the fugitive. Perhaps she had dropped somewhere, from fatigue and cold. Like their chief, the warriors knew there would be no trail as the rain had drowned out everything. Nevertheless they pretended to search, some of them with suspicious ardor. One, reaching the shore, shouted,

"One of the canoes is gone!"

Then Akroun recalled that the Tzoh women had come into the Ougmars' realm in a boat, and while his anger against the young girl increased, it became mixed with admiration.

"That Tzoh woman fought at Helgvor's side!" he murmured. "She has the heart of a man!"

He therefore desired to recapture her the more, for he recalled the glance glittering with hatred she had turned upon Heigoun. This made him think of his own grandmother, Awa, who had killed a warrior whom she had been forced to wed.

"Let two canoes go after her," he said. "But the warriors must return before the Sun is midway between the river and the top of the sky."

The prolonged absence of Heigoun and Shtra worried him.

The pursuing canoes returned before the scouts. Akroun mused, filled with regret, "The daughter of the Rocks is as clever as the lynx!"

Submitting to fate, and having but a poor notion of passing time, he squatted again, waiting. The Sun crossed the zenith and was starting westward when the watchers on the hills came back to camp from the north-east.

"Heigoun is in sight beyond the hills—returning."

The jaw of the chieftain protruded as he foresaw a victory for his rival.

"Heigoun is bringing prisoners!" another watcher announced.

The soul of the leader was bitter. His ears buzzed with the quickened flow of his blood. Heigoun would claim leadership now! Turning his face toward the hills he saw, standing on a crest, Heigoun waving his arms triumphantly, indicating two captive Tzohs and four women.

The Ougmars howled with frantic enthusiasm and one of them was bold enough to express the general belief, "Heigoun will make a great chief!"

All trotted to meet the newcomers. Three warriors, recognizing their women, leaped like wild sheep. Heigoun came straight to the chief and said with significant pride, "Here are two captives and four women; three Tzohs were slain."

"Heigoun is a skilled warrior!" Akroun tore the words from his heart. "How many Tzohs did he fight?"

"Five!" Heigoun answered. "Did I not state that there were two captives, that three had been slain?"

"Why were there but five Tzohs?" Akroun wondered.

"There were 20 Tzohs or more before, and ten women," one of the Ougmar women replied. "The flood drowned six women and 15 warriors. Then Heigoun came with his companions."

"Did the five Tzohs fight hard?" Akroun asked, cleverly.

"They were worn out, spent," the woman answered, without distrust.

Silent laughter creased the corners of Akroun's eyes, while Heigoun glared at the woman with indignation. But few of the Ougmars understood; all admired the skill of Heigoun.

The warriors crowded around the captives who appeared pitiful, covered with bloody mud, their lean bellies heaving, pupils dilated by fever, quivering with dread. Not a few insulted them and threatened them with death.

"The son of the Wolf wanted the Ougmars to see the faces of their foes," Heigoun stated. "Now they may be put to death."

"Why not?" the woman who had already spoken offered. "Did they not massacre the old men, the children of the Ougmars? Did they not beat their women?"

A warrior lifted his hatchet, wildly approved by vehement clamors, and already spears pierced the bellies of the unlucky fellows who lifted pleading hands. Clubs fell, stakes were pushed forward. The Tzohs, prone on the ground, struggled hopelessly, giving shrill yells.

Sickened, Akroun and a few of his men drew aside.

Heigoun, who had been peering about avidly for Glava, asked,

"Where is the foreign woman?"

"She fled," Akroun said nervously.

"The foreign woman has fled?" Heigoun said with rage. His huge shoulders swayed, his eyes menaced the chieftain. "Who let her go?"

"The chief shall say that later," Akroun said, shaking his head. He had straightened, hatred had given him back energy. Heigoun saw that he must not go too far.

"Let her be sought for!" he suggested.

"She has been sought for."

"Shtra did not come back as yet?" Heigoun asked. Already calm was returning to him, his voice was no longer gruff.

"Shtra did not come back."

Heavy laughter shook Heigoun's frame. He hoped that Helgvor had perished, and that hope made him joyous. Then fierce doubt assailed him; had the Tzoh left to seek the son of Shtra?

The Sun had slid down the sky and Shtra had not appeared. Keen anguish bit at Akroun's heart. Without Shtra, lacking Helgvor, the struggle became harder, victory uncertain. Meanwhile, the women had told their story, and it was known that an important troop of Tzohs was fleeing southeast, while another had remained close to the river.

A choice must be made, for it would have been dangerous to split the forces of the Ougmars. Heigoun and his followers insisted that the party go south-east. Akroun protested.

"We must await the return of Shtra!"

"Shtra will not return," laughed the giant.

A remote shout rose on the southern hills and a watcher waved his arms.

"There!" Akroun said. "We must wait."

He did not know whether the sentries announced good or bad news, and watched a man coming with long strides. The watcher shouted as he came nearer, "Shtra is coming back!"

"Does he bring back prisoners?" Heigoun asked, sarcastically.

"He brings back women—many women."

"Many women?" Heigoun repeated, his face paling.

"Twice as many as the fingers of one hand, at least."

The warriors, crowded to listen to the man, bellowed like a herd of aurochs. Some were saying, "Shtra is a great warrior!"

But Heigoun felt that Shtra was not the real victor, and murderous blood now pounded against his temples, while a quick joy animated Akroun.

Soon Shtra, Helgvor, Iouk, four other Ougmars, a score of women and the Gwahs appeared.

As when Heigoun had returned, all the warriors rushed to meet the scouts. Many, recognizing their wives, laughed with savage mirth as they ran. Shtra stepped before the chief.

"Here are those whom Helgvor, Shtra and the warriors bring back to the Ougmars."

"And what of the Tzohs?" the chieftain asked.

"Almost all are dead. Very few were saved. They were three times as many as the fingers of one hand."

As Heigoun laughed insultingly, Shtra, Iouk, Helgvor and the others silently threw at Akroun's feet the severed thumbs of the warriors. There were 24!

"It is well," the chief said. "Shtra is indeed a great warrior."

"Shtra is not a great warrior," the old man answered. "It was Helgvor, clever as a lynx, strong as a tiger. He killed more than 12 Tzohs!"

"Shtra lies!" Heigoun yelled.

"Shtra tells the truth!" Iouk said.

And the warriors who had followed Shtra shouted,

"Shtra tells the truth!"

Then many other warriors hailed Helgvor, and Akroun felt his power returning.

"Helgvor is mightier than Heigoun!" a voice said in the crowd.

"Heigoun shall crush Helgvor as the leopard crushes the doe!" roared the son of the Wolf.

"Helgvor does not fear Heigoun," the young man said. He faced the giant, spear and club ready, but warriors intervened while Akroun spoke.

"The Ougmars have not recaptured all their women! They need both Heigoun and Helgvor!"

"Heed Akroun, the chief!" 20 voices shouted.

The son of the Wolf controlled his anger. "Helgvor shall perish when the women are retaken!"

"Helgvor shall beat down Heigoun!" Then Helgvor, astonished not to see Glava, asked, "Where is the daughter of the Rocks?"

"The foreign woman fled!" the chief explained. "Rain drowned the camp, the fires were dead. It was so black that a herd of mammoths would have passed unseen. Even the dogs knew nothing."

Speaking thus, Akroun reassured and won to his side those who had watched Glava, for they knew that if Heigoun became chief, they would suffer. As had his rival, Helgvor said,

"She must be caught."

"The warriors sought her long."

The gloom which swept Helgvor was so intense that he forgot his recent victory. "Helgvor will go to seek Glava!" he stated.

"Not until the Ougmars have retaken their women!" the chief replied.

A longing to rebel shook the young man, but the Law of the Race won out. "Helgvor shall wait until the women are retaken!"

XVI. Battle Plans

Because the Sun was low, Akroun put off the start until morning. Now, only one path appeared good, for Shtra, Iouk and Helgvor agreed with Heigoun, and all the women advised it.

"Tomorrow we leave for the south-east," the chief said.

During the night, Helgvor awoke thinking of Glava. He knew she would undertake to find Amhao. If the coming expedition was quickly over, perhaps he would reach the Red Peninsula before her. That hope appeased him for a moment, then the fear of the perils she would run contracted his chest. He saw her being downed by a wild beast, drowning in the river, and infinite desolation seeped into him.

At dawn, Akroun called the older warriors together.

"The women could not follow quickly enough. They must return with a few guards to the Red Peninsula."

Some of the Ougmars received this advice with regret.

"Won't the Tzohs come back to capture them again?"

"The Tzohs won't dare. They've lost too many warriors."

When those who were to escort the women were selected, Helgvor asked Shtra to propose him for the mission. Both Akroun and Heigoun refused.

Beyond the hills of the south-east, the plain spread endlessly, an ocean of grass on which existed the great grass-eaters, mammoths, horses, aurochs, antelopes, deer, galloping under the rough glare of the Sun, under the drifting clouds, through storms and the white ferocity of the winters.

After a few hours' march the ponds were reached, around which the Tzohs had been found, and all searched for the tracks of the band which had started eastward. By evening a warrior named Akr discovered the ashes of an encampment and the stripped carcass of a stag.

The dogs sniffed about, the men bent low to scan spoors.

"The Tzohs camped here several days ago," Shtra stated.

A coppery twilight, fused with blues and greens, spread across the western clouds on which the crescent moon etched its slender horns. A warm wind caressed the men's faces. The chief was uneasy. The tracks by the ponds announced a strong party of Tzohs, and the glance of Akroun wandered often to count the Ougmars and Gwahs.

Because they were kept supplied with roasted meat, a happy confidence reigned. But there was no joy for Helgvor; the world seemed lost, his happiness had gone with the daughter of the Rocks, into the solitude.

"The eyes and ears of Helgvor must be keen," Shtra whispered. "Heigoun will make traps."

"The same soil can no longer bear us both!" Helgvor agreed.

"Shtra will fight for his son."

"Iouk also."

A brief tenderness shaped in those primitive souls, which mingled with dim shame within the rough instincts. Shtra had watched over the childhood of his companions. Irresolute man, mediocre warrior, he loved his own people, and Akroun, of whom he felt the superiority with a vague pleasure at being dominated. Iouk was much like him, and both, effortlessly, centered their family pride upon Helgvor. Despite his quicker passions, his deeper hates and his fiercer anger, Helgvor shared with them the weakness of being affectionate, and at times even merciful.

"Akroun is also Helgvor's friend!" Shtra resumed after glancing about cautiously. "He desires the death of Heigoun because Heigoun wants to take command and kill Akroun!"

"We are the chief's allies!"

A lion appeared upon a hillock, shook his mane and his enormous voice roared a threat to space; wolves, dogs and a panther were seen. Yet the men dominated the land; even the mammoth and the rhinoceros retreated before man, who ruled the Earth.

At times the glance of Helgvor turned toward the northern section of the camp where Heigoun and his followers rested.

Night followed day, and day followed night many times.

The men marched to their destiny. The plain was broken by clumps of trees, and sometimes by thick forests which warned of the proximity of the south-eastern jungle.

Had it not been for the ashes of fires, the tracks might have been lost. But the Tzohs lit fires each night. It had been ascertained from these that the troop numbered 60 warriors and a score of women.

Their march had been much slower than the progress of the Ougmars, and the time came when but a half-day's march separated the two hordes. To cut down that distance even more, the Ougmars marched several hours by the light of the Moon, which had become full.

Akroun then gathered the veteran warriors.

"Tomorrow the Ougmars fight!" he said.

And all understood that the battle would be bitterly waged.

"The Ougmars must surprise the Tzohs!" the chief added.

"During the march or in camp?" asked the oldest fighter.

"At twilight," Shtra advised. "Thus did Helgvor vanquish."

"If they must be surprised on the march," Akroun wondered, "must we not head them off?"

"Heigoun will surprise them!" the giant declared.

"Heigoun is powerful as the aurochs! But the aurochs is not as speedy as the stag or the wolf! Now, Helgvor is swift…"

Akroun allowed his words to sink in. "What Helgvor did was well done. The fleetest shall precede us, and because it will take one day to reach the Tzohs, it shall be toward night that we attack them. We shall have the light that lingers after the Sun has sunk into the lakes, and then the full light of the Moon. Therefore, Helgvor and the most agile Ougmars shall lure the Tzohs out of their camp, and we will surprise them. Heigoun will smash them up with his club."

The giant did not like the plan, but the others approved.

"Which of the warriors shall go with Helgvor?"

There were Akr, Houam and Pzahm, all three in their youth. Akr was the fleetest, Pzahm the slowest.

"Pzahm will fight with the clan," Helgvor decided. "There is no need of more than three men. Before daylight we shall leave, with my wolf and my dog; they know how to keep silent."

"So be it!" Akroun concluded.

But Heigoun turned a murderous stare upon the young man.

Helgvor rose an hour before dawn. The Moon was huge on the western sky, the hue of molten copper. Akr and Houam were ready, both thin, with weak arms and long legs. Akr had raced against Helgvor in the past. For many seasons their speeds had been equal, first one then the other won out. Then Helgvor had won all the time. It was not likely that among the short-legged Tzohs there would be any who could catch Akr, but Houam was not as fast, not as trustworthy.

XVII. Battle of the Clans

First, Helgvor and his two fellow scouts had to ascertain the strength of the enemy and report to the chief. Only toward evening, Akroun having prepared the ambush, should Helgvor lure the Tzohs to their doom.

The Tzohs had changed their route since the preceding night, striking westward, probably in the hope of finding the river again. On the terrain covered in the last few days, the flood had caused no damage. It was seldom that the ravines had been found flooded.

Helgvor, with his wolf and his dog, followed the trail as easily as if the foe had been in sight. The tracks were so clear that they had to proceed with care. Luckily, there were few thickets, and the grass was rather short.

At noon they came to a range of hills rising from the plain. As they climbed the slopes, Helgvor and Akr found many traces, and when they reached the crest, the scouts saw the enemy's band and the women. The sight of the women and the girls maddened Houam for the Men of the Rocks had taken away his mate and his young sisters. Hatred stirred Akr, although his wife was among those who had already been rescued by Helgvor. Because he had lived through a like adventure before, Helgvor remained calm, although his heart beat harder.

"We must go downhill by the ravine," he suggested, "then by the pools." Casting a glance at the sky to ascertain the time, Helgvor added, "Will Houam go back to our people and warn them?"

As agreed, the scouts had left clear traces of their march, and Akroun could have had no trouble following them.

"Houam will warn the warriors."

While Houam went back to the north-west, Helgvor and Akr passed through the ravine and circled the pools. Skilled at hiding themselves, nothing betrayed them. And the Tzohs walked without fear, confident because of their numbers. They marched slowly. The flood had reached this section and made the trip difficult. Many were obviously tired, not a few wounded. Moreover, the women had to be spared too great fatigue.

Through the grass, behind hillocks, bushes and trees, Helgvor and Akr followed the hostile horde. The Tzohs halted before the Sun grew red with approaching twilight. They had chosen a formidable position in which to camp. Protected by pools and boulders, it could be reached only through a gap in the rocks, easily fortified, easily defended. Pines and firs supplied wood for the fires.

"The Tzohs are mighty!" Akr said, doubtfully.

"The Ougmars shall not attack their camp!" Helgvor replied. He laughed low, and resumed, "They would be dangerous to attack with club and spear, with hatchets. Dangerous also against spears. For one would have to risk their weapons in return. But, with his bow, Helgvor can harm them without coming within their range."

He indicated his bow, and Akr, knowing his reputation, grinned. The Tzohs were still gathering wood, and a few came toward the bush behind which the two Ougmars had taken shelter. Although it was improbable that they would come this far, Helgvor and Akr retreated to the tall grass. The dog and the wolf, now accustomed to hunting man, imitated them without need of speech.

The Sun was setting in an enormous blaze of red against the west when Houam returned.

"The Ougmars are in the ravine," he said.

He related that Akroun had chosen a spot pitted with caves. But Helgvor went back to the main body. He addressed the chief.

"This place is too far to lure the Tzohs."

"Let Helgvor guide us."

And the son of Shtra led the Ougmars into a thicket within 1000 cubits of the Tzohs' camp. The Sun had vanished and light was dwindling on the plain.

"We must wait for moonlight," the chief said. "What does Helgvor wish now?"

"Another bow and many arrows."

Behind the fires of the Tzohs, glowing brighter as the twilight darkened, the swarthy faces of the warriors could be seen clearly. The women also could be discerned, and many of them appeared resigned to their lot.

Helgvor selected a second bow, that of a warrior with mighty arms, a weapon which few men could use well. Arrows were brought. Helgvor tested the bow, adjusted its tension. Then, patient as animals in ambush, the warriors waited in the shadow. The sky was overcast, and they saw neither the great blue star, the Northern Cross, nor the red star. Many closed their eyes and drifted into a light sleep. Then the Moon appeared at the edge of the plain, dipped its distorted disk into pools, while millions of frogs croaked like old men.

"The son of Shtra must prepare to go," Akroun said.

The orb, at first much like a red cloud, condensed and became like the polished blade of a hatchet, its light turned the plain into a limitless, silvery lake.

Already, followed by Akr, Helgvor crawled through the grass. When they had gone 500 paces, Akr hid, and permitted the son of Shtra to go on alone. The Tzohs were dropping off to sleep. A few sentries squatted near the entrance. Before so many warriors skilled in the use of hatchet and all weapons, what could be done by a lion, a tiger, or a gray bear? Spears alone would have riddled them. The Tzohs felt secure.

Suddenly, the only presence they would fear manifested itself. A tall man was standing in the grass!

At the first alarm, Kzahm, son of the Boar, stood. The warriors, startled from sleep, were puzzled and bellowed questions. And the resounding voice of Helgvor defied them.

"The Ougmars come to punish the skunks!"

Clubs whirled, spears were darted. Helgvor, with a savage laugh, took his bow and aimed. The arrow pierced the neck of a Tzoh. The outcry died out and deep surprise immobilized the Men of the Rocks; no Tzoh bow could have sent an arrow that distance. Advancing a few steps, Helgvor shot again; the arrow stabbed between the ribs of another man.

Upon an order from Kzahm, the warriors fell headlong to the ground. The third arrow missed, the fourth dug into a shoulder. Thus, Helgvor made the camp unsafe.

Seeing but a single warrior, Kzahm grew ashamed and ordered a pursuit. Not too trustful, nevertheless, he dispatched only 15 warriors against that odd adversary. Feeling that delay was dangerous, the warriors rushed headlong. Helgvor waited for them to come halfway, his bow hummed three times. The first arrow pierced a belly, the second knocked out an eye, the third missed. Several of the Tzohs returned his shots, and an arrow scratched his thigh, but the Ougmar ran, and increased the distance separating him from his pursuers.

The appearance of Akr worried the Tzohs and slowed them a while. He fired an arrow, missed, and pretended to flee, while Helgvor stood still. Five men headed for Akr, eight sought to surround Helgvor, who avoided them with ease.

Scattered in a semi-circle, fierce and desperate, for the fugitive's speed left them small hope, they kept on stubbornly. Then Helgvor raced to the right and, with a blow of his club, killed an isolated warrior. Then his arrows hummed again, and he faced the remaining five.

"The Tzohs are not even hyenas!" he derided them. "The Tzohs can't fight anyone but old men and women!"

Some distance away, Akr had reached the ambush. Twenty Ougmars leaped out, terrifying the Tzohs who were killed off almost without offering resistance, while Helgvor dropped two more of his foes.

Now, Kzahm was aware that the night of life or death had come. The Ougmars, the Gwahs and the dogs howled all together. Because they had appeared suddenly where they were not expected, they seemed the more formidable. Memories were stirred in the skulls of the veterans, the legends woven around the Ougmars. But the battle must be fought: the

Ougmars were coming. Around them were scattered the fierce dogs and the Gwahs with pointed ears.

Furious puzzlement quivered in the Black Boar's breast. He thought of rushing out to meet his enemies, but the numbers of the Tzohs and those of the Ougmars were now almost equal, and moreover there were those black men, those dogs with the terrifying bark. From the elders, Kzahm had heard of the Men of the River, knew their strength to be great, their agility extreme. He alone, he thought, was more formidable than any Ougmar. He decided to wait for the attack and had fresh branches piled across the gateway. The warriors could take shelter behind the heap of wood and bush.

But Akroun called a halt to inspect the Tzohs' camp. He saw that the storming would be hard to push through, and would cost many lives.

"It is wood that fire loves to eat," Helgvor said, coming near.

"Helgvor is as sly as he is valiant," Akroun smiled.

He ordered that dry branches and twigs be gathered, then, torches in hand, the Ougmars went forward once more. Close to the camp, they tossed the flaming bundles into the barrier. Smoke lifted.

Kzahm had guessed his foes' plan quickly. To avoid the spread of flames over the entire camp he ordered the barrier fired, and the two blazes clashed. On both sides, men waited until nothing but ashes remained. As the Ougmars had to cross a narrow spot or wade in the pools, Kzahm decided to stand his ground and wait for them.

"The Men of the Blue River seek to die!" he clamored to cheer his followers. "They shall die!"

The Ougmars replied with their war-cry, but still Akroun delayed an onrush. He preferred to order his best bowmen, Helgvor principally, to harass the enemy with arrows. This tactic could not fail. When several Tzohs had dropped, Kzahm realized that his wait meant disaster, and ordered an offensive movement.

It was like a mass of bodies, of hatchets, stakes, clubs and spears. Fearing panic, Akroun opposed onslaught with onslaught. The mass of the Ougmars dashed forward, while the Gwahs hovered on the flanks, pelting the Tzohs with sharp stones.

The two hordes collided. Young and strong men left life. Heigoun, Kzahm, Helgvor, with the more muscular of the fighters, struck with clubs, breaking bones. Others, armed with stakes, aimed for the body, disemboweled their antagonists. Many used the spear, striking for the soft places. While the spring of the Tzohs appeared to triumph at first, the Ougmars soon were masters.

Heigoun and Kzahm came face to face. Their bulks were alike. Both had the deep chest of the bear, monstrous shoulders and legs like oak branches. Their clubs clashed like rock on rock, and the impact was so terrific that both staggered back.

Astonished, each now aware of the strength of his enemy, they hesitated, eyed each other, and planned clever strokes. Rasher, Heigoun resumed the fight, and his swinging club would have crushed Kzahm's skull had not the other parried. The Black Boar swung on the flank, mightily. But an Ougmar warrior shoved the club aside, hitting Kzahm on the shoulder. Heigoun got home two blows immediately, one to the other shoulder, the other on the neck.

Kzahm fell to the ground and Heigoun shattered his ribs and his limbs.

The defeat of their chief discouraged the Tzohs, and only a few kept on fighting. The mass suddenly became as does under the claws of the leopards, like stags before the tiger, and perished without combat, struck down by the hatchets, the clubs and the heavy stakes.

Akroun looked down upon the corpses and the bodies of those not yet dead. The women had come to greet their men, who dripped with fresh gore.

"The Ougmars are mighty! The Ougmars have annihilated their enemies!" the chief proclaimed, tossing a spear into the air. All the warriors acknowledged his worth. His reputation would last a long time, for the hero of the day was much too young to command.

"Akroun is a great chief!" Shtra declared solemnly.

"Helgvor is a great warrior!" the chief replied.

Heigoun, somber, sullen, eyed Helgvor steadily.

The clan was taking the women back to the Red Peninsula, but Helgvor, with Iouk and Akr, sought Glava's tracks.

The left bank having proved fruitless, Helgvor had thought of the right shore and the islands, particularly of the tiny islets on which animals were scarce. Akr explored ardently, for he loved to seek for trails above all things, loved to direct the dog. Days passed without result, until one morning when Akr picked up a spear with a broken head. Poorly chipped, the stone point was not the work of Ougmar or Tzoh, while the Gwahs used only stakes and stones.

Later, a second indice was found on an island. Helgvor, Iouk and Akr found ashes, a squirrel skin, the shell of a tortoise blackened with smoke.

XVIII. Sacrifice to the Red Moon

Glava waited with her limbs stiff with horror. Terrorized, the little jackal had fled. There were pauses, absolute silence, then crawlings, creepings, heavy breathing. Stake in hand, ready to fight, Glava was moved by the instinct of hunted beasts, and felt in advance the anguish of death.

The attack was brutal as the leap of the leopard, sly as the onslaught of wolves. The Gwahs, springing together in a somber, moving mass, overpowered their victim. The only blow she contrived to deliver dropped a Gwah, but ten arms were around her like black reptiles, and collective strength vanquished individual vigor. Blows with sharp stones dazed her. Lianas were wound around her limbs.

"The Gwahs are the masters of the daughter of the Blue River!" Ouak clamored.

Because his ruses had succeeded, his authority increased. All the others thought merely of drinking warm blood, of eating flesh, but Ouak was sensitive to the mysterious allure of the tall, flexible maid, whose light complexion made her so startling among the black masks surrounding her.

"The foreign woman must be killed!" one of the men said.

"The Gwahs shall kill her," Ouak agreed, "but she shall be offered in sacrifice to the Red Moon!"

This was the most important of the rites performed according to ancestral traditions by the Men of the Night. The flesh of beings sacrificed to the Red Moon had particular virtues, and the mention of the sacrifice recalled evenings of absolute happiness. Even the greediest accepted the delay, and Ouak had gained time to think of some way to be alone with the captive.

"The daughter of the River shall perish beneath the Pointed Rock!" he added.

Then, four Gwahs carried Glava through the forest. She closed her eyes, unable to look at these men without frightened disgust. Perhaps she would have suffered less under the claws of the gray bear or the tiger. Racial instinct made the Gwahs more odious than Old Man Urm, than Kzahm with the bison's head, than even that gigantic Ougmar from whom she had fled. She felt the end approaching.

They passed between trees older than 100 human generations; grass died in their shade, in their clefts, large as caves, dwelt wild beasts. The trees grew scarcer, the soil was hard and red. Then they came to a pointed rock, in a cluster of black pines.

Gwahs, men, women and children, emerged as if from the ground, howling hideously, clawing toward the prisoner. Glava thought her life was finished. The hot blood of youth revolted against destruction. Amhao seethed to float in the sky, together with the tall Ougmar warrior who had saved her, the memory of whom made the Gwahs appear more ugly, more sordid.

The women, ardent as she-wolves, were for putting the captive to death at once.

"Ouak has heard the voice of the Red Moon," the chief said, to quiet them.

The women accepted this explanation but watched over the girl with bloodthirsty jealousy. In vain Ouak used all his ruses but could discover no reason for being alone with the prisoner. In any case, as this was a ritual question, his prestige availed nothing against the opinion of the old men, in whose heads were kept alive the obscure legends.

A stag was captured alive, and joy increased. It would be sacrificed at the same time as the foreign woman. And the time drew near when the Red Moon would swing into the sky.

Two men unfastened the lianas binding Glava. Five others came, armed with sharp stakes, and the girl knew she was to die. An old Gwah started a ritual chant, monotonous as the dripping of rain on stones.

"The Gwahs were born of the Night and the Red Moon yields them strength! The Gwahs are the masters of the forest, and those who walk on all fours fear the stakes and the sharp stones! When strangers come into the forest, the strangers must perish, and the Gwahs must drink their blood! The Gwahs were born of the Night and the Red Moon grants then strength!"

The men brandished their stakes, the women yelped horribly, and all repeated in chorus, "The strangers must perish, and the Gwahs must drink their blood."

Then the old man indicated Glava, and resumed his chant,

"That woman is a stranger. She shall perish!"

The stakes menaced the daughter of the Rocks.

There was a great silence; the Red Moon was about to be born anew. A pale light filtered among the western stars, a cloud was illuminated, and suddenly the Red Moon lifted her disk above the horizon.

The old man chanted, "Red Moon, Red Moon, who made a pact with our ancestors, here is the stranger! Her blood shall flow before thee, and thou shalt hear her cry of agony!"

He lifted both arms to give the signal, and his eyes dimmed with terror. Somber silhouettes had leaped from a clump of bushes, came on, numerous as the ants from a heap. Bellowing like bison, impetuous, they attacked.

They were the Upper Gwahs, whose legs were longer than those of the Lower Tribes, whose hair was spotted as the pelt of the panther, but whose skins were also porous and sweaty. Their thick lips were drawn back on sharp teeth. Often, a generation would pass on without their appearance, but their hatred was eternal.

Women fled, the males turned their stakes against the invaders, and the battle started, at the end of which the living would eat the dead. Alone beneath the Pointed Rock, Glava was paralyzed by surprise for a moment, then, understanding that her death had been delayed by fate, she sought cover.

Nearby ran Gwah women, so frightened that they did not recognize the stranger. But when they reached the shadows of the old trees, two of them instinctively leaped upon the daughter of the Rocks.

She dropped the first one with a blow and, grasping the other by the hair, dragged her to the ground. Bewildered, the others allowed the prisoner to escape, and soon she was a long distance ahead, out of their reach. She no longer felt fatigue nor pain. Drunk with the joy of living, she crossed an immense stretch, and only stopped when tired out.

The stars twinkled through the leaves, branches palpitated in the wind. She flung her arms wide and dropped to the soil. She slept there, at the mercy of prowling animals.

When she awoke, the patient Moon had reached the zenith. A night bird flew away like an enormous, dark butterfly. Nearby, animals grazed, and Glava, sitting up, saw herself surrounded by monstrous shapes. The nearest one was as bulky as seven aurochs and resembled a boulder covered with reddish moss. The block of the head ended in a long snake, twisting between white horns, large as the horns of ten bison, which were tusks. Four cylinders, thick as tree-trunks, supported chest and belly.

Glava recognized the mammoth. For thousands of years such beasts had not inhabited the Land of the Tzohs, and in the territories of Ougmars and Gwahs they grew rarer as the centuries passed. The daughter of the Rocks had first seen mammoths during her flight with Amhao. This one, standing in the moonlight, formed an imperishable image in the eyes of the fugitive.

Dull fear seized her. She looked at the other mammoths, under the low branches, with the light of the Moon drenching their backs, and because they were so like the first, her amazement did not increase. But the impression made by this giant stirred her to active fear.

Glava knew that she was in the center of immense forces, any one of which could crush her as she could crush a lizard. The formidable beasts were asleep, and she could hear the rhythm of their breathing. They feared nothing in the murderous forest, neither tiger, lion, gray bear, nor poorly armed Gwahs, and were endangered only when faced by the rhinoceros who occasionally clashed with them, and tried to pierce their bellies with his spike. But the mammoth more often than not crushed him beneath his tremendous weight. And those encounters were so rare that generations of mammoths knew nothing of them.

For several thousand centuries the ancestors of the mammoths had lived in a dreamy peace. Now the time had come when, upon a warmer Earth, their number dwindled. Those who were to exist for a long time were far north, on plains where water became stone as early as autumn.

120

The future did not exist for them: peaceful innocence filled their hearts. But the summers were becoming too hot for them, and on very long days, when the Sun consumed half the night, they plunged their hairy bulks into the river, into lakes, into pools, to refresh themselves. They felt better during the cool autumn months.

Dawn broke, dimmer than moonlight, then day came, with its bird songs and colored clouds. Glava was no longer afraid. While she had slept, exhausted, still as death, one of the mammoths had investigated her. As she did not move, the instinct of the animal supposed that she lacked that life which troubles other lives. And he readily granted her the small stretch of soil she occupied.

When the animals awoke, her scent was familiar. All that recurs without bringing annoyance or danger becomes indifferent or loved by the living. The mammoths accepted Glava as they would have accepted a tree or a stag.

She also felt, although differently, the security of repetition. When the mammoths strode away to seek better pasture, she followed them because she feared the Gwahs, keeping nearest the one who knew her best. The others, as time passed, grew accustomed to her presence. And a whole day elapsed. She found nuts, roots and mushrooms which fed her, while they ate bark, tender stems, grasses or the tufts of aquatic plants.

On the second day she circulated in the herd as if she had been with the mammoths for several seasons. Her scent was so well known that they forgot her. In all things they proved themselves better than men; none were inclined to kill her or to cause her suffering. They roamed at random through the forest and the marshes. The world entered through their tiny eyes, the hue of sod, and they had an intelligence special to them, which permitted them to know what was harmful and what was good.

Glava lived more at ease while with them than she had among the Tzohs, where the weak were sacrificed, or among the Ougmars, where she had met Heigoun. She was sad, however, for she needed Amhao, and although she did not know it, she missed the tall, tawny warrior.

Perhaps she could have become friendlier with the mammoths, by digging up roots for them or selecting tender twigs for offerings. But their bulk frightened her, that strange hairy snake swinging between the immense tusks, and their enormous legs which might crush her with ease. She kept her distance, and if they did not threaten her, they made no effort to know her better.

They marched uphill through the forest, farther from the river each day, so that she soon realized she would have to leave them. This was a hard decision to make for she feared the Gwahs, the Red Moon, the evening fires, death.

Nevertheless, she allowed them to go off without her one morning. The thickets screened them. Alone, she felt rising in her the horror of meat-eaters, and she hid a long while under branches. The numberless sounds, which she had not heeded when with the mammoths, resumed their ferocious significance. The shadows held lurking monsters. Armed with a clumsy stake and sharp stones, she traveled in this land of claws, of teeth and venoms, all her senses keyed for a brief future.

As after her flight from the Ougmar camp, she found herself lacking fire. The flints she found produced small sparks, but she could not set flame to grass. She encountered the wolf, the hyena, the brown bear, the panther. None attacked her. But she saw no lion, no tiger, no gray bear, beasts that retreat before none save the mammoth, the rhinoceros—or fire.

At last she reached the river and knew her way.

She walked and walked. At night, she sought shelter. And fate spared her.

At the end of a day, after seeking long, she selected a flat space on a steep rock, five arms' lengths above the ground. The stars were out, she was tired, and she trusted herself to the night. Wolves, hyenas, jackals passed by, ascertained that they could not reach her, and went their way. Glava would awake, watch for awhile, fall asleep again.

Toward morning a terrible life halted near the boulder. In the weak light seeping out of the east, by the lingering glow of the stars, the shape recalled that of the tiger. But it was a large, handsome lioness, full-grown and very strong. Her light-colored pelt, her eyes with round pupils were enough to distinguish her from the striped feline, the eyes of which are oval. But the manner was the same, that patient watchfulness in a huddling crouch.

As her scent was poor, chance had caused her to stop near. A gust of wind had brought the smell of Glava to her nostrils. Having eaten the women and children of the Gwahs, she knew human odors. Of late, her hunts had not been successful. Accumulated hungers twisted her belly. And there was a prey upon the boulder which would sate her craving.

But the needed leap worried her. If the prey fought, she would be in a bad position, and she recalled a blow from a sharp stick, flush on the nose, delivered by one of the women she had caught. With raging impatience, certain that the erect creature could not flee, she watched.

Finally, trying to surprise Glava, she stood up against the side of the boulder. Glava had watched her without showing herself. And she saw no lane of escape. When the lioness leaped, Glava would die. She saw the beast prowl about the boulder, smell the wind. Occasionally she heard heavy breathing or a low dull roar. Immobility was her defense. But when the lioness reared her body against the rock, immobility became dangerous, and standing in her turn, the girl spoke in a strident voice,

"The stake of Glava is sharp, it shall sink in the lioness's jaws! Sharp stones will put out her eyes!"

The animal, astonished, retreated as if to think the situation over. Glava had but one hope, that another life might pass, easier to catch. No life passed by, and the lioness sprang. The point of the stake broke off on her hard skull, and, one hip ripped open by a clawing stroke, Glava rolled helplessly from the flat surface down to the plain. She was helpless, closed her eyes, and waited for the lioness to devour her.

A shadowy form appeared near the boulder.

The feline, turning, beheld an immense and hideous beast. A horn jutted from its nose, another was planted in the middle of the ungainly head. Its skin was like the bark of very old trees, its eyes were tiny and stupid. Survivor of a formidable breed which had vanished almost altogether, evil-tempered and ferocious, the beast had probably been awakened by the noise of the struggle and had come to investigate.

The ancestors of the lioness, recognizing a rhinoceros, would have fled without hesitation.

But she was surprised, excited by the conquest of copious flesh, hesitated a moment, then it was too late. The enormous mass charged headlong. The lioness clawed at random, bit, but the rhinoceros, invulnerable, had but to pass. She was stretched out, ribs smashed in, entrails showing, moaning with pain. The huge animal turned, trampled her, scattered her bones, her flesh, her hide. Then, his rage vented, he trotted away, forgetting the other being.

Glava had crawled behind the boulder. Her blood spurted. Her head was light, her eyes no longer saw; she fainted.

XIX. Reunion

When she came to, a man was staring at her.

"Helgvor!"

He had come out of the limitless solitude. And despite her pain, despite her weakness, she knew the unfathomable happiness of not being alone. Two other men were nearby. When with the Ougmars she had learned that Iouk was a quiet man, and she guessed that Akr, slight, almost frail, would obey the others. For a time she took joy in not being alone, and a great tenderness went from her toward Helgvor.

Then she asked, "Amhao?"

"We'll find Amhao!" he said.

She trusted her destiny to the tall nomad, and sank into fever, fatigue—and faith.

The wound was deep and the fall had harmed the bones. Glava suffered, bravely. In the mystery of instinct, she felt that Helgvor was more tender than she had ever been. Her astonishment was limitless, that such gentleness was not a weakness, for was he not as brave as a tiger, as clever as a wolf, as skilled as the most feared warrior?

No other man resembled him. He was alone, as if sprung from an unknown race. Her horror of men who break off women's teeth, who beat them, or throw them in sacrifice to the Hidden Lives, did not extend to him.

And Glava was revealed to Helgvor. She was the eternal and ever-changing morning. For her, he would slay Heigoun. The fear of losing her was so violent that he would feel his heart grow cold at the thought.

As he watched by the fire, Heigoun's silhouette rose in the flames. Helgvor believed ardently in his own victory, but in a livid glow he sometimes felt himself crushed by the club, disemboweled by a hatchet. The cry that then died on his lips did not express fear, nor rage, but the supreme shame of not having known how to guard the daughter of the Rocks.

They traveled in the canoe by day, stopped at night. Glava was delirious for a time, then youth won out. And they whiled the time exchanging the legends of their tribes. After 12 days she was well, out of danger. And that night, when Akr and Iouk were asleep, Helgvor spoke to Glava.

"In a few days the canoe will reach the Red Peninsula."

A shudder rippled on Glava's flesh, as the poplars quiver before the wind. She recalled the colossal warrior with the cruel eyes: Heigoun.

"Glava cannot live on the Red Peninsula," she cried.

At the sound of her voice Akr stirred restlessly in his sleep and the wolf growled. A sharp pang lashed Helgvor's heart.

"Where can Glava go? The Men of the Rocks would kill her, and women cannot live alone on the plain or in the forest."

"Amhao and Glava lived thus!"

"Was not Glava stretched helpless upon the ground? Even jackals could have devoured her. And was not Amhao's canoe pursued by the Tzohs on the river?"

"The chief will give me to the giant warrior," she said, trembling. "Glava prefers the tiger's fangs."

"Helgvor killed twenty times as many foes as Heigoun," the nomad said proudly. "If Heigoun wants Glava, Heigoun shall die."

She lifted her head with a surge of faith and admiration.

"Helgvor is braver than the snow eagle!"

"Helgvor will not allow any man to touch Glava," he said excitedly. "For her he would fight the chief of chiefs and the whole tribe!"

Feeling that she would not be merely Helgvor's slave, Glava felt an intense tenderness.

The Moon was full when the canoe neared the Red Peninsula.

It was toward twilight that Iouk and Helgvor first saw the dark trees and the reeds faded by autumn. Since the preceding night, they had been on the alert for Heigoun and his men. Helgvor decided not to take Glava to the tribe as yet, but concealed her in the bushes. He addressed Akr, more subtle than Iouk,

"Akr shall go and see if the Tzoh woman, sister of Glava, is on the Peninsula. He shall also find out if Heigoun is hunting. Akr shall not allow himself to be seen."

Akr left, light and swift as a stag. When he returned, the Sun was rising over the forest.

"Akr walked among the Ougmars," he reported. "He was not seen! The Tzoh woman is on the Peninsula."

"Akr has seen Heigoun?"

"Heigoun is not there."

"Helgvor then shall go to see the chief," the nomad said, after a moment's thought. "Akr and Iouk will watch over Glava?"

"They'll watch!" Iouk assured him.

Glava listened, fearful. She did not wish Helgvor to leave her, but she knew his aim, and kept quiet.

"Let Glava fear nothing!" Helgvor said. "Before the Sun reaches the black hills, Helgvor shall return."

Helgvor reached the Peninsula, and the warriors who saw him shouted loudly. Other men, women, ran forward, then came Akroun. He considered Helgvor with fretful elation.

"Helgvor came back! Where are his companions?"

"Iouk and Akr are waiting away from here."

"Why did they not come with Helgvor?"

"They shall come," he answered, lifting his voice to be heard above the cheers of the warriors.

"And the foreign girl?"

"Helgvor saved the daughter of the Rocks," the tall nomad replied, his face set.

"He also saved our own women," the chief said, gently. "The Men of the River have not forgotten. What does Helgvor wish?"

"That no one shall be master of the foreign women without his consent."

"So be it," the chief promised gravely.

"And if Heigoun protests?"

"The warriors will obey the chief of chiefs."

Akroun's way was firm. No Ougmar now dared to question his judgment. But he distrusted the obscure twists of destiny, and he wished Heigoun to disappear.

"Helgvor always liked to obey Akroun, always shall obey him. But Heigoun will not obey. He will roam near the chief, roam near the daughter of the Rocks. Let the chief allow Helgvor to fight."

Akroun was perturbed. Should Heigoun win, all would fear him.

"The tribe needs strong men!" he said at last. "If Heigoun gives up the foreign woman, Helgvor must not fight him."

"Heigoun will not yield her."

"Then," the chief said after a long pause, "the combat is inevitable."

"It will be so," Shtra put in. "Heigoun will attack Helgvor!"

The spectators were silent. Almost all dreaded the defeat of their hero. Because Heigoun was escorted by ten men, Akroun gave ten men to Shtra to avoid a surprise, but he concluded,

"Ougmars must not fight Ougmars. Only Helgvor and Heigoun may fight!"

"Thus shall it be," Shtra agreed. "And if Helgvor wins, Shtra shall give him Glava for a mate!"

"The foreign woman shall be Helgvor's mate!"

Then Helgvor asked for Amhao, and added, "If Helgvor is vanquished, the foreign women shall not be slaves. They shall be permitted to go free."

The chief and the warriors having given their consent, Helgvor sought Amhao. She had lived somberly, for no Ougmar woman had befriended her. At the sight of the young man she trembled and wept. At first, poignant joy dominated her, then she feared the death of Glava, and she wept.

"Glava lives," he said. "Come."

She understood, cried out loudly. Then, submissive, filled with unutterable affection for her savior, she picked up her child and followed Helgvor.

"The son of Shtra returns," Akr said. "He is not alone."

Glava heard the light rustling of the bushes and, suddenly seeing Amhao, boundless joy dilated her chest and she threw herself upon her sister.

Then Helgvor said, "Amhao and Glava shall follow Helgvor, and when Helgvor has found Heigoun they shall remain by the river bank, ready to flee in the canoe."

Glava then feared Helgvor's defeat, and no longer desired the combat. But she knew that the clash was as unavoidable as the darkness which follows twilight.

XX. For Glava!

The endless world was the same, yet constantly died. The river rolled waters which were not the same waters, light succeeded light, and it was never the same light, night followed day, and it was ever another darkness, the beasts roamed the plains, and they were other beasts than the numberless beasts vanished into eternity.

Heigoun, son of the Great Wolf, roamed, furious beneath the sky. He had the brutal temper of the boar, the ferocity of the flesh-eaters and a merciless pride. His ambition had been born one day when Akroun, thrown far by the horns of an aurochs, had nearly died. While the chief of chiefs, in his hut, healed slowly, Heigoun dominated the others. His deception was bitter when Akroun lived. The son of the Wolf scorned Akroun, whose hair was dusted with the spray of old age.

After the kidnaping of the women, seeing his followers increase in numbers and influence, he had condemned Akroun in his own mind. But his men had been too few and too timid. Helgvor had defied him and dared to claim the stranger. Moreover, the exploits of Shtra's son had caused those of Heigoun to be forgotten.

Thinking of such things, rage shook the warrior, jealousy burned his entrails. He wished to annihilate Helgvor with invincible stubbornness. Finding neither Helgvor nor Glava on the Red Peninsula, he had started out to seek them. His hope was to meet them either on the river bank or along the stream, for he thought they would follow that path.

And one morning he halted in a cove. Five men who would become minor chieftains the day he won over Akroun followed him. All scanned the river and saw nothing but floating trees, grasses, twigs, leaves, carried away by the current. Heigoun wondered whether Helgvor had not reached the Peninsula since his departure. And as he mused, a voice hailed him, and he turned, astounded at what he saw.

Helgvor had come.

He stood on a hillock, armed with a solid stake and one of the bronze hatchets taken from the defeated Tzohs, bow hung over one shoulder.

The giant replied to his call with a shout loud as the roar of a lion. His five followers advanced carefully, wishing to surround the young warrior, but Shtra appeared with the men given him by Akroun, and Hiolg, the boy, who had contrived to accompany them.

"Why does the son of jackals come here?" Heigoun asked.

"Helgvor wants to live in peace within his hut."

"Heigoun wants the foreign woman!"

"Did Heigoun find her? Did he make an alliance with her?"

"Before Heigoun, Helgvor is like a stag before the lion! Heigoun shall become chief of chiefs, and all the Ougmars will bow before him."

"Helgvor will never bow to Heigoun, nor obey Heigoun."

"Did Heigoun go and dare the Tzohs within their camp?'' Shtra, irritated, spoke in turn. "Did he bring back 20 women? Did he kill 15 warriors? Helgvor shall be a great chief."

Heigoun brandished his stake, but when he saw Helgvor grasp the bow, he hid in the bushes. His men imitated him and an arrow hummed close to Helgvor's head. Then Helgvor, Shtra and their men took shelter in the thicket. Silence weighed on land and waters, beast no longer saw the erect beings. Then the voice of Helgvor rose.

"Does Heigoun want peace or war?"

"Heigoun wants Helgvor to submit or die!"

"It is well! Helgvor and Heigoun shall fight."

Then Helgvor took his bow in hand. He had six arrows, but Shtra and his warriors gave him 20 more. Before shooting, the young man warned,

"Helgvor is ready to fight!"

There was no reply, and the first arrow whistled. It shot through the leaves, near Heigoun, who laughed scornfully. At the fourth arrow, a roar of fury burst out, and the colossus appeared. Blood dripped from his ear, and his face was twisting; he rushed like a wounded leopard.

The twigs of the bush made the use of the bow awkward, and Helgvor was eager to fight. He showed himself, shot an arrow at random, for he was hurried, then his fire-hardened stake met the stake of the giant. The sense of fatality, submission to Destiny, held the other warriors aside.

The stakes clashed as Heigoun sprang upon Helgvor at top speed, but the young man avoided the lunge by leaping aside. He thrust out in his turn, and his point struck the giant's club hung from the shoulder.

"Heigoun is as heavy as an aurochs! Shall Helgvor have to kill him with arrows?"

It seemed that the son of Shtra was about to use the bow again, but the desire to clash hand to hand with his rival proved strong enough to make him retrace his steps.

Heigoun lunged for the belly. The weapon slid on the ribs, ripped off a strip of skin. But Helgvor, pushing with all his might, had already driven his stake into his foe's breast. Heigoun reeled and grasped his club. Because his stake was blunted, Helgvor changed it for the bronze hatchet.

Formidable despite his wound, Heigoun whirled his club, but carried away by his spring, he missed Helgvor. As he rushed by, the bronze hatchet split his skull. He fell, the hatchet dropped hard twice more, and death came. For a moment longer the immense body palpitated, then Heigoun was still forever.

"Helgvor is the mightiest of the Men of the River!" Shtra proclaimed in a resounding voice.

And the shrill voice of the boy, Hiolg, repeated, "Helgvor is mightiest of men!"

Glava and Amhao had waited, ready for flight, in the canoe hidden among the reeds. At intervals the girl was swept by cold shivers, she chattered as if winter had come suddenly into the sky. Her confidence died and was reborn. She saw Helgvor beaten constantly, saw him triumph constantly. Neither image effaced the other completely. She listened tensely, but the distance was too great, and she heard nothing save the monotonous voice of the flowing waters, the rustling of insects, and when she looked at Amhao, identical terror showed in their eyes.

Steps were heard. Unbearable impatience drove Glava from the canoe upon the plain. The universe spun, Glava uttered a wild cry and sank to her knees. Helgvor, her beloved, had come back.

She extended her arms, while her face dripped with tears.

"The hatchet dropped the son of the Wolf," Shtra said.

Helgvor held the girl against his chest, and with her, he seemed to embrace the river, the forests and the plains, all space and all time. She was weak from a happiness composed of the tests she had survived, of the death from which Helgvor had saved her, weak also from the immense faith she had in his strength.

Then Shtra said, according to traditions,

"The daughter of the Rocks shall live in Helgvor's hut. She shall be obedient, and he shall kill those who covet her."

THE GIANT FELINE

I. Aoun

Aoun, son of Urus, loved the subterranean country. There he angled for blind fish or livid crayfish, accompanied by Zouhr, son of Earth, the last of the Men-without-Shoulders, who had escaped the general massacre of his race by the Red Dwarfs.

For days together Aoun and Zouhr would walk along the borders of the river which flowed through the caverns. Often the bank became nothing but a narrow ledge; sometimes it was necessary to creep along the passages formed in the strata of porphyry, gneiss or basalt. Zouhr lit torches made of the wood of the turpentine-tree, and the purple light was reflected back from the vaults of quartz above and the everflowing water below. Then they would stoop down to watch the pale creatures swimming in the stream, determined to find outlets by which to continue their journey, until they came to the wall from which the waters gushed forth. There they halted for a long time. They would have liked to surmount that mysterious barrier, against which the Oulhamr had vainly hurled themselves during six springs and five summers.

Aoun, who was the son of Naoh, the son of the Leopard, belonged according to custom to his mother's brother, but he preferred Naoh, whose build he had inherited together with his untiring chest and his instincts. His hair fell in tangled masses like a stallion's mane, and his eyes were the colors of blue clay. His strength rendered him a formidable antagonist, but he even surpassed Naoh in sparing the lives of those he vanquished when they groveled before him on the ground, and this was the reason that the Oulhamr mingled contempt with the admiration which his courage awoke in them. He hunted alone with Zouhr, whose feebleness rendered him of no account, but who was clever in discovering the stones from which fire could be obtained, and in preparing an inflammable substance from the pith of trees.

Zouhr's slight form resembled that of a lizard, his shoulders sloped away so rapidly that his arms appeared to spring directly from his trunk; this build had always been that of the Wahs, the Men-without-Shoulders, from the time of their first origin till they were annihilated by the Red Dwarfs. His intelligence was slow, but more subtle than that of the Oulhamr. It was doomed to perish with him and only to be reborn in other men after a lapse of millions of years.

Even more than Aoun, he delighted in the subterranean country; his fathers and the fathers of his fathers had always lived in countries full of water, of which a part disappeared into the hills or was lost in the mountains.

One morning they found themselves on the bank of a river. They had seen the scarlet of the sunrise change to a golden yellow light. Zouhr knew that he derived pleasure from watching the flow of the stream, Aoun experienced the same pleasure without being conscious of it. They directed their steps towards the country of the caverns. A mountain lay before them, high and inaccessible; its summit formed a long wall. To the north and to the south, where the range was indefinitely prolonged, impassable masses arose. Aoun and Zouhr desired to scale the mountain; all the Oulhamr were anxious to do so.

They came from the northwest. They had been traveling for 15 years towards the east and south. At first they had been driven back by floods, then, seeing that the land became ever more and more desirable and more rich in prey, they had grown accustomed to that endless journey.

They grew impatient of the obstacle which the mountain placed in their way. Aoun and Zouhr rested by the rushes under the black poplars. Enormous yet benevolent, three mammoths passed by on the opposite bank. Antelopes ran away into the distance and a rhinoceros moved close to a promontory. Obscure feelings were stirred in the son of Naoh; his spirit, more vagabond than that of the storks, longed to conquer the universe. Then he stood up and went towards the rising ground from which he could see the frowning opening whence the river gushed forth. Bats flew about in the shadows; an intoxicating feeling came over the young man and he said to Zouhr, "There must be other countries beyond the mountains."

Zouhr replied, "The river comes from the lands of the Sun."

His sleepy eye, closely resembling the eye of a reptile, fixed itself upon Aoun's sparkling orbs. It was Zouhr who had interpreted the desire of the Oulhamr. A prey to the dreamy intelligence of the Men-without-Shoulders, which had caused the downfall of his race, he knew that streams and rivers have a source.

The blue shadow changed to black. Zouhr lit one of the branches which he had brought with him. He could have walked easily without light, for he knew the country very well. They continued their way for a long time, traversing passages, surmounting crevasses, and towards evening they slept, after eating some roasted crayfish.

They were awakened by a shock, as if the very ground at their feet were rocking. They heard a sound as of stones rolling, then all was silent again. The anxiety this had aroused was soon lulled, however, and they went to sleep again. But when they resumed their march they found their way impeded by masses of rock which had not been there before.

Then recollection surged up in Zouhr's mind, "The Earth trembled," he said.

Aoun did not understand and did not try to do so. His thought was alert, intrepid and short, it concerned itself only with immediate difficulties or with living creatures. His impatience grew and caused him to hasten his pace so that before the end of the second day they had reached the wall of rock where the subterranean country ended.

Zouhr lit a fresh turpentine torch so that he might see better; its light traveled along the gneiss and mingled the life of its flame with the mysterious life of the mineral.

The companions broke into loud exclamations, a large fissure had appeared in the wall.

"It is the Earth," cried Zouhr.

Aoun advanced and leant over the opening. It was wider than a man's body. Although he knew the danger that lurked in newly-riven rocks, his impatience urged him on towards the crevasse. Walking was difficult, at every moment it was necessary either to climb or leap over the blocks. Zouhr followed the son of Urus; there was in him a kind of latent tenderness which caused him to share the other's perils, and changed his prudence to audacity.

The passage grew so narrow that they had to walk slantwise, and a heavy air seemed to emanate from the rock. Then a sharp projection made the passage narrower still, and as they could not stoop the adventure appeared to be at an end.

Drawing out his axe of jade, Aoun struck out angrily as he would have struck at an enemy—the projection tottered. The two warriors understood that it would be possible to detach it from the rock. Zouhr fixed his torch into a fissure and united his efforts to those of Aoun. The projection tottered still more; they pushed against it with all their strength. The gneiss cracked, stones rolled down, they heard a dull thud, and the passage was clear.

It grew larger, they were able to walk without difficulty, the air became pure, and they found themselves in a cavern. Much excited Aoun began to run, until he was stopped by the darkness, for Zouhr remained behind with the torch. The halt was a short one. The Oulhamr's impatience had infected the Man-without-Shoulders, and he advanced with long strides.

Soon a light as of dawn filtered through and grew clearer as by degrees the entrance to the cavern became visible and revealed a defile hollowed out between two walls of granite.

High up a band of sapphire blue sky appeared. "Aoun and Zouhr have scaled the mountain," cried the son of Urus joyously.

He drew himself up to the full extent of his great height. An unconscious but profound pride vibrated through all his being; his nomad instincts carried him away with ungovernable ardor. Zouhr, whose nature was more secretive and dreamy, subordinated his emotions to those of his companion.

But that narrow defile, lost in the recesses of the mountains, bore too great a resemblance to the land of caverns; Aoun wanted to see the free earth again and would hardly take any repose. The defile appeared interminable. When they reached its extreme end the day was already dying, but their dream was accomplished.

Before them stretched vast pasture lands which seemed to blend with the distant firmament. The mountains rose sheer above it on either side, a formidable world made up of stones, silence and tempests. They appeared immovable, yet drops of water were forever undermining them, carrying them away and dissolving their substance. Aoun and Zouhr could hear the beating of their own hearts. Life with boundless possibilities lay before their eyes. It teemed in the fertile earth, and man's whole destiny was bound up with those black basalt cliffs, with the granite peaks, with the veins of porphyry, with the gorges where the torrents raged and with the gentle valleys where the stream murmured in tender tones: it hung also on the armies of fir-trees, the legions of beeches, on the pasture lands which had appeared amongst the rocky indentations, on the glaciers lost among the summits, on the deserted moraines...

The Sun was setting over a panorama of turret-like summits, cupolas and peaks; the forms of a few mouflon sheep appeared mysteriously silhouetted on the edge of an abyss, an old wolf was spying out the solitude from his vantage ground on a rock of gneiss, whilst a bald-headed eagle hovered slowly upon the edge of an amber-bordered cloud.

A new land called to Aoun's adventurous soul, and to the dreamy spirit of Zouhr, the last remaining Man-without-Shoulders.

II. The Saber-Tooth

Aoun and Zouhr walked for 14 days. A powerful force forbade their returning to the Horde until they had discovered savannahs and forests in which the Oulhamrs would find such meat and plants in abundance as were necessary for the nourishment of human beings.

It is impossible to live permanently in the mountains. The climate there forces men to abandon them at the end of summer; the earth becomes green again there much later, when the plains are already covered with fresh grass or new leaves.

More than once evening was upon them before they had killed enough game or discovered sufficient roots to appease their hunger. They were going towards the east and the lands of the south. On the ninth day the beech-trees became more numerous than the fir, then oaks and chestnut-trees increased in their path. Aoun and Zouhr knew that they were nearing the plains. Beasts roamed about them in greater numbers; every evening flesh and roots were roasting at their fire, and the nomads slept under warmer stars.

On the 14th day they reached the end of the mountains. The plain stretched out interminably along the banks of a giant river. Standing on a declivity of a basaltic promontory, which rose out of the savannah, the two companions gazed on the new country, which had never before been trodden by any of the race of the Oulhamrs or the Wahs. At their feet grew unknown trees: banyans, each of which seemed to form an arbor, palms with leaves like immense feathers; green oak-trees crowned the hillsides, and bamboos reared their giant grasses beneath. Innumerable flowers studded the expanse with hidden joys; all expressed the fertile love and patient voluptuousness of the vegetable world, on which all life depends.

But it was the animal life which Aoun and Zouhr were especially watching. The beasts appeared and disappeared according to the nature of the soil, the height of the grasses, the rushes or the tree ferns, and the lie of the hills, the trees and bamboos. They could see troops of lithe antelopes racing away, horses and onagers advancing towards them and zebus feeding peacefully. Deer and gaurs were landing at a turn of the river; a horde of Dholes surrounded an antelope; snakes were crawling cunningly among the grasses; the humped bodies of three camels stood out on an eminence; peacocks, pheasants and parrots appeared at the edge of the palm wood, while monkeys hid themselves among the branches and the hippopotami plunged into the river, where the crocodiles floated like logs. There would never be lack of meat each evening at the fires of the Oulhamr! The promise of a life full of abundance set the hearts of the nomads beating faster, and as by degrees they descended the promontory, the atmosphere became so warm that the stones seemed to burn under their feet.

They thought that they had only to cover a short distance to reach the plain, when suddenly a rocky peak arrested their progress.

The Oulhamr gave vent to a cry of rage, but the Wah said, "This land is full of pitfalls! Aoun and Zouhr have not enough spears. Here no man-devouring beast can touch us."

The silhouette of a lion appeared in the distance in the hollow of a hill.

Aoun replied, "Zouhr has said the right thing! We will fashion many spears and clubs and javelins to bring down our game, and to conquer the man-eaters."

The shadows grew long upon the promontory; the light became like the pale hue of honey. Aoun and Zouhr bent their steps towards a young oak, from which they could obtain suitable material for their arms. They knew how to make javelins and clubs, how to work in horn and how to sharpen stones and harden wood by fire. Their hatchets had become dull, and they had not been able to renew their tools since they left the caverns. They had an impression that it would be wise to arm themselves powerfully, before they entered that alarming country.

They hewed off branches until the Sun set over the distant landscape, like a vast red fire. Then they gathered together the horns, the bones and the stones, which they had brought from the mountains.

"Night is coming upon us," said Aoun. "We will work on when the light returns."

They had gathered some dry wood, and Zouhr began to make a fire with the aid of a marcasite stone and a flint, whilst his companion stuck a pointed stick into a leg of wild goat.

They sprang to their feet as a noise like something between a roar and the laugh of a hyena fell upon their ears. They saw a strange animal about 500 cubits from the promontory. It had the shape of a leopard, its fur was red striped with black, and its eyes were large and more brilliant than those of the tiger. Four teeth, very long and sharp, crossed each other outside its jaw. Its whole form indicated swiftness.

Aoun and Zouhr realized that it belonged to the carnivorous race, but it was unlike any of the wild beasts that were found on the other side of the mountains. It did not appear dangerous to them. Aoun could overcome a beast of that size with a harpoon, a club or a spear. He was as strong and swift as Naoh the conqueror of the Hairy Men, the gray wolf and the tiger.

"Aoun does not fear the red beast," he cried.

A roar sharper and more strident than the first surprised the warriors.

"Its voice is greater than its body," said Zouhr, "its teeth are sharper than those of any other flesh eater."

"Aoun will fell it with a blow of his club."

The animal made a bound measuring 20 cubits, and stooping down, Aoun perceived another monster, a giant, which was trotting along at the base of the promontory. Its skin was naked, its legs were like young willow trunks, and its muzzle was enormous and stupid looking. It was a male hippopotamus in full strength. It tried to regain the river. But the saber-tooth barred its way at every turn, and the hippopotamus came to a standstill, its gaping jaws uttering a growl.

"The animal is too small to overcome the hippopotamus," said Aoun. "The hippopotamus does not fear the lion."

Zouhr looked on without saying anything. An intense curiosity possessed the two men—all the passion for strife which lies dormant in man.

Suddenly the saber-tooth made its spring. It alighted on the neck of the hippopotamus and held onto it with its sharp claws. The pachyderm, howling with pain, galloped towards the river. But the sharp teeth penetrated the leather-like skin, and lodged in the thick flesh beneath. An ever-widening wound appeared in the colossal neck and the saber-tooth drank the red flood which flowed from it with sounds of joy and triumph.

At first the hippopotamus hastened his pace, he no longer howled, his energy was concentrated on regaining the river. There he would plunge into his native pastures and heal his wound, there he would find the joy of renewed life. His massive paws beat down the savannah, and despite the swaying body on his back, he still progressed as fast as a wild boar or an onager. The river was near, its damp smell raised the monster's courage. But the savage teeth were plunged in once more, a new wound began to open, the hippopotamus reeled. The short legs trembled, the rattle of death came from his monstrous muzzle, and the relentless teeth of his assailant struck ever-deeper.

Just as he had reached the margin of the rushes, the victim turned slowly around, he was seized with giddiness... He drew one more hoarse breath and then the immense mass subsided.

The saber-tooth reared himself on his lithe paws, gave forth a roar which caused the buffaloes to flee in the distance and settled himself to devour his yet living prey.

Aoun and Zouhr remained silent. They felt the approach of carnivorous night, an uncomfortable feeling shivered down their spines, they vaguely understood that this new world was a land belonging to another age, older than that in which the Oulhamr habitually roamed, a land where animals still existed which had lived in the time of the earliest men. The deep shadow of the past settled down with the twilight, and the age-old river flowed all red through the savannah.

III. The Fire in the Night

It took them two days to fashion their arms. The spears were tipped with pointed flints or sharp teeth; they had each a harpoon whose point was of horn, two bows which could shoot arrows to a distance, and finally the oak had provided clubs, of which the heaviest, wielded by Aoun, was calculated to be dangerous for even the largest wild animals.

They climbed down from the point of the promontory into the plain, helping themselves with thongs cut from the skin of a deer. When they were once on the savannah the horde of the Oulhamr seemed immeasurably distant. Aoun was carried away by the strength of his youth and the spirit of conquest which is innate in human animals. He only needed to hide himself in the grass to surprise the wild goat or the spotted deer or the antelope. But he did not kill herb-cropping animals wastefully, for flesh is slow in growing and man must eat every day. When the horde had abundance of provisions, Naoh, the chief of the Oulhamr, forbade hunting.

Moreover the newness of it all astonished the companions. They watched the gavial, which was 12 ells long, with its long slender snout. They could see it floating in the river or lying in ambush on an islet or among the rushes by the bank.

The dryopithecus[1] showed his black hands and human body in the branches of the trees. Troops of wild cattle, strong as the Urus and armed with horns which were capable of goring the chest of the tiger or crushing the lion, roamed at will. Black gayals displayed their massive stature and prominent withers.

A cheetah disappeared suddenly at the turn of a thicket; a pack of wolves, in pursuit of a nylghau, slunk along in a furtive and sinister manner, and the Dholes, with their noses close to the ground, followed closely on a trail or raising their fine heads in the air howled in chorus. Sometimes a tapir rose up terrified from its lair, or fled into the mazes of the banyan-trees.

Aoun and Zouhr, on the alert and with dilated nostrils, were on their guard against cobras, and in terror of the beasts of prey. These creatures, however, were sleeping in their dens or among the bamboos; only a red panther showed himself in the hollow of a rock towards the middle of the day, and fixed his green eyes on the two men.

Aoun lifted his club and straightened his muscular form, but Zouhr, remembering the saber-tooth, held back the arm of his companion.

"The son of Urus must not fight yet."

Aoun understood Zouhr's thought: he argued that as the saber-tooth had shown itself to be more powerful than the lion, even so this red panther might prove to have the strength of a tiger. Naoh, Faouhm and Goun of the Dry Bones, teach prudence as much as courage: one must know one's enemies. All the same the Oulhamr did not at once lower his cudgel: he cried, "Aoun does not fear the panther!"

As the wild beast did not stir from the cavern, the men resumed their way. They sought a place of retreat. In that torrid country, the night must teem with carnivorous animals; even near the fire, too many perils threatened the nomads. The Oulhamr had the custom and the art of homemaking. They

---

[1] An extinct genus of long-armed apes, remains of which are found in the Miocene beds of the south of France.

knew how to protect the mouths of caverns by the aid of boulders, boughs and trunks of trees; they could make shelters for themselves either in open ground or under overhanging rocks.

All day the companions found nothing, and towards evening they left the river bank. The first stars came out as they halted on a rising ground where only some sparse brush-wood and thin grass grew. Protected on one side by a wall of slate they arranged their fire in a semicircle. They were to take turns to watch. Aoun was to be on guard first, because his hearing was sharpest and his sense of smell most subtle; for the early part of the night is the most dangerous.

A gentle breeze wafted the disagreeable odors of the beasts and the pleasant smell of the vegetable world towards him. The young Oulhamr's senses were aware of the lightest shades of sound, phosphorescence or effluvia.

First the jackals showed themselves, furtive, uncertain and graceful. The fire at once attracted and alarmed them. They remained immovable for a time, then, gently pawing the ground, they drew near to the mystery. Their shadows leng-thened behind them, their brilliant eyes became alive with red light, their pointed ears were stretched in all directions. They recoiled altogether at the slightest movement that Aoun made. The moment he moved his arm they fled, giving vent to faint yelps. Aoun was not afraid of them even when they came in great numbers, but their strong smell incommoded him, by rendering the emanations from the other wild beasts less dis-tinct.

Not to waste his weapons he picked up some stones. At his first throw they dispersed. Then the Dholes appeared, their numbers and their hunger making them audacious. They prowled in clusters or darted forward with growls, which passed from one to another as if they were talking among themselves. The fire brought them up short. They were as cu-rious as the jackals and sniffed the smell of the roast meat and of the two men. A confused supplication seemed to be blended with their covetousness.

When Aoun threw stones at them the advance guard drew back and heaped themselves together in a corner, while threatening howls proceeded from the semi-darkness. They rallied when they were out of reach and sent out scouts, who searched cunningly for openings. The spaces which separated the sides of the fire from the ridge seemed to them too narrow; they returned to them, however, sniffing all the time in an irritating manner. Sometimes they feigned an attack, or a group would gather behind a rock and howl there, in the hope that a sudden panic would yield up the meat to them.

Little by little the jackals had come back, more crafty than ever, but kept at a little distance from the Dholes. They retreated before a dozen wolves who had appeared from the east, but who presently dispersed, leaving the place free for the hyenas. These animals trotted along in an exasperating way, with a convulsive motion of their sloping backs, giving vent at intervals to bursts of laughter like those of an old woman.

Two dwarf bats were circling around on their soft wings; higher up a roussette, whose wings were as wide as an eagle's spread, floated under the stars; near the fire the bewildered nocturnal insect world quivered in myriads, the gnats formed into humming columns and the foolish beetles fell among the glowing logs.

Two bearded monkeys' heads were peeping out from a banyan-tree; a marsh owl moaned on a hillock and a hornbill thrust its enormous beak through the feathered leaves of a palm-tree.

Aoun was beset by anxiety. He watched all those gaping jaws and sharp teeth, and those staring eyeballs, which shone in the firelight like living carbuncles.

Death was hovering about him. There was enough energy assembled there to destroy 50 men. The Dholes had the strength of the horde, the hyena's jaws were as strong as the tiger's: the tall wolves showed their muscular necks, even the jackals, with their pointed teeth, could have torn Aoun and Zouhr to pieces in the time it would take a branch to burn. The fire stupefied these staring animals; they were cunning but not audacious, and the difference of their species disunited their common covetousness.

They waited for some event to happen such as rewards those who watch and wait; and at intervals mutual hate threw them upon one another. When the wolves howled the jackals took refuge in the shadows, but the Dholes gave tongue together, and all fell back before the hyenas. These animals, who are but a slight menace to man, being averse to all risks and accustomed to prey on the dead or the defenseless remained there, held fast by the crowd around them and by the fascination of that strange light which emanated from the ground.

At last a leopard appeared and Aoun woke Zouhr up. The wild beast crouched before the Dholes. His amber colored eyes were riveted on the flames and on the tall forms of the two men.

Aoun exclaimed indignantly, "The son of Urus has killed three leopards."

The animal stretched out its paws with the long claws, and let its lithe flexible body lie at full length. It was of great height and more massively built than the spotted leopards which the Oulhamr were acquainted with. Its skin was loose over its muscles. It could easily have sprung over the fire and attained the ridge where the two men stood. It endeavored anxiously to recognize what those two upright creatures were. Their smell and the shape of their bodies reminded it of the gibbon, but the gibbon was smaller and had not the same appearance. The red light showed them to be taller than the gaur; their movements and the curious objects which they balanced at the end of their arms, awoke the leopard's prudence. Besides he was alone and these creatures were ready to face him.

Aoun shouted more loudly, his voice sounded like that of a powerful enemy... The leopard crept towards the left, hesitated a moment before the empty space which separated the fire from the ridge, then passed to one side and backwards. A stone struck him in the face. He gave vent to a howl of rage, but retreated. He crouched in a threatening attitude as if about to spring, then scratched the earth with his claws and swerved towards the river. He was followed by a party of jackals, the Dholes and wolves gave signs of fatigue, and the hyenas roamed in ever-increasing circles, and only appeared intermittently in the flickering light...

Suddenly all the hordes were on the *qui vive,* all their nostrils sniffed the air towards the west, and the sharp ears were pricked. Short strident roars broke the silence and made the men on the ledge start. Then a sinuous body rose up in the shadow and alighted in the full blaze of the firelight. The Dholes had gone away, tense excitement kept the wolves immovable and caused their eyes to flame, the hyenas came back at a trot, and two civet cats mewed in the half light.

Aoun and Zouhr recognized that red fur and those terrible teeth...

The beast crouched by the fire. He was hardly bigger than the leopard and not so large as the tallest hyenas, but all the other animals bowed before a mysterious power which emanated from his movements and his immense eyes.

Aoun and Zouhr held their weapons in readiness. The son of Urus had a harpoon in his right hand, his club was at his feet; Zouhr who was not so strong preferred the spears. They both considered the saber-tooth was superior in strength to the tiger, and perhaps even as much to be feared as the enormous wild beast from which Naoh, Gaw and Nam had made their escape some time ago in the country of the Men-Devourers. They already knew that he could cover 20 ells at a single bound, a greater distance than that which separated him from the ridge. But the fire stopped him. The red tail lashed the earth; the thunderous voice resounded in volleys; the two men's muscles stiffened as if they had been made of granite...

Aoun brandished his harpoon and took aim...the saber-tooth leaping sideways deferred the combat, and Zouhr said in a low voice, "Once he is struck the red brute will spring despite the fire..."

Although he was as skillful as Naoh himself, Aoun was not capable of inflicting a mortal wound on a wild beast 20 ells away. He took Zouhr's advice and waited.

The saber-tooth stood in front of the blazing fire.

He came near to it until he was only 15 ells from the warriors. They could see him better. His chest was covered with fur of a paler hue than that on the upper part of his body, his teeth shone like onyx stones, and when he turned his head towards the shade the fire of his eyes shone like glow-worms.

Two points of rock prevented him from making his spring, and also impeded the men in throwing their javelins or harpoon.

He must advance three ells. He prepared himself to do so; for the last time he gazed hard at his adversaries, while his bosom throbbed with ever-increasing rage, for he foresaw the courage of the human race.

Suddenly a pandemonium broke out in the ranks of the Dholes; the wolves were in a tumult, and the hyenas beat a retreat towards the banyan-trees. By the light of the stars they could make out an enormous heaving mass. Soon the red blaze disclosed a heavy muzzle towards the end of which grew a horn longer than that of the buffalo. The skin was like the bark of old oak-trees; wrinkled columns supported a body which was as heavy as that of six horses. Haughty, purblind and un-observant, agitated by some incoherent anger, the beast trotted along. All got out of his way; a wolf, whom panic had thrown on the rhinoceros' path, was crushed like a rat. Aoun knew that a lion or a cave wolf would have suffered the same fate. It seemed as if even the fire would not stop the monster. But it did stop him. The colossal body swayed before the scarlet flames, the small eyes dilated, the horn menaced those around it...

Then the saber-tooth appeared before the rhinoceros.

Stretched out so that he seemed like a snake, his chest flat on the earth, the carnivorous beast snarled without ceas-ing.

A vague recollection made the pachyderm uneasy but this quickly gave way to fury. On the steppes, in the jungle, far away on the moors, no life had been able to resist his weight; he had crushed everything which did not flee from him. His horn pointed towards the red beast, his heavy legs resumed their course... He was like an avalanche. It would have needed a rock or a mammoth to stop him. Another two steps and the saber-tooth would have been in shreds...but the saber-tooth effaced himself.

Before he had time to turn the colossus rolled up to the banyan grove, and the red beast was upon his shoulders. It gave vent to a hoarse roar, dug in its four sets of claws and began its work. The artery which it knew and which had been known to its ancestors millions of years before, was there under a fold of the skin, which was thicker than the bark of ancient cedar-trees, and as hard as the shell of the tortoise. It was impenetrable to the tiger's or the lion's teeth or to those of the giant feline of the caverns. Only *his* long incisive teeth knew how to force a passage. The skin and flesh were gashed open and a jet of blood gushed out, rising the height of an ell into the air. The immense beast tried to shake off its assailant, and being unable to accomplish this rolled upon the ground.

The saber-tooth was not defeated. With growls of pleasure he bounded to one side and defied that strength, which was twenty times as great as his own. An unfailing instinct told him that the beast's life was ebbing away with that hot stream and that he only had to wait. Already the rhinoceros was staggering, the Dholes, hyenas, jackals, and civet cats were approaching the antagonists, clamoring enviously.

The vanquished colossus would afford food for all of them for one day; the saber-tooth purveyed more than any other wild beast for the parasitic hordes that escorted the great carnivore.

One more effort. The fierce horn charged the enemy, the muzzle dribbled and the voice became hoarse, despair beat at the heart of the powerless mass... Then the end came. The hot flood ceased to flow; all energy was lost in the mystery of a swoon, the fear of death was wiped out by death itself. The rhinoceros sank down like a rock, and the saber-tooth enlarged the wound which had killed the monster, and devoured the yet warm flesh. Then the jackals licked up the blood from the ground, and the Dholes, hyenas and wolves waited humbly till the red beast was satiated.

IV. The Men and the Red Beast

After the saber-tooth's victory Aoun and Zouhr put fresh branches on the fire. Then Aoun lay down, guarded by his companion. The peril was past, that circle of hungry jaws which had threatened the two men, were now pressing around the rhinoceros. Zouhr could see the stars, which a little while ago touched the crests of the ebony-trees, sinking towards the river. More timorous than Aoun, he felt himself strangely enveloped by the unknown, in that new land, where a wild beast hardly larger than a leopard destroyed huge pachyderms...

The conqueror took a long time devouring his prey.

Either through caprice, or because he liked it, or in pursuance of an inherited habit, he tore away the skin in every direction, only remaining for a moment at each place. The more feeble animals, the jackals and the civet cats, slipped into the places he had left without interference from the victor, but he growled when the Dholes, the wolves and above all the hyenas pressed too closely upon him.

The Moon, which was in its last quarter, was rising on the opposite side of the river when the saber-tooth left his prey. Then the wolves, the Dholes and the hyenas threw themselves frantically upon it. It seemed as if they would exterminate each other: there were only a few inches between their tusks, and an immense chorus of howls went up to the stars... But a truce was made in the very heart of the tumult; the wolves took possession of the shoulders and chest, the hyenas tore at the vitals, the Dholes flung themselves on the back and the hindquarters. The jackals and civet cats knew their place and got away.

For a moment the saber-tooth turned his head towards the swarming mass of jaws. The blood was dripping from his lips, which he licked unconcernedly; his jaws were heavy with the effort of devouring, his eyelids half closed. He awoke with a start, and made a few steps towards the fire and towards that human being who irritated his instincts; then, confident in his own unvanquished strength, he laid himself down on the savannah and went to sleep.

Zouhr observed him with suspicion. He considered whether he ought not to take advantage of the beast's slumbers to make his escape, but thinking that no doubt the animal would sleep for a long time he did not arouse Aoun. The Moon grew smaller as she rose above the hills, making the starlight seem pale. The mass of rhinoceros flesh grew smaller among the swarming mouths; the dawn was near when the son of the Men-without-Shoulders touched Aoun's chest.

"There is no more wood," he said as his companion sat upright, "the fire is low...the red beast is asleep. Aoun and Zouhr must leave this place."

The tall Oulhamr considered the scene. He saw the motionless saber-tooth lying 200 ells off their encampment. A sudden hate seized him. He again saw the brute roaring before the flames, he saw the cruel teeth plunged into the skin of the colossal herbivore: the whole race of man and of those by whom he lives was threatened by that unfamiliar form.

"Could not Aoun kill the beast in its sleep?" he asked.

"It will awaken," replied the other, "it would be better to pass to the other side of the rock."

The son of Urus hesitated. The force which urged him to fight was one of the primary instincts of his species. Neither Faouhm nor Naoh would have suffered a wild beast of that size to dog his steps in order to devour him.

"Naoh killed the tigress and the gray wolf," said the Oulhamr somberly.

"The tigress and the gray wolf would have fled before the rhinoceros."

That reply appeased the warrior. He gathered together his harpoon and bow and spears, and took his club in his hand. After a last look at the beast they cleared the ridge and descended from the rock. They were dejected, having slept badly, and they thought of their horde on the other side of the mountains.

Day was about to break, the sunrise was pale, and the carnivorous voices were silent on the river bank; the leaves and flowers seemed more motionless than usual...

A hoarse sound broke the stillness. Aoun and Zouhr turned around and beheld the saber-tooth. Some trifling movement, or simply the two men's departure, had awakened him; instinct caused him to follow the two creatures who had surprised his confused mentality.

"Aoun should have fought the red beast when it was asleep!" said the Oulhamr, freeing his harpoon.

A feeling of sharp regret stabbed at his heart. The Wah hung his head, feeling that his prudence had been ill-timed, and he looked humbly at Aoun. But Aoun bore no malice; his great chest swelled at the thought of the combat, and Zouhr was like a part of himself. First they stood shoulder to shoulder, combining their strength. Aoun shouted his war-cry.

"The son of Urus and Zouhr will spear the red beast and crush its bones!"

The saber-tooth did not hurry himself. When the human beings stopped, he stopped too; he watched them make ready their bows and javelins and stretch out their limbs in a curious manner. As before, their articulated shouts surprised him: he began to move along a parallel track which did not bring him nearer to them.

"The red animal is afraid of man," shrieked Aoun, and he brandished his harpoon and club together.

A prolonged roar answered him, the saber-tooth made two colossal bounds. Before he could spring for the third time Aoun and Zouhr's bows had come into action. Struck by arrows in the neck and in the body the wild beast threw himself upon the men in a frenzy. The son of Urus threw a harpoon which lodged in his ribs, Zouhr's weapon flayed his hard skull... The beast was upon them.

In one bound it threw Zouhr to the ground and sunk its fangs in his chest. Aoun attacked it with his club. The oaken bludgeon struck horizontally and only met thin air; the saber-tooth had drawn back... The Oulhamr and the beast stood face to face. He avoided the first attack by a leap to one side, he repulsed the second by a whirl of his club which grazed the brute's shoulder. An irresistible mass threw him to the ground and itself fell headlong, overthrown by its own impetus. The man found himself kneeling on one knee at the moment when the saber-tooth came back to the charge. The fainting Zouhr flung his axe, while Aoun brought down his club with both hands. It resounded on the massive head, and the wild beast began to turn around and around as if he had become blind. A second blow paralyzed his neck. Then Aoun shattered his ribs, broke his legs, and crushed his jaws. The muscles continued to quiver for a long time, and the heart, which had been laid bare, continued to beat; it required two thrusts with a spear to finish its agony, and Zouhr sighed in a hoarse and feeble voice,

"Aoun has killed the red beast... Aoun is stronger than Faouhm... Aoun is as strong as Naoh, who won the secret of fire in the country of the Devourers-of-Men!"

The Oulhamr was intoxicated by his companion's words, pride dilated his nostrils, the sadness which had made his bones so heavy when he fled in the night had left him; his whole being was triumphantly elated by adventure, and turning towards the purple dawn he felt a passionate love for the unknown land that lay before him. Zouhr continued to stammer, "The son of Urus will be a chief among men!"

Then he uttered a cry, his face became the color of clay and he fainted. Aoun, seeing the blood flowing from the breast of the wounded man, was as concerned as if it had been his own, and the still face terrified him. The time they had lived together rose up before him in chaotic scenes. He saw again the sylvan solitudes, the brushwood, the marshes and the rivers, where their energies had joined, where each was for the other a living weapon. But Aoun gathered together leaves and herbs, crushed them with stones, and applied them to the wounds of his companion, and Zouhr opened his eyes. At first he was surprised to find himself lying there, then his eyes searched for the fire, then he remembered and repeated the words which had preceded his fainting fit, "Aoun will be a chief among men!"

Becoming conscious of his feebleness he wailed, "The red beast has pierced Zouhr's chest…"

Aoun continued to dress his wounds while the Sun rose in its grandeur beyond the river. The wild beasts of the night had disappeared. Some entellus monkeys were making the branches move; the white-headed crows were hovering over the carcass of the rhinoceros, two vultures soared in the breeze, and the herbivores rose up in their masses. The hour of peril had passed for Wah and the Oulhamr; the great destroyers slept in their dens or in the jungle.

But the day itself is an enemy when the light is too strong and the earth is roasted with heat. Zouhr must be carried into the shade. Like all the Oulhamrs, Aoun had an instinct for caverns. He scrutinized the landscape in the hope of discovering some rocks, but he could only see steppes and brushwood, a few palm groves, the clumps of banyan-trees and clusters of ebony or bamboo.

Then, having secured the leaves and herbs on his companion's chest, he took him on his back and started to walk. The journey was a hard one, because he had also to carry the weapons, but Aoun had inherited the strength of Faouhm, Naoh, and the Hairy Men. He walked for a long time, obstinately fighting his fatigue. Frequently he laid Zouhr down in the shade and without losing sight of him mounted a knoll or a boulder and surveyed the landscape.

The morning was passing, the heat became intolerable, and still no line of rocks revealed itself to him.

"Zouhr is thirsty," said the Man-without-Shoulders, who was shivering with fever.

The son of Urus directed his steps towards the river. At this sweltering time of day, only a few crocodiles were to be seen spreading their scaly bodies on an island, or some hippopotami would appear for a moment above the surface of the yellow water.

The river rolled on into the far distance. Its fertile waters had given birth to age-old forests, perennial grasses, and animals without number. Father of life, it had life's untiring energy; it hurried forward its hordes of waves over rapids and cataracts.

Aoun fetched some water in the hollow of his hands and gave the wounded man a drink. He asked anxiously, "Does Zouhr suffer?"

"Zouhr is very weak! Zouhr would like to sleep."

Aoun's muscular hand was laid lightly on his companion's head, "Aoun will make a shelter" he said.

The Oulhamrs knew how to protect themselves in the forest by an arrangement of interlacing branches. Aoun set himself to look for creepers, which he cut with his hatchet, and having chosen three palm-trees which grew on a little eminence, he cut notches in their stems and interlaced the flexible stalks from one trunk to the other. This formed a triangular enclosure, the latticework sides of which offered a supple but solid resistance. The son of Urus worked hard, and the shadows had grown long on the river before he took any rest. It was necessary that the shelter should be covered with creepers sufficiently strong to resist the weight of a wild beast until his stomach should be slit or his heart pierced by the point of a spear.

Zouhr's fever continued to run high; green lights traversed his pupils; he dozed at intervals and woke up with a start, muttering incoherent words. Still he watched Aoun's work attentively, and gave him advice, for the Men-without-Shoulders were more ingenious constructors than the Oulhamrs or than any other men.

Before resuming his work Aoun ate some of the meat which lad been roasted the previous day. Then he collected some thick creepers which made a roof for the refuge, and prepared two great branches which were intended to close the opening.

The Sun was approaching the crest of the highest ebony-trees when the men took refuge in their hut. It dominated the surrounding country. The river could be distinctly seen through the latticework, 300 ells away.

It was the hour of life. The monstrous hippopotami came up from their submerged pastures and clambered onto the islands. A long troop of wild cattle were drinking on the other bank. A file of gangetic dolphins, with pointed snouts, could be seen parting the water. A crocodile with two crests appeared out of the rushes and shut his jaws on the slim neck of a chital. The graceful creature struggled with death in the fearsome jaws, which gradually decapitated it. Rhesus monkeys were distractedly agitating their miniature human bodies among the branches, while pheasants of emerald sapphire and golden hues alighted among the rushes, and snowy flight of egrets fluttered on the flowered islands. At times, seized with panic, a horde of nilgai or axis would pass, fleeing before a pack of Dholes or a couple of cheetahs. Then some horses appeared, wild-eyed, anxious and tumultuous creatures, whose prudence kept all their muscles tense. They came on with sudden prancings which swayed the whole troop, pricking their nervous ears—terrified at every noise. A string of gayals gravely skirted a little forest of bamboos.

Suddenly a loud roar was heard and five lions bounded towards the river. Solitude resulted. The broad-chested beasts caused the herbivores to vanish into space. Only the crocodile who had torn off its victim's head had not fled. It was impossible to say whether it scented danger. Its body, covered with thick scales, measured 12 ells; it was as broad as a log, and its glassy eyes and stupid head seemed an uncouth mixture of animal and mineral. A confused instinct however, impelled its huge jaws towards the newcomers. It hesitated—then, seizing its prey by the middle of the body with its long rows of teeth, it plunged among the lotuses.

Two of the lions had manes. They were thickset males, whose heads were like blocks of shale, and though heavy in repose they could bound 20 ells at a time when hunting. The lionesses were not so tall, but they were longer and more lithe, and appeared to be more cunning. All of them had large yellow eyes, which looked straight before them like the eyes of man.

They watched the stampede of the magnificent flocks from afar, and filled with disappointment halted to growl and roar. The sound of the male lions' tremendous voice traveled over the surface of the river and made even the dolphins tremble. Panic was rife amongst the palm groves, the rushes and the banyan-trees; it reached to the little landing bays, the promontories, and onward to the confluence of the stream and the river. The monkeys chattered frenziedly among the branches.

When the carnivores had given vent to their anger they continued their way. The males sniffed the faint breeze, the more nervous lionesses stretched their muzzles towards the earth. One of them winded the men. She advanced crouching towards the hut, half hidden by the high grasses; the other two females followed her while the male lions waited.

Aoun watched the brutes come towards him. Each of them had five times the strength of a man; their claws were sharper than arrow heads, and their teeth were more efficacious than harpoons. He realized his weakness and the horror of being alone, and he regretted having left the country where his kind had numerical strength in their favor.

Zouhr lifted up his head; in his wounded breast fear mingled with pain and regret that he was unable to fight.

The first lioness was now close to them. She could not get a good view of the singular animals sheltered by the creepers, so she circled warily around the enclosure. Now that she was so close to him the son of Urus was no longer afraid; the blood of the warriors who knew how to die under fierce claws without ceasing to fight, coursed tumultuously through his veins; his eyes glowed as fiercely as the lioness', and brandishing an axe, he shouted from his deep chest the defiance of the human, "Aoun will scatter abroad the lions' vitals!"

But Zouhr said to him, "Let the son of Urus be prudent! Lions do not fear death when once their blood is up. You must hit him on the nostrils while you shout your war-cry!"

Aoun realized the Wah's wisdom; it was greater even than that of Goun of the Dry Bones. Craft veiled the light in his eyes.

Motionless now, the lioness tried to see the being distinctly from which that menacing voice proceeded. First one of the lions roared, then the other; Aoun responded mightily; all five brutes were now in front of the creeper covered arbor. They were aware of the superiority of their strength and of their numbers, and yet they delayed the attack because their prey defied them and remained hidden.

It was the youngest lioness who attempted to force her way through. She came quite close, sniffed and gave a blow with her claws. The creeper yielded but did not break, while the blunt end of a harpoon struck hard against her nostrils; she leapt back with a mew of rage and pain, her companions surveying her with anxious surprise. There was a pause. The five motionless lions seemed no longer to be thinking of the men. Then one of the males snarled, and with a terrific bound the tawny mass landed on the creeper roof, which sagged.

Aoun had stooped down. He waited till he could reach the beast's muzzle; then he succeeded in inflicting three blows on its nostrils. Mad with pain the animal rolled about as if it were blinded and finally fell back to the ground and crawled away.

The son of Urus threatened, "If another lion bounds onto the men's heads Aoun will tear out his eyes."

But the lions remained pensive. Those who had not attacked retreated like the others. The hidden human beings appeared more enigmatical to them than ever, and altogether terrible. Neither in their way of fighting nor in their voices did they in the least resemble the prey which the lions were accustomed to attack in their ambushes or at the drinking places. The blows which they dealt were strangely intolerable.

The lions were afraid to approach the hut, but tenacious rancor kept them on the watch. Couched among the tall grasses or under the arches of a banyan-tree, they waited with their peculiar nonchalant and terrible patience. From time to time one or other of them would go down to the river to drink, and the herbivores were already reappearing in the distance.

Birds teemed. The pale bodies and black heads of the ibis could be seen outlined against the hollow of the bays, the marabous danced ridiculously on the islands, the cormorants made sudden dives, a flotilla of teal passed furtively, cranes flew noisily over a band of white-headed crows, while the parrots hidden among the palm-trees made a deafening clamor...

Slowly an ever-increasing sound arose in the west. One of the lions bent his head to listen to it, then a lioness sat up quivering. They all growled; the thunderous roar of the males seemed to tear the air.

Aoun listened in his turn; he thought he heard the tramp of a herd, but his attention always came back to the carnivore. Their excitement increased, they assembled by the hut and began to attack it all together. Aoun's voice stopped them; those who had been struck on the nostrils drew back; a reverberation rose up from the depths of the earth.

Then the son of Urus realized that an immense herd was advancing towards the river. He thought of the aurochs which pastured on the plains beyond the mountains, then of the mammoths with whom Naoh had made an alliance, in the land of the Devourers-of-Men.

A sound of trumpeting was heard.

"It is the mammoths!" declared Aoun.

Despite the fever which made him shiver, Zouhr listened attentively.

"Yes, it is the mammoths," he repeated, but with less conviction.

159

The lions had all risen. For a moment their massive heads were bent towards the west, then with slow steps they went downwind, and their tawny bodies were lost in the brushwood.

Aoun was not afraid of the mammoths. They crush neither men nor grass-eaters, not even wolves or leopards; it is only necessary to remain motionless when they pass, and to keep silence. But would they not be irritated to find men hidden in this bower of creepers? With a single blow one of these colossi could break through the enclosure and annihilate the son of Urus.

"Must Aoun and Zouhr leave the creeper cavern?" asked the Oulhamr.

"Yes," replied the Man-without-Shoulders.

Then Aoun moved the creepers arranged over the opening, crawled out onto the plain and helped Zouhr to follow him. Trees crashed. In the distance massive forms, gray in color like clay, became visible. Trunks stood out at the end of their heads, which were like rocks. The herd formed into three groups, preceded by six colossal males. They pounded the earth, crushed the cannas, and pierced the curtains of the banyan-trees. Their skin was like the bark of old cedar-trees, their legs were as thick as Aoun's body, their bodies like the bodies of ten aurochs.

The Oulhamr said, "They have no manes, their tusks are almost straight, they are larger than the largest mammoths!"

"They are not mammoths!" said the Man-without-Shoulders. "They are the fathers of mammoths!"

For the Men-without-Shoulders, knowing their own feebleness, believed in the superior strength of ancestral life.

Aoun felt his insignificance much more than when he was in the presence of the lions. He felt himself as defenseless as an ibis confronted with crocodiles. His pride was annihilated; motionless, stooping over his wounded comrade, he waited.

The advance guard was near. The six leaders approached the refuge; their brown eyes never ceased gazing at Aoun, but they showed no distrust, perhaps they knew human beings.

Death or life—the decision was near; if the leaders did not turn aside, it would require but ten steps before the men were pounded into the earth like woodlice, and the creeper enclosure swept away. Aoun gazed fixedly at the most powerful male elephant. Fifteen ells high, his trunk would have stifled a buffalo as easily as a python would have strangled an axis.

He stopped in front of the men. As it was he who gave the line of march all the other leaders imitated him, and an army of giants spread out in a vast heaving curve. His club at his feet, with head bent low, Aoun accepted his fate.

At last the chief trumpeted, and turned towards the right of the enclosure.

All followed. Each full-grown elephant, because those ahead of him had stepped aside, stepped aside in his turn; none, not even the youngest ones, touched the men or their refuge. The earth trembled for a long time. The grass had become a green pulp, the reeds and lotus perished under the tread of the advance guard, the hippopotami had fled; a crocodile 20 ells long, had been thrown aside like a frog, and on a rising ground the five lions could be seen lifting their roaring muzzles towards the red Sun.

Very soon the whole herd had plunged into the river. The waves ebbed, the trunks sucked up the water and threw it back in douches, then these moving rocks submerged themselves: the monstrous heads and huge spines seemed like erratic blocks washed down from the mountains with the glaciers, the torrents, and the avalanches.

"Naoh made an alliance with the mammoths," murmured Aoun. "Could not the son of Urus make an alliance with the ancestors of the mammoths?"

The day was dying, the lions disappeared from the rising ground; the ponderous gaurs and the graceful axis hastened towards their nocturnal shelters. Then the Sun touched the hills beyond the further bank of the river, and the carnivores awoke in their lairs. Aoun went into the creeper hut and dragged the Man-without-Shoulders in after him.

V. The Python

Three days passed; the lions had not returned and the elephants had disappeared down the river. Under the rays of the terrible Sun and with the help of the nocturnal vapors, the crushed grasses and shrubs were busy remaking their green flesh. Inexhaustible life, that outstripped all the hunger of the herbivores, sprang up from the damp soil and spread itself upon the waters of the inlets. Prey was so abundant that Aoun had only to throw a javelin or dart a harpoon each day to ensure their subsistence. Naoh's spirit was upon him, forbidding him to kill more than was necessary to stay his hunger.

His companion's shivering fits and delirium troubled Aoun for a long time. But his wounds were healing and the green light was leaving his eyes. On the fourth day they were joyful. The shade of the creepers and palm-trees made a pleasant freshness. Seated at the entrance of their shelter, the Oulhamr and the Man-without-Shoulders enjoyed a sense of complete repose and the luxury of abundance. The sight of the teeming animal life around moved them deeply, for it gave promise that they would not starve, and there is satisfaction in beholding the world's strength. Purple herons swooped down on the water chestnuts, two black storks got up on the opposite bank of the river, a marabou danced in a strange and unmeaning manner, and the pendant legs of a flight of yellow-headed cranes were visible, while black-footed geese with thick wattles and scarlet ibis were seeking adventures among the lotus.

A python emerged from the mud and climbed on the bank, unfolding his lithe body, as thick as a man's and five times as long. The wanderers gazed with disgust at the loathsome beast, which was unknown to the Oulhamrs. Although it was capable of the speed of a wild boar, it progressed heavily and uncertainly, still numbed by sleep and more suited to the night than to the day.

Aoun and Zouhr had taken refuge in the creeper hut. No previous experience enabled them to judge the strength of the reptile, or to know whether its fangs were poisonous, like those of the serpents which they had met in western countries. It might be as strong as a tiger or as venomous as a viper…

Little by little it approached the enclosure. Aoun kept his club and spear in readiness but did not think of shouting his war-cry. He was conscious of life which resembled his own in the great brutes, but this long slimy body without any limbs, the head which was too small in proportion—the motionless eyes, seemed stranger to him than grubs and earthworms.

When the python was close to the refuge it reared itself up and opened its flat jaws.

"Should I strike now?" asked the son of Urus.

Zouhr hesitated; in his country the Men-without-Shoulders killed serpents by crushing their skulls, but what were the serpents he knew in comparison to this huge monster?

"Zouhr does not know," he replied. "He would not strike until the beast attacks the hut."

Its head had reached the creepers and was seeking for an opening. Aoun pricked its muzzle with the point of a spear. The python bounded back with a loud hissing noise, twisted itself dizzily together and started off to return to the river. At the same moment a young antelope crossed the plain. Either the reptile saw it or it gave way to its natural indolence: it became motionless. The antelope lifted up its humped forehead, the smell of man made it anxious and it left the neighborhood of the refuge. Then only did it see the python; a trembling seized its limbs, its eyes became fixed on the cold eyes before it, it was paralyzed. The scene was short. The antelope tried to escape, but the long soft body flung forward with the rapidity of a panther. The antelope tripped over a stone and was knocked down by the attack of the reptile. It recovered itself before the python could envelop it and fled at random. This brought it to the edge of a creek, where the sinuous brute again barred its way.

Shivering with terror the antelope gazed into the distance. Life was there, the life of the vegetable world through which its agile body leaped so joyously. Two successful bounds and it would be saved. It tried to pass between the bank and the serpent, then in despair it leapt the obstacle. It was struck by a giant blow, the tail of the python was lashed around its panting body, and the little creature, feeling the approach of death, bleated dismally... In another instant the graceful form was struggling in the grasp of the long ice cold muscles; then its moans were changed to the death rattle, and hanging its head, vanquished, with mouth open and tongue lolling out, it drew its last breath.

This scene awoke a strange hate in Aoun. A leopard, wolves or a hippopotamus might have killed the antelope without his feeling any emotion, but the victory of this cold-blooded creature seemed to menace even human beings. Twice the warrior stooped down to leave the refuge, but Zouhr held him back.

"The son of Urus has abundance of meat, what will become of us if he gets wounded?"

Aoun yielded, he did not understand his own anger; it seemed to him like the fever of a wound. And what did he know of the great serpent's strength? One blow of its tail had felled the antelope and would certainly overthrow a man.

He remained moody, however, and the creeper hut became unbearable to him.

"Aoun and Zouhr cannot live here," he cried, when the python had carried off its prey beyond the rushes. "The Oulhamrs need a cavern..."

"Zouhr will soon be able to get up," his companion replied.

VI. The Giant Feline

Two more days passed. Zouhr was weak, but he could stand up; his young blood rapidly healed his wounds. Aoun could leave the hut for longer periods and explore down the river. Although he had traveled 15,000 ells, he had found no place to shelter them. Between their present habitation and the furthest point he had explored, rocks rose near the bank, but their fissures were too narrow to shelter men or even Dholes. Zouhr thought of digging a ditch, as was the custom of the Men-without-Shoulders, but it was slow work, and the Oulhamrs inhabited such lairs with reluctance. He contented himself with strengthening the creeper enclosure. More clever than Aoun in the art of construction, he made it impenetrable for wild beasts; but the elephants, rhinoceroses, hippopotami or a herd of cattle would have been able to trample it down; and it had the disadvantage of attracting the prowling beasts of the brushwood.

More days passed. The end of spring was near, fierce heat beat down upon the river, fever-breeding vapors rose up under the starlight and shrouded the landscape long after day had dawned. One morning Zouhr realized that he had regained sufficient strength to continue the journey. He said to his companion, who was impatiently looking at the vegetable growth which luxuriated around their refuge with invincible strength, "The son of Earth can follow Aoun."

The Oulhamr stood up joyfully; the wounded man was like a creeper twined around his shoulders, hindering his every movement.

Mist still hung about the river; young hippopotami grunted as they played near the inlet; birds were pursuing their active lives. Aoun and Zouhr went downstream. As the Sun rose higher they searched for shade; they were obliged to be careful not to stumble against the snakes that awoke with the heat and to detect the smell of carnivorous animals asleep in the dusk of the thickets. In the middle of the day they rested under some turpentine-trees. They had dried meat, roots and mushrooms, which they roasted over a fire made of sticks. The mere smell of the hot meat made Aoun laugh; he devoured it with the joyful haste of a young wolf, while Zouhr lingered over his meal and savored every morsel. A great numbness came over all the creatures. Only the distant voice of the waters and the humming of insects was to be heard; war was suspended; the two men gave themselves up to the sweetness of life, the strength of their youth and the intoxicating effect of the pictures which rose up before their minds, like the water chestnuts on the river.

Zouhr who was still weak became drowsy, while the son of Urus watched; his watch resembled sleep, moved only by the echoes of instinct, but his senses were awake to every variation of his surroundings.

They resumed their journey when the shadows began to grow long on the plain, and did not halt till twilight was upon them. The next day and the day after they continued in the same manner. They had to pass through a jungle, skirt the marshes, swim a river, and push their way through brushwood. Zouhr's feebleness had disappeared: he patiently followed his broad-chested companion. There was never any question of a quarrel or rancor between them; each one found in the other the resources which were lacking in himself. Aoun's strength reassured Zouhr and astonished him; Aoun valued Zouhr's cunning and the secrets which he held from the Men-without-Shoulders.

On the morning of the ninth day, rocks appeared almost on the bank of the river. They formed a chain which extended for more than 1000 steps, broken by two fissures; the highest ones rose to more than 300 ells, and extended backward to the border of the jungle; the crevices sheltered eagles and falcons.

The son of Urus gave a cry of joy at the sight, for he inherited from his ancestors the love of rocks, especially when they were near to a stream. Zouhr examined the site more calmly. They discovered several overhanging masses of rock, like those under which the horde were accustomed to shelter themselves in default of caves. But the shelter which was adequate for a band strong in numbers was insufficient for two warriors alone. They stopped frequently and carefully examined the walls of basalt, knowing that a small opening may lead to a spacious cavern.

At last Aoun's sharp eyes discerned a fissure as high as a man; it was only two handbreadths wide at the base, but it grew larger higher up. In order to reach it they had to lift themselves onto a horizontal projection, then to climb to a ledge where three men could stand upright.

The warriors easily reached the projection, but in order to get to the ledge of rock Aoun had to climb on Zouhr's shoulders. Then the Oulhamr penetrated into the fissure, but not straight: he had to crawl along sideways for a distance of five ells... The passage then grew larger, and the wanderer found himself in a low but spacious cavern. He went slowly along it, until he was stopped by a depression, a rapid declivity which ended in gloom. Before pursuing his exploration Aoun preferred to hoist Zouhr onto the ledge. He crawled out again sideways as he had gone in.

"The cave is big, perhaps it has two entrances," he said, "Aoun has not seen the end of it yet."

Stooping down he stretched out a spear. Zouhr managed to seize the end of it and pulled himself up along the face of the rock, his feet clinging to the unevenness of the surface, thus facilitating his efforts and those of his companion. As Zouhr climbed up, Aoun gradually straightened himself and backed towards the fissure.

When Zouhr had reached the ledge the Oulhamr conducted him to the cavern and led him down the declivity. The increasing darkness made them go more slowly, an odor of wild beasts made them anxious, and they were thinking of going back when a light broke through.

"There is another way out," murmured Zouhr.

Aoun shook his head deprecatingly, but without stopping. The slope became more gradual, the light, though still faint, grew stronger. It came from a very long zigzag crack,

which was too narrow to admit the passage of the two men...
Bats flew out with shrill cries.

"Aoun and Zouhr are the masters of the cave," murmured the son of Urus.

Zouhr put his head through the crevice; a roar resounded, a giant *beast* rose up from a spacious lair. It was impossible to say whether it most resembled a tiger or a lion. It had a black mane and its chest was as broad as that of a gaur; its body was long and sinuous though thickset; it was of taller stature and its muscles were thicker than those of all the other carnivores. Its immense eyes seemed to shoot out yellow or green fire according to the play of the shadows.

"It is the lion of the rocks!" whispered Zouhr.

The beast, taking its stand against the crevice, lashed its sides with its shaggy tail.

Aoun gazed at it in his turn and said, "It is the tiger from the country of the Kzamms."

He had seized his spear and prepared to fling it through the fissure; he opened his mouth to shout his war-cry. Zouhr stayed his uplifted arm:

"Aoun cannot strike hard enough through the fissure to kill the lion of the rocks, and it would be difficult for him to reach it at all."

He pointed out projections which would turn aside or arrest the course of the weapon. The Oulhamr understood the danger there would be in uselessly irritating the beast. It might leave its lair and seek its aggressors. Besides it was already becoming passive again, and it was unlikely it would hunt the next night, for abundant remains of a wild ass were bleeding on the ground, which was covered with the skeletons of previous kills.

"Perhaps Aoun and Zouhr will be able to make a trap for him," murmured the Wah.

For a moment longer they could hear the hard breathing of the wild beast, then he stretched himself carelessly among the dry bones. He knew no fear, so his fury gradually subsided. No beast was audacious enough to attack him, unless it were the purblind rhinoceros. The elephant did not fear him, but also did not attack him; the leaders of the gayals, the gaurs and the buffaloes, who defend their herds from the tiger and the lion, quailed before him; his strength exceeded that of all other carnivores.

The animals whom he now smelt on the other side of the wall of basalt reminded him of the odor of the gibbons, the rhesus and the entellus monkeys, all weakly creatures that he could crush with a single blow of his claws.

Aoun and Zouhr returned towards the top of the cavern. Here was no immediate danger and they did not look far ahead, but the mere neighborhood of the feline animal was alarming to them. Although its home was on the other side of the rocks, and no doubt it hardly ever hunted in the daytime, some chance might put it on their track. Therefore this refuge, which had seemed so secure, accessible as it was only to men, vampires and birds, was rendered unsafe.

They resolved, however, not to leave it until they should have discovered another.

The son of Urus said, "Aoun and Zouhr will not go out until the Kzamms tiger is asleep in its lair."

"The lion of the rocks is too heavy to climb trees," Zouhr added. "There are branches everywhere in which we can hide ourselves."

They were not afraid of being surprised while they were hunting. Aoun's sense of smell was as keen as that of the jackals, and Zouhr's cunning was ever on the alert.

For several days their life remained tranquil. Zouhr, guided by the instinct of his race, brought in provisions of mushrooms and roots; Aoun provided meat and collected wood for the fire. They lit it on the ledge and in the evening it glowed with a red light, surprising alike the prowlers on the plain and the vampires, owls and eagles of the chain of rocks.

There was abundance of food. The men ate joyfully, safe from the beasts who watched them from below, and not deigning to notice the rapacious birds that hovered over their heads. Zouhr went down several times each day to spy out the den.

The wild beast no longer displayed anger, or even impatience. The smell of the young warrior had become familiar to it and did not even disturb its sleep. If it was not sleeping it would sometimes stand up against the crevice and its fiery eyes would vaguely scan the height and face of the human being.

After some time the son of Earth said to him, "Aoun and Zouhr are not enemies of the rock lion."

The brute, surprised by the sound of an articulate voice growled and tore at the rock with its claws.

"The lion of the rocks is stronger than Zouhr," continued the warrior, "but Zouhr is cunning... If the lion of the rocks, the son of Earth and the son of Urus made an alliance, no prey could escape them."

He spoke in this way without any real hope, and only because of old memories which stirred in him. Often the Men-without-Shoulders had lived side by side with the wild beasts, taking part in their hunting, and Naoh, son of the Leopard, of the Oulhamr tribe, had made an alliance with the mammoths. Descended from a race which had been declining for generations, Zouhr often lost himself in dreams. He had many more recollections than his companions, and these recollections, fired by his youth, took on strange shapes on days when he was safe from peril and want.

It was the first time that he had found himself in the constant vicinity of a dangerous animal. On the steppes and in the forest animals were inaccessible or menacing. Besides, when Zouhr thought of imitating Naoh or any of his ancestors, Aoun and his other companions came and dissipated his dream. Naoh himself had not continued the experiment of living with the mammoths. When he became chief of the horde he forgot his journey with Nam and Gaw, and only thought of leading the Oulhamrs to lands favorable for them. The Horde was too numerous and too keen on the chase to give the animals confidence; they kept their distance and could only be approached by cunning or taken in ambushes.

Here Zouhr could have touched the lion's nose by merely reaching his outstretched arm down the fissure. Although he would perhaps have preferred a less formidable wild beast, his imagination was working slowly. Moreover the habit which links beings together was growing. Everything that repeats itself harmlessly ceases to seem terrible. That large chest, that head like a block of basalt, those fiery eyes, no longer made Zouhr tremble. His subtle, youthful senses became aware that he himself had grown familiar to the carnivore. He was no longer considered as possible prey; he would no doubt cease completely to be regarded as such when his smell became gradually more intermixed with the odors of the den.

Summer was approaching. Scorching heat had settled down upon the earth. It burnt up the waterless steppes, it intensified the terrible energy of vegetation in the forest, jungles and savannahs, and the monstrous green life that enveloped the banks of the river. The teeming animal life became intolerable. Worms, spiders, insects, crustaceans, swarmed on all the folds of the leaves, the stalks and the flowers; the viscous flesh of the worms, reptiles and mollusks, frogs and toads accumulated in the bays; herds of herb-cropping animals came up from the arid plains, and despite the presence of the great feline, the tiger and the lion hunted in proximity to the chain of rocks. Aoun and Zouhr only went out in the early morning, and never dallied till the evening twilight. They knew that a black lion with two lionesses occupied the northern jungle, and from the top of their post of observation they saw that a tiger and tigress had invaded the confluence of the great river and the stream. It would be necessary to walk the third part of a summer's day to reach their lair and rather less to arrive at the jungle. Sometimes, as night fell, the sound of the lion's roars came nearer, or the strident voice of the tiger; the great feline of the cavern would then give vent to his thunderous voice.

At times Aoun and Zouhr thought of leaving their refuge. But when morning dawned they forgot that hungry clamor, prey became ever more and more abundant, rendering their hunting invariably successful; and the nocturnal carnivores slept before the dawn broke, drunk with meat and blood.

171

Zouhr said, "Further on there are more tigers, lions and other tawny beasts. Would Aoun and Zouhr find such a good cave elsewhere?"

The son of Urus did not reply. His soul was more nomadic than Zouhr's: he was curious about new countries. This desire was only occasionally a clearly conscious one, it appeared and disappeared like an appetite. Some mornings he would go alone to the confluence of the river, and observe the rocks where the lions slept. A sudden desire to fight would possess him, or a great longing would fill him to know what savannahs and hunting grounds and animals were hidden from his view in the distance. Sometimes he would follow the upward course of the river, putting 2000 or 3000 ells between him and the lions. Again he would manage to cross the river, partly by swimming and partly by jumping from one erratic block to another. Then his chest would swell with the lust of travel, and he would gaze longingly at the blue depths of a forest barring the horizon. On his return a deep feeling of unrest would make his flesh creep.

During these absences, Zouhr would dry slices of meat in the Sun, or else lay in a fresh store of roots. He was desirous to keep a good reserve of provisions, so that they might be masters of their movements and hours of repose. At intervals he would go down to the fissure, and if he found the feline awake, he accustomed it to the sound of the human voice.

One afternoon, when the shadows of the rocks had passed to the other bank of the river, he was surprised because Aoun did not return; and as he was tired of inaction, he climbed down with the help of leather thongs, which enabled him to reach places otherwise inaccessible to all but birds and vampires.

First he went towards the confluence, but a long string of buffaloes barred his way. Zouhr knew that their tempers were uncertain, and that at the least alarm the males became dangerous. He made a great circuit towards the west, and was about to turn southwards when a rhinoceros appeared among the high grasses. The son of Earth tried to efface himself under the vaults of a banyan-tree: the heavy beast followed him. Then he climbed up a hillock, turned along the edge of a pool, lost his way in the brushwood, and found himself once more in sight of the chain of rocks, but on the side which was inhabited by the giant feline.

The rhinoceros had disappeared. Zouhr studied this place, where neither of the companions had ever ventured before. The chain of rocks was more rugged and had deeper hollows than near the river. Two falcons rose in spirals, with hardly a stroke of their wings, towards a froth-like cloud. Despite the approach of sunset the light beat fiercely down upon the rocky desolation and the luxuriant verdure. Lying flat on his face in the shade, the Wah tried to discover the great beast's lair. He thought it must be down there among the great black hollows, where the shadows were indistinguishable from masses of rock. To the left, the pool was hidden behind a jungle of rushes; to the right there was a series of ravines, with archipelagoes of hillocks, and towards the chain of rocks there were lines of basalt, forming low ridges, ruinous walls and prisms... Doubtless the brute was sleeping until the hour when carnivorous voices were wont to make themselves heard.

Suddenly Zouhr's hair stood on end. A thickset lion had appeared on the top of one of the hillocks below him. It was not a yellow lion like those which had attacked the creeper hut, but it was a huge black lion of a kind that was unknown to him. The grass was short under the tree which gave Zouhr shade; the animal caught sight of the man...

Zouhr remained lying on the ground paralyzed. He did not possess Aoun's strength or impetuosity. He could not drive his lance so deeply into a hard chest, and his club would not break the animal's vertebrae or crush its limbs. He must take to flight; the tree was too low to give him safety. Below him he saw a crenelated wall which led by a sharp turn to the chain of rocks and was inaccessible to the carnivore.

He started off and bounded down the nearest passage, between the lines of basalt, while the lion descended the hillock with a roar. When Zouhr had reached the passage the brute could no longer see him. Without slackening his speed he took note of the crevices and fissures with great care... He had gone more than 1000 ells before he turned around: his trail was deserted; the lion must have hesitated. Perhaps he was nonchalant like all of his kind and had given up the pursuit. Zouhr hoped he had done so, and went on towards the wall. A loud growl made him tremble all over, and with the corner of his eye he recognized the dark form of the brute. It came upon him with leaps and bounds, more fierce and determined than the tawny lions. Zouhr could hear its panting breath... It was too late for him to reach the chain of rocks. A few more bounds and Zouhr would feel his bones being crushed...

At this moment three projections attracted the fugitive's attention. They stood out like broken branches, and would allow him, with the aid of a fourth projection, to reach the top of the passage.

The ascent was only possible for an animal with hands or one of light weight. Zouhr jumped and reached the first projection, pulled himself up to the second and then to the third on his hands and feet, and hauling himself onto the last found himself on the crest of the ridge. The lion followed...it made a tremendous leap, and fell back; the rock, which was almost vertical, offered no hold which could support its massive build. Three times it tried the escalade, then with a furious roar gave up the attempt. Its huge face was turned towards Zouhr, the yellow and the brown eyes stared fixedly at one another, full of fury and terror.

The son of Earth asked himself whether he should remain on the crest or descend the other side of the ridge.

There were two ways, one nearer the plain, the other close to the rocky chain, by which the lion could reach the man... So long as the lion remained motionless Zouhr hesitated. The moment he saw it begin to prowl, he decided upon flight, and descending the slope, he started in a northerly direction. He did not run at random, but examined the chain of rocks with the hope of discovering a refuge. His head was giddy and he seemed to see the cavern and the outline of the giant feline.

The lion had again disappeared; perhaps, with the patience of the carnivore, it was lying in wait; perhaps it did not notice the way in... Zouhr scarcely asked himself the question, the urgent need for a shelter absorbed all his sensations; he unconsciously drew nearer to the rocks...

He was 50 steps from his goal, when he realized that the pursuit had begun again. The black lion, retracing its steps, had caught sight of the man once more; its bounds made depressions in the long grasses; the rocks revealed no means of escape, and Zouhr now only followed the instinct of flight... At last the basalt wall was close to him; again a panting sound arose among the rustling of the disturbed vegetable life. Zouhr stopped. His heart was bounding in his breast even as the lion bounded on the plain. The world was swimming before his dilated eyes. Life, which his young body loved, and which up to a moment ago seemed imperishable, was there; death was there also, made suddenly present by the approach of the wild beast... The son of Earth felt as feeble as the ibis in the clutches of the eagle... He no longer had any weapons even; he had only limbs without claws; the cruel fangs would dissect him like a fruit.

That one moment seemed as long as a whole twilight. Zouhr had his choice. On one side was the black lion and on the other the lair occupied by the giant feline. There was no longer time to hesitate. The devourer was six bounds distant from him. Then, in a second, with a giddy suddenness Zouhr resumed his flight; to die—but in the cavern—close to his refuge.

He was engulfed in the jaws of basalt rock, like a sparrow in the mouth of a cobra.

Two roars challenged each other. The massive black form of the lion stood out against the red light, and a creature of enormous stature stretched itself at the back of the lair. Then two bounds, the clashing of claws, the crashing of jaws and the giant feline had conquered. The black lion stumbled, rolled over, and conscious that it had met an unconquerable antagonist, groveled and fled, its lifeblood flowing from a gaping wound.

The other stood motionless, with its rock-like head held high; it watched the invader's flight, and sent forth a thunderous roar towards the west.

Zouhr had hardly seen the battle. He only knew that the conqueror was the one in whose den he had taken refuge. Lying prone, with his hands on the ground, he waited silent and immovable. He had so completely abandoned the contest that even his fear was numbed; the giant feline destroyed both hope and despair; Zouhr resigned himself to what would follow, as he had resigned himself to pain when the saber-tooth ripped his chest.

The colossus growled for another moment, then with heavy steps and licking a gash which had been made by the enemy's claws, it went back into its cave. It sniffed at the body of the man lying prostrate at its feet, and put a foot down on him, heavy as that of a gaur. It might tear that quivering flesh without the man making any movement. But the brute did not attempt to rend him, its breath came quite gently; Zouhr guessed that it recognized the smell which had penetrated each day through the fissure in the basalt. Then hope revived, a revolution took place in his young flesh which brought back the thought of life and never ceasing desires... He looked up at the monstrous muzzle and remembering that the brute was accustomed to listening to the human voice, he murmured, "Zouhr is like an antelope under the paw of the lion of the rocks!"

The animal breathed harder, and gently removed its paw. The habit which had grown up between them when they were separated by the rock took on a new form. The Wah divined that every interval of peace increased his chances. All that continues is continued by repetition. As the carnivore had not already devoured the man no doubt it would now never devour him. Zouhr would now never be its prey; there would be an alliance between him and the animal...

Time passed. The crimson fire of the Sun was about to disappear behind the hills. The giant feline had not struck. It listened intermittently to that changing voice which spoke to it. Crouched down before the son of Earth, it sometimes smelt him in order that it might know him better, sometimes it touched him with a velvet paw, as gently as it used to play with those who were born on the same day with it in the maternal lair. Fear coursed like lightning flashes through Zouhr's body, but each time with less violence...

Darkness was slowly creeping over the eastern clouds, and the entrance to the cave was filled with a violet hue; two stars twinkled and the night breeze blew against the chain of rocks.

Then the giant feline rose up. The ardor of the chase flamed in its eyes, the night air with its smell of prey filled its nostrils. Zouhr knew that once more the moment of life or death was upon him. If the brute confused him with the trembling herb-croppers hidden in the jungle, the son of Earth would never see Aoun again. Several times the great form came back towards the man. The fiery green eyes, that the darkness surrounded as with a halo, fixed themselves on the frail human being... With a final snarl the carnivore left the cavern and gradually diminishing, disappeared into the night.

The warrior said to himself, "The lion of the rocks has made an alliance with Zouhr."

He went towards the fissure and shouted with a loud voice, "Aoun!"

A short time afterwards he heard the step of his companion; the light of a torch shone red about him, the son of Urus saw Zouhr at the entrance to the cave and gave a cry of terror, "The tiger of the Man-Devourers' country will tear Zouhr in pieces!"

"No," replied the Wah.

He told the tale of how the lion had pursued him and how he had come to the cave. Aoun listened with stupefaction to the story, first so wild, then so gentle, more wonderful than that of Naoh and the mammoths. The nomad soul, always

177

ready for adventure and eager about unknown things, opened out.

He said with pride, "Aoun and Zouhr are now equal to the chief of the Oulhamrs!"

Then anxiety seized hold of him. He announced, "Zouhr cannot remain in the cavern any longer. I will go around and meet him."

The two men met again to the south of the chain of rocks; then, having lit a fire on the ledge, they tasted the joy of a complete sense of security; while all around them in the brushwood and the jungle, ambushes were being laid from which the plaintive herb-croppers fled in the darkness, hiding themselves amongst the vegetation or dying under the claws of the carnivore.

VII. The Tiger and the Flame

Aoun and Zouhr often went down to the fissure. When the giant feline was awake, they let it look at their faces and bodies, and spoke to it each in their turn. Aoun's presence at first aroused its impatience, a deeper breath would expand its heavy chest, sometimes a snarl would mark its distrust and anger. At last the brute got accustomed to mingling the two odors, and when it approached the fissure it did so from a certain confused sense of sympathy, because even wild creatures feel the dullness of solitude.

One evening Aoun said, "It is time to renew the alliance; Aoun and Zouhr will go into the cave on a day when the tiger of the Kzamms has had a successful hunt."

Zouhr did not refuse, although he was less prompt than his companion in risking his life. The alliance was his work; he often thought of it with satisfaction, and he told himself that there would no longer be any danger for them if they were certain never to be menaced by the lion of the rocks...

One morning they saw the body of a large antelope in the cave. One of its legs had been sufficient to appease the carnivore's hunger; it was sleeping heavily, tired with hunting and gorged with meat.

"We will go and see him when he wakes up," said Aoun, "he will not require any prey for two nights."

They thought of it as they wandered near the river, or rested in the shade of the rocks. The fierce sunlight burnt up the dry ground and gave endless life to the damp places. Hardly a sign of animal life was to be seen on the plain; eagles and falcons hid themselves, cranes and herons remained invisible; only from the distance came the snorting of a hippopotamus as it plunged back into the water, or the form of an alligator could be seen lying on the water in torpid repose.

Towards midday Aoun and Zouhr became drowsy. Then they fell into vague reveries, sitting on the ledge. The rock, which at first had been broiling, grew cool as the shadows lengthened, and a gentle breeze sprang up and played about the men's chests. They were conscious of many things within themselves which they were unable to express. It was the voluptuous feeling of youth and abundance, the sudden melancholy moods called forth by the thought of their faraway Horde, by the remembrance of hunting scenes, of the departure of the Oulhamrs towards the southeast, of mountains and the subterranean river, and the wonderful pictures which their imaginations drew of the unknown land.

When Aoun half shut his eyes, he could see again the Dholes, hyenas and wolves before their fire screen, the sabertooth killing the rhinoceros, and himself killing the sabertooth. His heart began to beat again; victory flowed before his eyes like a river, and the desire to continue his conquests tightened all the Oulhamr's muscles. He thought of the lions as they prowled around the creeper hut, of the elephants stamping down the soil, the python devouring the antelope. Zouhr's imagination was haunted by similar pictures, but they took on other forms and details; he preferred to think of the giant feline. Aoun thought of it also and was impatient for the hour of dusk.

When the Sun began to grow red, they went down to the depths of the cave. The beast no longer slept, it had caught hold of the antelope again and was gnawing its shoulder.

"Let us go towards it," said Aoun.

The son of Earth yielded to the desire of the Oulhamr. His courage was of slower growth, but when a project had once taken root in his mind he was as ready to risk his life as Aoun.

They re-ascended the ledge, then descended to the foot of the chain of rocks. The herds had drunk their fill and were looking for a place in which to spend the night; parakeets made the dusk hideous with their strident shrieks; a gibbon crouched on the ground, then bounded back among the palm-trees. In the sunset light, Aoun and Zouhr walked around the rocks and came close to the cave.

Then Aoun said, "I will go first."

That was always his way; he went in front of Zouhr and exposed himself first to any danger. This time Zouhr resisted, saying, "The lion of the rocks knows me best. It is better that I should be between him and Aoun."

There was no pride between the two men. Each one valued the resources that lay within the other and reaped security from them. Aoun considered that Zouhr was right.

"Go," he said.

He held his club in his left hand and his strongest spear in his right. At that moment he had a better idea of the danger than the son of Earth. They looked at each other; an eagle gave its war-cry on a summit of basalt; six enormous gaurs fled in the glen. Zouhr walked quietly and his form stood out before the shadowy hole. He disappeared. Again he was face to face with the sovereign beast. It stopped tearing the antelope's flesh; the green fire of its eyes seemed to envelope the form of the Man-without-Shoulders. He said in a low voice, "The men have come to renew the alliance... The time of the rains is approaching, when prey will be hard to find and difficult to take. Then the lion of the rocks will have the cunning of Aoun and Zouhr on his side!"

The giant feline half shut and reopened his eyes, then it rose in its nonchalant strength and came towards the man. Its head brushed against Zouhr's shoulder, and he passed his hand along the stiff mane. When they are touched, the most savage animals feel confidence. There was no longer any fear in the breast of the son of Earth. Several times he repeated the movement and even slowly rubbed the animal's spine. The wild beast remained motionless breathing quietly...

Zouhr still hesitated to call his companion when a shadow appeared before the cave. Aoun was there, still holding his club and spear. The giant feline ceased to purr, its thickset muzzle with its shining fangs opened. The skin on its head made great pleats, its muscles contracted and the green fire of its eyes shone phosphorescent.

"Aoun is also the ally of the lion of the rocks," murmured the Man-without-Shoulders. "Aoun and Zouhr live together in the cave above..."

The monster gave a bound; the Oulhamr grasped his club; but Zouhr placed himself in front of his companion, and the immense chest ceased to heave; the alliance was complete.

They came back on the following days; the giant feline became accustomed to seeing them and desired their presence. The immense solitude of the world was distasteful to him; he was young, and from his birth until the previous autumn he had lived with others of his kind. Down the course of the stream he had had a den on the border of a lake, with his mate. His little ones had already begun to hunt. One night the lake rose tumultuously, the waters overflowed the brushwood, a cyclone carried away the palm-trees, a torrent engulfed the mother with her young, and the male lion, carried down with the big trees, was washed up in the open country...

The old den remained under water for a whole season... The desolate male, had searched for it at first with vehement and dogged anxiety; his roars had summoned his race in the autumn rains; vivid memories had shot through his dull brain... Days went by; the giant feline discovered the chain of rocks and took refuge there from the cataracts of the clouds. An obscure sadness made his sides grow lean; when he woke in the morning he smelt all around the cavern, and when he brought back his prey, he looked all about him as if he expected to find those who used to share it with him. In the end these recollections became dim and finally disappeared. He grew accustomed to smelling no other creature at his side, but his body could not resign itself to the dullness of being alone...

One evening Aoun and Zouhr accompanied him in the chase. They all three passed into the jungle, where the light of the half moon made patterns on the earth. Alarmed by the smell of the carnivore, the herb-cropping animals awoke in their lairs. They all retreated to the innermost recesses, or climbed into the branches of trees. Those of them who lived in herds warned each other mysteriously of the danger. In the midst of these innumerable lives, he remained as if in a desert. The power of immense bulk was always defeated by the keen senses, the ruses, the agility and the subtleness of the feeble ones. With one movement he could kill the wild ass, the antelope, the wild board or the nilgai; with one bound he could overthrow a horse or even a gaur; but they knew how to hide in impenetrable places, or to vanish into the distance. It was only their numbers that favored the sovereign beast, for it caused them to swarm in every part of the plains, the woods and the jungle.

In spite of all his advantages, when day dawned it often found the great feline, tired with his efforts and out of patience, returning famished to the chain of rocks. On this particular night he was unable for a long time to capture an axis or an antelope. His strong pungent odor, to which was added the more delicate scent of the men, enlarged the limits of the area into which the fugitives took care not to intrude.

At last he lay in ambush on the confines of a jungle and a marsh. Strongly scented flowers spread their smell around, the earth was redolent of musk and rottenness. The men had separated themselves from him and had also hidden, one among the rushes and the other in a clump of bamboos. All the animals had fled. Enormous batrachians roared like gayals; in the distance there was the sound of a galloping herd; an owl flew by on downy wings; then a wild boar passed, tearing up the soil with its tusks...

It was a heavily-built animal, with thick neck and shoulders and slender legs, and it came on in a surly manner puffing and grunting. It knew its own strength, and a slow heavy kind of courage animated its gray, bristle-covered body. It had put the leopards to flight, it disdained the hyenas, routed the Dholes and the wolves; it would stand up to a lion if flight were impossible or a wound had infuriated it. The consciousness of having defeated all who had attacked it, made it less vigilant.

The wild boar reached the rushes where Zouhr was standing and, suddenly smelling his presence, stopped. The scent reminded it of the gibbon or the rhesus monkey, from whom it knew that it had nothing to fear. It merely grunted and passed on towards the bamboos. Then, in order to turn it towards the giant feline, Aoun shouted his war-cry, which was at once repeated by the son of Earth. The wild boar retreated, not because it was afraid, but from motives of prudence. A trap lurked always in the unknown! Neither the rhesus nor the gibbon had that singular voice. At the second cry it flung itself in the direction where the giant feline lay in ambush. A colossal form rose up; the wild boar thrust furiously with its tusks, but the beast which was upon it had almost the weight of a buffalo. It stumbled, its sides were torn open, and a pair of granite-like jaws were sunk in its throat... The red flow of life gushed out, and the wild boar sank on the grass in the throes of death.

When the prey was safely in the cave, Aoun wished to test whether the alliance was complete. He took his axe and cut off a leg of the wild boar; the giant feline did not interfere.

The men knew then that their strength had become as great as that of a horde.

They hunted many times with the great feline. Often they went long distances from the den, or their prey kept ever-further away from the domicile of the terrible inhabitant of the rocks. Aoun's heart beat high. He aspired to yet more distant expeditions; impatient curiosity urged him on. One morning he said to Zouhr, "It is good that we should know the hunting grounds... Perhaps many beasts will go further off in the autumn. Will Zouhr accompany me beyond the haunts of the tigers?"

Zouhr had never refused to accompany his companion. Although his curiosity was less vagabond, it still was great, and intensified by youth.

"We will go and see the lands where the river goes," he said.

They sharpened their weapons, dried and smoked some meat, roasted some roots, and set off just as the Sun, in all its grandeur, was rising above the further bank, deeper in color than the reddest of minium. Zouhr did not leave the cave without some regrets. He had lived in security and abundance there, and he had concluded an alliance with the great feline. But the soul of Aoun urged on his steps towards unexplored regions.

They advanced without difficulty until the middle of the day, and even after the noonday sleep, which the beat of the Sun made obligatory. Aoun's sharp eyes and his Dhole-like sense of smell discovered the reptiles on their path; the carnivores slept, and only insects troubled them. Red-headed flies buzzed unbearably, and followed the odor of meat in myriads; stinging gnats flitted in the shade, and the wanderers had to guard against the great hornets, six or seven of which could kill a man. When they halted, the neighborhood of the white ants had to be avoided.

It was late when they reached the confluence. Aoun knew the river, having crossed it many times. He guided Zouhr over the line of erratic blocks, and brought him to the tigers' hunting grounds. Then everything became terrible. During the day the lion is in his lair. Like man he prefers a fixed abode, to which he always returns. But the tiger prowls everywhere, and makes his resting place wherever the fortunes of the chase or the chance of his wanderings may lead him; he is content with places which would repel other wild animals... Therefore man cannot foresee his movements and cannot tell which way to take to avoid him...

The Oulhamr and the son of Earth walked at a little distance from each other, so as to increase the area of their observation. At first the presence of the herb-cropping animals assisted them: antelopes, saigas, gaurs and panolia[2] deer would not have had their feeding grounds in the neighborhood of the tigers. When the land became empty around them, the nomads suffered tortures of anxiety. The country was varied; in some parts the jungle opened out into clear spaces, savannahs and marshes, in others the bamboos and palm-trees grew close together. Aoun thought it better to return towards the river, because the many islands in it promised safety. The solitude of the land became ever more profound, while the water was teeming with life. The wake of long alligators could be seen among the islands; hordes of webfooted creatures and waders dabbled in the coves, and sleeping pythons displayed their clammy coils.

"We have come near to the tigers," said Zouhr in a low voice.

Aoun, listening intently, advanced at a slow pace. The jungle, which at first had lain far from the bank, was now close to it, a tangled mass of prickly growth covered with creepers.

The son of Earth stopped and said, "It is here that the tigers come down to the river to drink."

He pointed out an opening in the brushwood. Other signs revealed themselves and Zouhr bent down to examine them more closely. They still exhaled an acrid odor. He whispered, "They have passed this way." Zouhr was trembling with excitement. Aoun anxiously made ready his spear. It seemed as

---

[2] *Cervus eldii* or Eld's Deer.

if something of the wild beasts themselves had remained there with their emanations... A crackling sound was heard in the thicket. The two men became as motionless as trees. Flight was useless. If the wild beasts were near, there was nothing left but to fight... But nothing appeared. Aoun sniffed the gentle breeze wafted from the jungle and said, "The tigers are still far away."

They resumed their journey, making haste to pass the danger zone. Soon the jungle joined the actual river bank and as it became still more impenetrable at the edge, the men were obliged to change their direction and plunge inland among the bamboos.

Finally they reached a place where some herbivores were feeding. As twilight was coming on they tried to find a suitable place for a camp. There was no sign of a rock as far as the eye could reach, and it was no longer possible to reach an island. The country was enveloped in jungle; evening would be upon them before they could reach the water.

Zouhr discovered a group of seven bamboos, which, as they grew close together, formed a kind of enclosure. Three of the interstices were so narrow that a man could not pass between them; Aoun and Zouhr could just squeeze in sideways through two of the others, but it would be impossible for a lion or a tiger to make its way through them. The two last were more than an ell wide at the base, but grew narrower towards the top, so that it would be necessary to close them with branches or creepers up to twice Aoun's height from the ground.

They quickly tore up some creepers and young bamboos which would make a solid barrier. The son of Urus prepared them, while Zouhr, who was more clever at constructing things, tied and interlaced them according to the custom of his ancestors.

Twilight had come when their work was finished, and no suspicious form had appeared about them. They then made a fire and roasted dried meat and roots. It was a pleasant repast, for effort had augmented their hunger, and they tasted the joy and pride of their manhood. No animal, not even among those that knew most about construction, would have been able to protect itself from the carnivores so quickly and so securely. When they had eaten, they remained for some time at the entrance of their refuge.

The Moon, which had completed nearly half its course, was moving westward. A few stars shone in the sky, and Zouhr asked himself what sort of men lit them every evening. Their minuteness was surprising. They seemed like the points of feeble torches, while the Sun and Moon resembled fires lit with branches. But as they burnt for so long, it must be that their flames were continually fed: Zouhr tried to make out the forms of those who piled wood on them, and could not understand why they remained invisible… Sometimes he wondered about the immense beat of the Sun, which was stronger when it shone high in the sky than when towards evening it grew much larger. These dreams soon mystified and wearied Zouhr. He abandoned them, and even completely forgot them. This evening he remembered the clouds which had become filled with flames after the Sun's departure. There were more fires in the west than if all the fires lit by the Oulhamrs during a whole winter had been united in one evening… And all those fires produced less light and heat than the Sun. Zouhr thought about it for a moment, then his reflections almost frightened him. None of the Men-without-Shoulders or the Oulhamrs had ever seemed to be moved by this thought.

He said mechanically, "What men light the sky when the Sun is gone?"

Aoun, after dreaming of tigers, had fallen into that sort of torpor which did not prevent his senses taking note of all the perils of the night. Zouhr's question awoke him.

He did not quite understand it at first, and he was not surprised, for Zouhr had ideas which were strange to other men.

Lifting his head towards the zenith, he considered the stars.

"Is Zouhr speaking of the little fires in the sky?"

"No, Zouhr is speaking of the big red and yellow fires which have just gone out. Are they lit by hordes?... If so they must be more numerous than the Oulhamrs, the Kzamms and the Red Dwarfs."

Aoun's brow contracted. He vaguely imagined beings hidden above him, and the idea was a disagreeable one.

"Night puts out the fires," he replied with hesitation... "Night makes our fire shine more brightly!"

This reply disconcerted the son of Earth, and he continued to think of it long after Aoun had forgotten the question which did not interest him.

Meanwhile the breeze freshened and brought sounds from far off. Furtive animals moved over the moor and disappeared. Some of them stopped to look at the fire, the light of which shone ever more brightly. Five or six Dholes prowled around stealthily, smelling the odor of roast meat, but they soon disappeared. Suddenly some panolia deer came out of the jungle and ran wildly away.

Aoun sat up. He sniffed, listened and whispered, "It is time to go into the refuge."

Then he added, "The tiger is near!"

They slipped between the interstices of the bamboos.

The brushwood had been pushed aside at a little distance from them. A striped animal appeared in the silver and ash-gray colored light. It was as large as a lion in bulk, but it was not so high, and its body was longer and more supple. The Oulhamrs and the Men-without-Shoulders dreaded it more than any other living creature, for the lion had less cunning, fury and swiftness, the saber-tooth was unknown on the other side of the mountains, and among the Oulhamrs two old warriors, Naoh and Goun of the Dry Bones, were the only men who had met the giant feline.

The tiger moved without haste, with sinuous undulations that had a terrifying effect. It halted at the sight of the flames, lifting its thickset head and displaying a pale chest, while its eyes shone like glow-worms. It was the largest tiger that Aoun and Zouhr had ever seen. Despite the anxiety which made the blood course faster through his veins, the son of Urus admired it, for he had a predilection for powerful animals, even when they were his enemies.

He said however, "The tiger of the Men-Devourers is stronger than this one."

Zouhr added, "He is as a leopard in comparison with the lion of the rocks."

Notwithstanding this they felt that, for a man, the tiger was as much to be feared as their brute companion of the cave.

The tiger halted a moment and then approached obliquely in a diffident manner. It feared the fire; it had fled before it when the prairie was struck by lightning, but this glow more resembled the light which appears at the end of night. It came so close that it began to feel the heat, and at the same time it saw the dancing flames and heard their roaring and crackling. Its mistrust grew; it walked around the fire at a safe distance and this movement brought it near the bamboos. It caught sight of the men at the same moment that their smell made it aware of their presence.

It snarled, and gave two hunting cries like those of the Dholes.

Without thinking, Aoun replied by shouting his war-cry. The tiger gave a start of surprise and looked sharply at its adversaries. Their odor resembled that of its most timid victims, their size seemed hardly greater than that of wolves.

Now all those that could stand against it were of immense stature. These, however, were unknown to the tiger, and age having endowed it with experience of surprises, it practiced prudence. The proximity of the fire added mystery to the strangeness of the men. The tiger approached the bamboos slowly, then it walked around them. Its long life in the jungle had perfected its instinct for judging distances, that instinct which invariably enabled it to make sure of its prey when it could be attained at one bound. It knew also the strength of the bamboos. It did not attempt to force the narrow interstices; it stopped in front of the interlaced branches and creepers. It tried them with its claws and attempted to tear out the thinnest ones, when Aoun's spear all but came in contact with its no-strils. It drew back growling and stood undecided. This attack made the unknown creature more strange to it. Its anger rose, a furious growl rattled in its throat, and gathering itself up for a spring, it attempted an overwhelming attack. This time the spear caught an angle of its jaw, for the oscillation of the branches and the carnivore's movement had not permitted Aoun to take good aim. The assailant realized the resistance offered by the obstacle and the man's courage; it drew back again, crouched on the ground and waited.

It was not the hour for hunting. The tiger was thirsty. Had it not seen the fire it would have gone first to the river. After a time its anger cooled; it felt again that dryness of the glands which only fresh water could appease...

Then with a long snarl, it got up, walked twice around the refuge and went away. There was a gap in the jungle which led to the river bank. Aoun and Zouhr saw it disappear.

"It will come back," said Zouhr, "perhaps with its mate."

"Not a single creeper has been torn away," replied the son of Urus.

They thought of their late peril for some time, but they felt no anxiety about the future. The refuge had protected them and would protect them again. It was unnecessary even to watch, and as soon as they lay down they were lost in slumber.

VIII. The Attack of the Tiger

Aoun woke when a third of the night had passed. The Moon had gone down behind the western jungle, and its light reddened the vapors which were condensing on the branches. The moor was covered with pale gray shadows; the fire shed only a faint light near the seven bamboos.

At first the warrior only saw the motionless vegetation, but his sense of smell warned him of a living presence. Then a shadow emerged, became detached from a clump of palm-

190

trees and approached cautiously towards him. Aoun knew it was the tiger from the moment he opened his eyes, and he watched it come with anxiety and anger. The daring spirit which worked in him like a storm on the waters dilated his chest. Although he knew the tiger's superiority over man, and despite the secret horror which possessed him, he desired to fight. Had not Naoh conquered the gray wolf and the tigress, had he not himself overcome the saber-tooth, the victor of the rhinoceros? For a moment he felt giddy, but this soon passed, the prudence of his ancestors calmed his blood; he knew that neither Naoh nor Faouhm nor the Hairy Men would have attacked the tiger unless their own lives had been in danger...

Besides, one had awoken who would restrain him. The son of Earth became aware in his turn of the terrible presence. He looked at his companion, who had raised his club, and said, "The tiger has not found any prey."

"If he comes near us," said the other in a quivering voice, "Aoun will fling his spear and harpoon."

"It is dangerous to wound the tiger. Its fury is greater than that of the lion," was the reply.

"And if it will not go away from our refuge?"

"Aoun and Zouhr have provisions for two days."

"We have no water and the tigress may join him."

Zouhr did not reply. He had already thought of that. He knew that the wild beasts would sometimes take turns in watching a difficult prey. After hesitating a moment he replied, "The tiger has been alone since last night. Perhaps the tigress is far from here."

Aoun could not see sufficiently clearly into the future to insist; his attention was concentrated on the tiger, which had come within five ells of the bamboos.

They could distinctly see the thickset muzzle, fringed at the back with stiff hairs, the eyes shining more brightly than before. Aoun had a strange horror of their green light, and they made Zouhr tremble. At intervals growls could be heard on the moor. The tiger came closer; then it began to prowl up and down and around the shelter, with an awful and exasperating

191

patience. It seemed as if it expected that the interstices would grow bigger or the interlaced creepers and bamboos become relaxed. Each time it came close to them the two men trembled as if the wild beast's hope was about to be realized.

Finally it crouched in the dry grass. From there it observed them patiently, and from time to time opened its great jaws, so that the dying light of the fire shone upon its fangs.

"It will still be there in the morning," said Aoun.

Zouhr did not reply. He was looking at two little branches of the turpentine-tree which he had exposed to the fire, for he always liked to have some dry wood ready. He split the thinnest one down its whole length and gathered together some twigs.

"Zouhr is not going to make a fire!" exclaimed the son of Urus reprovingly.

"There is no wind; the ground of our refuge is bare; the bamboos are young," said Zouhr striking the stone flint against the marcasite… "Zouhr has only need of a little fire!"

Aoun did not insist. He watched the sparks rise from the twigs, while his companion lit the end of a turpentine stick. It soon threw out a bright light. Then, leaning towards one of the openings, the son of Earth flung the burning brand towards the tiger…

The flame described a parabola and fell among the dry grass. It was the most arid part of the moor, where the nocturnal vapors had not yet formed…

The tiger started as he caught sight of the glittering projectile, which disappeared among the tall grass stalks. Aoun laughed silently. Zouhr was carefully considering whether he should light another torch.

Only a twinkling red glow remained among the vegetation. The tiger lay down again.

After a moment's hesitation Zouhr lit the second turpentine stick. The fire had just caught the point of it, when a livid jet appeared where the first had fallen, ran up the grass stalks, and made a line of light. The wild beast rose up with a roar, and was about to spring when Zouhr flung the second burning brand.

It struck the brute on the chest. Maddened, it turned around and around and bounded from side to side in zigzags. The fire, with a dry crackling sound, seemed to gallop its way through the tall grass; then it disseminated itself in sheafs and enveloped the wild beast... The carnivore gave a cry of fury, plunged through the flames and fled.

"It will not come back," Zouhr asserted. "No beast returns to the place where it has been burnt."

His companion's cunning delighted Aoun. His laugh was no longer silent but rang out over the moor, like a joyous war-cry.

"Zouhr is more cunning than Goun of the Dry Bones," he said enthusiastically.

He laid his muscular hand on the shoulder of the son of Earth.

The tiger did not return. Aoun and Zouhr slept till daybreak. A mist covered the moor and the jungle; silence and stillness lasted till the full dawn. Then the day animals began to stir. A loud clamor rose from the river and the trees of the forest. The son of Urus came out of the refuge and studied the landscape. No suspicious odor alarmed his nostrils and some axis passed by, which reassured him still more.

He went back to Zouhr and said, "We will continue our journey; but we will first go in a westerly direction so as not to meet the tiger."

They started before day had fully dawned. The mist slowly rolled away and was lost in the pale sky, which rapidly turned blue. At first there were few animals to be seen; then their numbers increased and the warriors conjectured that they had left the domain of the tiger behind them. Aoun however sniffed the air anxiously. Feverish heat hung over the foliage; red-headed flies tormented the two men; the Sun's rays shot through the branches and seemed to bite into their flesh like white ants; monkeys made faces at them, and parrots shrieked in strident and furious tones.

"There will be thunder in the forest!" said the son of Earth.

Aoun stopped to consider the western sky. They were at the entrance of a clearing and could see a long stretch of firmament, of the color of lapis lazuli, without a single cloud. Notwithstanding this the two men felt a vague uneasiness, which seemed to pervade the air like an unseen terror.

It lasted for a long time. Aoun and Zouhr turned aside towards the river, following the lines indicated by the various kinds of undergrowth. At midday the storm was still far off. They made no fire, but ate, without enjoyment, a slice of meat they had cooked on the previous day. Their rest was disturbed by the attacks of insects.

When they resumed their journey, the first mists were appearing in the west. A milky color spread itself among the blue; the uneasy belling of the swamp deer was heard, and the lowing of buffaloes; cobras slipped by among the grasses. For a moment the warriors hesitated to start, but their halting place was not a favorable one: immense old trees lifted crests that were dangerously high; the ground was spongy at their feet; they could see no shelter against the thunderbolts that would ravage the forest. At intervals gusts of air passed over the crests of the trees with a sound like that of a river, or rose up in spirals, brushing aside the foliage. This was followed by deep, heavy silence. A wall of vapor rose towards the zenith, black smoke that became phosphorescent towards the edge. Then furious livid gleams of light shot through the world of trees. They had their origin very far from where Zouhr and Aoun stood, so they did not add their clamor to the tumult of the storm. When the wall shrouded the middle of the firmament and began to descend towards the east, a growing terror took possession of all living things; here and there only a fugitive animal could be seen seeking its lair, or a frightened insect trying to reach some crack in the bark of a tree. The life of the creatures was enveloped by another life, that life which, subtly diffused, creates and nourishes the forest life, but which if it is unchained destroys alike trees, grass and animals.

The wanderers had experienced these convulsions of nature. Aoun only thought of a refuge; Zouhr lifted his head from time to time possessed by the idea that monstrous wild beasts were raging in the clouds. Already their roars could be heard. Distance made them solemn, like the Sound of lions' voices lost among the hills. Then the thunder broke and the glare of the lightning became intolerable. A sound of running water was heard, which soon grew to the roar of rapids and of torrents. The jungle opened upon a lake which was preceded by marshes; no shelter was visible in the reeking ground, and the thunder rolled on at intervals. Under the arcades of a banyan-tree where the two men stopped, a leopard crouched; sharp cries were heard from the monkeys in the branches above. Water flowed as if an ocean had broken through dykes in the sky; the smell of thunder and the scent of plants was borne on the squalls of wind... In an hour the lake had risen; the marshy pools were full; one of them overflowed and began to invade the forest.

The wanderers were forced to retreat; but other waters came on with a roar which added to the noise of the storm. They were forced to flee as best they could towards the east. The raging waters harassed them. They had barely escaped from the floor on one side when it appeared unexpectedly on the other. Aoun galloped like a stallion, and Zouhr followed him, bent down and hardly lifting his feet, as was the custom of the Men-without-Shoulders. When they had put a space between themselves and the inundation they continued their way towards the east, in the hope of reaching the river.

They traversed moors, and threaded their way through bamboos, palms and creepers. A marsh which had overflowed obliged them to turn towards the north. The storm was abating, the gusts of wind howled less loudly, and they finally reached a clearing where a torrent formed by the rain was racing along...

There they stopped, trying to estimate the depth of the water.

The lightning struck a group of ebony-trees; on the other bank the long body of a terrified animal rose in great bounds; Aoun and Zouhr recognized the tiger. It turned around and around for a time in terror, then it stopped and perceived the human beings...

Aoun's instinct told him that it was the one which had prowled around the refuge. Zouhr was certain of it when he saw that its chest was singed, and knew it must have been done by the burning grass... More vaguely the tiger recognized the prey that had escaped him, made memorable by the fire, the barricade of creepers and the burning grass. He found them again at the moment when another fire struck the ebony-trees. Their forms thus associated in its mind with terrible things, made the wild beast hesitate.

All three remained immovable for a time. There was too small a space between the men and the beast to make flight possible.

Aoun had already got ready his spear, and Zouhr, fearing that flight might be followed by pursuit, also prepared himself to fight.

It was he who first hurled his weapon. It whistled above the waters and hit the brute close to its right eye. With a terrible roar it made its spring, but blood impeded its sight: its bound had not that awful precision which condemned to death all within its reach. The long body fell into the torrent, turned around and around, and clung to the bank by its front paws. Aoun threw himself upon it, his spear struck its breast, missing the shoulder... Maddened with rage the brute hoisted itself onto the bank and charged the men. It was lame, and it moved slowly; Zouhr pierced its side with a second spear, while the son of Urus wounded it on the neck...

Then, holding their clubs in readiness, they waited. Aoun faced the attack and brought down his weapon on the tiger's head, while the Wah attacked it from behind and aimed at the vertebrae... One of its claws tore the Oulhamr's body, but by stepping aside he made it slip, and the club, crashing down on the tiger's nostrils momentarily arrested its course... Before it could spring again, Aoun's club came down for the third time with such force that the tiger remained motionless, as if it slept. Then, without pausing for a moment, the two companions belabored its vertebrae and legs with blows. The enormous body sank down, with terrible convulsions, and the son of Urus having put out its left eye, the wild beast was at the men's mercy.

A spear thrust let out its heart's blood.

IX. The Forest of the Lemurian Men

The weather was mild on the following days. The warriors advanced confidently through lands where the river was as broad as a lake. The joy of the conqueror was upon them, which made the recollection of past perils almost agreeable to them, without diminishing their prudence. They found temporary homes in the jungle, on the river bank, among the rocks, in the hollows of trees thousands of years old, in thickets where the thorns were so strong that after having cut a passage for themselves with their axes, and stopped up the entrance, they could defy the carnivores.

Their way was barred by a lake, which made them turn aside from the river, and they found themselves at the foot of a mountain. It was not a high one. After walking for a quarter of a day, they reached a plateau, which began with a savannah, and became a forest; it stretched from northeast to southwest, and was dominated on the northeast by another chain of mountains where two rivers, which fed another lake, took their rise.

Aoun and Zouhr did not get close to the forest till near sunset. A crevice in a porphyry rock gave them shelter and they barricaded the opening with branches. Then they lit a great fire on the savannah and roasted an iguanoid. The heat was not so great as on the plains, and a breeze which blew from the neighboring mountains refreshed the air of the plateau. The two men enjoyed the coolness after so many torrid nights; it reminded them of their nightwatches with the Oul-hamrs. They took almost as much pleasure in breathing it in as they did in eating. The rustling of the forest was like the sound of running water in the distance. At times they heard the roar of a wild best, the hyenas' sinister laugh, or the howling of a pack of Dholes.

A sudden clamor arose, then strange forms appeared in the trees. They resembled dogs and at the same time Red Dwarfs. Their over-mobile faces were lit up by round eyes placed too close together. Their four legs ended in hands.

Aoun and Zouhr recognized them. They were the rhesus monkeys, who have green hair on their backs, and yellow on their chests, and whose faces are as red as the setting Sun. They looked at the fire. The son of Earth did not dislike them. In one sense he considered them like himself, as he did the Men-Devourers. Aoun shared this belief. Since their arrival in this new country, the wanderers had met them almost every day, and knew that they were inoffensive. But on account of their resemblance to the Red Dwarfs, the rhesus inspired them with a vague uneasiness.

About a dozen of them could be seen in the last rays of daylight. Having watched the flames for a moment, they bounded from branch to branch, and from tree to tree, with giddy rapidity; then they stopped and again began to take note of the unusual spectacle. At last a big male—he was like a wolf in build—slowly descended to the ground and advanced towards the fire. When he had covered a distance of about ten ells, he stopped and gave a sort of gentle whimper, which was at the same time an appeal.

Aoun had lifted his spear, remembering the treachery of the Red Dwarfs, who were hardly larger than the rhesus. He let it fall again when he heard the cry. After waiting a moment the monkey advanced another few ells. Then he seemed to have stopped for good, rendered motionless by a combination of fear and curiosity.

Loud howls resounded; three wolves appeared on the summit of a mound. As the wind blew away from them neither the men nor the rhesus had noticed their approach.

The rhesus tried to reach the trees. The most active of the wolves got ahead of him, the two others barred his retreat. Only the way to the fire remained free. The great monkey stood for a moment distracted, while his companions in the trees chattered despairingly. He turned his anxious face to-wards the men, saw that the wolves were drawing nearer, and mad with terror, dashed forward.

At the moment when he got near the fire, the three pur-suers were converging upon him; the most active of them was only ten ells distant. The rhesus gave a mournful cry. There was no space left between the flesh-eaters and the fierce flames. Death was before him and the simian felt its cold hor-ror. He turned first towards the forest, towards that ocean of leaves where he could so easily have escaped from the teeth of his enemies...then a second time his distressed face was turned imploringly towards the men.

Zouhr rose, his spear held high in his hand. A race in-stinct boiled within him; he bounded towards the monkey. The wolf recoiled before the man's form, and Aoun in his turn sprang to his feet. The wolves howled; though they still kept their distance, they feigned attack, with lips turned up mena-cingly.

Aoun disdainfully threw a stone. Struck on the shoulder the nearest wolf fell back towards the others.

"Wolves are not worthy of spears or javelins," mocked the son of Urus.

Among the trees one could see the other monkeys bound-ing from branch to branch, while the motionless fugitive looked anxiously at the men who had just saved his life. His long arms trembled. Fear had taken possession of him; he was afraid of the unknown fire, afraid of the wolves, afraid also of those forms which stood up so straight, and of that strange voice which differed from any of the voices of the forest or the steppes. By degrees his heart beat less quickly, and his round eyes sought those of the men. He began to feel reassured; when the stronger one does not strike first, after a little while the feebler one thinks that he will not strike at all. The rhesus was now afraid only of the fire and the wolves. Then the fire ceased to alarm him, as it remained within the pile of heaped-up branches.

Aoun and Zouhr, having chased away the wild beasts, took stock of their guest. He was sitting down like a child, and his little hands completed the resemblance; also his chest, which was nearly flat.

"The wolves shall not eat the little green dwarf," said Aoun with a laugh which made the monkey start.

"Aoun and Zouhr will take him back to the trees!" added the Wah. He began to tremble again as they approached him. Their slow movements, the tones of their voices, no longer loud as when they were threatening the wolves, calmed the rhesus, and there was a feeling of gentleness between them. For Aoun and Zouhr there was pleasure in the thought of having a new companion, who excited their curiosity and made life less bleak.

Time passed. The wolves still watched; they howled at intervals; they were furious with the fire, the men, and the prey that had escaped them, not by cunning or swiftness, but through an incomprehensible intervention. At last they disappeared. They faded into the night and, as they were no longer downwind, it was impossible for their approach to be unobserved should they return.

The rhesus did not go away at once. He began to grow accustomed to the fire: the breeze blew more chill from the mountains; the sky was too clear, it absorbed the heat; the beast imitated man and took pleasure in the hot breath which came from the flames.

Then the rhesus gave a little cry, looked fixedly at his hosts and bounded towards the trees.

Aoun and Zouhr regretted his departure.

The next day the two men returned to the forest. It astonished them by the enormous size of its trees and undergrowth. There were fewer serpents than on the plains; the tribe of white-headed crows croaked in the tops of the trees; gaurs passed across the clearing, while black bears showed themselves on the forks of the big branches. Sometimes a leopard would come forth towards the close of day, without daring to attack the men. Then a horde of long-tailed entellus monkeys, with bearded faces, would appear. They assembled in clusters in the branches, with weird cries, enjoying the feeling of companionship and the sense of security which they derived from uniting to defend themselves and their territory.

On the fourth night, Aoun became aware of a peculiar smell. No other odor which he had smelt since his arrival in this new land so much resembled the human effluvia. He shuddered; fear made his hair stand on end. Neither the odor of the tiger, the lion, the saber-tooth, nor that of the giant feline would have seemed so alarming to him.

He wakened Zouhr so that they might be ready to fight, and both of them kept all their senses on the alert. The Wah's power of smell was not so strongly developed as that of the Oulhamr, he only noticed a faint odor, but Aoun affirmed with dilated nostrils, "The smell is that of the Kzamms."

The Kzamms were the most ferocious of men. Tufts of fur, in color like that of the fox, covered their faces and bodies; their arms were as long as those of the Tree Men, their legs were short and bowed, their thighs hung in three fleshy folds and their toes were enormous. They ate the vanquished Oulhamrs, and had devoured the few Men-without-Shoulders who had escaped extermination.

For a little while the smell seemed to grow weaker, the mysterious being appeared to be going farther away. Then it became stronger again and finally Zouhr whispered, "The son of Urus speaks truly; it is like the smell of the Kzamms."

An agony of impatience made Aoun breathe quickly. His club was at his feet; he readied his bow, in order to shoot to a great distance…

It now became certain that more than one of the mysterious creatures was near; the smell came from two directions.

He said, "They see us and we do not see them. We *must* see them…ourselves!"

Zouhr, always more in favor of temporizing than the Oulhamr, hesitated.

"The light of the fire shows us up," continued Aoun.

He had picked up his club. The Wah once more tried to pierce the darkness; he could discern nothing, and thinking that the unknown enemies might attack them unexpectedly, he approved the action.

The son of Urus went forward, and Zouhr followed him in silence. They bent down and carefully examined every detail of the ground as they passed, stopping at intervals. Aoun swept their surroundings minutely with his eyes, his ears, and above all with his delicate sense of smell. He held his club in one hand, and his bow with the arrow ready strung in the other. He advanced, observing the odors all the time, and was gradually convinced that there were only two beings…

There was a rustling sound. A bush moved, then a light step was heard upon the mould. Aoun and Zouhr could discern an indistinct shape in the low underwood, but it was so dim that they could not tell whether it was standing upright or on all fours. The sound of footsteps, however, was that of only two paws; neither the rhesus, the long-tailed monkeys nor even the gibbons would have fled in this manner.

Aoun said in a low voice, "They are men."

They stopped as if transfixed. The shadowy form took on a terrible significance. In face of this new peril Aoun suddenly and almost involuntarily shouted his war-cry. Then a second set of footsteps was heard parallel to the first; after that the sound and the smell diminished. The Oulhamr started in pursuit. He was stopped first by some creepers, then by a marsh; Zouhr asked, "Why did Aoun shout his war-cry? Perhaps those men do not wish to fight us."

"They smelt like the Kzamms!"

"The smell of the Blue-Haired Men is also like that of the Kzamms."

The Oulhamr was struck by this reflection. An instinct of prudence kept him motionless for a moment; he sniffed for a long time in the half darkness and said, "They are gone!"

"They know the forest and we do not!" said Zouhr. "We shall not see them tonight. We must wait for morning."

Aoun did not reply. He made a few steps to the left and lay down with his ear to the ground. He became aware of all sorts of faint noises, and among them the son of Urus could only just distinguish the footsteps of the unknown beings. They grew fainter and became indistinguishable, while the sound of a small pack of prowling Dholes came nearer.

"The Men-of-the-Forest did not dare fight!" he said rising to his feet, "or else they have gone to warn their brothers."

They came back to the fire and threw on more branches: their hearts were ill at ease. Then silence settled down on the world of trees; the danger seemed very far away; the Oulhamr slept, while Zouhr watched by the crimson flames.

Morning found them irresolute. Should they continue their journey or turn back? Zouhr, always less ready for adventure, wished to return once more to the bank of the river, by the chain of rocks, where the alliance with the great feline rendered them invincible. Aoun however, elated by what he had already accomplished, was averse to retreat.

He said, "Will not the Men-of-the-Forest know how to follow us if we go back? Why should there not be others in the country through which we have passed?"

Zouhr was all the more ready to agree to these ideas because they had occurred to him before Aoun had given expression to them. He knew well that men wandered further than jackals, wolves, or Dholes. Only birds roamed over greater distances. That they had met no hordes on their way, did not prove that there had been none on their right hand or their left, and that they would not find them in the path of their return.

Zouhr agreed to take the risk. He was more foreseeing than Aoun, less ready to fight; his courage was equal to that of his companion, but he was more willing to accept the inevitable. The fatality of his race lived in him; all his own people having perished, he sometimes wondered at finding himself still alive. He would have been quite alone without Aoun; all his happiness was bound up in his alliance with the young Oulhamr, and there was no danger he might encounter which could compare with the loneliness of living without his companion.

The day passed without any alarms: when they had chosen their resting place no peculiar presence was revealed.

It was in the depths of the forest, but the lightning had set many of the trees on fire and burnt up the grass. Three blocks of schist supplied a refuge which could be sufficiently strengthened with thorns. Aoun and Zouhr roasted a leg of antelope, the flavor of which was pleasant to them; then they laid themselves down beneath the stars. Dawn was near when Aoun awoke. He saw that the Wah was standing up, listening intently, his head inclined towards the south.

"Has Zouhr heard the lion or the tiger pass?" he asked.

Zouhr did not know; he thought he had smelt a suspicious odor... Aoun sniffed the air and affirmed, "The Men-of-the-Forest have returned."

He pushed aside the thorn barricade, and went slowly towards the south. The smell had vanished; it was only the trail left by the mysterious beings. It was impossible to pursue them in the dusk. The two men went back into the refuge and waited for daylight. A gray light began to spread among the clouds in the east. A bird filled its little chest and twittered. Shifting lights appeared among the clouds. Then day dawned. Amber-colored lakes, emerald rivers, and purple mountains were born and died in the land of trees. Then a scarlet shape appeared, glinting through the forest roves...

The Wah and the Oulhamr had already started. They were going towards the south, attracted by the unknown. The danger of being taken by surprise appeared to them greater than that of going in pursuit of those who were spying upon them. Their instinct told them that they must know the nature and strength of those beings, so that they might organize their defense, and Zouhr's prudence agreed with Aoun's ardor.

They walked quickly. There was little to impede their progress. It seemed as if paths had been made by the frequent passage of individuals or hordes. Aoun continued to wind the trail. For a long time the scent remained weak, then in the middle of the day, it strengthened. Aoun pursued his course impatiently. The forest began to grow lighter. A moor appeared, studded with trees, bushes and ferns at rare intervals, and with a few stagnant pools...

Aoun hesitated for one moment, then suddenly he gave a cry: he had discovered quite fresh footprints in the soft earth. Traces of broad feet with five toes were there, which more resembled men's feet than the feet of the dryopithecus.

The son of Urus stooped down and examined these footprints for a long time: then he announced, "The Men-of-the-Forest are near, they have not yet regained their covert."

The companions started once more. Their hearts beat fast, they did not go near any bush without having first made the circuit of it. When they had gone 3000 or 4000 ells, Aoun pointed out a thicket of mastic-trees, and said in a low voice, "They are there!"

A shudder ran through them; the sympathy which united them after so many days spent together was now blended with profound anxiety. They had no means of gauging the enemy's strength. All that Aoun knew was that there were only two of them. He considered himself as strong as Naoh, the strongest of all the Oulhamrs, but Zouhr was feeble; nearly all the warriors of the tribe could wield heavier clubs, and move more rapidly. They must try to carry on the fight from a distance; and if the others had no bows, the advantage would be on the side of the Oulhamr and the Wah.

"Is Zouhr ready to fight?" asked Aoun with gentle anxiety.

"Zouhr is ready...but we must try first to make an alliance with the Men-of-the-Forest, like the Wahs did in old days with the Oulhamrs."

"Both hordes were enemies of the Red Dwarfs."

Aoun advanced first, as he had the keenest sense of smell and he wanted to stand the first shock. His fighting instinct, and the wish to preserve his companion's life, made him desire this.

When they were about 100 ells distant, they began to make a circuit around the mastic-trees, stopping from time to time so as to get a good view of the clear spaces in the thicket. No animal form became visible among the trunks or branches.

At last the Oulhamr lifted up his loud voice, "The Men-of-the-Forest think they are hidden from us, but we know their retreat. Aoun and Zouhr are strong—they have killed the red beast and the tiger!"

The thicket kept its secret. Not a sound excepting the light sough of the breeze, the droning of the flies and the far off song of a bird broke the silence. Aoun grew impatient.

"The Oulhamrs have the noses of jackals and the hearing of wolves! Two Men-of-the-Forest are hidden among the mastic-trees."

Yellow-headed cranes fluttered down close to a lotus-covered pool, a hawk hovered above the crests of the trees and the glaring sunlight, which burnt up the grass, revealed a herd of graceful antelopes passing in the distance. Fear, prudence or cunning counseled the unknown beings to keep silence.

Aoun had fitted an arrow to his bow. Thinking better of it, he gathered some thin branches and trimmed them. Zouhr did the same.

When they had finished their work they did not at once make up their minds as to further action. Zouhr would have preferred to wait. Even Aoun was full of indecision… The idea of latent danger became unbearable to him, he fitted one of the sticks to the bow and shot it off. It produced no effect. Three times they renewed their efforts without any more success. A dull cry was heard after the flight of the fifth missile; the branches were pushed aside, and a hairy being came into view in front of the mastic-trees.

Like Aoun and Zouhr he stood on his hind legs, his back forming a convex arch; his shoulders, which inclined forwards, were nearly as narrow as those of the Wahs; his chest projected outwards like that of a dog; his thick head had an enormous mouth, and a retreating forehead, and his pointed ears were reminiscent of those of the jackal and also of those of men; a tuft of hair formed a crest on his skull, while a short bristly growth covered his sides; his arms were shorter than those of a monkey. The newcomer held a pointed stone in his hand.

Shorter than the Oulhamrs, taller than the Red Dwarfs, he was muscular and wiry. For a moment his round eyes were fixed upon the warriors; the skin of his forehead swelled with fury; they heard the grinding of his teeth.

Aoun and Zouhr measured his height and watched his movements. Their last doubts vanished, the creature that stood before them was evidently a man. The stone which he held in his hand had obviously been cut; he stood more firmly on his hind legs than the Men-with-Blue-Hair; there was some indefinable quality in his gestures which is not to be found in the entellus, the rhesus, or even in the gibbons or the dryopithecus...

Zouhr remained anxious, but the great Oulhamr, comparing the weapon of his adversary to his own club, spears and harpoons, and measuring his own tall straight figure against that crouching form, decided that he was the superior. He made a few steps towards the mastic bushes shouting, "The son of Urus, and the son of Earth, do not wish to kill the Man-of-the-Forest!"

A hoarse voice answered him, which was like the growl of a bear, but it had some attempt at articulation. Another softer voice was heard, and at the same time a second form emerged from the covert. It was more lanky, the chest was narrower, the belly was swollen, the legs were knock-kneed, the round eyes were shifty, and an aggressive fear distended the jaws.

Aoun began to laugh. He displayed his weapons, and held up his muscular arms.

"How do the long-haired man and woman expect to fight against Aoun?"

His laugh astonished the others and lessened their fear. Curiosity appeared on their heavy faces, and Zouhr spoke gently, "Why should not the hairy men make an alliance with the Oulhamr and the Wah? The forest is vast, and there is abundance of prey."

He expected that they would not be able to understand, but he trusted like Aoun to the power of articulate speech. He was not mistaken; the hairy man and woman listened with great curiosity, which presently grew into confidence.

When Aoun was silent, they remained in a stooping posture, still listening intently; then the woman made some sounds which, though they were nearly akin to those of an animal, had a human rhythm about them. Aoun began to laugh again in a friendly manner, and throwing down his weapons, he made peaceful signs to the pair. The woman laughed in return, a stiff, broken, embryonic laugh, heavily imitated by the man.

Then the Oulhamr and the Wah approached the mastic-trees. They went slowly halting at intervals, taking only their clubs with them. The others watched them approach with occasional starts of fear and preparation for flight; then the Oulhamr's laugh would reassure them. Finally they were within two paces of each other.

That was the dangerous and decisive moment. The flat faces of the aborigines once more displayed great mistrust; their eyes rolled, their foreheads swelled. The man involuntarily lifted his stone, but Aoun stretched out his enormous club towards him and began to laugh again.

"What harm can the little pointed stone do to the big club?" he asked.

The Wah added in a low musical tone, "Aoun and Zouhr are neither lions nor wolves."

The anxiety of the others was already abating. The woman made the first advance. She touched Aoun's arm murmuring semi-articulate words. Then, as the danger had not materialized, it seemed impossible that it should do so. Animal confidence, which follows all harmless contact, began slowly to grow. Zouhr held out a slice of dried meat which the man devoured, while Aoun gave the woman a cooked root.

Long before the day was ended, it was as if they had lived months together.

The fire did not alarm their new companions. They watched it catch one stick after another, and soon became accustomed to warming their limbs at it. The cool wind had subsided. The heat of the soil rose rapidly through the pure light air towards the stars. The wanderers were pleased to see the strange beings sitting near the fire. It reminded them of evenings with their horde, and they felt the sense of security engendered by numbers.

Zouhr tried to understand the strange sounds and gestures of their new companions. He had already made out that the man was known by an appellation which sounded like Rah, and that the woman answered to the cry of Wao, and he tried to learn whether there were other men in the forest and whether they formed a horde. Several times the newcomers' gestures seemed to coincide with their own, but it was only a glimpse of real understanding and soon disappeared or became uncertain.

During the following days the friendship grew closer. The hairy man and woman did not distrust them. A habit had established itself in their brains, which were more embryonic than those of Aoun and Zouhr. There was in them a native gentleness, and a tendency towards submissiveness which was only changed to brutality by fear or anger. They gave way before the big Oulhamr's ascendancy and Zouhr's subtle patience. Their sense of smell was equal to that of the son of Urus. In addition to this they were nyctalopes and could see as distinctly as a panther in the dark. The rhesus and entellus monkeys hardly surpassed their agility in climbing trees. They ate meat readily, but they were able to keep themselves alive on leaves, young stalks, grasses, uncooked roots, and mushrooms. They could not run as fast as Aoun, but about equaled Zouhr. Their muscular strength surpassed that of the Wah, but was far inferior to the big Oulhamr's. They had no weapons except their pointed stones, which they used also to cut stalks and bark, and they did not know how to make a fire or keep it up.

In old days, in the tertiary forests, their Lemurian ancestors had invented speech and cut the first stones. They had spread themselves over the world. While some were learning to make use of fire, and others discovered the art of extracting it from stones and dry wood; while tools and weapons were being perfected by cleverer hands than theirs, they themselves, having led an easier and more abundant life, remained always the Lemurian men of ancient days. In the course of ages their speech had hardly changed, though it had perhaps lost a few of its articulate sounds; their gestures remained stationary, and though they could adapt them partially to new conditions they lost in doing so some of the qualities they had possessed in the past.

As it was they could hold their own against the leopard, the panther, the wolves and the Dholes, who rarely attacked them. Their agility in climbing put them out of the power of the lion or the tiger, whose presence they smelt far off. Their aptitude for nourishing themselves with various kinds of food made them almost ignorant of hunger. Even in winter they discovered many useful roots and mushrooms without much difficulty. They were not called upon to endure the terrible cold to which the Oulhamrs, the Wahs, the Red Dwarfs and the Kzamms were subjected on the other side of the mountains, in the lands of the north and of the setting Sun.

Notwithstanding this their race was becoming extinct, after having inhabited many different forests and jungles.

Mysterious causes had destroyed it in the east and the south.

Other and stronger men, who could make better use of articulate speech, fashion more formidable weapons and employ fire, had pushed back the Lemurian men to the plateau. For 1000 years the conquerors of the plain had only attacked it two or three times in each generation, and had not remained there. The primitive men fled to the recesses of the forest at their approach. These were periods of horror, the recollection of which was deeply engraved on the instinct rather than the brains of the race, and they were the only times when the life of the Lemurians became sad...

Rah and Wao knew nothing of these vicissitudes. They were young and had not suffered from an invasion. They had seen the fires of a camp two or three times at the extreme end of the plateau. It was a vague picture which revived in their minds when they saw Aoun and Zouhr's fire.

Zouhr and Wao began to understand each other better and better. The Wah now knew that there were other Lemurian men in the forest and he had warned Aoun of it. The son of Urus received the news unconcernedly. He thought that as he had made an alliance with Rah, there would not be war between him and the others, and he also imagined they would not dare to fight him. Zouhr did not share his unconcern. He did not imagine that the Lemurians would be inclined to fight—Rah and Wao did not hunt any dangerous beasts—but he feared they might think they were attacked.

One night the fire was burning brightly among the dry sticks. Rah and Wao looked at it with beatitude and, instructed by Zouhr, amused themselves by throwing on branches. The hunters had spitted a haunch of fallow deer, which began to spread abroad the intoxicating scent of roast meat. Mushrooms were cooking on a flat stone. Through the leafy arcades the horns of the waxing moon could be seen among the stars. When the food was ready Aoun gave a portion to the Lemurians, and divided the rest with his companion. Although their shelter was not very good, they felt secure. They were surrounded by trees the trunks of which were too high for tigers to scale, and in which they could take refuge before a carnivore could get near enough to attack them.

It was a pleasant time. No feeling of mistrust divided the wild beings: inoffensive to each other, ready to combine against any surprises from without, they enjoyed the great happiness which belongs to healthy bodies, repose, and abundant food... Suddenly Aoun and Rah, then Wao, started. A furtive smell was borne past them.

Rah and Wao gave a kind of laugh; the Oulhamr said anxiously to Zouhr, "More men are approaching us."

The Wah turned towards the woman. She bowed her head, her nyctalopic eyes were fixed on the darkness. He touched her shoulder and questioned her by voice and signs. The question which he put to her was plain, events made it still plainer. Wao nodded her head, held out both arms, and made an affirmative sound.

"Aoun is right," said the son of Earth, "other Men-of-the-Forest have come."

The Oulhamr rose up; Rah crawled in the grass; there was an anxious moment. Mistrust made Aoun set his jaws, and Zouhr depress his eyebrows. Rah however had begun to move on. Zouhr called him back; the Lemurian's face was undecided, and his appearance was that of a man who hesitates. He would have liked to bound towards his kind, but he was afraid of Aoun.

After a pause the son of Urus seized his weapons and walked in the direction from whence the smell came. It became stronger and multiplied. The warrior counted that there must be six or seven men in the grove; he accelerated his pace. At one moment the emanations seemed quite close, then they scattered. In the gray light which filtered through the branches the Oulhamr thought he distinguished the outline of figures. They disappeared immediately. The warrior ran as quickly as possible, delayed sometimes by the brushwood. Suddenly he stopped: a sheet of water 200 ells broad stretched out before him; frogs leapt into it, and others set up their senile croaking among the lotus leaves; the waxing moon threw a long track of shining light on the water...

On the other bank, several forms bounded up one after another, as if they had sprung from among the water weeds. Aoun addressed them,

"The son of Urus and the son of Earth are the allies of the Hairy Men."

The fugitives paused to look at Aoun when they heard his resounding voice. Then they made a dull threatening clamor and shook their sharpened stones. They were about to resume their way towards the south when Rah intervened in his turn. His voice answered those of the men of his race. He showed them Aoun and then put both his hands on his breast. Shrill voices resounded in answer and arms gesticulated wildly. With their nyctalopic sight the fugitives could see the Lemurian and the Oulhamr as plainly as by daylight; Rah missed nothing of the dumb show of his people.

When Wao and Zouhr appeared the clamor became louder. Then there was a kind of pause.

"How did the Hairy Men pass over the pool?" exclaimed Aoun.

The Wah turned towards Wao, and succeeded in making her understand the question. She began to laugh and dragged Zouhr away to the left. Then, under the transparent water, he saw a gray line and Wao, in response to a sign, quitted the bank. She stepped into the water up to her thighs and began to walk along a sort of causeway under the water. Aoun followed without any hesitation; Rah preceded Zouhr.

For a moment the Lemurians on the other bank remained motionless, then they were seized with panic, and a woman having given the signal they took to flight... Rah spoke to them in sharp tones. A male, the most thickset of the troop, stopped first; by degrees they all ceased to flee. They could be seen forming a long zigzag line.

When Aoun landed there was another panic, which was quickly arrested. Rah, having landed in his turn took the initiative. The thickset man waited. It was an exciting moment. all the Lemurians fixed their eyes on Aoun's great height. Those who had met the Men-of-the-Fire did not remember ever having seen so tall a man. The picture of implacable massacres rose before them; remembering defeat their bodies shook with terror. By degrees, as Rah continued his signs, they were reassured. The thickset man, after recoiling at first, allowed Aoun to place his hand on his shoulder. Zouhr, who had just landed, made the signs of alliance which he had learnt from Wao. Then these poor creatures were carried away by their joy, and also perhaps by a kind of pride that they should ally themselves with this giant, who surpassed in size the most terrible of their vanquishers. The women were the first to join the thickset man; Aoun laughed his great laugh, full of the joy he felt at once more forming part of a horde after so many days spent away from his own tribe.

X. The Men-of-the-Fire

For several weeks Aoun, Zouhr and their allies wandered in the forest. They lived a life of abundance and ease. The Lemurians were clever at discovering springs of fresh water, detected the presence of wild beasts a great way off, and knew how to dig up edible roots and extract the pith of the sago palm. Around the fire in the evening a sense of complete security reigned. The little horde defied attack; Aoun and Zouhr had cut axes and clubs for their companions, which after a time they wielded skillfully. They all seemed ready to defy the carnivores, under the able leadership of the Oulhamr. They were of a gregarious nature like the entellus monkeys, and became formidable when inspired with confidence. Little by little Aoun gained complete ascendency over them. They had a naïve love and admiration for his colossal chest and irresistible arms; his thunderous voice moved them to laughter; in the evening, when the coppery gleam of the fire danced on the grass and under the arches of the trees, they crowded around the Oulhamr shouting for joy. Everything that terrified them about the Men-of-the-Fire was changed to a sense of security... Zouhr's presence was almost equally agreeable to them. They realized his ingenious cunning and knew that the giant listened to his counsels; he understood their signs and confused speech. There was, however, a kind of equality between Zouhr and them; they liked him in almost the same manner that they liked one another, while their predilection for Aoun was more in the nature of worship for a superior being...

As they advanced further towards the south, the Lemurians displayed hesitation, which almost took on the appearance of fear. Wao explained that they were nearly at the end of the forest. The plateau sloped downhill; the heat became greater; palm-trees, lianas, banyans and bamboos began to be more numerous again.

One afternoon they were stopped by a declivity which was almost perpendicular. A torrent ran through a narrow valley. On the other side the bank sloped upward without attaining so great a height as that on which the wanderers stood. They could distinguish a large savannah interspersed with groups of trees.

The Lemurians, who had remained crouched among the bushes, looked at the savannah with shifting eyes. Zouhr having interrogated Wao, said to the son of Urus, "It is the land of the Men-of-the-Fire!"

Aoun gazed at it with fierce curiosity.

Zouhr added, "When they come into the forest, they kill the hairy men and eat them, as if they were spotted deer or antelopes."

Then anger rose in the Oulhamr's breast, for he remembered the Kzamms, who were men-devourers, from whom Naoh had reconquered the secret of fire.

The place was well suited for their encampment. There was a long cave in the rock, easy to defend against wild beasts or men, and a clear space in front of it where a fire could be lit which the thick brushwood would render invisible from the other bank. With the assistance of the Lemurians, Aoun and Zouhr fortified the entrance to the cave. When evening came it was strongly protected and would resist the attack of 30 men.

The son of Urus said, "Aoun, Zouhr and the Hairy Men are stronger than the Men-of-the-Fire!"

He began to laugh, his ringing victorious laugh, and his gaiety spread among the others. The Sun's scarlet disc was reflected back from the waters of the river; the clouds were filled with trails of glory: they were like those red rocks which rise in the north of the Wah's country, and stood out from purple moors and abysses of sulphur. The fire was magnificent among the lengthening shadows. A cool breeze helped to kindle the branches and bark; a whole antelope was roasting for the horde; the Lemurians cooked their roots, their beans and their mushrooms under Zouhr's directions…

As the repast ended, Rah, who was near the brushwood, started up suddenly, making confused sounds. His arm was stretched out towards the opposite bank.

Aoun and Zouhr penetrated into the thicket and stood aghast: to the left of their encampment, but on the other bank, a fire began to glow… It was still very feeble, and the branches and twigs were not yet well alight. Then it caught on and flames burst out. A red smoke hung about it. The flames grew and seemed to conquer the darkness; their light was thrown over the steppe; black or copper colored forms were indistinctly visible, their color varying according to whether they passed on one or the other side of the fire.

All the Lemurians had followed Aoun. They watched their enemies' movements with feverish anxiety, gazing between the interstices of the brushwood. At intervals a shudder of fear crept over them. The oldest among them remembered wild flights, and saw again in imagination their companions being killed by spear-thrusts or blows from a hatchet.

As they looked, Aoun was able to take in the scene better. The Men-of-the-Fire were preparing portions of game and roasting them at the flames. There were seven of them, all males. No doubt they formed one of those hunting expeditions which were frequent among the Oulhamrs, the Red Dwarfs, the Kzamms and in old days among the Wahs. One of them was warming the point of a spear at the fire so as to harden it. It did not seem as if they were aware of the presence of another fire. Their encampment was situated lower down than that of Aoun and Zouhr. The brushwood formed an almost impenetrable curtain. Soon, however, Aoun guessed that they had noticed something. Now and then one or the other would turn towards the rock plateau and look hard at it.

"They see the light of our fire," said Zouhr.

Their calm surprised him. Perhaps they thought that the encampment was occupied by men of their horde. He interrogated Wao. She pointed to the river, then to the descent on their side and the ascent on the other, and made him understand that there was no way of getting across, unless by going around a long way. The current was so strong that no man or beast could swim across the river. It would be necessary to walk till daybreak to reach the enemy's camp. Security for both sides was complete for the moment.

Aoun observed these beings for a long time. They were nearer to his race than the Lemurians, and yet they more resembled the Kzamms than the Oulhamrs. Despite the distance he could see their short legs, and note that their bodies were thicker than they were broad, but he could not make out their heads, which were narrower than those of the Men-Devourers, their heavy jaws, and their enormous arched eyebrows.

"The Men-of-the-Fire will not attack us tonight!" affirmed Aoun. "Will they dare to attack us tomorrow?"

His bellicose heart did not shrink from battle; he was confident of victory. Though the Lemurians might be weaker than their enemies, they outnumbered them, and the Oulhamr counted on his own strength and Zouhr's cunning.

He asked, "Have the Men-of-the-Fire, spears and javelins?"

The question was put to Wao by the son of Earth; she took some time to understand it, then she inquired of one of the oldest of her companions.

"They fling stones," said Zouhr when he had unraveled the meaning of the Lemurian's gesticulation.

"And they do not know how to extract fire from stones!" exclaimed Aoun joyously.

He had succeeded in making out two small fires, at a little distance from the big fire, which burned in cages of stone. If their fire were extinguished by their enemies, as had happened to the Oulhamrs before Naoh brought back the secret from the Wahs, they would be forced to return to their horde.

The night was peaceful. Aoun, who took the first watch, found his task of observing the enemy all the easier because the Moon set later than the evening before. Two Lemurians watched with him. They had learnt the need for vigilance and they relieved one another naturally when any danger threatened. Nothing alarmed them more than the proximity of the Men-of-the-Fire.

When it was Zouhr's turn to watch the Moon had set and the fire on the opposite bank only threw pale glimmers. All the warriors were asleep except one who could be seen walking up and down in the half light. Soon Zouhr could no longer see him, but the nyctalopic eyes of Rah continued to follow him despite the distance... The night wore on. Hundreds of stars had set in the west, others continued to shine, mounting everhigher in the sky. One red star only remained motionless in the north. Towards dawn the mist formed on the river and gradually veiled the opposite slope. The encampment of the Men-of-the-Fire became invisible.

The fog remained until after daybreak, when the morning breeze made rents in it, and the Sun evaporated it. Gradually they could see the opposite shore. First only the crest was visible, then the mist rolled back, in long trails, and allowed the whole slope to come into view once more.

The Lemurians gave a kind of wail; there were no more Men-of-the-Fire! Only a few ashes and blackened marks showed where they had camped.

XI. The Invisible Enemy

Aoun, Zouhr and the Lemurians spent a great part of the day fortifying the cave in such a manner as to render it impregnable. The precautions which sufficed to defend it against carnivores, who would always end by going away, were insufficient as a defense against men. The Oulhamr and the Wah knew well that the Red Dwarfs or the Kzamms were capable of besieging their enemies for weeks together. If they shut themselves up in a cave, surrounded by numerous adversaries, it meant condemning themselves to death. Against a dozen enemies however—and they had only seen seven on the previous evening—the cave might serve as a trap.

They killed several antelopes in the afternoon, the flesh of which was to be dried by the fire and in the Sun; the Lemurians collected provisions of vegetables.

At the same time they all kept a good look out. It came naturally to them as it did to the Dholes and jackals. The position was a difficult one to invade: to the south there was the river and the rocks; to the east a long moor, and to the west marshy ground. There was only one way which was really accessible, that of the forest, which stretched away backward, but which left space between it and the cave which was easy to watch. In fact no surprise attack was possible. In order to reach the shelter the Men-of-the-Fire would have to traverse from five to 900 paces of open ground, which could be swept by arrows, javelins and spears.

Until evening no suspicious smell presented itself to give warning of an enemy's approach. At twilight the Lemurians dispersed in a radius of about 3000 ells. Aoun climbed onto the highest rock, but could not discover anything. If the enemy had returned he must still be at a great distance.

The Oulhamr began to be reassured. He said to Zouhr, "The Men-of-the-Fire were only seven; they have gone away."

He meant to convey that the existence of so great a fire must have made their pursuers think that they were a group of men numerous enough to defend themselves. Zouhr remained anxious. He had more foresight than the Oulhamr, and even perhaps than all other men of his day, and was a prey to undying distrust on account of the annihilation of his race by the Red Dwarfs. He replied, "If they have not returned it is because they have gone to fetch the warriors of their horde!"

"Their horde is far away," said the Oulhamr unconcerned. "Why should they return?"

"Because the Men-of-the-Forest do not know how to light a fire. They will want to know what new men are in the forest."

Aoun was impressed by this answer, but having disposed the watchers so as to guard against all surprises he was reassured. As usual he took the first watch. The waxing moon, which grew ever-bigger and gave increasing light, would not set till about the middle of the night. This circumstance, which was important to Aoun, mattered little to the nyctalopic Lemurians, who had rather the advantage in the darkness. Nothing beyond the occasional sound of some wild beast hunting broke the stillness in the depth of the night. Aoun, seated by the fire, neither thought nor dreamed; only his senses were alert. The three Lemurian watchers were still more somnolent, but the slightest suspicious odor would have made them start up... Their sense of hearing and of smell, which was as infallible as that of the Dholes, stretched over their surroundings like a network of fine wires.

The Moon had accomplished two-thirds of its course when Aoun lifted his head. He saw that the fire was reduced to red embers, and mechanically he threw on an armful of wood. Then, sniffing the air uncertainly, he looked at the watchers. Two of them had sat up and the third soon followed their example.

A faint scent came from the forest. It so much resembled the smell of the Lemurians that Aoun thought it must mean that some of the prowlers of that race were near. He walked towards Rah; Rah was listening with all his ears, his wide nostrils were distended, and his shoulders shivered nervously.

When Aoun got near to him, he extended his hand towards the forest, stammering incomprehensible syllables. Aoun understood that the Chellian[3] men were there!

Hidden in the dense thickets, they could see the fire, they could see the Oulhamr, while they themselves remained invisible.

An immediate surprise did not, however, seem possible. All around the cave there was short grass, the even expanse of which was only broken by an occasional isolated tree or a thin clump of bushes.

Aoun's sharp eye could see all the details of the position as it lay in the gray light of the Moon. He was bursting with daring, and had great difficulty in restraining himself from giving his war-cry. Hate boiled up within him, because the Men-of-the-Fire had crossed the river and skirted the moor in order to attack the encampment. They had thus displayed their tenacity, courage and hostility.

Before awakening Zouhr he prowled around the area which surrounded the cave, trying to locate the emanations and to make out the number of the enemy. He held a bow in his hand, two javelins and a harpoon were hung around his shoulders. He desired to entice the Chellians out of the forest; for as they only knew how to throw stones with their hands, he could kill or wound several of them before they were near enough to wound him in return.

The Lemurians came out of the cave one by one, having become aware of an unwonted presence. Zouhr accompanied them. Thanks to Wao, he at once knew the danger.

The great Oulhamr gazed alternately at his allies and the moving bushes. Those who were concealed in them could not number more than seven. He had eight men on his side, four women who were almost as good as the men, besides himself

---

[3] Name given by the French anthropologist G. de Mortillet, to the first epoch of the Quaternary period. The word is derived from the town of Chelles, in the Department of Seine-et-Marne, where human remains of that epoch have been found.

and Zouhr. If the Lemurians displayed courage, the chances were on the side of the allies. It was however obvious that the greater number of them were so terrified that they would not stand before a determined attack. Only the thickset one, Rah, Wao and a young man with eager eyes showed any courage.

"Are there as many warriors as there were around the fire yesterday?" asked Zouhr.

"There are no more!" replied Aoun. "Should I shout my war-cry?

Zouhr preferred an alliance to a battle. He said finally, "The forest is vast... The prey is sufficient for all. May Zouhr speak to the Men-of-the-Fire?"

Despite his irritation Aoun accepted the proposal, and Zouhr lifted up his voice and spoke in musical tones, which made his utterance even more gentle than usual, "The son of Urus and the son of Earth have never fought with the Men-of-the-Fire! They are not their enemies."

The forest remained silent. Aoun called to them in his turn, "Aoun killed the tawny beast! Aoun and Zouhr killed the tiger... They have clubs, and spears and javelins! If the Men-of-the-Fire desire war, not one of them will live to return to the horde."

Only the gentle sough of the breeze was heard. Aoun took 100 steps towards the forest and his voice rang out more loudly, "Will not the Men-of-the-Fire reply?"

Now that he was closer to them their smell became plainer. Knowing that he was being watched, he was seized by a growing fury. Beating his chest with his fist, his cry went up like the sound of wolves howling.

"Aoun will slit your bodies from top to bottom; he will give your carcases to the hyenas."

A kind of growl re-echoed from the somber arches. The Oulhamr took another 100 steps. He was now only 300 ells from the edge of the forest. He called to Zouhr not to follow him, and threatened, "The son of Urus will crush your faces!"

He hoped that the enemy, seeing that he was isolated from his band, would take the offensive.

For a moment the smell of the aggressors seemed to come closer, then it seemed farther off. Aoun, having advanced another 150 ells, drew himself up to his full height. He could have sent an arrow into the wood.

A cry of alarm rang out. Three men appeared suddenly from behind an advanced bush. They started to run across the open space in a transverse direction so as to cut off Aoun's retreat. The wanderer saw them... With a defiant laugh, he retired slowly, having slipped an arrow into his bow... At the same moment three other men appeared on the right... Terror made the hearts of the Lemurians sick. Half the band scattered, but Rah, Wao, the adolescent, the thickset man and a gray-headed one stood firm. Wao even ran to call back a woman who was escaping to the forest.

The six Chellians tried to join forces, so as to cut off the Oulhamr's retreat. The bow twanged, an arrow was planted in the shoulder of an aggressor; Zouhr and Rah feigned an attack. Surprised at the distance from which the Oulhamr had struck, marveling to see the Wah leading the Lemurians, and fearing a surprise, the Men-of-the-Fire retreated.

Those on the right had captured Wao.

XII. The Wolf-Women

The Truce was short lived. Rah gave vent to furious lamentations; the abduction was intolerable to Aoun, to whom it seemed like a defeat; even Zouhr forgot all prudence. Five of them began a pursuit.

The scent had disappeared, as the abductors had gone downwind. For a little while it was impossible to detect it. When the pursuers winded it again the Men-of-the-Fire had a long start; the trail which the Oulhamr's band picked up among the thickets and marshes was difficult to follow and only became clear after they had made many detours.

A fierce ardor animated the big Oulhamr. Confident in his own strength he advanced far ahead of his companions. Zouhr and Rah tried to follow him; the thickset Lemurian displayed endurance and tenacity…

At last the scent became stronger, and the trail, after leading them into the forest, took the direction of the river. Then it diverged and the son of Urus hesitated, finally choosing the trail in which the smell of Wao mingled with that of her captors.

The trees grew more sparsely; a plain covered with dry grass spread out before them, and a flame shot up which ran along the open space. Aoun was forced to retreat towards Zouhr. A sharp cry was heard, and after leaping up in several places the fire died down. Aoun and his companions continued their way southwards; all trace of the trail was lost.

When they emerged from the forest the moor stretched drearily before them, and at a distance of 2000 ells they saw the light of a fire. Seated on a stone a man was watching. He rose to his feet as he caught sight of the pursuers. Six other men appeared at almost the same moment; they were dragging Wao along, and one of them was walking painfully, holding his hand to his shoulder…

Aoun began to run forward again. He bounded along for about 1500 ells, then stopped with a cry. A gulf lay before him, a deep fissure in the ground, at the bottom of which raged a torrent… The Men-of-the-Fire hooted at him and laughed derisively.

The distance which separated Aoun from the fire was four times greater than the flight of an arrow. Deep disappointment took possession of the wanderer; he met the mocking laugh of his adversaries with shouts of hate.

They arrayed themselves in force, superior in numbers and full of disdain for Aoun's allies. The Lemurians were less to be feared than wolves; Zouhr with his barrel-like body and short arms seemed despicable to them; only the big Oulhamr surprised them. Were they not, however, in their unconquered might, themselves endowed with the strength of the bear? Less tall than Aoun, their chief had a broad chest and long arms, strong enough to suffocate a panther... He turned his enormous face towards the son of Urus, and laughed in a sinister fashion.

Large blocks of stone lay scattered around the fire, thus strengthening the position of the Chellians. All the advantage was on their side, excepting the missile weapons. Aoun saw this plainly and Zouhr was even better aware of it, but they were both overexcited. The Wah had conceived a kind of tenderness for the Lemurian woman; Aoun was smarting under a sense of defeat. They remained on the alert, however... Darkness was coming on. The red disc of the Moon was already disappearing in a cloud which grew ever-larger in the west. A rough wind blew in gusts. Suddenly the son of Urus made up his mind. He skirted the edge of the abyss and returned to the forest. At the end of about 2000 steps, the fissure contracted, then it disappeared.

"I will go first," said Aoun to his companion. "You will follow me at a distance, until the fire is in sight. The Men-of-the-Fire will not take me by surprise. Their pace is not as rapid as mine."

When he emerged again upon the moor the Chellians had not moved. Three of them stood among the interstices of the boulders and gazed into the distance; the others were near the fire. They all had javelins, hatchets and stones ready to throw. When they saw Aoun appear, they howled like Dholes and the chief, lifting his spear, made as if to attack him. The Oulhamr slackened his pace. He knew well it was useless to think of an assault; he cried out, "If you will give up Wao to us, we will let you return to your hunting grounds."

They could not understand his words, but his gestures, which were the same as those of all nomads, made them aware that he was reclaiming their captive. A surly laugh was the reply. The broad-chested chief seized Wao by the hair and felled her to the ground by a blow on the head with his fist. Then, pointing in turn to her prostrate form, the fire and his own jaws, conveyed to Aoun that the Chellians would roast and devour the woman's body...

Aoun bounded like a leopard. The Men-of-the-Fire disappeared behind the boulders. Meanwhile Zouhr was approaching. When the companions were within an arrow's flight of the enemy the Wah said, "Let Aoun go to the right, some of those who are hiding will become visible."

The Oulhamr went to the right of the fire. Two of the Chellians, seeing that they were discovered, tried to retreat. A spear whistled through the air, and a loud cry rang out in the stillness.

The Wah shot in his turn, and a second Chellian sank to the ground, hit in the thigh.

"The Men-of-the-Fire have now three wounded," shouted the Oulhamr's ringing voice.

The black storm clouds mounted ever-higher; the men were enveloped by the eternal forces of earth and sky as it were in deep, intangible, fierce waves. The Moon had disappeared, there was now only the waning glow of the fire and dazzling flashes of lightning. The Chellians had become invisible, fearing to expose themselves to the enemy's spears and javelins; the Oulhamr, the Wah and the Lemurians realized the impossibility of attacking an enemy entrenched behind masses of rock.

There was a pause in the mysterious rolling of the storm. The wind had fallen, thunder was not yet heard; the animals couched in the forest were still. Then the clouds growled like a drove of aurochs; water, the mother of all, began to fall in heavy drops, and fury seized upon the Chellians. Their fire would be put out; they could not protect it even in the stone cages where they preserved it for future use; they would find themselves on the savannah and in the forest in no better case than a pack of wolves.

The chief issued orders. The Men-of-the-Fire attacked, all shouting together. Four of them, two being the wounded men, directed their steps towards Zouhr and the Lemurians. The deep-chested chief and the strongest warriors bounded towards Aoun. Two arrows whistled past them, followed by two others, which the darkness and the pace of the assailants rendered ineffectual. Aoun retreated towards the river, in order to gain time to enable him to fling his spears, while Zouhr and the Lemurians turned towards the forest.

The spears only inflicted slight wounds: the Chellians quickened their pace with cries of victory; the Oulhamr continued his retreat, and the Wah was approaching covertly. Suddenly water poured from the sky like a thousand torrents, the fire sputtered; only the warrior who was wounded in the thigh remained at the camp and protected the fire cages under the stones.

Zouhr and his party were surrounded. The youngest of the Lemurians, who was terrified, tried to flee to a tree for safety; his body was laid open by a javelin stroke and a stone crushed in his head. Rah and the thickset man defended themselves with the clubs which the Oulhamr had fashioned for them; Zouhr felled the Chellian who was wounded in the shoulder with a blow of his axe, but another came stealthily behind him, seized the Wah by the back of his neck and threw him to the ground.

As soon as Aoun saw that the aggressors were separated by a distance of 15 ells, he made three enormous bounds and brought down his club.

The first blow shattered a javelin, the second split a man's head. The Chellian chief and the Oulhamr found themselves face to face. They were both of formidable build. That of the chief was reminiscent of the bear or the wild boar: woolly hair covered his body; his round eyes shot fire. Aoun was of taller stature, his broad chest did not resemble that of any animal, and his body was firmly poised on stout legs. He held his club in both hands. His antagonist's javelin was made of ebony wood, heavy and very pointed, capable of inflicting a deep wound or breaking a bone.

The Chellian struck first, and his weapon hardly touched the son of Urus. Aoun whirled his club. It only met the ground, while a growl burst from the Chellian's lips. His enormous face expressed hatred, murder and insult.

For a moment they watched one another, each of them having retreated a little. Torrential rain enveloped them in mist, the last embers of the fire gave hardly any light; each of the combatants felt death was passing near them as they heard the peals of thunder, and felt the moor tremble beneath their feet.

Aoun resumed the offensive. The club whirled and grazed the tawny body of the Chellian, while the sharp point of the javelin lacerated the Oulhamr's shoulder. Then their weapons became entangled. The javelin touched Aoun's chest at the moment when he was bounding back. Blood flowed from two wounds. Aoun, shouting his war-cry, seized the javelin with one hand and struck with the other. The blow descended full on the Chellian's head, and paralyzed him; a second blow broke his collar bone; more heavy blows were rained upon him and fractured his ribs...

The fire had just gone out; darkness was over all. The flashes of lightning became more rare and feeble, and hardly seemed to pierce the dense blackness. Aoun searched in vain for Zouhr and the Lemurians; the storm had blown away all odors.

He called, "Where does Zouhr hide himself? The son of Urus has overthrown his enemies!"

He was answered by a far away growl, which came from the forest and did not at all resemble the voice of the Man-without-Shoulders. Aoun felt his way in the darkness or ran when the lightning flashed. The form of Rah emerged when he came to the border of the forest, then vanished in the shadows. The Lemurian stammered obscure words, and Aoun guessed that the Wah had disappeared. Sometimes a flash of lightning showed him some gesture more expressive than words. At last the thickset Lemurian appeared also. His attempts at explaining something he wished to say were even more confused than the stammering accents of the other.

228

All action was impossible. The men were enveloped in the unceasing rain; they were more powerless than insects hidden under leaves or in the hollow bark of trees, and the big Oulhamr was in the greatest distress he had ever known. His groans and lamentations rent the air, his chest heaved with great sobs, his tears mingled with the rain. His whole past was bound up with Zouhr. He had loved him since the days when Naoh had brought him back from the country of the Red Dwarfs. Just because Zouhr preferred him to all other beings, Aoun also preferred Zouhr. Sometimes he shouted a loud call and hope would cause his shoulders to heave. Hours passed; the rain ceased; a pale light showed in the east; he could just see the body of the Man-of-the-Fire whom Zouhr had killed, the young Lemurian, whose mangled body was hideous to behold, and also the bodies of the chief and of the warrior whom Aoun had felled. Near the cinders of the burnt-out fire a Chellian lay groaning, his leg pierced by a spear. Wao lying crumpled up near a mass of rock, had fainted so long ago that she had not heard Aoun and Rah's calls. Weak and shivering she gave a hoarse laugh when she saw her companion and the son of Urus.

The Chellian threw himself in front of Aoun beseeching for mercy. The gentleness for which his tribe reproached him inclined the son of Urus to pardon him. But two of the Lemurians were already striking the man with their clubs; they crushed his neck and fractured his skull. Aoun was indignant but he knew it was the law of war.

Wao, who had learnt the meaning of the Oulhamr's gestures better than Rah, remembered a few words which Zouhr had taught her. She listened to the Lemurians and made Aoun understand that the Chellians had carried off the son of Earth into the forest. But the rain had made it impossible for their nyctalopic eyes to see clearly at that time. Rah had lost his way, and so had the thickset Lemurian, who was also wounded and in a fainting condition. So the Wah's fate remained uncertain; hope and fear alternated in Aoun's breast. He searched for the trail all morning. They might find it some distance off, or Zouhr might be dead. The Lemurians scattered in all directions; those who had fled on the previous day returned, and the help of so many sharp eyes and keen noses was inestimable... Finally one party went up the river and the other took a downward course, and both were to cross to the other bank. Aoun was with those who went downstream. He walked two-thirds of the day and forded the river... Wao stopped and gave a sharp cry: the trail was found! They saw the trace of footsteps in the clay, they detected Zouhr's presence.

Joy welled up in the heart of the Oulhamr, but it was at once mingled with fear. The trail was no longer fresh; the Chellians had passed in the morning, and it would be impossible to overtake them till the following day. Moreover it would be necessary that Aoun should go on alone. The Lemurians would be unable to keep up with him, even at a distance. He made sure that all his weapons were intact: three javelins recovered on the field of battle, two spears, his exe and club. He did not forget the flint and marcasite stone with which to make fire... He stood still for a moment, with a beating heart; he felt a kind of tenderness for these feeble, badly armed men, with their imperfect speech, and rudimentary gestures. They had hunted with him, lived by his fire, and many of them had displayed real courage in the struggle with the kidnappers.

He murmured gently, "Rah, Wao and Olin are the allies of the Oulhamrs... But the Men-of-the-Fire have a long start of us, and they go swiftly... Aoun alone can overtake them."

Wao understood his signs and explained them to the others. Deep depression weighed down the Lemurians.

Wao wept and Rah made a sound like that of a wounded Dhole when Aoun began to ascend the slope. They accompanied him to the crest where the plateau began. The Oulhamr sped away like a wolf; the Lemurians shouted after him, and he halted a moment to console them, "The son of Urus will see the Hairy Men again!"

Then he resumed his course. At times the trail became uncertain, then it was strong again. At the spots where, owing to the fugitives having halted for some time, the earth was impregnated with their effluvia, the wanderer found grasses which Zouhr had held for a long time in his hand and then had thrown away: Aoun recognized the Wah's subtle ruse. He was surprised that the Chellians had not killed their prisoner, who, being less active than they were, must hinder their flight.

He only halted twice to rest, and then for a very short time, until the evening. Then he continued to seek the trail by the light of the Moon and stars. It grew ever more and more recent. When he lay down exhausted among the rocks however, he was still far from the fugitives.

He made the circuit of a little lake in the early dawn, and found himself back in the forest. More than once he was in doubt and missed the way, and towards midday, when he was about to rest, he was perturbed by a new discovery. The trail had become much plainer; a small hunting party had joined those who were carrying off Zouhr, doubling their number. Aoun could even distinguish the way by which the newcomers had arrived. There were now six adversaries to fight and no doubt he was approaching the territory of the horde.

To fight seemed to be impossible. No Oulhamr other than Aoun or Naoh would have continued the pursuit. The son of Urus was carried away by an instinct which was stronger than prudence, and he relied partly on his fleetness of foot, which equaled that of the wild ass; the short-legged Chellians would never be able to catch him.

The hours slipped by; the second day was declining when, despite the numbers of those he was pursuing, Aoun found he had lost the trail at the passage of a river. As it was quite shallow the wanderer had crossed it without difficulty, but on the other side there was no trail... He searched desperately: evening was far advanced and still he had discovered nothing. Then he sat down, tired out and wretched, with no courage left even to light a fire.

After a short rest, he started off once more. He traversed an uneven country where clear spaces alternated with woods, and here he became aware of slight odors, which a favorable wind rendered more intense. They were certainly the emanations of the Men-of-the-Fire and yet he seemed to perceive a difference. There was nothing to be betoken Zouhr's presence.

He picked his way carefully among the brushwood and the bamboos; crawled through the high grasses, and found himself close to those whom he sought... A menacing sound made him start; two human forms rose up whose presence he had not expected, for the wind had carried their smell in the opposite direction.

They had seen him. It was necessary to be prepared to fight. The Moon, already at the full, lit up the two forms vividly. He became aware that they were not men but women. Thick-set, short-legged, with the stout bodies and thick faces of the Chellians, they each held a long and heavy spear.

The Oulhamr women seldom bore arms. Although the wanderer had seen the Lemurian women almost equal to the males in strength, he was surprised to see these two forms in a threatening attitude. He felt no anger and spoke in friendly tones, "Aoun has not come to kill women."

They listened, their anxious faces cleared. Aoun began to laugh so as to further reassure them, then he advanced slowly, holding his club low. One of the women recoiled, and with a bound both of them took to flight, either from fear or in order to warn their companions. But their short legs could not compete with Aoun's long limbs: he caught them up and passed them... Then they waited side by side, their javelins pointed towards him.

He shook his club unconcernedly murmuring, "The club would easily break the javelins..."

With a movement in which there was more of fear than animosity, one of the women darted her weapon. Aoun turned it aside, and broke its point; then without retaliating he went on, "Why do you make war on the son of Urus?"

They understood that he had spared them and gazed at him abashed. The one who had not made use of her weapon, lowered her javelin and made signs of peace, which were soon repeated by the other. Then they resumed their way. Confident of his own powers and activity Aoun followed them. All three advanced against the wind to a distance of 4000 ells. They reached a place covered with ferns, where by the light of the Moon the wanderer became aware of the presence of more women... They had risen up when they saw the man, and were gesticulating and uttering cries, which were answered by the new arrivals.

For a time, Aoun feared a trap. He could have fled, the way was open, but fatigue, solitude and pain had made him listless. When anxiety awoke in him once more, he had already reached the camp, and the women had surrounded him.

There were twelve of them, including those that had brought in the wanderer; several children were among them, and two or three quite little ones lay asleep. Most of the women were young, heavily-built, with enormous jaws, but one of them fascinated Aoun because she had the flexible figure of the daughters of Gammla, the most beautiful among the Oulhamr. A dazzling mane flowed over her shoulders, her teeth shone like mother of pearl. A gentle and timid force penetrated the warrior's heart; brilliant memories awoke within him and united themselves to the fresh form of the stranger...

The women drew their circle closer. One of them, with brawny arms and shoulders, was face to face with the son of Urus. Energy seemed to exude from her sparkling eyes, and her muscular cheeks. He understood that she was offering to make an alliance with him, and as he knew of no race in which men and women form separate hordes, he looked around for the male members of the tribe. Not seeing any he made gestures of acquiescence. They then all laughed and followed this up by friendly signs, which he understood better than those of the Lemurians.

Nevertheless they remained much astonished. They had never before seen a warrior of such great stature or one whose speech was so different from their own. Their horde only knew three kinds of human beings: those who formed the hunting party whose prisoner Zouhr was; the Lemurians, whom they had seldom seen and whom they did not fight; and the beings of their own race, where the men and women did

not usually intermingle, and whose marriages were conse-
crated by fierce rites. Even if Aoun had belonged to their own
race, they would have rejected him or subjected him to hard
trials. They only accepted him because they were attracted by
the novelty of the adventure and because they were passing
through an inauspicious time. Half of them had perished in
consequence of various disasters or under the weapons of the
Chellians; most of the children had died.

In addition, having lost their fire, they wandered miserably on the earth, crushed by the sense of their downfall and
full of hatred against their enemies.

It was pleasant to them to have this tall stranger as an ally, for he seemed as strong as the gayals. After crowding
around him for a long time, trying to understand his gestures
and to teach him theirs, they finally understood that he was
seeking for a companion whose trail he had lost. It was a satisfaction to them to know that the Oulhamr's adversaries were
the same men that they themselves execrated. Aoun, guessing
that their fire had been put out, set himself to collect dry
grasses. With the help of twigs and his stones he brought the
flame to life. The younger ones leapt around him with enthusiastic cries, the words they pronounced, repeated in chorus,
making a kind of chant. When the red life spread to the
branches their cries became frenzied. Only the girl with the
fine cheeks did not lift up her voice: she contemplated the fire
and the wanderer in silent rapture, and when she spoke it was
in a timid and seductive manner.

XIII. At the End of the Lake

Every morning Aoun resumed his search for Zouhr's
trail. The women followed him, full of an ever-growing confidence. By dint of taking part in the same acts and exchanging
gestures they understood the Oulhamr's object quite clearly.
He too became familiar with their signs. His strength and ac-

234

tivity amazed them; they admired his weapons, especially his harpoons and spears, which killed animals at a distance. Weakened by misery and defeat, they rallied humbly around the stranger and liked to obey him. Their help was not to be despised. Four of them were more robust, lithe and swift than Zouhr; they were all capable of enduring great fatigue. Those who had little children could carry them all day without being tired. The boys and girls had the endurance of jackals.

Had it not been for the loss of Zouhr, their evenings would have been very pleasant. Every night, when Aoun struck sparks from the stones, the women showed the same ecstasy as on the first occasion, and their joy delighted the big Oulhamr. Above all he loved to watch Djeha, with her long beautiful hair, her bright eyes reflecting the flames: he dreamed of returning with her to his native horde; his heart began to beat...

At the end of a week the trees became still more sparse; a long steppe stretched out before them with only a few thickets, spinneys and brushwood to break the monotony.

They went forward in the hope of discovering a height from which they could scan the horizon. Towards midday, during the hour of rest, a woman who had wandered towards the east called the others. There was no need for explanations: they all recognized the traces of a fire.

"The Men-of-the-Fire!" said Aoun.

The women displayed great emotion. The one who was in command, Ouchr by name, turned towards Aoun with angry gestures: he understood that the Chellians were his companions' enemies. Not only had they been decimated by them, but no doubt the Chellians had also destroyed the male horde which was allied to the women, as it had not reappeared since the autumn.

The camp had been used several days before; there was no scent left to guide them. They took some time to assure themselves that it did not imply a numerous band; there was nothing to show that Zouhr was with them... Meanwhile, thanks to some slight indications, Aoun and the women were able to organize the pursuit. Little by little the trail became clearer: it was all the easier to follow because the Chellians were moving in an almost straight line towards the north. Twice the ashes of a fire showed that their presence had been recent.

On the third morning, a young woman who walked at the head of their band turned around with an exclamation. When Aoun came up with her he saw the print of many footsteps in the light soil: he trembled with joy when he recognized the trace of Zouhr's. Indeed the pursuit was becoming easy: the soil revealed emanations, a proof that they were gaining ground. That night they prolonged their march, although the Moon had not yet risen, for two of the women were nyctalopic, although to a less degree than the Lemurians. Their way was barred by a range of hills. They climbed halfway up the highest of these, and Aoun lit a fire in a dell, so that it might be invisible from a distance. The enemy's proximity demanded ever-increasing prudence.

Aoun had killed a swamp deer, and the women were busy roasting its quarters. The safety of their shelter, abundance of food, and the brilliant firelight, raised the spirits of the little horde. It was one of those happy interludes when human beings forget the cruel law of life and the snares of the world. Even the Oulhamr would have been blissfully happy had it not been for Zouhr's absence. Djeha of the fine eyes sat by him, and he thought vaguely that perhaps Ouchr, the woman chief, would give her to him in marriage. The rugged soul of the young Oulhamr was full of secret tenderness. When Djeha was near him he felt a dread which made his heart beat quicker: he wanted to be as gentle to his companion as Naoh was to Gammla.

When the children and those of the travelers who were most tired had fallen asleep after the evening meal, Aoun set out to climb the hill. Ouchr and Djeha rose to accompany him, as well as several of the other women warriors. It was not a difficult ascent, and they soon reached the crest of the hill. They had to go through some brushwood before they could see the other side. A long plain lay stretched out under the stars, and a lake shimmered almost at the foot of the slope.

At the northern end, but on the further shore, they saw the light of flames. Aoun's whole attention was concentrated on them. The fire lay about 4000 or 5000 ells distant in a straight line, but they would have to go around by the shore of the lake and perhaps avoid some obstacles.

The wind blew from the south. They would therefore be able to approach the camp without being discovered... They must get there before the Moon rose, and only Aoun was swift enough to accomplish this.

He looked earnestly at the fire and the figures, sometimes purple and sometimes black, which hovered around it. There were five of them: the son of Urus could distinctly see Zouhr seated by the side of the lake, and a seventh man lying on the ground.

Then he said to Ouchr, "Aoun will go to the Men-of-the-Fire and demand Zouhr's freedom..."

Ouchr understood and replied, "They will not give up the prisoner..."

The Oulhamr continued, "They took him away as a hostage, they were afraid of Aoun."

"They will dread him still more when they no longer have a hostage."

The wanderer remained undecided for a moment. He could see no other way by which he could deliver Zouhr than by cunning, violence or gentleness: in any case he must approach the Chellians' camp.

"Aoun must deliver his companion," he said darkly.

Ouchr agreed with him. She had nothing to say in reply. He added, "Aoun must go towards the fire!"

"Ouchr and the Wolf-Women will follow him!"

Aoun, after looking long at the plain, acquiesced, "The son of Urus will wait down there for the women to come," he said. "He will be alone, but the Men-of-the-Fire cannot reach him by running, and he can fight them at a distance!"

Ouchr commanded her youngest warrior to fetch rein-
forcements. The Oulhamr was already descending towards the
plain. It was an easy slope, almost level, without crevices and
covered with grass. When he reached the plain, the wind was
blowing the odors towards the north and the lie of the ground
favored his enterprise. The Moon was still hidden; he soon
found himself on the same bank as the Chellians, less than
1000 ells from the camp...

Clumps of trees, high grasses and low hillocks allowed
him to continue his way unobserved for 400 ells, but then he
had to face open ground. Nothing could further conceal his
movements from the piercing eyes of the enemy. A prey to
anxiety, not for himself but for Zouhr, he remained motionless
among the vegetation. Would the Chellians kill the Wah if
Aoun appeared suddenly, or would they on the contrary spare
his life, the better to preserve their own? If they offered them
his alliance would they mock him?

He waited for a long time. The Moon rose, red and mis-
ty, from the depths of the savannah. Five Chellians had lain
down on the ground. The sixth was watching, sometimes
standing up to listen, his mobile eyes and nostrils quivering.
Zouhr was awake also, at the other end of the little camp, near
the fire. The Chellian took hardly any notice of the prisoner,
who was neither strong nor active, and therefore could not
think of flight.

A project haunted Aoun's imagination. He knew that
Zouhr, so slow in running, was, like all the Men-without-
Shoulders, a clever swimmer. He could outstrip the most active Oulhamr in a river or a pool; he could dive like a crocodile and remain a long time under water. If he leapt into the
lake, he could reach the other shore, which at that point was
not very far off... Aoun would lure the enemy on to fight. It
would, however, be necessary that the Wah should see him
and understand his signal; the least alarm would make his rescue impossible.

Now the watcher looked chiefly towards the north, because of the wind. He turned his face every moment towards

the bush which concealed the son of Urus. The Moon rose ever-clearer, brighter and more steely. The wanderer's breast was bursting with the fury of his impatience, and he was almost in despair, when a loud roar reverberated from the direction of the south, and the form of a lion was outlined on a hillock. The watcher gave a great start; the Chellians stood up around the fire and turned their faces towards the carnivore...

Zouhr, almost motionless, was peering in all directions, full of the desire for rescue, which was rendered keener by all the vicissitudes he had gone through.

Suddenly Aoun showed himself, his hand stretched out towards the lake... The moment was propitious: a distance of 30 ells separated the Wah from the nearest of his captors. They were thinking only of the great brute.

The lake was 20 steps from Zouhr. If he started promptly he could reach it before any of the Chellians.

Zouhr had seen the outstretched hand. Uncertain and puzzled, he walked furtively towards the bush. Aoun again pointed towards the lake; the Wah understood and began to walk carelessly in the direction of the water, then his step changed and with great bounds he leapt towards the bank.

Just as he flung himself into the water one of the Chellians turned around. He was more surprised than anxious, he only gave the alarm when he saw the Wah striking out for the opposite shore. Two warriors gave chase, and one of them tried to catch Zouhr by swimming after him. When he found he could not overtake him, he returned to the bank and began to fling stones at him. Zouhr, having dived, was invisible.

The lion's proximity paralyzed the resolution of the band. One man alone was sent in pursuit. He thought that by running around the end of the lake he must inevitably meet Zouhr, who would be an easy capture, for he was unarmed, slow and weak of muscle.

Aoun, seeing the warrior come towards him, laughed silently and withdrew. He remained invisible for a little while, then an open bit of ground revealed him to the enemy. He waited with his spear held high in the air...

The Chellian was one of those who had fought in the stormy night. He recognized with great alarm the big wanderer who had killed his chief, and with a loud outcry he beat a retreat.

Aoun, who was anxious about Zouhr's fate, did not attempt to pursue him. He directed his steps to the end of the lake and went around the point. The Wah had not yet landed; he could see him swimming like a reptile with writhing movements. When he reached him the son of Urus lifted him up with joyful murmurs, and they remained looking at each other, dumb with the joy of his deliverance.

At last the Oulhamr shouted his triumph, "Aoun and Zouhr mock the Men-of-the-Fire."

Meanwhile the lion had disappeared. For a moment the Chellians continued to watch the hillock, then, at a sign from their chief, they directed their steps towards the north.

"They are more active than Zouhr," said the Wah sadly, "their chief is as strong as a leopard!"

"Aoun does not fear him…and we have allies."

He dragged his companion along with him, and when the pursuers arrived at the turn of the shore a clamor arose from the hill. Ouchr and seven other Wolf-Women had appeared; the Chellians, discouraged, gave up the pursuit.

The women came down to Aoun, and Ouchr said, "If we do not kill the Dhole-Men they will return with their horde."

The Oulhamr understood her after she had repeated her gestures and phrases.

"Have they spoken of their horde?" he asked the Wah.

"It is two long days' marches from here," Zouhr replied, and after gazing at the women he added, "If we attack them they will kill many of the women, and some of them will doubtless succeed in escaping."

Aoun's blood boiled, but the fear of again losing his companion prevailed, and he also had a benevolent feeling towards the Chellians because they had not killed their captive.

XIV. The Flight from the Chellians

Aoun, Zour and the women were fleeing. They had been chased by the Chellian horde for more than a week. A woman had noticed them first, and Aoun, stationed on a high rock, had counted 30 men. The fugitives' march was delayed by the Wah, who could not go fast, but Ouchr knew of winding ways through the forest where Zouhr, aided by the marshy land, invented stratagems to lead the enemy astray. Every time they came across a shallow water course, they walked up or down its bed for some distance; on several occasions Ouchr and Aoun set fire to the dried grasses through which they had passed. So the Chellians lost their trail: but they were numerous and obstinate, and dispersed in different directions to find it again. On the eighth day, the band crossed the torrent on the bank of which Aoun had left the Lemurians. The Oulhamr would have liked to go up stream, but Ouchr pointed out a safer way, and they turned again towards the south of the plateau.

The day of the new moon came, and they had not seen the Chellians. Their halt that day was a happy one. It was in the jungle, for gradually the fugitives had neared the plain and were approaching the river. Enormous bamboos surrounded the open space. There was still daylight, and men and women were busy cutting wood for the fire, and constructing a refuge with thorns, creepers and saplings. A red glow succeeded the amber light; a fine mist rose towards the clouds; wind murmured in the luxuriant vegetation and Aoun's soul was full of solemn yet gentle feeling. The same weakness that caused him to spare the life of his vanquished foes, made him tender in his manner towards Djeha of the supple shoulders. His strength became feeble in the presence of her magnificent hair and the wonderful light in her eyes; her timidity was more intoxicating to him than victory. Fleeting dreams came to him, which he did not understand. Sometimes, when he reflected that

241

Ouchr's consent was necessary, and the possibility of a refusal crossed his mind, the violent spirit of the Oulhamr possessed him and shook his whole being. In reality, however, he was prepared to submit himself to the customs of these women, who shared his perils.

When the stars came out above the bamboos, he went to the woman chief, who was finishing her repast, and asked, "Will Ouchr give me Djeha to wife?"

When Ouchr understood she was undecided. The laws of her race were very old, and by dint of repetition they had acquired strength and preciseness. The women of the horde were not to unite themselves with the Chellians or the Lemurians. Disaster, however, had engendered profound uncertainty. Ouchr did not know if any men of their race still existed. And Aoun was her ally.

She answered, "This is what we will do: first we must escape from our enemies; then Ouchr will strike Djeha on the chest, and she shall be Aoun's wife."

The Oulhamr only understood a part of this reply; fervent joy took possession of his heart. He did not notice that Ouchr was sad; she did not understand why he preferred this lithe young girl to the woman chief, of the muscular hands and heavy jaws...

They continued their flight next day, and the day after that. They were now quite close to the river. A line of rocks appeared, like those where the giant feline had his lair. There was nothing to indicate the presence of their enemies; even Ouchr began to think they had given up the pursuit. In order to make quite sure, she clambered up a high rock with Aoun and Zouhr, from which a good view of the surrounding country could be obtained. When they reached the top they saw the river winding around a bend between two steppes, then, still further off, some human beings on the edge of a jungle, who were advancing towards them.

"The Dhole-Men!" said Ouchr.

Aoun made sure that their number had not diminished, and said, "They are not following our trail."

"They will find it," said Ouchr.

Zouhr added reflectively, "We must cross the river!"

It was an attempt in which even the strongest swimmers could hardly hope to succeed; crocodiles abounded in the mud, on the islands and about the promontories. The Wahs, however, possessed the art of crossing water by means of big branches and split trunks of trees, bound together by creepers and withies. Zouhr led the troop down to the bank of the river, where black poplar-trees abounded. Two trunks stranded in a cove made their work more rapid. Before midday the raft was ready, but the enemy was near. They could see their advance-guard at the turn of the river, 3000 or 4000 paces off. When their improvised raft left the bank, the Chellians set up a great clamor. Aoun answered them with his war-cry, and the women howled like wolves. The fugitives drifted obliquely from the shore. As they were being taken downstream they got closer to their enemies, and the two bands found themselves at last face to face. They were separated by a distance of only about 200 ells. The Chellians were assembled on a promontory, to the number of 29, all thickset, with Dhole-like jaws and muscular hands. Their round eyes were lit up by a violently ferocious light. Several of them made as if they would throw themselves into the water and swim after the raft, but a python and several crocodiles appeared among the lotus leaves.

Meanwhile Aoun and Zouhr and the women, with the aid of branches, changed the course of the raft. It passed between two islands, spun around, returned for a moment towards the bank where the Dhole-Men were standing, then took a south-westerly course… Ultimately it went aground on the opposite bank, and the women shouted insults at the Chellians.

The band plunged into the jungle until it was stopped by a tributary of the river. It was a shallow water course, the bed of which was easy to walk in. But before they started Zouhr made them cut the skin of a swamp deer into pieces, and he explained that when they left the river bed, each of them was to wrap up their feet in the bits of skin. They disembarked on a rocky cape and having all of them wrapped up their feet, they splashed water over their halting place.

"Zouhr, is the most cunning among men!" exclaimed the Oulhamr... "The Dhole-Men will think a herd has passed here!"

The Chellians had however so often recovered the trail that the fugitives thought it wise to walk on until nightfall without stopping.

XV. In the Defile

The ground became marshy. They had to plunge through mud, or toil along the bank. For two days the fugitives advanced no faster than creeping beasts. Then the river was locked between steep banks, and an enormous wall of schist barred their way. It was 3000 ells long, and 600 high; to the west it rose out of the river, and on the east it was rooted in an impenetrable marsh. There was only one outlet, a narrow defile which was hollowed out at a height of 200 ells, and access to which was gained by slopes interspersed with reddish masses of rock. Aoun, who was walking at the rear of the band, came to the entry of the pass, and stopped to consider the place. Meanwhile Ouchr had gone on. She soon returned and announced, "The marsh spreads out on the other side of the rock."

"We must cross the river again," said the Wah, who had followed the woman chief. "There are trees, we can make a raft."

Aoun gave an exclamation, and stretched out his hand. Men had appeared below them, between two pools. There were seven in number, and their appearance was too characteristic to leave any doubt as to their identity.

"The Dhole-Men!" cried Ouchr.

Their number continued to increase. Aoun's chest swelled. He sniffed the feverish breath of the marsh waters and gazed at the abyss.

"Long before the raft is built," he said, "the Dhole-Men will be upon us!"

Heavy stones lay around him. He rolled several of them to the entrance of the pass, while Ouchr, the Wah and the women carried others... Between the two pools, they saw the Chellians crawling along. Death lay in the advance of those somber figures.

Aoun said, "The son of Urus and three women will defend the pass. Zouhr and the other women will build the raft."

The Wah hesitated. He fixed his trembling eyes on his companion. The other, understanding his fear, added, "There are four spears, and two harpoons. I have my club and the women their javelins. If we are not strong enough, I will ask for assistance. Go, only the raft can save us."

Zouhr gave way. Aoun chose Ouchr and another deep-chested woman to remain with him. When he turned around to choose a third, he saw Djeha, who advanced towards him shaking her hair. He wished to put her aside, but she looked at him with eager gentleness. Love was upon him, the tender choice which, among the Oulhamrs, only Naoh had experienced. The old story repeated itself; he forgot peril and death.

The Dhole-Men approached. Having threaded their way between the pools they spread out over the rocky bank. One of them, whose body was as hairy as that of a bear, displayed enormous arms; he wielded without difficulty a spear which was heavier than Aoun's club. They scattered as they approached the mass of rocks, so as to discover a way round. There were several gullies hollowed out of the mass, but they all ended in perpendicular walls of rock; the defile seemed to be the only way out.

Aoun, Ouchr, Djeha and the third woman were completing its fortification; they also collected boulders with which to crush the assailants. There were two ways of gaining access to

245

the pass: either directly by the bed of the water course through which the spring and autumn rains made their way, or obliquely through a labyrinth of boulders. The direct way would allow of an assault three or four men deep; the roundabout way forced the besiegers to adventure themselves one by one, but the attack could be made from above on those below...

The Chellians stopped 100 ells from the rock. They watched the movements of Aoun and the women; their large faces mocked them and their blue lips showed brilliant white teeth. Suddenly they set up a lugubrious howling, which was reminiscent of the howling of wolves and Dholes. Aoun displayed his harpoon and his club!

"The Oulhamrs will take the Men-of-the-Fire's hunting grounds from them!"

Ouchr joined her hoarse voice to that of the son of Urus; she cried, "The Dhole-Men have massacred our brothers and sisters. Our allies will destroy the Dhole-Men down to the very last..."

Then there was a long silence. A warm damp wind came up from the marshes. Eagles and vultures hovered over the crests. Monstrous gavials could be seen on the islands; the sound of the river was heard in the vast solitude, fresh, living and unending as in the first days of the world...

The Chellians divided into two bands. The chief led the first among the maze of boulders; the others tried to reach the defile by the direct way, hiding themselves in the fissures and behind boulders...

Aoun's sparkling eyes counted the enemy. He lifted up his bow ready strung; Ouchr and her companions, at the first signal, were to stone the assailants... But they remained invisible or only appeared among obstacles which made it almost impossible to hit them. A Chellian did however show himself; the bow twanged and an arrow pierced his ribs. Hoarse shouts were heard; the wounded man disappeared... Aoun was on the alert and was ready with a second arrow.

Soon they returned to the attack, especially those who were trying to make their way by the indirect road, where several warriors had reached the height of the defile. They could not be seen. To carry out their plan they would have to get even higher and scale a narrow ledge, from which they could jump down one by one...

Meanwhile the direct way was invaded; a powerful voice thundered and 15 men hurled themselves forward in a furious dash. Arrows whistled, boulders were pushed down and rebounded, ferocious and plaintive cries re-echoed from the rocks... The Chellians had not been arrested in their course. Despite endless stones hurled at them and the flinging of a spear, they succeeded in getting to within eight ells of the pass. Three had rolled down into the ravine, two others were wounded; Aoun saw the mass of faces coming ever-nearer to him; he could see the fire in their eyes and their panting breath. Then with a desperate effort he flung an enormous boulder, while the women made the stones roll wildly. A lugubrious howling resounded from the rocks; the besiegers retired falling over each other, and Aoun was about to detach another boulder when a stone hit him on the skull.

He lifted his head; a face surmounted by red hair mocked him; four forms bounded down in quick succession. Aoun had fallen back. He held his club in both hands. Ouchr and Djeha brandished their javelins. There was room for three pairs of combatants to meet face to face.

There was a momentary truce. Fear of the stranger kept the Dhole-Men motionless; Aoun pondered whether he should call for help... He was confronted by the enemy chief, who stood before him a picture of massive strength. His javelin was an ell longer than that of his companions; power and the habit of victory seemed to exhale from his whole being...

He began the attack and his javelin tore Ouchr's side. But Aoun, with a weighty blow, beat down his weapon, and his club crushed the shoulder of a warrior who had sprung forward to assist his chief.

The man fell to the ground, and was at once replaced by another; new assailants came up from behind. Then Ouchr gave the cry for help, which was repeated by Djeha and the other woman, while the Chellians flung themselves upon them with wolf-like growls. The son of Urus struck down three javelins in as many strokes, breaking two of their points; Ouchr wounded a Dhole-Man in the chest, but the third woman sank down with a deep wound in her body...

The aggressors had recoiled before the colossal club. They were massed at the entrance to the pass; the chief with uplifted spear, stood an ell's length in front of his men, the places of those whose weapons were damaged being taken by others.

With a fierce laugh and grinding his teeth, while his piercing eyes kept watch on every moment of his adversary, the Chellian chief charged. The Oulhamr avoided him, but the javelin tore his thigh and he stumbled; the chief gave a victorious cry... He was answered by the club. The thick skull of the tawny man was cracked; he fell backwards with a hoarse cry into the arms of his companions.

For a moment the Chellians hesitated; but their numbers continued to grow, and they charged again. The terrible club broke the points of their javelins and crushed their chests; Ouchr and Djeha fought without ceasing. They were forced to give way however, being outnumbered, and they were nearing the point where the defile grew wider and the Chellians' attack would become more effective.

The son of Urus succeeded by an immense effort in breaking the javelins on every side of him, and the enemy became motionless ... A furious clamor arose from the other end of the defile, the Wolf-Women appeared; twice Zouhr's bow twanged and his arrows were imbedded in the shoulders of the enemy. Aoun raised his club for a supreme blow.

Panic set in; the Dholes retired in a mass, dragging their wounded and even their dead with them; they overthrew boulders, rolled down the slope, took refuge among the rugged rocks and fissures. Only one dead man and one wounded one, who was groaning miserably, were left upon the ground. The women finished him off...

Uncertainty kept the besieged motionless at the entrance to the defile. The Chellians had once more become invisible; dead bodies lay among the blocks of schist.

Then the women became elated by victory. They stooped over the boulders, they shouted wildly. Aoun, despite his wounds, was filled with a proud joy. Was it not he who had broken the shock of the javelins, struck down the chief and spread terror among the Dhole-Men? He had also saved Djeha from the javelin which was about to pierce her breast; his look met that of the woman warrior and a subtle emotion mingled with his triumph, in the presence of those beautiful dark eyes and that magnificent hair, which was more beautiful than the finest plants of the savannah or the jungle...

The Wah said, "Zouhr and the women have found wood in abundance... The raft is almost finished."

"It is well! The son of Urus will remain with six Wolf women to defend the defile... Zouhr will finish the raft with the others."

A sound of lamentation arose. The wounded woman felt a mysterious horror creeping over her, the icy breath of complete nothingness. Turning her dilated eyes towards the heavens, she saw great vultures and white-headed crows hovering over the dead bodies... Her small and narrow soul swelled with an immense desire. The forests and clear dawns passed before her eyes, the days of abundant life, the evenings when the fire shed its warm life around it. The memory of the past was hers, that memory which is born of speech and resuscitates the days which have been spent, a possession which the gaurs, the Dholes and the lions do not enjoy. For a moment she experienced bitter regret, the burning fever of remembrance. Then she became unconscious. The flash of insight which had laid death bare before her had faded away. She was only a dull animal which goes out, leaving the vast world undisturbed, and her face became rigid. Her companions set up a solemn wail, a confused melody which foreshadowed the rhythm and songs of a later humanity.

Time passed. It seemed as if the Chellians had disappeared, but Aoun heard them moving on his left, and knew that they were making their way over the crests to cut off his retreat at the other end of the pass. If they succeeded their victory would be certain. Despite their losses they were still superior in numbers, strength and agility. The Oulhamr alone dominated them, and among the women Ouchr alone equaled one of their warriors; but Ouchr and Aoun were weakened by their wounds. The Oulhamr listened with growing anxiety to the enemy's movements.

At last several Chellians became visible. They had reached to within five ells of a ledge, sometimes by climbing on their companions' shoulders, sometimes by hollowing out steps in the friable schist. To reach the ledge it would only be necessary to cut five or six more steps on a smooth slightly inclined slope. They began to cut the two first. Aoun flung his last spear in order to stop them, but the weapon ricocheted from a projection; he also threw some stones but the distance rendered them innocuous.

A direct attack appeared to be impossible. The struggle lay between those who were building the raft and those who were cutting the steps. As no attack on the defile was imminent, Aoun sent back two of the women to hurry on the Wah's work.

The third step and then the fourth was cut. One more and the Dhole-Men would reach the ledge from which they could storm the crest. The last step appeared to be more difficult to cut than the others, but already a Chellian, mounted on the shoulders of one of his companions, was at work upon it.

Then Aoun said to those who waited with him, "Go and rejoin Zouhr. The raft must be finished... Aoun will defend the passage alone!"

Ouchr, having scrutinized the rocks, called the other women; Djeha cast a supplicating look towards Aoun and went off with a faint wail... Bending over the crenelated top, he threw stones, without being able to stop the Chellians. The work was finished. The first warrior dragged himself up to the ledge and was followed by another. Even the chief, who had been stupefied by Aoun's club, crawled along the schist. Aoun reached the other end of the pass in a few bounds, and went down to the river. The first Chellians were already swarming over the crest.

"The raft is not finished," said Zouhr, "but it will bear us to the other bank."

At a sign from Aoun, the women seized the extemporized interwoven mass of branches and creepers, and took it down to the river. A prolonged shout was heard: the Chellians were coming... The women hustled one another onto the raft, and the enemy was only 50 ells away when Aoun and Zouhr followed them.

"Before eight mornings are past we shall have annihilated the Dholes!" growled the son of Urus as the water carried their raft away.

XVI. The Return to the Cave

The raft drifted. The eddies of the stream made it turn around and around, or else the current carried it away with alarming swiftness. Several times the Wolf-Women had flung themselves into the water to lighten the raft which, being hastily constructed, was in danger of breaking up. But this expedient had to be abandoned on account of the crocodiles.

Meanwhile they approached the further bank. Far away in the distance they could see the forms of the Chellians. They would have to cross the river in order to continue the pursuit, and they could not do so in any other manner than that which the fugitives had employed.

Aoun said to Zouhr, "We must walk till evening. Before four days are over we shall have reached the cave."

They looked at each other; the same thought was at work in both their brains.

"Aoun and Ouchr are wounded," said the Wah sadly.

The Oulhamr replied, "If we do not get ahead of them the Dhole-Men will exterminate us!"

Ouchr shrugged her shoulders disdainfully; her wound was slight. She picked some herbs which she laid upon her hurt, while Zouhr dressed that of his companion. Then the little band moved on again. The road lay through marshy ground and was very rough, but towards evening Aoun and Zouhr began to recognize it. The following day and the one after passed without alarms; they were two days' march from the chain of basalt rocks; Zouhr multiplied devices to hide their trail. On the fifth morning the chain of basalt rocks appeared. From the top of a hill, near a bend of the river, they made out the long crenelated ridge. Aoun, who was shivering, fixed his ardent eyes on the dark mass and seized the Wah's shoulder murmuring, "We shall see the tiger of the Kzamms again!"

A low laugh distended his lips. The refuge in which they had passed days of security, the enormous beast who was their friend, the clear mornings, and the evenings when the red light of the fire played about the platform, came back to him in incoherent and happy pictures... The great Oulhamr turned his face, emaciated by loss of blood, towards Djeha and said, "We can brave 100 Dhole-Men in the cave."

Ouchr gave a stifled exclamation. She pointed downstream and they all distinctly saw the Chellians 700 or 800 ells away. They resumed their flight as rapidly as the wounds of the Oulhamr and the woman chief would allow. If they did not reach the chain of rocks before their enemies, they could not save themselves. There were at least 20,000 ells to cover.

They had gone half the distance, but the Chellians had gained 4000 ells. They were swarming like jackals. The man they dreaded most among their enemies was weakened by his wound: they saw him limping along behind the little band and they shouted their war-cry in joyful triumph.

There was a short halt. Aoun fixed his eyes on Zouhr, mental as well as physical fever burnt in them. In that terrible moment the Oulhamr held back the Wah by his shoulder...

But the howls came nearer; Aoun looked at Djeha, bowed his head towards his bleeding thigh, and measured the distance which separated him from the Dhole-Men.

He loosed Zouhr's shoulder with a great sigh, his companion bounded towards the giant feline's lair, while Aoun conducted the women and children to the cave.

XVII. The Giant Feline

When they reached the cave's mouth, Aoun and the women were only 2000 ells in advance of their enemies. He climbed up to the platform first, with Ouchr, to organize the escalade; then the others arrived in succession. First the children were hauled up; the women followed; the last three were already halfway up when the Dhole-Men threw a shower of sharp stones. They rebounded from the rock. Aoun brandished his last spear; Ouchr and her companions threw stones. The Chellians were still too few in number to attempt an assault, so they retired out of reach of the projectiles, and when the rear guard came up, the Wolf-Women were all safely in the cave.

It was impregnable. One man or one woman alone could reach the ledge at a time; after that they would have to climb on their companions' shoulders. One or two javelin thrusts would defeat each attempt.

The Chellians understood this. They were examining the chain of rocks in the hope of finding another way, but all around the cave the wall of rock was uncompromisingly unscaleable.

The Dhole-Men did not care. They had only to wait. Hunger and thirst would yield up the besieged to them. Down at the defile they had been able to escape and cross the river. Death would be their portion the day they attempted to leave the cave. What could 11 women and two men do against 20 stalwart warriors?

When the women were in safety, Aoun placed two of them to watch on the platform and forbade anyone to follow him. Then, having lit a torch, he went down to the deep cavern. He was tortured by anxiety. He thought it was impossible that the giant feline should not have recognized Zouhr, and yet he doubted.

Halfway down the sound of a growl hurried his footsteps. The fissure was there, through which he had so often spied upon the beast... Suddenly he breathed freely; he had seen Zouhr by the side of the carnivore, two enormous eyes glowed, and a halting whisper greeted the Oulhamr.

"The lion of the rocks is still the ally of the son of Earth and the son of Urus," said the Wah.

It was a moment of dull joy and vast hopes.

"The Dhole-Men have not followed Zouhr's trail?"

"They did not see him separate himself from the others: Zouhr had hidden himself among the boulders."

After having sniffed at Aoun for a long time, the giant feline lay down again and began to go to sleep.

Aoun resumed, "Zouhr will only go out at night, with the Kzamm tiger...he will attempt nothing against the Dhole-Men till Aoun is strong again... In the daytime Zouhr will only go as far as the pool...the pool is near... Aoun and the women will need water."

Aoun sighed. He saw the pool, the river and springs. He was parched with thirst, which was increased by his wounds. He could not help saying, "Aoun is burnt up with thirst...but he will wait till evening."

"The pool is close!" Zouhr repeated. "Aoun must drink in order to get well again. I will go to the pool."

He went towards the entrance to the den. The giant feline hardly opened its eyes, for it scented nothing unusual. Zouhr glided to the pool. The lie of the land rendered him invisible from a distance. First he drank, then he dipped a primitive leather bottle into the water. It was made of antelope skin and the upper part was fastened together with thorns. It contained sufficient liquid to quench the thirst of several men. Zouhr

254

filled it and got back to the den. Aoun drank the life-giving water in long draughts, and his energy, freshness and confidence returned.

"Ouchr is wounded also," he said, "the others can drink tonight."

He carried the leather bottle into the upper cave, but, when Ouchr had drunk, he gave some of the water to Djeha also.

He slept till evening, and his strength and youth worked for him while he slept. The fever decreased, and his wound, which only required rest, began to heal. When the twilight had died down over the jungle, Aoun rose so as to spy out what the Chellians were doing. They had lit a big fire; their thick faces were turned towards the chain of rocks; it was easy to see that they were obstinate in their determination to conquer and destroy.

The women were racked with agony. Tired out by their long flight they too had slept. They were awoken by a terrible thirst more than by hunger. All turned their distressed eyes towards the Oulhamr, and thought of the water which he had brought in the skin bottle, of which only Ouchr and Djeha had had a share. The confidence of the weak in the strong alternated with fear.

Ouchr asked, "Where has Zouhr gone to?"

The son of Urus replied, "Zouhr will bring us meat and water before the night is over."

"Why is he not with us?"

"Ouchr will know that later."

He added, noticing that the woman chief turned toward the darkness, "Aoun alone will go down to the depths of the cave! Otherwise we shall be hungry and thirsty."

Their feeble brains were at first excited by the mystery, then the women became resigned. It was sufficient that Aoun had given them hope. All the Wolf-Women had experienced times of scarcity and want, all, even the children, had endured long privations and dreadful periods of suspense.

The stars in the sky continued their eternal course and the Dhole-Men slept. Most of the women had gone to sleep again; even Aoun was resting.

Towards midnight the sound of a call came up from the abyss and woke the Oulhamr. He lit a torch and went down. The giant feline and the Wah had returned from hunting; the carcass of an enormous swamp deer lay on the floor of the den. The Man-without-Shoulders had already cut off a haunch, which he passed up through the fissure, then he went to get a first leather bottle full of water...

When Aoun returned with the meat and water there was excitement among the women and a confused re-awakening of hero worship. The cave still contained some wood, left there by the two companions before their exodus. Aoun, after having gone back to fetch more water, lit a fire and had the venison cooked. It was an imprudent defiance. The Chellian watchers informed their chief, who stood up stupefied. The thing was too complex for him. He guessed that there had been wood in the cave, but he thought the flesh must have been that of an animal killed during their flight. Had there been a second entrance the fugitives would have escaped by it... To make sure he sent some warriors to the other side of the chain of rocks.

They went around the southern spur and tried to make out the crevices and caverns by the light of the Moon. They found nothing but narrow fissures, small crevices and one or two places of shelter under overhanging rocks. They were stopped for some time by the deep gully by which Zouhr had escaped from the lion; when they had passed it they saw a dark cavern... A strong smell was wafted to them on the night breeze; the warriors realized that a wild beast was near and halted. Their own scent spread towards the den. A massive form advanced towards them, a loud roar shook the air, and the terrified warriors fled wildly, having recognized the presence of the most dreaded of the carnivores.

The chief was confirmed in his opinion that no other outlet was open to the besieged besides the one which his warriors were watching. If any doubt remained in his mind it was dissipated during the following days, for Aoun and the women showed themselves at regular times on the platform: therefore flight was impossible. He needed only to wait and watch. He prepared for the hour to come when he could massacre them all.

The Oulhamr's recovery was rapid: his hot blood quickly healed his wound, the fever had disappeared and he spent his time teaching the women to sharpen the stones which served them as missiles. Below, in the cave, Zouhr continued to provide the refugees with meat and water. He accustomed the giant feline to follow him: the beast, obscurely conscious of the useful cunning of the man, consented to be guided. Zouhr foresaw its impulses, and guessed what its actions would be according to circumstances; he fathomed the shades of its moods, and conformed himself to them with so much cleverness that the wild beast attached itself to the Wah more surely than it would have done to one of its own species.

On the eighth night, Aoun having gone down to take the meat said, "My wound has healed. The son of Urus can now fight the Dhole-Men. Tomorrow night Zouhr will bring the Kzamms tiger to the other side of the rocks."

The Wah remained silent for a time. Then he replied, "Listen!... Zouhr noticed this morning that one of the stones in the fissure shook. If we could pull it out, the opening would be large enough to let a man pass, and too narrow for the lion of the rocks to get through."

He put his hand on the lowest projecting stone and shaking it, caused it to oscillate. First it moved almost imperceptibly, but gradually it gained in impetus... Aoun, full of admiration, joined his efforts to those of the Wah: his muscular arm made the stone rock. Then he pulled with all his strength, while Zouhr pushed with both hands. First one fragment became detached, then two others. The Oulhamr threw them behind him, and lying flat on the ground penetrated into the den. The giant feline, impatient of this commotion, had ceased to devour his prey. He sprang up in a manner that was almost menacing; but a caress from Zouhr at once appeased him and he sniffed Aoun amicably.

"We can surprise the Dhole-Men," cried the Oulhamr.

The Wah showed him, at the entrance to the cave, a dozen javelins which he had fashioned during his long solitary days, "We will fight them at a distance," he said.

On the following day, Aoun and Zouhr made two more javelins, so that their total number was 14. At twilight, the Oulhamr said to Ouchr and her companions, "Aoun and Zouhr will fight the Dhole-Men tonight! Let the Wolf-Women hold themselves in readiness..."

Ouchr heard with astonishment, "How will Aoun and Zouhr meet?" she asked.

He began to laugh, "We have enlarged the passage between two caves... We will pass to the other side of the rocks and we will attack the Dhole-Men with our ally,"

"Aoun and Zomhr have an ally?"

"They have made an alliance with the tiger of the Kzamms!"

Ouchr listened, stupefied. Her soul being simple she did not long attempt to understand. Her confidence in the great Oulhamr was stronger than all possible surprise.

The warrior went on, "The women must not come down to the plain until they hear Aoun call! The tiger would tear them in pieces."

Djeha, who was more surprised than the other women, turned her eyes, bright with curiosity, towards Aoun, "Cannot the tiger pass from one cave to the other?" she asked.

"The entrance is too small for him!" was the reply.

The wonderful afterglow began to fade in the sky; a pale star began to twinkle. Aoun went down to the lower cave.

The Chellians' fire now only shed an uncertain light. Three men however still watched. The others were asleep in a rocky enclosure which made them safe from all surprises. Two of the watchers were dozing; the third, obeying the orders of his chief, prowled around the fire, and lifted his eyes often towards the cave.

The Chellian had just thrown some small branches on the embers, when looking up he caught sight of a form on the ledge. It was a woman. She bent over the ledge watching him. The warrior stretched out his hand, armed with a javelin, towards her and mocked her silently. His laugh however quickly ceased. At the base of the chain of rocks another human form had come into view, whose tall stature and broad chest it was impossible to mistake. The Dhole-Man considered it for some rime in speechless amazement, and asked himself how the man had dared to descend to the plain. He called the other watchers, who all three brandished their weapons and shouted their alarm cry.

Aoun now left the rocks. He boldly approached the fire, and when he was within range he flung a pointed stone. It hit one of the watchers on the head, making only a slight wound, for the Oulhamr had thrown it from too far away. Another stone grazed the shoulder of another warrior.

Vociferous cries resounded, and dusky forms surged from the rocky enclosure on all sides... Then Aoun rose to his full height and replied by giving his war-cry. There was a short pause, during which the Chellians alternately considered the Oulhamr and the place. Two women had now joined the other on the ledge; Aoun alone, and armed only with his club and a few stones, was to be seen upon the plain. The bewildered Dhole chief tried in vain to understand; his certainty that Aoun was alone was blended with vague distrust. The instinct of war triumphed; a guttural voice gave the order to attack and they flung themselves forward. Twenty active bodies converged upon the son of Urus.

He threw one last stone, then took to flight. His pace seemed to have diminished; the swiftest among his pursuers were gaining upon him, and the others, excited by the imminence of the capture, followed with great rapidity. At times it seemed as if the Oulhamr stumbled; sometimes again he appeared to make a great effort to gain ground, which he immediately lost. The chief was only 30 ells from the fugitive when he approached the spur which terminated the chain of rocks.

The Chellians howled with triumph... Aoun, with a sort of lamentation, swerved and took refuge among the rocks. They formed a series of gullies, which all ended, towards the south, in a wider pass.

The chief stopped, threw a rapid glance around, and commanded several warriors to bar the other outlet while he sent eight men in direct pursuit.

A fierce laugh rang out, then a roar, and a huge body sprang down among the rocks.

"The Dhole-Men are about to die!"

The giant feline was already upon the Chellians. Three men fell, their bodies ripped up, a fourth rolled on the ground his throat torn open...

Aoun and Zouhr had climbed a flat rock; their bows twanged; arrows pierced the enemy's chests, their thighs and shoulders, while the carnivore emerged from the rocks, crushed one fugitive and tore another to pieces.

Panic seized the Dhole-Men. Bewildering mystery mingled with the horror of death in their dull brains. The chief himself fled. Aoun had regained his full strength. Bounding like a leopard he overtook the rear guard, and his club crashed on their hard heads...

When the Chellians got back to the circle of rocks there were only eight of them left: the others lay stretched on the grass, either dead or incapable of taking any further part in the struggle.

"Let Zouhr stop the tiger of the Kzamms," cried Aoun.

Sheltered in their stronghold, the vanquished men again became formidable. Despair was upon them; wielded between the crenelations their spears might kill the brute.

The giant feline allowed himself to be restrained. He saw his prey scattered all around. He calmly seized a dead body in his jaw and went towards his den.

For a little while uncertainty held the son of Urus motionless. Then he said, "Zouhr will accompany the Kzamm tiger. He will then come back by the higher cave and tell the women to hold themselves in readiness!"

The Wah and the giant feline disappeared behind the rocks: Aoun began to pick up the spears and to withdraw them from the bodies, then he went slowly towards the Chellians. He caught sight of them between the interstices of their wall; he could have killed several of them, but the soul of Naoh was in him, full of deep pity: "Why did the Dhole-Men attack the Hairy Men... Why did they want to kill Aoun and the Wolf-Women?"

His ringing voice had a sad tone in it; the Chellians listened to him in silence. The deep chested chief rose up between two boulders and made as if he would attack him. The Oulhamr lifted his bow and went on, "Aoun is stronger and quicker than the Dhole chief! And he can kill him at a distance."

Up above them the women were uttering shouts of triumph. They had watched the vicissitudes of the struggle, the extraordinary apparition of the wild beast, and their souls were full of mystic confidence. Djeha was the first to go down, then Ouchr, then the others, except one who stayed to guard the cave.

They clustered around Aoun, and gazed at the rocky circle with somber interest; remembering their sufferings they cast insults at the Chellians. The Dhole-Men remained silent, but they were strong and resolute, holding their long spears in readiness. Their position was impregnable; without Aoun's presence, they would have been the strongest. With the exception of Ouchr, not one of the women could have resisted their attack; they knew it, and despite their hate, moved about with great caution.

When the Wolf-Women drew nearer the fire, however, they took pleasure in throwing branches, brushwood and grass on it. It soon revived and the flames leapt up magnificently. The women brought wood from all directions, crying, "The Dhole-Men dare not fight! They will die of hunger and thirst!"

Gradually, as the stars turned towards their setting, or rose in the east, anxiety and impatience began to grow. The besieged appeared more formidable. The besiegers feared a

261

trap; none of the women dared sleep... Even Aoun and Zouhr began to think it would be necessary to fight.

The Wah said, "We must force the Dhole-Men to leave their refuge."

By dint of hard thinking an idea had come to him.

"They cannot resist fire... Aoun, Zouhr and the women will fling flaming brands at them!" he said.

The Oulhamr gave an enthusiastic cry. Both of them began to cut branches and expose their points to the flames. Then they called the women, and the Wah having explained the proposed stratagem to them, they all took burning brands in their hands and flung themselves upon the stone circle.

A rain of fire fell upon the Chellians... At first they resisted, but their chests swelled with fear and fury. Suffocated by the smoke, made giddy by their burns, little by little any peril seemed preferable to that which threatened to destroy them without giving them a chance of fighting...

The thickset body of the chief rose up on a boulder, he bounded forward with a hoarse howl, and seven warriors rushed after him. Aoun ordered the women to beat a retreat. Twice the bows twanged and two Dhole-Men fell. Five of the remaining six charged the group of women and the Wah; the sixth rushed upon Aoun, who stood apart. The son of Urus flung a new spear which grazed his opponent's shoulder, then, rising to the full of his magnificent stature, he waited. He might have fled, and so tired out his adversary; he preferred to fight him. It was the broad-shouldered chief, with a head like a block of granite, who advanced upon him. He brandished his spear and also an enormous horn. The weapon came in contact with the club, swerved, turned aside and returned to earth like a thunderbolt. Aoun's chest was bleeding, but his club broke the chiefs bones. He fell on his knees and dropped his spear, with the resignation of a vanquished wild beast, knowing that his end had come. Aoun had picked up his club and did not lower it. His breast contracted with a strange feeling of disgust; that movement of pity which was his weakness, and the weakness of Naoh, came upon him...

Below them two women lay stretched on the grass, but Zouhr's spears and javelins had done their work: three Chellians groaned in the agonies of death; the Wolf-Women finished them off. A fourth, the youngest of the party, mad with terror, ran towards Aoun. When he found himself in close proximity to the enormous club, his muscles gave way and he fell prostrate.

The women rushed forward to kill him; the son of Urus spread out his arms crying, "His life is in the hands of Aoun."

They stopped, their faces contracted with hate; then, hearing the groans of those who had been wounded in the first encounter, they went off to hack their bodies to pieces. Aoun listened gloomily to their cries of agony and vaguely rejoiced that Djeha had not followed her companions.

XVIII. The Horde

Aoun, Zouhr and the Wolf-Women remained for a month in the chain of rocks. Only one woman had died; four others were hurt; Aoun's wound was not serious. Now that they were delivered from the Chellians they were masters of the savannah, the jungle and the river. The giant feline eliminated all other wild beasts by his mere presence. Thus life was ample and easy. Aoun and Zouhr tasted the pleasure of repose in full measure after all the perils they had passed through. Zouhr loved those dreamy hours when all kinds of remembrances and pictures surged up in his mind. His soul knew the sweetness of thoughts of the past which had been transmitted to him by a race destined to extinction. He only woke up to devise traps for game, or to gather edible roots.

Even in repose Aoun was a prey to tumultuous instincts and to confused desires, which filled his whole being. His senses were continually surprised by the subtle curves of Djeha's young body, by her lovely floating hair, and the changing lights in her eyes. Everything about her seemed perpetually to renew itself, like the early mornings on the river, and the flowers on the savannah. Sometimes a movement of revolt shot through the wanderer's breast. He became like other men, and despised weakness; his instinct of tenderness changed to a rough and bellicose mood, and he turned towards Ouchr, prepared to ask her to celebrate the marriage rites of her race, by flinging Djeha on the ground and wounding her bosom with a pointed flint.

The women asked for no other existence than their present one, which gave them such profound security. They lost the desire for liberty, and were content to place their destiny in the hands of the great Oulhamr. The future had no place in their limited imaginations; after their many misfortunes they desired nothing but the tranquil abundance which they enjoyed at present, and which was renewed every morning and evening. They even allowed Aoun to liberate the two prisoners. He had conducted them himself to the place where the stream and the river divided.

The rainy season was now only five weeks distant. Aoun thought more often of his horde, of Naoh, the conqueror of the Kzamms, the Red Dwarfs and Aghoo the Hairy, of the evening fires, and of his rough companions, of whose ferocity, however, he did not approve.

One morning he said to Ouchr, "Listen: Aoun and Zouhr are going to visit their horde; the Wolf-Women will choose a cave close to the mountains... After the cold weather, the Oulhamrs will come... They will be the Wolf-Women's allies."

Ouchr and the other Wolf-Women felt the weight of impending destiny. They were on the plain near the bank of the river. They thronged around the son of Urus; the younger ones wailed... Djeha had bounded to her feet. Her breast heaved, her great eyes were full of tears. Aoun, deeply moved, regarded her for some time in silence.

He said, "Ouchr has promised that Djeha shall be Aoun's wife. Djeha will obey."

He turned towards Ouchr, and trembling slightly murmured, "Give me Djeha as my companion."

Ouchr threw Aoun a long melancholy glance, then she seized Djeha by the back of her neck and flung her on the ground. With a pointed stone she then made a long wound, which reached from the shoulder to the middle of the girl's chest. Blood gushed out, and Aoun put his lips to it. Ouchr pronounced the words which their ancestors had used long ago, and which gave the woman to the man.

The next day the little band started off. Aoun and Zouhr had left the giant feline sadly. The Wah felt the parting more than his companion, having no love of woman in his heart. His race would die out with him; he bitterly regretted leaving the cave and that alliance with the great wild beast which he had made. Nothing attached him to the Oulhamr horde; he was a stranger in it, and the young Oulhamrs despised him...

They passed the place where the yellow lions had fled before the elephants; they passed close to the granite ridge where the saber-tooth had devoured the rhinoceros and where Aoun had killed the saber-tooth; then they came to the rugged promontory which the mountains threw out towards the land of the Chellians.

From that high promontory they had discovered the river, and the strange red beast which lived before the time of the giant feline, itself a precursor of the lion and tiger. It was there that the Wolf-Women chose a spacious cave in which to pass the rainy season. Then they helped Aoun and Zouhr to find a way towards the mountain.

The separation was a hard one. The women would no longer have near them that strength which had delivered them from the Chellians; they would be alone in a world full of dangers. When they reached the foot of the ravine, where the travelers were to leave them, they made a long lamentation. Aoun cried out, "We will come back to the banks of the great river."

His own heart was heavy. The land he was leaving was indeed full of ambushes and enemies, but he had triumphed, he had overcome the perils; men and beasts had given way before his strength. He was carrying off Djeha.

Zouhr dreamed of no other joy than that of returning to the chain of rocks.

One day succeeded another. Aoun, Zouhr and Djeha went up the rugged mountain paths. Aoun was impatient to see his horde again. Every stage they accomplished brought back the remembrance of former joys to his young soul.

The time came when they found again the lofty defile through which they had passed when they left the mountain; then they arrived before the fissure. As it had grown larger they had less trouble in passing through it. The caverns were there, re-echoing the sound of water. In them they slept, and two days passed before they could find the horde.

They found them at last at the decline of day, at the foot of a hill, under an enormous overhanging porphyry rock. The women were heaping up dry branches, which Naoh was to set a light to. Their watchers shouted, and Aoun was the first to appear before the son of the Leopard. There was a great silence. The women gazed at Djeha with malevolent eyes.

Naoh said gravely, "A whole season has passed since you went away."

"We have crossed the mountain and we have discovered vast hunting grounds," replied Aoun.

Naoh's face lit up. He remembered the fierce days when he set off with Nam and Gaw to reconquer fire; he lived over again his battle with the gray wolf and the tigress, his pursuit of the Men-Devourers, his alliance with the chief of the mammoths, the perfidy of the Red Dwarfs and the gentleness of the Wahs, the forest of the Blue-Haired men, the surprise of the Bear of the Caves, and, on their return, the terrible encounter with Aghoo the Hairy... He had brought back fire, and the secret of extracting it from stones, which he had learnt from the Men-without-Shoulders.

"Go on," he said, "Naoh listens to the son of Urus."

He set fire to the pile of branches and encouraged his son to speak.

Gradually, as he heard the recital, his adventurous soul became excited. The red beast filled him with surprise, but he revolted when Aoun maintained that the elephants were bigger than mammoths, "No beast is bigger than the mammoth, with whom Naoh lived in the country of the Kzamms."

He recognized the wild beast which lived among the chain of rocks, and asked Aoun, "Does he not kill the tiger as easily as the lion kills the panther?"

He was full of enthusiasm over the alliance with the giant feline. He turned his benevolent face towards Zouhr and said, "The Wahs were the most clever among men. It was they who found out the secret of obtaining fire from stones. They could traverse rivers by means of interlaced branches, and they knew the waters which flow underground!"

His breast heaved with excitement as they told of their fights with the Chellians; his eyes sparkled, he laid his hand on the young man's shoulder saying, "Aoun has the heart and the strength of a chief!"

The Oulhamrs around them were listening, but they remained full of distrust; they were thinking that Naoh had reconquered the secret of fire, and saved the horde when they were dying of cold on the rocks, while Aoun had only brought back a strange girl with him, and that weakly companion whom no one liked.

Khouam, son of Aegager exclaimed, "Did not Aoun say that those lands were much hotter than ours?... The Oulhamrs will not be able to live in them... When we traversed the Burnt Plain, the warriors and women died like grasshoppers in autumn."

Dull voices approved his words. Aoun understood that the horde loved him even less than before he went away.

For a week, the son of Urus tasted the sweetness of being among the men of his race. He hunted with the others, or else stayed near Djeha, to whom the women of the horde would not speak. Little by little sadness took possession of his breast. He felt he had accomplished a task which was as great as that of Naoh, for though he had not brought back the secret of fire, he had told his horde that an immense land, teeming with animal life, existed beyond the mountains. He knew himself to be superior to all the young men, and as strong as the chief. He could see that the Oulhamrs did not admire him at all. All of them preferred Khouam, whose club and spear could not have fought against those of Aoun. Khouam would be chief if the son of the Leopard died, and he would have to obey Khouam. That would be hard for Aoun, for Khouam would incite hatred towards him, Djeha and Zouhr, which would grow rapidly.

Even before his departure they had reproached the son of Urus with preferring the Wah's company, and now he had united himself to a maiden from a country into which they had never penetrated. Thus he became a stranger to them. The women especially hated him. They turned away from Djeha with insulting words, and when several of them passed her together a hoarse murmur showed their dislike. Even Aoun's sisters fled from her.

When he found himself alone in the twilight with the young Wolf-Woman and the Wah, Aoun felt his humiliation most keenly. Terrible impatience burnt in his veins.

After a few days he revolted. He no longer tried to draw closer to the others, but obstinately isolated himself with Zouhr and Djeha; when they were hunting he went off alone whenever he had received no special order from Naoh to stay with the horde. He wandered for days together near the underground river, and often, compelled by an impulse which was too strong for him, he found himself again by that fissure which led to the land of adventure.

One morning he set out in pursuit of a leopard. Leopards abounded in the neighboring forests. Powerful, circumspect and audacious, voracious and active, they exterminated the deer, antelopes and onagers, and even killed young aurochs. Naoh did not hunt them, being bound to them by an obscure totemism; many Oulhamrs feared them because they defended themselves madly when wounded; few solitary hunters dared to attack them.

Aoun prowled for a long time in the forest without finding the trace of one. A small water course trickled on a flinty bed; the wanderer became aware of the smell of a leopard. He lay down among the ferns and waited, motionless.

He noticed upstream, under long leafy arcades, a little rocky eminence, the advanced part of which formed a sort of cave. A beast lay asleep there in profound security, its head on its paws. Despite the distance and the waning light, Aoun could see it was a leopard. About 1200 ells separated the man from the beast. The warrior advanced 800 ells before the beast was disturbed from its slumbers. As he plunged into a tangle of high grass, the round head was raised, two fires of amber and emerald were lit up in the shadow of the rocks.

Aoun lay flat on the ground, while the wild beast sniffed the air for a long time. The sparkling eyes gazed around for a moment, then the muzzle dropped, and the spotted body again became inert. Aoun allowed many minutes to elapse before moving on. He had still about 200 ells to cover. Then he could shoot an arrow from his bow. His weapon could not inflict a mortal wound at that distance, even if it reached its mark, but Aoun hoped that the beast, becoming enraged, would accept battle.

A gentle breeze sprang up, which carried the smell of the hunter away from the animal. He hastened his steps and gained 150 ells, then he hid behind a tree.

Again the leopard lifted its head to listen. Then it came out of its lair, the better to sniff the suspicious smell.

Suddenly a belling was heard, a doe bounded out between the sycamores and the leopard dashed after it. The doe took a turn towards the tree which hid Aoun from view; the warrior rose, his bow twanged. The leopard, wounded at the back of its neck, gave a frenzied howl. It hesitated, gazed at its adversary and slipped away among the ferns.

Aoun placed himself in an open space, in order to guard against a surprise, holding his club in one hand and a spear in the other. The leopard seemed unable to make up its mind to attack him. It could distinctly see the man through the thick vegetation, and it tried to find a way of approaching him under cover and leaping on his back.

Its fury had abated; it hardly felt its wound, and although it had proved itself too clever for all the Oulhamrs' traps, it realized that it now had to do with a dangerous adversary. It tried to improve its position, but found itself several bounds length from its enemy in whichever direction it turned. Aoun, having a good view of its spotted fur, flung his spear. It fell among the ferns and the leopard retreated into the deep thickets.

Other creatures had for some time been moving in the forest; the hunter became aware of the approach of a band of men. Shouting a rallying cry he dashed off in pursuit of the leopard. Heads appeared here and there; spears were flung without result. Suddenly Khouam showed his muscular body, and brandishing his bow let fly an arrow. Hit in the flank, the leopard sprang up and turned, ready for battle... Khouam had vanished; all the other heads had hidden themselves; only Aoun remained visible.

The leopard hesitated no longer; it was within reach of the son of Urus in three bounds, then it sprang... Aoun's club stopped it and threw it to the ground; he shattered its skull, and the beast rolled over and expired with a hoarse cry.

Then Khouam and his companions ran up. Aoun watched them come, leaning on his club. He thought that they would admire his strength; an amiable gentleness and the attraction of race rose in him. But the faces were hard. One of the men who followed Khouam, like Zouhr followed Aoun, exclaimed, "Khouam has conquered the leopard!"

There were loud grunts of approval. Khouam drew himself up by the body and showed his arrow, which was deeply imbedded in the beast's ribs. Aoun revolted, "Khouam did not conquer the leopard."

The Oulhamrs mocked him and displayed the arrow; the man who had first spoken went on, "It was Khouam! Aoun only finished the victory."

The son of Urus raised his club; anger raged within him; he shouted disdainfully, "What is a leopard? Aoun has conquered the red beast, the tiger and the Dhole-Men. Only Naoh is as strong as he!"

Khouam did not give way. He felt the support of his companions' presence around him.

"Khouam fears neither the lion nor the tiger!"

A bitter sorrow gnawed at Aoun's heart. He was like a stranger to the men of his race. Seizing the carcass he flung it towards them, "There. The son of Urus will not strike the Oulhamrs. He gives them the leopard."

They no longer mocked him; their ferocious eyes were fixed on his tall stature and his enormous club; they were all cunningly aware that his strength was like that of the great carnivores. But they detested it, and disdained his gentleness.

Aoun returned to the camp full of disgust and annoyance. When he got near to the overhanging rock, he found Djeha all alone, crouched upon a rock. She rose when she saw him, with a wail... her cheek was bleeding.

"Djeha has hurt herself?" he said passing his arm around her shoulders.

She replied in a low voice, "The women threw stones."

"They threw stones at Djeha?"

She nodded her head; a shudder ran through the wanderer. "Where are they?" he asked, seeing that the camp was deserted.

"I do not know."

He bowed his head sullenly. The pain which he felt became intolerable. In the silence which succeeded he realized that he no longer wished to live with the horde.

"Would Djeha like to return to the Wolf-Women with Aoun and Zouhr?" he murmured.

She lifted her face towards him full of joy, which she tried to hide. She was a submissive and timid creature. She suffered acutely among the Oulhamrs; she endured their hate, the disdain and mocking laughs of the women, and was the more overcome because she hardly understood their language.

She dared not complain, and would not have spoken of her wound if Aoun had not interrogated her.

She exclaimed, "Djeha will go with Aoun wherever he goes."

"Does she not prefer to live with her horde?"

"Yes," she whispered.

"Then we will go back to the bank of the great river."

She gave a sigh of relief and leant her head on the man's shoulder.

When the Wah returned from the underground lands, the son of Urus drew him to a distance from the camp, for the women and the hunters had returned.

"Listen," he said abruptly, "Aoun wants to see the Wolf-Women, the Kzamm tiger and the high cave again."

Zouhr lifted his vague eyes; his lips opened with a laugh. He knew that his companion was living through bad days in the horde, and his own heart was heavy, "Zouhr will be happy in the high cave," he said.

His words dissipated the wanderer's last indecision. He went to Naoh, who was resting apart from the horde, under a jutting rock of porphyry, and said, "The warriors do not like the son of Urus. He wishes to go back to the other side of the mountain. We will live with the Wolf-Women and be the ally of the Oulhamrs."

Naoh listened gravely. He was fond of the young man, but he was aware of the horde's aversion for him, and foresaw painful struggles.

"The horde is displeased to see Aoun consorting with strangers," he said. "If he stays with the horde they will not forgive him. The Oulhamrs respect their allies. They have fought with the Men-without-Shoulders. They will like Aoun better when he has left the horde. Listen! In the spring Naoh will conduct his people to the other side of the mountain. He will occupy the plateau while the Wolf-Women occupy the plain. If he comes down to the plain during the cold season, he will not hunt on the same side of the river as Aoun. So the alliance will be secure!"

He laid his hand on the young man's shoulder and added, "The son of Urus would have been a great chief among the Oulhamrs, if he had not preferred the Wah to his own men, and a strange woman to the women of his tribe!"

The son of Urus understood the truth of those words. He, however, regretted nothing: more than ever he preferred Zouhr and Djeha. The separation from Naoh would be his only sorrow.

"Aoun will bring teeth and shining stones to the son of the Leopard," he murmured.

Twilight came on. A sweet melancholy feeling came over the two men; their souls were as much alike as their destinies were different; each one had carried his strength and audacity very far. Yet almost identical acts had made a chief of the father and an exile of the son.

Epilogue

Since the previous day a couple of saber-tooth tigers had established themselves among the rocks, 300 paces from the Wolf-Women's cave. They knew the agility, strength, cunning and audacity of these devourers of pachyderms. None of the women dared venture out. During the night the red beasts had prowled for a long time about their refuge. Sometimes they came nearer, and their snarls and rough growls could be heard. Then the women shouted all together and threw sharp stones. The projectiles had no effect, however, and were lost among the boulders, thorns and branches accumulated for the defense of the cave. At last other prey claimed the attention of the tigers, but during the day, the male or the female would return, between two sleeps, to watch the enigmatical beings.

The rainy season was near.

As they took refuge behind their barricade, in the shadow of the porphyry rocks, the women thought of the wanderer whose terrible arms had vanquished the Dhole-Men, and their agony was increased by the thought. He would have struck down the red beasts with his club and his spear...

There was no doubt that the saber-tooth tigers must have captured insufficient prey on the previous night, for they came to spy upon the cave long before twilight. The day was already darkened by the clouds that had covered the sky; a cutting wind came up from the plain and howled dismally among the rocks; some of the children were crying, and the Wolf-Women, crowded together near the opening, were looking out mournfully on the landscape; Ouchr was thinking that the wild beasts would continue to inhabit the rocks.

The wind hurled itself with greater fury against the mountain, the saber-tooth tigers appeared together before the refuge and lifted up their voices in a roar. Ouchr, much distressed, went forward to prepare the defense.

Suddenly a long weapon whirled through the air and one of the wild beasts, the male, hit in the back of the neck, flung himself towards the Wolf-Women. Spears were thrust firmly through the rocky openings, and a second javelin was imbedded in the red body; a clamor arose above the noise of the wind, a great form appeared and a club whirled formidably.

Falling over each other in the attempt, the women thrust aside the boulders that defended their den... The male saber-tooth was lying on the ground, the female, terrified by its cries of agony and the sudden appearance of so many enemies, fled towards the river.

The Wolf-Women, growling with joy, pressed around their savior. All the massive faces lit up; the large eyes were fixed upon Aoun with excited worship. He brought with him security, the certainty of conquering the elements, beasts and men... The son of Urus, feeling that he should never go back to his life among the Oulhamrs, cried, "Listen! Aoun and Zouhr have returned to the Wolf-Women. They will not leave them again. They will live all together in the big cave near to which they exterminated the Dhole-Men!"

As he spoke, their joy became deeper: the Wolf-Women bowed before him as a sign of love and obedience. His heart swelled, he forgot the bitter disappointment he had suffered on his return to the men of his own race, and only thought how a new horde would grow up under his leadership.

"Ouchr and the Wolf-Women will be your warriors," said the woman chief. "Where you live they will live. They will do your will and follow your customs."

"They will become a horde to be feared," said Aoun. "They will learn to make and wield harpoons, spears, hatchets, bows and arrows. They will fear neither the Dhole-Men nor the Red beast."

The women collected branches; a magnificent fire lit up the darkness; the night hours were no longer full of ambushes, and the happiness which spread over those youthful hearts seemed to extend itself over the great river and to know no bounds!

Zouhr alone was melancholy; he would not feel satisfied until he saw again the chain of rocks and the giant feline.

The wind howled as the little horde reached the cave on the 12th day. Fox bats had sought a refuge there, but they flew away when they saw Ouchr; a falcon took wing with a hoarse cry. Standing on the platform, Aoun stretched out his hand towards the savannah and jungle. They teemed with animal life; a never-ending population of fishes, tortoises, crocodiles, hippopotami, pythons, purple herons, yellow-headed cranes, black storks, ibis, cormorants and black-footed geese lived in the river or on its banks; the savannah, jungle and forest were overpopulated with swamp deer, axis, antelopes, fallow deer, wild asses, horses, onagers, gaurs, buffaloes and wild goats; numberless parrots, doves, birds of the sparrow tribe and pheasants filled the branches; the rich vegetation would supply them with roots, tender stalks and fruit. Aoun felt himself to be stronger than the great carnivores, and rich in the blood of a conquering race that coursed in his veins... Around him, Dje-ha, Ouchr and the others seemed the continuation of himself...

The Wah went slowly down towards the deep cave. He went to the fissure and looked in: the den was empty... Zouhr shivered, crept through the opening, and began to explore the deep shadows of the cave. Fresh bones mingled with the dry ones, the smell of the giant feline hung about in the darkness. The son of Earth left the cave and wandered about for a long time in great anxiety, without heeding the wild beasts that might be hidden in the underwood... He had hardly entered the jungle when his face cleared.

"The Lion of the Rocks!"

There among the bamboos, the colossal form was couched on the body of a swamp deer... The feline raised its great head at the sound of the man's voice, then with a gentle roar it bounded towards him...

Zouhr's joy was complete. When the animal came close to him, he passed his two hands through its mane, and a pride equal to that of Aoun swelled his feeble breast.

Afterword

The turn of the 20th century was a time of great highs and abysmal lows. The Paris Universal Exposition of 1900, The Armory Show of 1913, Marie Skłodowska Curie's two Nobel Prizes[4] shared center stage with the Dreyfus Affair, the rise of New Imperialism and the First World War.

Writing from within this maelstrom of history was J.-H. Rosny *Aîné* (1856-1940). This member of the distinguished Goncourt literary academy was the first writer to straddle the line between themes used commonly in mainstream and academic literature and those used in science fiction. He was also the single French-language author who best embodied the evolution of modern science fiction away from the juvenile, one-dimensional scientific anticipations of Jules Verne, or the pulp serials of Paul d'Ivoi, Jean de La Hire and Gustave Le Rouge, to a more mature, literary form of pulp or popular fiction. Needless to say, his genre fiction was neglected by literary scholars.

Many years later, two individuals, one in a smoldering France, the other in McCarthyist America, one a philosopher, the other a writer, picked up the jet-tipped arrows fired by Rosny. They were unknown to one another and yet so alike in their admiration for this sophisticate who wrote pulp fiction, this great miscegenationist who wrote a philosophy book on pluralism that went through two printings.[5]

Philosophy should be like a type of science fiction, suggested the philosopher Gilles Deleuze (1925-1995) in the preface to his magnum opus *Difference and Repetition* in 1968, for we "write only at the frontiers of our knowledge, at the border which separates our knowledge from our ignorance and

---

[4] Physics (1903) and chemistry (1911).
[5] *Introduction* by Brian Stableford in Rosny, 2010a: 53.

transforms the one into the other." Apologizing to future detractors, he adds wryly: "We are therefore well aware, unfortunately, that we have spoken about science in a manner which was not scientific."

In terms of science fiction there is no writer more indebted to Rosny, and none more worthy of the honor, than Philip José Farmer (1918-2009). From beginning to end, both Farmer and Rosny ceaselessly experimented with alchemical transformations of ignorance and knowledge, writing like men possessed, "so gabby, so sloppy, so pagan, so wild, so cynical, so drunk (should I say, crazed?) with learning."[6]

It is a short step from Rosny's giant bats of "The Depths of Kyamo" and "The Wonderful Cave Country" to Farmer's humanoid bat-couple, Ghlikh and Ghuakh, in *The Stone God Awakens* (1970), a lost land adventure replete with love affairs of a genuinely cross-cultural and inter-racial nature, fecund worlds within worlds, and a modest even reluctant hero for whom the avoidance of shameful (human) actions is more important than notations of evil in a morally relativized universe. Unlike Ghlikh and Ghuakh, however, Rosny's giant bats form something of a symbiotic alliance with humans and other animals whose blood they are dependent on. The hosts may not have offered themselves, but the Nature to which they are subject provides the necessary conditions for its will to be done. Save for a lethargy just before and during transmission, there are no adverse side-effects for the hosts. This idea is given a twist by Farmer in *The Wind Whales of Ishmael* (1971) where it is the carnivorous flora that will insert its vegetable probosci into human jugulars, again, with no adverse side effects.

Rosny's "The Navigators of Space" and its sequel "The Astronauts"[7] depict human *astronauts* (his term) traveling to Mars in a spaceship powered by artificial gravity and made of an indestructible, transparent material, not unlike Larry Ni-

[6] Farmer, 1999: 32.
[7] Written concurrently but only published in 1960.

ven's spaceships. On Mars, the humans come into contact with an intelligent and peaceful, six-eyed, three-legged dying race. A young Martian female, capable of bearing children parthenogenetically by merely wishing it, eventually gives birth to a child after falling in love with one of the human explorers, undoubtedly the first romance ever written between a man and an alien female. This colorful, poetic ode to the power of love and plea for understanding between races, was a sharp departure from the xenophobia celebrated by Wells with his *War of the Worlds*.

The most celebrated miscegenationist tale in the tradition set down by Rosny is Farmer's short story *The Lovers* (1952).[8] Hal Yarrow, a tyrannical, "terrocentric" and "hidebound"[9] earthman is in the process of breaking out of his spiritual prison in an unprecedented act of apostasy.[10] Having fallen in love with a woman named Jeannette Rastignac, the two conduct a clandestine love affair. Whilst Jeanette may look human, she is in fact of the species "Chordata pseudarthropoda"[11] who are also known as "lalitha...Nature's most amazing experiment in [mimetic] parasitism and parallel evolution."[12] Tragedy almost ends the relationship, but being a mimetic parasite Hal's lalitha is *the* woman he wishes *any* lalitha to be, and Jeannette had sisters...

Farmer and Rosny also shared an interest in substances both synthetic and natural, conveyed by beings organic, mystical, or natural. Stableford notes the appearance of both ama-

---

[8] Expanded into a novel published by Ballantine Books in 1961.

[9] These expressions do not appear in the 1961 edition of *The Lovers*. We are quoting from the Baen Books edition (2008: 84). We have not seen the 1952 magazine version.

[10] In the Iranian Sufi tradition the word "hal" means "spiritual state," as in divinely inspired agitation (Wilson, 1988: 203).

[11] Farmer, 2008: 198.

[12] Farmer, 2008: 201. Lalitha is also the name of the Hindu Goddess *Lalita Devi*, or, the *Divine Mother*.

nita and ayahuasca (DMT) in Rosny's work.[13] For his part, Farmer's *Unreasoning Mask* (1983) features a planet whose atmosphere necessitates the wearing of masks by humans so as to "strain out the psychedeligenic spores."[14]

Many a strange or violent event in their fiction could easily be read as moments of expanded consciousness due to the ingestion of psychoactive substances. But as a testament to their virtuosity as writers of exceptional vision and daring, these same stories can be read as transliterations of ideas gleaned from specialist areas of inquiry.

An excellent example in Farmer is the short story "St. Francis Kisses His Ass Goodbye" (1989). This story was first discussed by Carey[15] within the context of Farmer's interest in the Sufi mystical tradition. St. Francis finds himself the unwitting subject of a scientific experiment which transports him through time during a violent storm. Once his transposition has occurred, he encounters a mysterious figure known variously as al-Khidr or "the Green One." Carey suggests that this was not a chance meeting in Farmer's imagination, but a creative elaboration of the little known fact that "St. Francis of Assisi had knowledge of Sufi doctrine, and... based much of his own teaching upon it." The limitation of Carey's account however is the implication of his analogy between Elijah and al-Khidr, for Elijah-as-al-Khidr then "is known in eastern European folklore as being responsible for bad weather."

In their *Green Gold: The Tree of Life, Marijuana in Magic and Religion* (1995), Bennett *et al.* note that "Attar and other Sufis are reported to have used el-Khidr (Khizr), the green man, as a hidden reference to hashish and bhang." Given that some forms of hashish have the equivalent effect of a staggering "500 micrograms of LSD,"[16] the *storm* assumes an

---

[13] Stableford in Rosny, 2010c: 328.

[14] Farmer, 1983: 10.

[15] Carey, 2009.

[16] Wilson, 1988: 204.

entirely different meaning to that associated with meteorological phenomena.

Al-Khidr (Khizr or Khezr) originates in and appears throughout both mainstream and mystical Islam, with variant spelling and interpretation of function. Wilson describes al-Khidr as the "hidden prophet of Sufism" an "initiator of Sufis who have no human master, a vegetation spirit in whose footsteps flowers and herbs sprout by magic."[17] This latter extrapolation seems to fit both Farmer and Rosny's extensive interest in flora as always containing more than itself and being a cipher for alternate "sentient" life. In a later study, Wilson adds that "one of [al-Khidr's] functions is to convince skeptics of the existence of the Marvelous, to rescue those who are lost in deserts of doubt and dryness."[18]

So this story could easily be seen as a cipher for the effects of the more powerful, hallucinogenic strains of hashish and cannabis manifested through the presence of al-Khidr. But it is equally a thermodynamic mystery/suspense with a potentially explosive pay-off. As Carey puts it, "al-Khidr, calling himself 'Kidder,' appears to the shocked friar, helping him make his way to the scientists whose experiment will end in a world wide disaster if St. Francis is not sent back to his past with the exact matter-mass which he brought with him to the future." In other words, how to reverse the division of matter—that is, St. Francis—in time, so precisely as to avoid the extensive properties of mass and total volume exceeding their ratio with the intensive properties of pressure, density and temperature;[19] or in the words of Kidder, how to avoid a "mass-temporal energy explosion."[20]

---

[17] Wilson, 1988: 213.

[18] Wilson, 1993: 139.

[19] "Thermodynamic properties can be divided into two general classes, namely intensive and extensive properties. If a quantity of matter in a given state is divided into two equal parts, each part will have the same value of intensive properties as

281

For his part, Rosny was saturated in the ideas of his age and so it comes as no surprise to read his account of the division of thermodynamic properties in "The Givreuse Enigma" (2010e). Here the setting is closer to the science of warfare than to the mysticism of a violent storm. It is at the moment of an artillery explosion in a First World War battle that Pierre de Givreuse is divided in space, that is, into two contemporaneous bodies in a way we would today refer to as bipartition or cloning. His double is given the name Philippe de Givreuse. What strikes the scientist handling their case is the "anomaly of their density... the respective weight of the young men was no more than 45 kilograms. This weight was in flagrant disproportion to the volume of flesh and bone. According to appearances, Philippe and Pierre should each have weighed about 70 kilograms—and it was known, with utter certainty, that before his departure, Pierre had weighed 73."[21]

Brian Stableford's trenchant commentary accompanying the preceding 6 volumes of this series bears witness to Rosny's laboratory of creative inventions and experimentations where transformations of the real, as outlined above, form an unscientific or romantic type of science fiction. In fact, experiments with many different results scatter Rosny's fiction, making his writing appear strategic and calculating, that is, political, rather than theoretical and didactic. His novels and stories portray scientists battling with problems that challenge and perhaps require the overturning of orthodoxy, rather than portraying orthodoxy being brought to bear on problems and the lives of scientists. In "Mysterious Force," physicist Gérard Langre, is described as a man leading "a disconnected life,"

---

the original, and half the value of the extensive properties. Pressure, temperature, and density are examples of intensive properties. Mass and total volume are examples of extensive properties" (Van Wylen in Beistegui, 2004: 369).

[20] Farmer, 1989: 292.

[21] Rosny, 2010e: 48.

one full "of genius, endowed with the stubbornness and skill of great experimenters," who "worked with such rudimentary apparatus and such restricted materials that he only obtained any results by virtue of the miracle of his obstinacy, his vigilance and his professional acumen. A lofty vision made up for the wretchedness of his laboratories."[22]

Rosny's understanding of politics was just as doggedly determined or strategic, that is, innate, intimate and global. Justice was an immanent requirement of everyday ethics and not a transcendent right to be applied by The Law from on high. For more than 30 years, from the 1887 "Manifeste des Cinq"[23] denouncing Zola, to his American trip of 1927, Rosny would embody, live and write his understanding of politics as a hatred as well as a terror of dissimulation, the masking of truth. It was "dissimulation and hypocrisy that [was] rotting the soul of America" he stated for *TIME* magazine.[24] For him, dereliction of creative or scientific duty, the perjury of a writer or scientist deserting the imperative of experimentation (personal or otherwise)—all were ciphers for actual *desertification*, the harshest idea informing "The Death of the Earth," one of his most disturbing works: "The impotence of human beings was structural: born with water, they were vanishing with it."[25]

Listening to Rosny describing the Russian émigré of Paris in 1891 in a journalistic piece he wrote for *Harper's New Monthly Magazine*, could just as easily be a summation of his own writing: a politics of scientific method (which at first glance does not appear to be very political or scientific): "His life is an exposition of principles or a perpetual discussion,

---

[22] Rosny, 2010c: 32.

[23] Bonnetain, *et al.* 1887.

[24] Rosny was scathing in his denunciation of what he felt were the "humiliating experiences" suffered by Americans at the hands of their own mores, and social and economic conditions (Rosny, 1927).

[25] Rosny, 2010a: 250.

and all the time we spend with him he is theorizing, comparing dates and events, describing a skeleton Russia wherein there seems to be neither men, women, nor children, but only an abstract population of problems.[26]

Farmer shared Rosny's sense of politics[27] as that which "precedes being" as Deleuze and Guattari put it.[28] When Hal "stepped out into the open air of the first habitable planet discovered by Earthmen" dissimulating scientific neutrality and good will so as to hide his mission objective of genocide, he is reminded of Columbus, and wonders if "the story will be the same?"[29] Similarly, Rosny's narrator in "The Treasure in the Snow" says: "Nine times out of ten—as I am not the only person to have remarked—one can reach an understanding with savages; the brutality almost always comes from the side of the white man."[30]

---

[26] Rosny, 1891: 430. It is of some importance to acknowledge the hidden hand of the philosopher Henri Bergson here: "The idea that problems, even more than theories and concepts, are the genetic element in the development of thought, keeps coming back in Bergson's works suggesting the stronger claim that his philosophy, more than any other in the beginning of the Twentieth-century, may provide the philosophical grounds for a non-positivist conception of problems themselves" (During, 2008). See also Chapman (1984) on Farmer: "parallels with Bergsonian vitalism...are fairly obvious" (86).

[27] Both Farmer and Deleuze entered politics, so to speak, at around the same time: "After his return to Peoria in 1969... [Farmer] developed a self-defined role as a resident liberal gadfly commenting on political issues" (Chapman, 2009). And Deleuze: "I, for my own part, made a sort of move into politics around May 68" (1995: 170).

[28] 1988: 203.

[29] Farmer, 2008: 59.

[30] Rosny, 2010b: 159.

In 1976, Farmer adapted Rosny's lost land adventure *L'Etonnant voyage de Hareton Ironcastle* (1922).[31] As Stableford informs us, Farmer's version stripped away the religion Rosny had placed strategically so as to appease what he believed was a bible-thumping American audience, but maintained the political intent: "our civilization...is the most homicidal that has ever appeared on Earth...we have caused the disappearance of more peoples and populations than all the conquerors of antiquity and the Middle Ages."[32]

Our uniquely human patrimony is the inheritance of shameful actions, and both writers knew that shame is not always where the consensus says it is. "Better sleep with a sober cannibal than a drunken Christian" reasons Herman Melville's Ishmael to himself when weighing up the prospect of sharing a room and bed with Queequeg.[33] This is the same inversion of a dubious morality that prompts Rosny to criticize by appeasement (as in *Ironcastle*) or direct attack (as in "Companions of the Universe"[34]). Farmer's invocation of, and paean to, the great Herman Melville through the words of Captain Ahab in his *The Wind Whales of Ishmael*, acts as a shared conception of this anti-dissimulationist political intent: "All visible objects, man, are but as pasteboard masks. But in each event—in the living act, the undoubted deed—there, some unknown but still reasoning thing put forth the moldings of its features from behind the unreasoning mask. If man will strike, strike through the mask!"[35]

---

[31] Farmer and Rosny, 1976.

[32] Stableford in Rosny, 2010c: 269.

[33] Melville, 1994:43.

[34] Rosny, 2010f: 205-206.

[35] Farmer uses this particular quotation in both *The Wind Whales of Ishmael* and *Unreasoning mask* (perhaps elsewhere, too). In the former though, he substitutes "still reasoning thing" for "still unreasoning thing" (156). Unless this is a misprint, we assume Farmer refers to the nature of time itself as

In 2007, *Collapse,* an independent journal of *Philosophical Research and Development* with a print run of 1000 copies per issue, embodying that *largesse* of spirit, invention, principled exposition and perpetual discussion Rosny might well have admired, published an issue titled *Unknown Deleuze.* Filed under "Rosny" was a translation of "Another World" preceded by a short introductory essay on the legacy of the author by the journal's editor and publisher, Robin Mackay. This short and incisive piece of scholarship introduces us to an equally *Unknown Rosny,* viz., Rosny the Philosopher and his unmitigated centrality to the strange and difficult philosophy of Gilles Deleuze.

Rosny's philosophical work was published by Félix Alcan, by all accounts a remarkable publisher whose authors, instead of embodying the common ethos of an exclusive or doctrinaire club, "saturated, through a sort of philosophical chromaticism, every philosophical possibility of the epoch offered to the field."[36] Such a politics of multiplicity—that is, one premised on the compulsion to experiment, to continually overthrow the reign of unity or science with new data, and to begin all over again—is otherwise known as pluralism.

Both Farmer and Deleuze pay homage to a writer for whom the very latest developments in science and philosophy, not to mention politics, always found a voice in his univocal choir—politics, philosophy and science sounding more romantic than political, philosophical or scientific. Deleuze acknowledges Rosny's central contribution to philosophy,[37] one which establishes pluralism (or the multiple) as the manifesta-

---

"unreasoning." Still, the point remains: "That inscrutable thing is chiefly what I hate" (Melville, 1994: 167).

[36] Mackay, 2007: 256.

[37] Mackay (2007: 256) cites Jules Sageret's *La Revolution Philosophique et la Science: Bergson, Einstein, Le Dantec, J.-H. Rosny Aîné.* Paris: Alcan, 1924, to give an idea of the stature of Rosny at the time.

tion of differences (and not the other way around). As Charles Gourlande puts it in "The Givreuse Enigma": "the individual, wherever it might be, is multiple"[38]—it is not the multiple which is constituted by already formed individuals (for that would simply be the anthropocentric dream of unity). Such a dream is achievable only through acts of exclusion. Like science, unity 'continually neglects, totalizes, symbolizes'.[39] But unlike science, unity has inherent, structural problems. Racism and xenophobia are the illnesses of anthropocentrism, the biological rites of exclusion applied as some sort of substitution for problems of integration or alliance.

Rosny went so far as to include *inorganic beings* or a "material form of energy"[40] as part of his pantheon of fictional "peoples," giving them equal, "organic" status. Writing in *Le sciences et le pluralisme*, he states that "there is no reason why the terrestrial surface, since it is traversed by immense energies, should not have produced organic systems equal in complexity to our own. No more than there is any reason that it might not produce another organic realm once ours has disappeared. My Xipehuz, Moedigen and Ferro-Magnetics are perhaps pale symbols of anterior and future realities."[41]

When Deleuze said of Rosny that "he invents a kind of naturalism in intensity which, at the two extremes of the intensive scale, …leads into the prehistoric caverns and future spaces of science fiction,"[42] he meant that between the bond of primitive alliance displayed in works such as *Helgvor of the Blue River* (2010g) and *The Giant Feline* (2010g) on the one hand, and the *inorganic beings* of "Another World" and "The Xipehuz" on the other, lay the immense creative energy of a

---

[38] Rosny, 2010e: 129-130.

[39] Mackay, 2007: 258.

[40] Rosny, 2010c: 117.

[41] Rosny in Mackay, 2007: 260.

[42] Deleuze, 1994: 329.

writer for whom "experimentation indefinitely dominates speculation."[43]

Rosny wrestled long and hard with many an "abstract population of problems." Perhaps at times, this "great bad writer"[44] got his facts and narratives wrong, perhaps, late at night, the frontiers of ignorance and knowledge blurred behind the tired eyes of one who believed with the Jesuit philosopher-paleontologist Teilhard de Chardin that "the history of the living world can be summarized as the elaboration of ever more perfect eyes within a cosmos in which there is always something more to be seen."[45]

Rosny's great contribution will be to advance a better idea than unity, an experimental idea par excellence, namely, of alliance between his fictional *peoples* be they animals, plants, aliens or energies. This acknowledgment of the richness of heterogeneous alliance over homogenous, anthropocentric unity (such as colonialism and other declarations of war), is something Deleuze built his philosophy upon, and Farmer, his fiction.

Paul Wessels and Jean-Marc Lofficier

---

[43] Mackay, 2007: 259.
[44] Stableford in Rosny, 2010f: 281.
[45] 1959: 31.

REFERENCES

Bonnetain, Paul, J.-H. Rosny, Lucien Descaves, Paul Margue-
ritte and Gustave Guiches. "Manifeste des Cinq" *Le Figa-
ro* (August 18, 1887). Available online (in French with
French commentary):
http://siecle19.freeservers.com/Manifeste_Cinq.html

Bennett, Chris, Lynn Osburn, and Judy Osburn. *Green Gold:
The Tree of Life, Marijuana in Magic and Religion*. Frazier
Park: Access Unlimited, 1995. Available online:
http://www.alchemylab.com/cannabis_stone1.htm

Beistegui, Miguel. *Truth and Genesis: Philosophy as Differen-
tial Ontology*. Bloomington and Indianapolis: Indiana University Press, 2004.

Carey, Christopher Paul. "How Much Free Will Does A
Pumpkin Have? Philip José Farmer and Sufism" *Planet
Stories* (July 12, 2009). Available online:
http://planetstories.wordpress.com/2009/07/12/how-much-
free-will-does-a-pumpkin-have-philip-jose-farmer-and-
sufism/

Chapman, Edgar L. *The Magic Labyrinth of Philip José Farmer*. Rockville: Wildside Press, 1984,

-------. "Remembering Philip Jose Farmer" *Bradley Hilltopics*
(Summer 2009, 15:3). Available online:
http://www.bradley.edu/hilltopics/09summer/notebk/.

Deleuze, Gilles. *Difference and Repetition*, tr. Paul Patton.
NY: Columbia University Press, 1994.

Deleuze, G. *Negotiations, 1972-1990*, tr. Martin Joughin. NY:
Columbia University Press, 1995.

Deleuze, Gilles and Félix Guattari. *A Thousand Plateaus: Ca-
pitalism and Schizophrenia*, tr. by Brian Massumi. London: The Athlone Press, 1988.

During, Elie. "A History of Problems: Bergson and the French
Epistemological Tradition" *Journal of the British Society
for Phenomenology* 35: 1 (January, 2004). Available online: http://www.ciepfc.fr/spip.php?article56

Farmer, P.J. *The Lovers*. NY: Ballantine Books, 1961.

-------. *The Stone God Awakens*. NY: Ace Books, 1970.

-------. *The Wind Whales of Ishmael*. NY: Ace Books, 1971.

-------. *Unreasoning Mask*. NY: Berkley, 1983.

-------. "St. Francis Kisses His Ass Goodbye" in Rucker, R., Wilson, P.L. and Wilson, R.A. *Semiotext(e) SF*. NY: Autono-media, 1989.

-------. *Nothing Burns in Hell*. NY: Tor, 1999.

-------. "The Lovers" in Farmer, P.J. *Strange Relations*. NY: Baen, 2008.

Farmer, Philip José and Rosny, J.H. *Ironcastle*. NY: Daw Books, 1976.

Mackay, Robin. "Rosny and the Scientific Fantastic" *Collapse: Philosophical Research and Development*, Volume III (2007). pp. 255-265.

Melville, Herman. *Moby Dick*. London: Penguin Books, 1994.

Rosny Aîné, J.-H. "Nihilists in Paris" *Harper's New Monthly Magazine* (August, 1891). pp. 429-442. Available online: http://www.harpers.org/archive/1891/08/0036600

-------. "Foreign News: Humiliating Experiences" *TIME Magazine* (July 25, 1927). Available online: http://www.time.com/time/magazine/article/0,9171,736799,00.html

-------. "The Navigators of Space," "The Astronauts," "The Death of the Earth," "Another World" and "The Xipehuz" *in* Rosny Aîné, J.-H. *The Navigators of Space and Other Alien Encounters*, tr. by Brian Stableford. Encino: Black Coat Press, 2010a.

-------. "The Depths of Kyamo," "The Wonderful Cave Country" and "The Treasure in the Snow" *in* Rosny Aîné, J.-H. *The World of the Variants and Other Strange Lands*, tr. by Brian Stableford. Encino: Black Coat Press, 2010b.

-------. "Mysterious Force" and "Hareton Ironcastle's Amazing Journey" *in* Rosny Aîné, J.-H. *The Mysterious Force and Other Anomalous Phenomena*, tr. by Brian Stableford. Encino: Black Coat Press, 2010c.

-------. "The Givreuse Enigma" *in* Rosny *Aîné*, J.-H. *The Givreuse Enigma and Other Stories*, tr. by Brian Stableford. Encino: Black Coat Press, 2010e.

-------. "Companions of the Universe" *in* Rosny *Aîné*, J.-H. *The Young Vampire and Other Cautionary Tales*, tr. by Brian Stableford. Encino: Black Coat Press, 2010f.

-------. "Helgvor of the Blue River" and "The Giant Feline" *in* Rosny *Aîné*, J.-H. *Helgvor of the Blue River/The Giant Feline*, tr. by Georges Surdez, and Lady Whitehead. Encino: Black Coat Press, 2010g.

Teilhard de Chardin, Pierre. *The Phenomenon of Man*, tr. Bernard Wall. NY: Harper & Row, 1959.

Wilson, Peter Lamborn. *Scandal: Essays in Islamic Heresy*. NY: Autonomedia, 1988.

-------. Sacred Drift: Essays on the Margins of Islam. San Francisco: City Lights Books, 1993.

SF & FANTASY

Guy d'Armen. *Doc Ardan: The City of Gold and Lepers*
G.-J. Arnaud. *The Ice Company*
Aloysius Bertrand. *Gaspard de la Nuit*
Félix Bodin. *The Novel of the Future*
André Caroff. *The Terror of Madame Atomos*
Didier de Chousy. *Ignis*
C. I. Defontenay. *Star (Psi Cassiopeia)*
Charles Derennes. *The People of the Pole*
Harry Dickson. *The Heir of Dracula*
Sâr Dubnotal *vs. Jack the Ripper*
Alexandre Dumas. *The Return of Lord Ruthven*
J.-C. Dunyach. *The Night Orchid. The Thieves of Silence*
Henri Duvernois. *The Man Who Found Himself*
Henri Falk. *The Age of Lead*
Paul Féval. *Anne of the Isles. Knightshade. Revenants. Vampire City. The Vampire Countess. The Wandering Jew's Daughter*
Paul Féval, *fils. Felifax, the Tiger-Man*
Arnould Galopin. *Doctor Omega*
V. Hugo, Foucher & Meurice. *The Hunchback of Notre-Dame*
Michel Jeury. *Chronolysis*
O. Joncquel & Theo Varlet. *The Martian Epic*
Jean de La Hire. *Enter the Nyctalope. The Nyctalope on Mars. The Nyctalope vs. Lucifer*
G. Le Faure & H. de Graffigny. *The Extraordinary Adventures of a Russian Scientist Across the Solar System* (2 vols.)
Gustave Le Rouge. *The Vampires of Mars*
Jules Lermina. *Mysteryville. Panic in Paris. To-Ho and the Gold Destroyers*
Jean-Marc & Randy Lofficier. *Edgar Allan Poe on Mars. The Katrina Protocol. Pacifica. Robonocchio. Tales of the Shadowmen* (anthos.; 6 vols.)
Xavier Mauméjean. *The League of Heroes*
Marie Nizet. *Captain Vampire*
C. Nodier, Beraud & Toussaint-Merle. *Frankenstein*

Henri de Parville. *An Inhabitant of the Planet Mars*
Polidori, C. Nodier, E. Scribe. *Lord Ruthven the Vampire*
P.-A. Ponson du Terrail. *The Vampire and the Devil's Son*
Maurice Renard. *The Blue Peril. Doctor Lerne. The Doctored
Man . A Man Among the Microbes. The Master of Light*
Albert Robida. *The Adventures of Saturnin Farandoul. The
Clock of the Centuries.*
J.-H. Rosny Aîné. *Helgvor of the Blue River. The Givreuse
Enigma. The Mysterious Force. The Navigators of Space. Va-
mireh. The World of the Variants. The Young Vampire*
Brian Stableford. *The New Faust at the Tragicomique. Fran-
kenstein and the Vampire Countess. The Shadow of Frankens-
tein. Sherlock Holmes & The Vampires of Eternity. The Stones
of Camelot. The Wayward Muse.* (anthologist) *The Germans
on Venus. News from the Moon*
Kurt Steiner. *Ortog*
Villiers de l'Isle-Adam. *The Scaffold. The Vampire Soul*
Philippe Ward. *Artahe*
Philippe Ward & Sylvie Miller. *The Song of Montségur*

MYSTERIES & THRILLERS

M. Allain & P. Souvestre. *The Daughter of Fantômas*
Anicet-Bourgeois, Lucien Dabril. *Rocambole*
A. Bisson & G. Livet. *Nick Carter vs. Fantômas*
V. Darlay & H. de Gorsse. *Lupin vs. Holmes: The Stage Play*
Paul Féval. *Gentlemen of the Night. John Devil. The Black
Coats: The Cadet Gang. The Companions of the Treasure.
Heart of Steel. The Invisible Weapon. The Parisian Jungle.
'Salem Street*
Emile Gaboriau. *Monsieur Lecoq*
Steve Leadley. *Sherlock Holmes: The Circle of Blood*
Maurice Leblanc. *Arsène Lupin vs. Countess Cagliostro. Lu-
pin vs. Holmes: The Blonde Phantom. The Hollow Needle.*
Gaston Leroux. *Chéri-Bibi. The Phantom of the Opera. Roule-
tabille & the Mystery of the Yellow Room*

William Patrick Maynard. *The Terror of Fu Manchu*
Frank J. Morlock. *Sherlock Holmes: The Grand Horizontals*
P. de Wattyne & Y. Walter. *Sherlock Holmes vs. Fantômas*
David White. *Fantômas in America*

SCREENPLAYS

Mike Baron. *The Iron Triangle*
Emma Bull & Will Shetterly. *Nightspeeder. War for the Oaks*
Gerry Conway & Roy Thomas. *Doc Dynamo*
Steve Englehart. *Majorca*
James Hudnall. *The Devastator*
Jean-Marc & Randy Lofficier. *Royal Flush*
J.-M. & R. Lofficier & Marc Agapit. *Despair*
Andrew Paquette. *Peripheral Vision*
R. Thomas, J. Hendler & L. Sprague de Camp. *Rivers of Time*

NON-FICTION

Stephen R. Bissette. *Blur 1-5. Green Mountain Cinema 1*
Win Scott Eckert. *Crossovers* (2 vols.)
Jean-Marc & Randy Lofficier. *Shadowmen* (2 vols.)
Randy Lofficier. *Over Here*

HEXAGON COMICS

Franco Frescura & Luciano Bernasconi. *Wampus 1*
Franco Frescura & Giorgio Trevisan. *CLASH*
 Luciano Bernasconi, Jean-Marc Lofficier & Juan Roncagliolo
Berger. *Phenix 1*
Claude Legrand, Jean-Marc Lofficier & Luciano Bernasconi.
Kabur 1
Franco Oneta. *Zembla 1*

Lina Buffolente, Jean-Marc Lofficier & Jean-Jacques Dzia-lowski. *Stangers 1: Homicron*
Danilo Grossi. *Strangers 2: Jaydee*
Claude Legrand & Luciano Bernasconi. *Strangers 3: Starlock*

ART BOOKS

Jean-Pierre Normand. *Science Fiction Illustrations*
Raven Okeefe. *Raven's L'il Critters*
Randy Lofficier & Raven OKeefe. *If Your Possum Go Day-light...*
Daniele Serra. *Illusions*